TEMPERING THE BLADE

BY

FRANK ROCKLAND

A Canadian Expeditionary Force Novel

1917

Designer: Jonathan Relph
Copyeditor and Proofreading: Allister Thompson
Proofreading Editor: Britanie Wilson

Other Books by Frank Rockland

Forging the Weapon
A Canadian Expeditionary Force Novel
1914

Who knew? In the fall of 1914, Canadians had earned a reputation as hard-drinking and poorly disciplined troops. No one expected much from them. Certainly not the British! All they wanted was a sharp salute as the men did what they were told.

Prime Minister Sir Robert Borden and his Minister of Militia and Defence, Colonel Sam Hughes, had different ideas. Borden had no choice! When England declared war, Canada was automatically at war too. Hughes, however, was eager to get his boys bloodied before the war was over. He would do anything in his power to get the Canadians into the fight.

As the guns sounded in August, the first contingent gathered at Valcartier. Corps of Guide Captain James Llewellyn had trained for this moment, and he was not about to miss out. Gunner Paul Ryan had volunteered to escape his family and to impress a girl. Nursing Sister Samantha Lonsdale had answered the call because she needed a job, and going to war was an adventure.

As the months rolled by, it was at Valcartier and Salisbury Plain that they helped forge the Canadian Expeditionary Force into one of the most formidable weapons of the First World War.

Hammering the Blade
A Canadian Expeditionary Force Novel
1915

The Canadians are being hammered on two fronts.

On the home front, Sir Robert Borden's government is being rocked by scandals. First it was the soldiers' bad boots, then charges of graft and corruption in the militia department's contracts, followed by the shell crisis. With an election in the air and the opposition pounding his minister of Militia and Defence, Major-General Sam Hughes, Borden is fighting desperately to save his government.

On the western front, after six months of constant harsh training, the CEF finally enter the trenches in France. Infantry Captain Llewellyn struggles to keep his men alive as snipers take their toll, and the Ross rifle fails its first combat test. Nothing prepares him for the chlorine gas attack at Ypres. A frustrated Gunner Paul Ryan watches helplessly as his comrades-in-arms suffer. He can't help, since artillery shells are in short supply. As the battles rage, nursing sister Samantha Lonsdale is nearly overwhelmed as she cares for the sick, the wounded, and the dying.

As the hammer blows fall, the blade is being tempered into cold steel.

Sharpening the Blade
A Canadian Expeditionary Force Novel
1916

In 1916 the Canadians' rough edges were being honed off.

First, in February, there is the tragic loss of the Parliament Buildings' Centre Block by a suspicious fire. Then, in May, Lieutenant-General Alderson's leaked memo damning the Ross Rifle ignites a political firestorm. After the Canadian Corps' disaster at St. Eloi craters, it doesn't take long for Major-General Sam Hughes to replace Alderson with Lieutenant-General Julian Byng. Within days, the Corps is struck by a devastating blow at Mount Sorrel. In October, Sir Robert Borden tires of crossing swords with his mercurial minister of Militia and Defence and issues a do what you are told ultimatum! A defiant Hughes quits.

At the sharp end, Major Llewellyn and his men continue to learn the use of the hand grenade, the rifle, and the bayonet as they are grounded in the terrible carnage at St. Eloi, Mount Sorrel, and the maw of the Somme. Gunner Paul Ryan will have to live with the tragic mistake as his shells decimate his own countrymen. Matron Samantha Lonsdale continues to use all her skills to put back the pieces of men torn apart by devastating new weapons. In the fall, Lonsdale is sent to Russia, where she is soon plunged into the Russian Revolution.

By the year's end, they have been sharpened to a razor's edge.

Fire on the Hill

What really happened on the night of February 3, 1916, when a fire destroyed the Centre Block of the Canadian Parliament buildings?

Inspector Andrew MacNutt of the Dominion Police's Secret Service, his wife Katherine, and Count Jaggi know, since they were there in the reading room when the fire started.

Ever since the war began, MacNutt has been struggling to secure Canada's borders against acts of sabotage organized by German military attachés based in New York City. The good news is that the Americans have finally ordered them back to Germany. The bad news is that Berlin has sent one of their best operatives, Count Jaggi, to replace them.

Using his cover as a Belgian Relief representative, Count Jaggi visits Ottawa, where he meets and is attracted to Katherine, who is helping him organize a local fundraiser.

Unaware that Inspector MacNutt has intercepted his secret messages and is hot on his trail, Count Jaggi takes a final trip to Ottawa to see Katherine, with tragic consequences.

Author's Note

Tempering the Blade is a work of fiction. All incidents, dialogue, and characters, with the exception of historical and public figures, are products of the author's imagination and are not to be construed as real.

Where real-life historical or public figures appear, the situations, incidents, and dialogue concerning the person are fictional.

In all aspects, any resemblance to the living or the dead is entirely coincidental.

CHAPTER 1

"**N**o!" replied Sir Robert Borden.

"What do you mean no?" demanded Sir Charles Ross, who was sitting across from him in his office.

The last two days had been busy but pleasant for Sir Robert, until today. On the 1st, he had been in his office dealing with correspondence, mainly replying to New Year's greetings from foreign dignitaries. After, he had addressed a large group of children at the Dominion Methodist church on duty and service. Then he went to the governor general's lévee. He had finished his day with a supper, sponsored by the Grand Trunk Railway, at the Château Laurier honouring a hundred wounded soldiers who had returned home. This morning he had even found time to visit his doctors.

Sir Charles had been grumbling for the last half hour about how his competitors were trying to smear him and his rifle to put him out of business. Sir Robert had agreed to the noon-hour meeting out of courtesy. Sir Ross, the 9th Baronet, besides being the inventor of the Ross rifle, was also one of the richest men in England. In Scotland, three thousand tenants lived on nearly 360,000 acres of land that he owned.

He then made an outrageous demand for an additional order for 200,000 rifles on top of the 100,000 his government had contracted with him last March.

"I'm afraid sir, the Canadian government will not be ordering additional Ross rifles," Sir Robert replied firmly. He was already thinking of cancelling last year's order, since Sir Ross had not even met that contract's terms. There had been substantial delays in deliveries.

Borden was well aware of Sir Ross's reputation. While he could be quite charming, he was rather ruthless when it came to money. After all, he had sued his own mother for misspending his inheritance. Borden wasn't intimidated by the man himself. Sir Ross was a large man. He weighed nearly 220 pounds and was only a couple of inches shy of six feet.

"What am I going to do with the factory?" he demanded as he brushed his thick moustache with a knuckle.

Sir Robert understood Sir Ross's position. He was trying to save his Cove Fields plant at the Plains of Abraham; he had expanded his factory to meet the flood of contracts from the Department of Militia and Defence, the War Office, and the Russians. Borden had heard he was going to Washington shortly to try to entice the Americans into buying his rifles. With the Canadian Overseas Force replacing the Ross with the Lee-Enfield, the War Office cancelling their orders, and the Russians' lack of interest, his plant was now idle. Most of the workers had been laid off, and the few that remained were filling orders for Sir Charles Ross's civilian rifles. The .280 version was well regarded by hunters and sportsmen.

But he wasn't about to spend nearly six million dollars to keep the plant going, although it might help the Conservatives' prospects when he called the next election. He already had gone through a political crisis last April when Lieutenant-General Anderson's report on the Ross's deficiencies was released to the public. The Liberals would rake him over the coals when they found out he had wasted six million dollars of taxpayer money on a weapon that no one wanted. The money could be used for much better purposes such as caring for the returning wounded.

"Sir Charles," Borden replied, "I'll be meeting with several of my ministers this afternoon. We'll be discussing several options concerning your plant."

"What options?" he demanded. Robert could see the gleam of interest in Sir Ross's eyes.

"That I cannot say at the moment," Borden replied. He didn't want to give him anything that he could use to his advantage.

"So that is your final word concerning any future contracts?"

"I'm afraid so," replied Borden in a firm tone.

"Very well," replied Sir Charles with a displeased look. "It will have to do for now. I'm looking forward to what you and you ministers may have in mind."

Sir Robert sighed with some relief when Sir Charles finally left his office. He made a note to discuss the matter with Kemp, the minister of militia and defence. He was proving to be a good choice after Borden had fired Sir Sam Hughes last October. He'd have to include Meighen as well. He wasn't looking forward to the ongoing drama. He wanted this Ross rifle fiasco done with.

CHAPTER 2

"So, what do you think?" asked Captain Laraway, who stood beside him as the Fusiliers marched past. A couple of raindrops fell off Lieutenant-Colonel Llewellyn's steel helmet. He didn't mind the light rain. It meant he and his men wouldn't be eating dust on the force march Brigadier-General Loomis had ordered for today since his Fusiliers had been designated as the rear guard. However, mud was another matter.

"I thought they would be in better shape," replied Llewellyn. He could see his men were slowing down as they started to get tired. The wet overcoats and the muddy boots added extra weight to the standard loads they had to carry. The steel helmets, while they kept the rain off his men's heads, added to their fatigue. He had orders from HQ that the Brodies were to be worn at all times especially when the men were on parade or in the field. He frowned when he noticed Sergeant Ellis was starting to hobble. It was obvious that he had pulled a muscle, but he was a stubborn man. He loathed riding in the horse drawn ambulances reserved for the stragglers in the rear.

For much of December, the 2nd Brigade had been in the reserve. The first few weeks were with the 1st Division. Since mid-December, they had been assigned as the Corps' reserve. Most of their time had been spent on individual and unit training. All the men had brushed up on their bayonet skills and everyone had gone through the bomber training using live grenades. Luckily, without any incidents. Captain Laraway had been sent to the Fusiliers to help improve the skills of his signal and intelligence sections. They were going to need it in the coming months. Llewellyn had noticed a marked improvement in their performance ever since. He was planning to ask Brigadier-General Loomis if he could keep him. The rest of the instructors who had come with Laraway hadn't impressed him as much, so he was sending them back to the Corps' school.

"We should be near Camblain-Châtelain," said the captain. Llewellyn couldn't help noticing the thirty-year old officer was breathing hard. "We've about two miles left."

Llewellyn glanced at his wristwatch. It read four-thirty. They should be done in just about an hour's time. They had been on the road since ten this morning. When the brigade started on their forced march from Ourton to Divion, he had some concerns about the state of the roads. As the crow flies the distance was only two miles, but the general had chosen a circular route from Ourton to Pernes to Camblain-Châtelain then to Divion, a total of eight miles. He had expected to complete the march in about three and a half hours. Since they were the rear guard, they had crossed the start line at ten thirty. Brigadier-General Loomis's headquarters staff had been the first unit out. The remaining battalions had marched after them in ten-minute intervals. They also had taken ten-minute breaks at the top of the hour and the one-hour break at noon to rest the men.

The roads had been in better shape than he expected. It had rained heavily a couple of days prior to New Year's. It had caused flooding forcing him to move A company to new billets. The gravel roads seemed to drain well as the ditches were full. In the low sections of the road, they had to wade through ankle deep cold water.

When he heard splashing, he turned his head to see that Private Watters was hurrying towards him. When he had slid to a stop, he gave Llewellyn a sharp salute, then said, "Colonel, Major Gavin requests your presence at the front of the column."

"Is there a problem?" Llewellyn asked.

"Not a problem sir," he replied quickly as he tried to catch his breath. "He wanted to let you know that General Byng's staff car is parked at the crossroads up ahead."

He heard Captain Laraway suck his breath in. The colonel noticed some of the men had overheard and were passing the word along. He could see his men straightening and picking up the pace.

"Let the brigade-major know that I will be along shortly," replied Llewellyn.

He hadn't been told that Lieutenant-General Byng, the commander of the Canadian Corps was visiting them today. To be honest, it wouldn't have made much of a difference if he had. He sighed. He knew he would be facing some constructive criticism.

JANUARY 5, 1917
THE OVERSEAS MILITARY FORCES OF CANADA
HEADQUARTERS, ARGYLL HOUSE, LONDON

Sir George Perley's limousine couldn't park in front of the main entrance of the four-storey Classical Greek sandstone building that dominated Little Argyll Street. Several khaki-painted White trucks with Canadian markings, red Cs in each corner of a triangle, were already there unloading desks and filing cabinets. His limo parked further down, and the bearded sixty-year-old Sir George stepped out and walked to the two soldiers that stood guard in front of the entrance. The polished brass letters *246 Regent* were gleaming in the morning sun on both sandstone panels framing the double golden oak doors. *Argyll House* was carved in the stone rectangle above the doors and below the stone Grecian A-framed window. When Perley approached the guards they saluted, then stopped two men carrying a desk to allow Sir Perley to enter before them.

Once inside he could see to his left, in the large high ceiling chamber, clerks and support staff answering phones and pecking at typewriters. He knew that the rest of the building was being filled rapidly with staff as they consolidated the Canadian military offices that were scattered across London. Argyll House was the new headquarters of the Canadian Overseas Force. He was happy they were able to lease the building since it was centrally located in Soho and was conveniently ten minutes away from the War Office, the Colonial Office, and Westminster.

The building didn't have a lift, so he took the stairs to his office on the top floor with the brass plate that read, "Minister of the Overseas Force in Canada and Britain." His secretary greeted him when he entered his office in an anxious tone, "Minister, they are waiting for you in the meeting room."

"I'm afraid I was delayed at the Colonial Office," Perley said as he handed Prichard his hat and coat. His secretary who always fussed over him, was in his mid-forties, with a receding hairline. He was born in Nova Scotia, but he had moved to England about twenty years earlier. Perley was glad that he was efficient since he did feel harried and overworked. It wasn't surprising since he had two jobs, he was the new minister for the Overseas Military Forces of Canada as well as the Canadian High Commissioner.

Perley gave Prichard a brief nod as he tugged on his dark suit jacket then headed to the meeting room. In a sea of khaki, he was conspicuous in the hallway since he was the only one in civilian dress. The officers assembled at a gleaming oak table rose to their feet when he entered the conference room. He couldn't help noticing the ribbon bars on their left breasts as he took his seat reserved for him at the head of the table.

"Please be seated gentlemen," he ordered.

At the opposite end of the table Major-General Turner took his chair.

He adjusted his wire-framed eyeglasses then said, "Let's begin. We have much to cover this morning."

Perley glanced at the stack of papers that had been placed before him with a tired sigh. It had been a month since he had appointed Major-General Turner as the GOC of the Canadian Forces in Britain. One of the first things he and Turner had agreed on was to get rid of most of Lieutenant-General Sam Hughes's, the former Militia and Defence minister, cronies. Especially the generals MacDougall, Steele, and Carson who were responsible for most of the current mess they were in.

He had been a touch concerned when Turner had appointed as his Chief of Staff, his adjutant-general, and his quartermaster-general officers he was familiar with. So far, they had proven to be quite efficient and competent.

When Borden asked him to head the new ministry created to administrate the Canadian Forces overseas; Perley knew he needed to find a seasoned and experienced officer as his second in command. Preferably, one who had the respect of the men. He had asked Lieutenant-General Byng for his recommendations. Currie had been Byng's first choice, with Turner as his second. He had gone to France to interview both, being careful not to indicate what he was interviewing them for. Currie had impressed him the most and he had offered him the job. When Currie turned him down, informing him that he would not put up with political interference in how the CEF would be run, he had been rather put off. He then turned to Turner with an offer. Perley was well aware of the friction between Turner and the former Corps commander, Lieutenant-General Alderson. After the St. Eloi defeat, if Sir Max Aitken hadn't used his influence to keep the major-general as the GOC of the 2nd Division, Turner would have been fired. Last October's Courcellete battle had rehabilitated their reputations. He had been well liked and respected by the men of the 2nd Division. Perley had expected that Turner would jump at the chance to be the GOC of the Canadian forces in England when he made his offer, but Turner said he needed a couple of days to consider it. When he finally replied, he had informed him that he would take it on one condition, that he be considered for command of the Canadian Corps when the position became available. After consulting with Borden, he had agreed.

When Turner had glanced at Major Harold McDonald, his chief of staff, Perley turned his attention to the tall thirty-two-year-old blue-eyed officer with a dark complexion and hair. His left sleeve was pinned up to his shoulder. He had lost the arm the first week the Corps had been deployed at the Somme. McDonald had been cleared by medical for light duty, but he would never lead a unit at the front again. As Turner's GS01, he had been tasked to look into the Forces training and intelligence policies. "The training syllabus were even worse than I thought," he said. "We have forty-six training camps in England with no standardization. A fair number of the instructors have never even been to the front. And, they've been training the recruits using outdated manuals. Some, for God's sake, go back as far 1907!

"One instructor I spoke to was surprised to hear the Corps was now using Lewis machine guns. He was even more surprised to learn that four of them were being issued to each battalion."

"You're joking!" sputtered Colonel Percival Thatcher. Thatcher had been Turner's chief administrative officer for the 2nd Division. He was forty-one years old, a graduate of RMC, and was a permanent force member. He was one of the few Canadian officers who had attended the Chamberley Staff College before the war.

"He didn't seem to be embarrassed by that fact either," replied McDonald.

"Good God," muttered Thatcher as he shook his head, his black hair was fringed with grey.

"I relieved him on the spot," McDonald stated. "We're going to have to bring experienced men from France to instruct our reinforcements with the latest methods and tactics."

"They aren't going to like that," stated Major Montague.

Turner nodded in agreement. No one liked losing experienced men. "They'll stop complaining once we start turning out quality reinforcements."

"And, half the recruits' training time was spent on fatigue duty which I have ordered to be stopped. It didn't make any sense. Also, I've been looking at cutting the depots in half and sacking any COs who refuse to comply with the new syllabuses."

"Agreed," Turner stated. "One thing General Byng wants us to emphasize is the men's saluting, appearance, and the care of their service arms. He told me he has found our men to be natural at bayonet fighting and bombing, so we can cut back on some of the hours we spend there. More time is needed on discipline and smartness in the drill."

"I'll make a note of it," said McDonald. "I'm afraid there's going to be some discontent from the COs and the senior officers as we cut back on their positions. It will add to our surplus officer problems."

Perley knew the new policy would mean there would be more complaints being forwarded to Ottawa. He glanced at Major Montague who had been tasked with the problem. The major had been a prominent lawyer in Winnipeg and had been on Turner's staff during the St. Eloi disaster. He coughed to clear his throat, then said, "I've been looking at the criteria for creating a gradation list for the senior officers and NCOs."

It was explained to Perley that before the war the Militia and Defence Department regularly published a directory, modelled after the British Army list, of all the army's senior officers and NCOs. The list provided a summary of each officer's career and any special postings he had been assigned to; from the date he became an officer to his current rank.

He had been getting an earful from aggrieved officers on how promotions were being granted. Perley knew most of the problems had been caused by Sam Hughes's habit of promoting officers according to his whims. He was also well aware how competitive the army officers were and how jealously they guarded their prerogatives. Turner had assured him that the gradation list would go a long way to reducing some of the friction among the men. It would also help make the promotion's list a bit more transparent.

"I've been looking at the start date for the gradation. Normally, we would use when the officer joined the service. However, with the overseas force we would need to get all the personnel records from Ottawa. It'll take quite a bit of time and resources to get them and compile an accurate list," Montague said.

"You have a suggestion?" asked Turner.

"I've been leaning towards using as the start date when they embarked to England. We have all the records here and we can compile the list quickly and efficiently. Some of the officers would complain that it isn't fair. Either way we'll get complaints. But if we're consistent and open about it, it will reduce some of the friction."

Turner paused to consider the idea then replied, "Hmm. Let me consider it for a few days then I'll let you know what I decide."

"Yes, sir."

Perley saw Turner turn to Brigadier-General McRae and cocked an eyebrow. The general was forty-three years old, balding, with what was left of his hair brush-cut. Alexander Duncan McRae was one of the bright spots in the previous administration. Sam had appointed him as an honorary lieutenant-colonel because of his business experience and had sent him to England in 1914 to purchase horses for the 1st Contingent. He had then stayed to clean up the mess at the Remount Commission. Now, he was their director of Supplies and Services. "I've discovered a few things that should save us some money. The first, we've been paying rent to the War Office when we had an agreement with them that they wouldn't charge us for the use of some of their facilities."

"Oh," said Perley in surprise. It was news to Perley. "How much?"

"I don't have the final figures as yet, but it'll be in the thousands of pounds. Also, I've been looking at our messing arrangements. It appears that each unit has made their own. When I was in France I did the same, simply because our men moved billets frequently. Here in England our units are stationary, for the most part, so what I want to do is centralize our purchasing. We'll be able to demand discounts and with the current shortages it will help reduce wastage."

"That sounds good," Turner replied pleased. "Go ahead with it."

"Also, I've looked at our program to reclaim surplus equipment. It seems several tons of clothing were initially declared beyond repair and were slated to be used for rags. When they were examined most of the uniforms were quite serviceable. All they needed was minor repairs and steam cleaning. And…" McRae said with a grin. "We found several hundred pounds of bills and loose change in the pockets."

Everyone at the table chuckled. Perley said in an amused tone, "That will help with the deficit."

"I'm sure it'll make a dent," replied McRae. "The other thing I have to look at is what to do with our surplus horses. We're reducing our reliance on them as we become more mechanized."

Turner frowned at McRae. "Unfortunately, I think you're right. But we still need a healthy supply for reinforcements."

"I know," replied McRae with a nod. "We need to do further analysis to determine how many we actually need."

"Okay. Keep me informed," replied Turner. "I guess that covers everything we needed to address today." He then looked at Perley. "Do you have anything to add, Minister?"

"I do," he replied. "I just came from the Colonial office, where I've been informed that Prime Minister Lloyd George has called for an Imperial

War Conference in March. So, I will be calling on you and your senior officers for reports and analysis on our current efforts and what we can provide in the future to help prosecute the war effort," Perley stated.

"We're at your service, Minister," Turner replied. "We have plenty of work to do, gentlemen. Let's get at it."

CHAPTER 3

When Samantha stepped into the main lobby, she couldn't help noticing that the guards that had been stationed in front of Count Dmitri's apartment were gone. She didn't have very much time to consider the implications when she saw Christine Steward, one of the Anglo-Russian nursing sisters, coming down the staircase. Samantha could see she was bursting with news.

"Hi Sam, you're late," Christine said as she greeted her.

"Yes, I was looking into the menu for tonight. It's Christmas Eve," Samantha replied. The Russians still followed the Julian calendar. It meant Christmas fell on the 7th of January, not on the 25th of December. "I was hoping to get something special for the men besides borscht."

They were lucky to have even that. The food supply was tight and was getting tighter. It was one of the unfortunate consequences of the Russians' peasant army. With so many being drafted, there was no one left to plow, seed, and harvest the fields. Food production had dropped considerably. Then, coupled with the poor distribution system, it had resulted in shortages and exorbitant prices.

"Were you able to find anything?" Christine asked.

"Just cabbage and salted fish. I was afraid to ask what kind," Samantha replied with a shrug. At least the salted fish didn't spoil easily. "The cooks can make a nice soup."

Christine then leaned forward and whispered, "You noticed the guards are gone?"

"I did," Samantha whispered back. She glanced around the wide expanse of the open staircase. She felt rather conspicuous whispering in the open as she started climbing the staircase to the wards above. "What happened?" she asked, speaking just above a whisper.

Christine whispered something that Samantha appeared to not have heard. "Can you talk a bit louder?" Samantha asked, hoping Christine would get the hint.

She replied in a slightly louder voice, "At nine thirty this morning, Count Dmitri was escorted out of the building."

"They took him to prison?" Samantha asked.

Christine shook her head. "They took him to the train station. He's being banished."

"Banished?"

"That was what I was told," she replied. "You know some of the guards are sweet on me." Samantha almost sighed. Christine had questionable taste in men. "I was really surprised when the guard told me what really happened that night."

"What did you hear?" Samantha stated. There were so many rumours of what happened.

"The count and another aristocrat had picked up Rasp…" Christine paused when Samantha gave her a sharp glance. No one spoke the mad monk's name. One never knew who could be listening.

The euphoria that swept the city when the news broke that Rasputin had been killed ended when they learned of the czarina's reaction. She had shocked the aristocracy by arresting Count Dmitri. No member of the Imperial family had been arrested in two centuries. Maybe the rumours that Rasputin had been her lover were true. Since then, there had been a number of arrests and disappearances. It also put the Anglo-Russian Hospital under a cloud, since it shared the same roof as the count. "What the guard told me was the Count had picked up the person at his home and then drove him to a palace he owns on the Moika Canal. Around three o'clock in the morning, several bobbies heard shots and screaming coming from the palace gardens. When they investigated, they found blood in the snow but no body."

"How did they find the body in the river?"

"Someone noticed a hole in the ice and blood, so they called the police. They put divers in the water and found the body. They think they had wrapped the body in a fur coat then drove him to an island in the Neva. There, someone cut the hole and dropped him in it."

Samantha nodded. She had heard he was shot in the head.

"So, what do you think we need to do?" Christine asked.

"Do?" Samantha asked. "What can we do?"

"Well…" Christine paused, at a loss. She couldn't think of anything.

"What we need to do is our jobs," Samantha stated firmly. "I'm afraid we still have patients to take care of. This unfortunate incident has put us under a cloud. Especially since the czarina is one of our patrons, and if things become difficult, she may withdraw her support."

Christine stopped and stared at her. "You don't think she would do that?"

"I really don't know. I'm hoping that it will simply blow over," replied Samantha when they reached the top of the stairs. "We'll have to talk with Meriel and her father, the British ambassador, for advice. In the meantime, we still have a lot of work to do today. Let's not dawdle. We want the men to at least have an enjoyable festive day."

"I guess you're right," Christine said with her back straightening a touch. "I just don't know if I can be that cheerful."

"You'll just have to try. Try very hard," replied Samantha. She knew how she felt, but it was important to give their patients a touch of cheer, even if it was only for a moment.

JANUARY 8, 1917
VOIE SACRÉE, SOUILLY

Lieutenant-Colonel Llewellyn watched as a stalled truck was pushed off into the snow-covered field. Men in blue French uniforms were removing wounded from the back of the green canvas-covered vehicle. The stretchers were being distributed to the rest of the convoy that had to stop until the road was cleared. The horn blasts behind the four idling staff cars sounded their impatience. He knew the French had orders that the traffic on the critical supply route, the Voie Sacrée, between Bar-le-Duc and Verdun should never stop. The heavy traffic going the other way didn't even slow down a notch to take a gander. They had timetables to keep and the French 2nd Army to feed and supply. Llewellyn didn't need to imagine what the traffic was like a month ago when the French had launched a fresh assault to take back its lost territory.

Through the slight frosting on the car's window, he could see his French driver shivering as he hunched his chin into his overcoat. The Panhard & Levassor limo was built more for passenger comfort than the driver's. The weather was unusually cold for France. There was even snow on the ground. By Canadian standards, it was a light dusting, barely an inconvenience. However, in the trenches it made life more miserable than usual.

"How are we for time?" asked Major-General Currie, who was sitting beside him.

Before Llewellyn could reply, Major R.T. Hammick in the front seat answered, "We have plenty of time to catch our train back to Paris. We'll get to the train station in about an hour and half." The major was a Royal Field Artillery officer who was seconded to the Canadian Corps. He was currently the brigade-major to Brigadier-General Thacker, the GOC of the 1st Canadian Divisional Artillery.

"Okay," replied Currie as he glanced out of his window at the stalled truck with its stylized *Berliet* nameplate on its grill. It had distracted him from the reports he had been reading. Llewellyn knew Currie quite well, since he had once been one of his staff officers. Llewellyn also knew Currie would never project a warrior image with his clean-shaven jowls and pear-shaped body.

"So, what were your impressions?" he asked Currie. He noticed Hammick give Currie and Llewellyn a quick glance. Some of the British officers could never get comfortable with the easy familiarity among the Canadian officers.

"It's been an interesting three days," Currie answered. Llewellyn raised an eyebrow. Currie had been in his element during their visit to the French 2nd Army. They had been part of a delegation of six officers who had come to study their recent operations at Verdun. The three of them had visited the Fort de Souville while the other three officers, from the British Army, had visited Fort de Vaux.

Llewellyn had to admit he had been impressed by Fort de Souville, even though he found being underground uncomfortable. He could still vividly recall when a German artillery shell had buried him alive last September during the fighting at Albert. The fort was part of a defensive system built after the Franco-Prussian war to defend their border. The upper structure had been pretty much reduced to rubble, but the underground system of offices, barracks, ammo dumps, and tunnels had been dug deep enough to be bombproof. The fort had been built several miles northeast of Verdun on a hill that gave the French an excellent position to observe the Germans.

When the Germans had launched their offensive last February, they knew Verdun had a special significance to the French. Its capture would have demoralized the French Army, and it very nearly succeeded.

"I'm surprised at the extent they use photo reconnaissance and how far down they distribute them," Currie stated as he placed his leather portfolio on his ample stomach. "That is on my list to look at when we get back to headquarters. I'm wondering if we can increase our own production of them. It would help enormously when planning our operations."

Llewellyn nodded. "I must admit I'm impressed by their planning. They even distribute maps down to the platoon level. We'll have to take a look at whether we should do the same. Currently, we have strict instructions not to bring battle maps into the trenches."

"You have a point," replied Currie. "That's one of the things I want to change as well. We tend to try to capture trenches. What the French have been doing is selecting an objective then letting the commanders plan how to go about capturing it. They study the terrain in detail, identifying the gun emplacements, machine-gun posts, and anything else that might slow the advance."

"General Guillaumat did say that Paris hadn't given them any additional troops for their assault," Llewellyn stated. General Guillaumat, who was Général de Division, the equivalent of a British lieutenant-general, had replaced Général Nivelle, who had led the 2nd Army for much of 1916. In mid-December, Nivelle had replaced Marshal Joffre to become the French commander-in-chief. They had just left the général after they had lunched with him at his headquarters in Souilly's town hall, twelve miles south of Verdun.

"I like the fact that they train their men to get across No Man's Land *en masse* and fast. I think we're getting too set in our ways by attacking in waves. They said they found the German artillery would start up when they're assembling for the attack. They were catching the third and fourth wave out in the open, decimating them. By the time they all got to the German trenches, they were so depleted they couldn't exploit any successes they may have achieved."

"I've noted that as well," replied Llewellyn. "They also said they used their first-class troops in the assault. They kept them well trained and fresh. Most of their fatigue work is done by their second-class units."

Currie snorted. "I know. I remember what happened at St. Eloi." The 2nd Canadian Division got mauled partly because they were so exhausted before they even got to the battlefield.

Llewellyn shook his head at the memory.

"One other thing they also do is give their junior officers plenty of latitude to do their jobs. Their platoons are self-sufficient and can take care of themselves. They've been giving them specific targets to capture, and they've been letting the platoon leader figure out how to do it. With all these specialists we now have, we have kind of forgotten how we used to train our NCOs and junior officers before the war," Currie stated.

Llewellyn paused to consider Currie's comment. "I think we may have to. One of the French officers told me about their fire and manoeuvre tactics that I liked. They used their artillery and machine guns to keep the Germans' heads down as their platoons manoeuvre around them to take them from the rear. We're doing some of that, but not enough. What frequently happens is that we call on the artillery to pound a position first, which then slows us down, and we lose momentum.

"No offence, Major," Llewellyn said when he saw the major's frown.

"None taken, Colonel," replied Hammick. "I did find it interesting that they didn't register their guns like we do. They prefer to observe each shell as it lands then make adjustments."

Currie nodded in agreement. As a former artillery officer, Currie appreciated the nuances between the French and Canadian artillery. "They give control of all their guns in the target zone to the local commander. It's his job to prepare the ground for the infantry. The use of gas shells to bombard the German artillery is a nice touch. We'll have to use that. They said, it helps reduce the Germans' artillery efficiency by at least sixty percent."

"Our own gunners can attest to that," answered Hammick.

"What they also do is once they've put a gun out of action, they keep shelling it. Lightly, mind you. It keeps the Germans from making repairs."

"We'll have to add that to our own plans," replied Hammick.

Llewellyn suddenly chuckled. Both men turned to him in surprise. "Sorry, a thought came into my head. There's one thing the French do that most of our men would love, but we'll never do it."

"Which is?" asked Currie.

"The second water bottle they provide their men," Llewellyn said with a grin. The French soldier's second water bottle usually contained wine.

"Ah, yes," Currie said with a chuckle just as the car was put into gear. "I'll mention it in my report. I'm sure that will go over well in Ottawa."

JANUARY 15, 1917
26TH TRAVELLING ORDNANCE WORKSHOP UNIT, RUITZ

"You lost our 18-pounder!" demanded Lieutenant Paul Ryan.

"Oh God, no!" replied Captain Leslie, the harried CO of the workshop. He was in his mid-thirties, clean-shaven with hazel eyes. "We definitely have it somewhere. I just can't seem to find the paperwork. You wouldn't happened to have a copy, hmm…"

"Nooo…" Ryan drawled. He glanced at Sergeant Ramus, who had accompanied him to the 26th Travelling Ordnance Workshop with six heavy draught horses. They had come to retrieve the 18-pounder that they had dropped off a week earlier for repairs. The workshop was near the railroad tracks on the outskirts of Ruitz. It had been easy to spot, since there were about a dozen guns, a mixture of 18-pounders, 60-pounders, and 4.5- and 6-inch howitzers parked out front waiting for service. Across the cobblestone street in front of the workshop, there were a half-dozen trucks and GS wagons that belonged to the Canadian Corps. Painted on the trucks' hoods and the wagon sides were triangles with a 'C' at each point. They looked like he felt at times, tired and worn out.

The workshop was a beehive of activity as craftsmen were busy stripping an 18-pounder to its frame. Whether they were stripping for parts or rebuilding, he couldn't tell. One of the craftsmen was using an acetylene torch to weld a crack in a gun carriage. Nearby, a burly corporal was pounding a broken wheel spoke with a short-handled sledgehammer.

"Hold on a minute." The captain rose from his chair and shouted to be heard over the din. "Corporal Mackay! Heh, Corporal Mackay!"

The corporal, who had been wielding the sledgehammer, looked up. "Yeah, Cap. What do you want?"

"Did you sign off on the 65th's 18-pounder?"

"Yeah," the corporal replied as he waved the heavy hammer in an easy circle. "She's out back, as good as new."

"Where's the paperwork?"

"On your desk at the bottom of the pile," the corporal replied, pointing at the captain's desk with his hammer.

A chagrined captain dug out the report and glanced at it, then said, "Follow me."

Leslie led them out of the rear entrance, past the corporal, who had returned to his hammering. Paul had to squint as his eyes adjusted to the bright sun. It was a pleasant, clear day but a bit on the cold side. The motor from one of the four trucks parked nearby caught his attention. The White five-ton trucks had been converted for ordnance use. Two of the lorries had their side panels lowered and were being supported by three legs. A craftsman wearing safety goggles was slowly turning the wheel on a lathe set up in the truck's bed. Metal shavings from the steel bar locked in place on the lathe fell to the wooden floor. Ryan assumed the truck's engine was generating the electrical power to run the lathe, the drill press, and the grinders that were tucked in the vehicle's corner. The lathe in the other truck was idle, but a private was using a drill press to drill a hole through a metal plate. The other two had their rear doors lowered, and he could see metal shelving arranged on both sides with various parts suspended from the walls.

The captain noticed Ryan's gaze and informed him, "Yeah, they're our spare parts lorries. We try to carry what we can. We're a mobile unit. When we have to move, everything comes with us."

"I noticed the trucks and GS wagons out front when we rode in," Ryan stated.

"Yeah, by the time we get them, they're so worn out, we can't do anything with them. We strip them bare for parts."

When they had passed the trucks, Ryan saw a train slowly come to a stop on the nearby tracks. Lashed to the flat-cars were four 60-pounders. The captain stopped the private, who was walking by, carrying a fender. "Let Corporal Mackay know that the 60s have arrived and to get a squad so we can unload them."

"Yes, Cap," replied the private, who then headed quickly to the workshop.

"They're going to be a bitch to offload," Ryan said. The 60s weighed nearly ten thousand pounds.

"You want to help?" asked Captain Leslie.

"Sure, our horses can help, but we only have six," replied Ryan. The 60s normally needed twelve horses to move them. But it was a good idea to build up some credit with ordnance. You never knew when you needed a favour. Ryan studied the 60s for a moment then said, "They look new."

"Yep, fresh from the factory. We have to inspect them, then we have to make some modifications before we can release them to the heavies."

"What modifications?" asked Ryan.

"They sent us a long list. We need to make twenty-seven of them before we can put them into service."

"Why didn't they make them at the factory?" Ryan snorted.

"That's what I said," replied the captain. "As if I've got nothing to do."

"Well, here's your 18-pounder," the captain said when they finally spotted four of them neatly lined up. The captain checked that the gun's serial number matched. "Yep, she's yours."

"She's looking pretty clean," Ryan said as he walked around the gun.

Leslie looked at the report that he was carrying. "We replaced the breech block with one that we had. It isn't new, but it's solid. Corporal Mackay is a superb craftsman. He knows his way around a gun. He found cracks in the buffer chamber, so he replaced it. It had some life in it, but it would have failed in a month or two. You wouldn't want that. He stripped her down to the carriage, inspected, cleaned, and greased all the parts. She's as good as new."

"You couldn't swap the A tube?" Ryan suggested.

"I wish," Leslie said. "There's some barrel wear, so you'll have to retest and recalibrate it. We can't replace the A tube here. It's a factory job. We're planning on sending the worn barrels to them for refurbishing once they start shipping new ones to us. We have plenty of carriages for them. We can swap them easily enough. Well, relatively easily."

"I'm glad to hear that. My CO's worried about the barrel wear."

"Yeah, everyone is."

Ryan nodded. "Reggie bring the horses around. We'll help them offload the 60s."

"Sure thing," Reggie said as he turned and headed to the front of the workshop where they had tied the horses up.

"Is there any way you can come to us for minor repairs?" asked Ryan.

"We've been looking into that. You know how it is. Finding craftsmen. Good ones are like pearls," replied Captain Leslie.

"I kind of figured that," replied Ryan. "In the meantime, let's get those 60s off that train."

CHAPTER 4

"So how did you cut your hand?" Samantha asked as she used a pair of scissors to slice the end of the cotton wrap into two ends. She then used them to tie and knot the wrap tightly around the bandage the woman was clutching in her hand. The cut had been deep and the length of her palm. If it weren't taken care of properly, she would be at risk of losing it.

While she had been looking at the woman in the face, she was actually addressing Anton, the sanitor the refugee had assigned to translate for them and to keep an eye on her and Dorothy Cotton as they provided medical care for the sick in the refugee camp.

"She said she cut her hand cutting food for her *deti*," Anton replied after he had translated the woman's answer. He pointed to four children sitting on the nearby bunk bed who were watching her every move with wide eyes. Samantha stifled the urge to snort. She didn't believe the woman's story. She knew that Meriel Buchanan's mother, Lady Buchanan, headed the refugee committee that supplied the camp with food to help feed the war refugees who had been pouring into Petrograd ever since the war started. A slice of black bread and a bowl of porridge wasn't enough to feed growing children. The women did what they could to earn a few kopeks to buy extra bread. There were always lineups at the bread shops, and the prices kept going up. There was no meat in the city, and there were only two weeks of flour left. Seeing the shivering children's thin frames, she wasn't surprised that desperate women had broken the windows at the bread shops to steal food. She knew that malnutrition made the little ones more susceptible to rickets, scurvy, and scarlet fever, but there was nothing she could do.

"Okay," Samantha said slowly as if the woman could understand her English better. "Wash, every morning. Clean." The woman turned her babushka-covered head to Anton, who translated.

"*Da*," she replied with vigorous nodding.

Samantha sighed. Considering the conditions of the camp, she doubted the woman could even if she wanted to. The barracks they were in, more of a shed, had been built for two hundred, with three tiers of bunk beds running along the length of the two walls. Now, it was filled with twice if three times that many. In the centre, there was a masonry stove that was providing some rather anaemic heat, since coal was scarce. Even she couldn't get her flat's temperature higher than fifty degrees. She needed to wear wool socks to keep her feet warm.

She rose and picked up her doctor's bag at her feet. What supplies she had brought with her were long gone. Nurse Cotton, who was at the far end of the barracks, was holding the bare feet of a ten-year old in her hands, rubbing them with a salve. Dorothy spoke soothingly as she massaged the girl's feet. All the refugees were in desperate need of shoes, especially since January had been extremely cold. The British embassy's refugee committee had donated clothing, but most of them were essentially rags. The peasants still made do with what they could get. After two years of war, there wasn't much left.

Dorothy wrapped the girl's feet with a linen wrap and told the mother, "Keep them on for the next couple of days and don't allow her to walk outside in bare feet." The girl's mother, a large woman with missing teeth, nodded in agreement after Anton's translation.

Dorothy turned to Samantha. "It's time already?"

"I'm afraid so. We have to go back to the hospital," Samantha replied. The Anglo-Russian hospital was about three miles from the camp that was set up near the Warsaw train station.

"Okay," she said as she repacked her black medical bag. Dorothy put on her heavy jacket then wrapped a wool scarf to cover her head. She tied it securely with a knot under her chin.

As they headed to the exit, Samantha stared straight ahead, trying to avoid eye contact. There was so much that needed to be done. But there was so little that she could do.

"Have things changed much since you left?" Samantha asked as the streetlights threw shadows on the nearby buildings. It was nearly five o'clock, and the sun had already set. Samantha still hadn't gotten used to how short the day was here. In Sudbury, it was usually light by seven thirty, but here the sun didn't rise until nine thirty. It did help explain a bit of the locals' dourness.

"No, not much. But the city seems to be quite tense," Dorothy replied as they passed the queue that was huddled together to escape the easterly wind. They were lined up to obtain a ration token from the camp's refugee office. The token entitled them to a slice of black bread and a bowl of porridge.

Samantha glanced at Dorothy and saw she too was studiously avoiding looking directly at the refugees as they made their way to their car. Dorothy hailed from Almonte, Ontario. She was nearly thirty, six years older than Samantha. She was tall, five ten, with dark hair and eyes. She had recently transferred back to Petrograd after a stint at the Moore Barracks Military Hospital in Shorncliffe. They knew some of the same people at the Shorncliffe, but many of those Samantha knew had been transferred to other units. Samantha had seniority, since she had joined the service eight months before Dorothy had volunteered in March of 1915.

"I think the cold has kept everyone indoors. It makes everyone moody," Samantha said as they approached their waiting car. When the driver spotted them, he clambered out and went to the front to use the crank to start the engine. They were nearly at the car when it finally roared to life.

"I don't know if that is it or not," Dorothy replied as she climbed into the back seat. When Samantha had settled into the car, she wrapped a wool blanket over her and Dorothy's legs.

Samantha nodded. "The czar firing the Jews in the government isn't going to help."

Dorothy shook her head. "I saw the military police come to the hospital to take the Jewish soldiers to the train station. Supposedly, they're being transferred to Siberia."

"I know," Samantha replied. There wasn't anything that the hospital could have done, especially since the czar and czarina were their sponsors.

"Thing is. It's the kids," Dorothy stated. "I don't know how many are going to survive the winter."

Samantha sighed. "We can only do what we can."

FEBRUARY 14, 1917
FOSSE 10, ANGRES

Lieutenant-Colonel Llewellyn could see that snow covered the superstructure of the Fosse 10 mine shaft a couple of hundred feet distant. The main shaft, so he had been told, dropped nearly twenty-seven hundred feet down. He could see workmen repairing the battle damage to the roof that extended above a siding where railway cars were waiting to be loaded with coal.

It was a dull, cloudy day that was dampening his mood somewhat. He couldn't help noticing A company was similarly dull and listless. His men were not their usual boisterous selves, even after several days out of the right subsection trenches. Their time in the trenches had been relatively quiet, suffering only one day of machine gun and artillery fire. He had been pleased that the Fusiliers hadn't suffered any casualties.

Today, A Company was scheduled for a refresher on bayonet fighting. He had decided to change things up by bringing in the top bayonet man, Sergeant Dickenbush, from the 1st Division to take his men through their paces.

Llewellyn nodded to the sergeant to begin. The sergeant was in his mid-thirties, five feet nine inches or so tall, with a coarse brown moustache and shorn hair under his Brodie helmet. He was standing in front of two wooden beams nailed in an X frame that supported four hanging bayonet dummies. The sandbags behind the sergeant, Llewellyn knew, had been filled with straw and thick wooden sticks to give the feeling of striking bone when the blade penetrated and when it was being pulled out. Rough, cream-coloured cloth circles had been placed as targets on the dummies. Each had a circle where a man's heart was while the arteries were also targeted.

"I'm here to teach you how to use the bayonet. Let me tell you boys that the only time you're going to use this," he said as he tapped the bayonet fixed to his Lee-Enfield, "is when things have gone into the crapper."

Llewellyn raised an eyebrow in surprise. It was true, but most instructors wouldn't have admitted it. "If I've my druthers, I'd just shoot the poor fucking bastard in the gut." Most of the men in A Company chuckled in agreement.

"So, when you're stuck in the middle of shit, what I'm going to teach you'll help keep you alive. Colonel, may I borrow you for a moment?" he requested.

"Sure," Llewellyn replied as he took a guard position with his bayonet pointing at the sergeant's throat. From the corner of his eye, he could see the men studying him. Some commanders acted as if they were gods and would never stoop to be made foolish during training. Llewellyn knew at times he needed to be god-like, but he had made his fair share of mistakes during training. He had lost count how many times he had been killed. If he didn't lead by example, how could he demand his men continue to learn and improve?

"If you'd try to stick me, sir," the sergeant said as he bounced slightly on his feet.

Llewellyn took a step forward as he thrust at the sergeant's head. The sergeant stepped out with his left foot. He used his Lee-Enfield to direct Llewellyn's bayonet into the empty air to his right then swung his scabbard-covered bayonet in a flat arc to rap lightly the back of Llewellyn's head. Dickenbush then said the words he dreaded most: "You're dead, sir."

When Llewellyn took his guard position again, Dickenbush asked, "Do you want another go, sir?"

"Okay," Llewellyn grunted.

Llewellyn set up again on the balls of his feet as he waited for the sergeant to give the signal. Llewellyn thrust out again when Dickenbush said, "Go!"

This time the sergeant pulled his left foot back behind his right foot as Llewellyn's bayonet slid once again into the empty air to the sergeant's left. But this time Dickenbush's bayonet swung at his neck, stopping just an inch short of Llewellyn's cathartic artery. "You're dead again, sir."

When the sergeant returned to his relaxed stance he said, "Thank you, sir." He turned to A Company, then said, "You'll have seen this before. The basic moves and countermoves. But there's to much mucking about with this." The sergeant motioned with his rifle.

"Colonel, if you'd mind one last time."

As Llewellyn took his guard position, the sergeant suddenly leaned forward, then rapped the lieutenant-colonel's left hand holding the front stock. Llewellyn yelped in pain, causing the rifle's muzzle to drop downward. He shook his left hand for a moment as he tried, with his right hand still on the grip, to keep the muzzle up.

"Forget about sticking it in a poor bugger's chest. It's too much work, and I'm a lazy bastard. Look!" he said as he raised his rifle and touched Llewellyn's chest gently with the bayonet.

"What's fucking closer? The fucking bastard's chest or his hands? So cut the bastard's hands off!" he exclaimed. Dickenbush then wrapped Llewellyn's right hand holding the grip, causing the rifle to clatter to the ground. "If he ain't got hands, he's a right fucking useless bastard."

FEBRUARY 15, 1917
THOMPSON CRATER, ANGRES

The wracking cough bent Paul Ryan over. The spasms in his chest nearly caused his supper to come up. It hadn't been much, only thin vegetable soup.

"Are you going to live?" asked Lieutenant-Colonel Masterley as he handed him a gunmetal flask.

"It's still too early to tell," Ryan replied as he took as sip of the flask. The strong rum soothed his sore throat as it went down. A few moments later, he could feel beads of sweat on his forehead. He hoped it was the rum killing off his fever. At least, he was thankful that his stuffed nose had cleared.

After Ryan had returned the flask, Masterley wiped its mouth before he screwed the cap back on then slid it into his overcoat. He then asked, "How many have come down with it?"

"Nearly half so far," replied Ryan. "I had three report for sick parade this morning."

"The MO sent me a report this morning on the rest of the 65th," Masterley said. "It doesn't look good for the next couple of days." With the bad winter weather, a bad cold as well as the flu, there have already been a couple of deaths.

Hearing slushy boots behind them, they turned to see, in the half-moonlight, a work party arriving, weighed down by Yukon packs. They were hauling wooden boxes of 18-pounder shells from the tramlines about five hundred yards behind them. The men slid their arms out of the rope straps as they bent their knees to gently drop their loads near the closest gun pit. They unlaced the boxes from canvas stretched between two wooden staffs. The Corps had been experimenting with what was the best method to haul material and supplies to the front lines. The packs familiar to the Canadians, especially those who had gone to the Yukon during the Klondike gold rush, were cheap and easy to make. Up north, the Indigenous porters using such packs easily carried loads of seventy-five pounds over rough terrain for twelve to fifteen miles.

Ryan, feeling another cough coming, tried to hold it off, but it was too late. When he finally lifted his head, he saw Masterley looking at him with concern. "Are you sure you're okay?"

"We have orders for tonight," replied Ryan as he took a handkerchief from his pocket to wipe his mouth.

Order 7 from Corps HQ instructed the heavies and the divisional artillery to bombard the roads, communication trenches, and billets behind the German trenches in front of the 1st Division. The heavies were hitting from Cité de L'Abattoir to the Central Electric Generating Station. The divisional artillery was to strike at all the roads in Angres, the crossroads at

Liévin, and the roads from Liévin to Cité de Caumont. The 65th had been allotted five hundred shells per gun. They were scheduled to start firing at midnight, which his watch's luminous dial said was in five minutes. Ryan had spent most of the afternoon in his dugout making the calculations based on the map coordinates Corps HQ had provided.

He knew his cold was getting progressively worse, since it had taken him twice as long to make the numbers work. He was trying to keep going till morning. After the job was done, he could then collapse into his cot. If he felt this bad already, he had concerns for his men. Sure, they had plenty of experience being tired and exhausted, but when you were this played out was when things usually went wrong. He hoped that would not be the case tonight.

As the minute hand swept to twelve o'clock, his 18-pounders opened up. He let a groan slip when his headache throbbed in pain each time a shell was detonated. It was going to be a long night.

CHAPTER 5

"Confounded!" swore Sir Robert Borden as he eyed in disgust the far corner of his cabin. He turned on the lamp beside him, fixed to the night table. He darted a glance to the port window to check that the blackout curtains had been drawn. The ship's captain was strictly enforcing the blackout regulations. He groaned when he read his watch. It was only two in the morning.

The noise from the loose expansion joint in the corner of the former chief gunner's berth was driving him mad. He muttered to himself as he rose that he should have requested a new cabin; after all, he was the prime minister, and there were plenty of cabins. The HMS *Calgarian,* built for the Liverpool–Quebec City–Montreal route, had two hundred first-class, five hundred second class, and a thousand third class berths. When the Royal Navy had converted her into an armed merchant cruiser, she had lost some of her berths to the gun crews manning the eight 6-inch guns installed on her top decks. It also might have explained why his room was so cold. It had been cold enough that the water pipes in his bathroom were frozen the night he had boarded her in Halifax. If he had switched cabins, someone else would be enjoying the musical tones of the expansion joints.

He nearly tripped over the small cloth bag of necessaries he had packed earlier in the evening in case he needed to get to his assigned lifeboat. They were to rendezvous with a couple of Royal Navy destroyers for the final leg of his journey to Liverpool, since they were now sailing through the danger zone. The *Calgarian* was a fast ship, top speed twenty knots, and could easily outrun any German submarine. However, the Royal Navy wasn't taking any chances with him aboard, especially after the Germans had announced on January 31st unrestricted submarine warfare against Allied and neutral ships that were sailing in British waters.

He frowned at the thought. He didn't envy the American president. He knew that Woodrow Wilson was doing his damnedest to stay out of the war. But Borden knew sooner or later a German sub would sink an American flagged vessel and the Americans would retaliate. When they did, it would bring them into the war. It was not a matter of if but when.

He sighed as he buttoned up his vest then put on his jacket. He picked up a couple of files he wanted to review before he handed them to Rogers and Hazen for their comments. They were accompanying him on his voyage to London. Besides the files he had brought with him, the ship's wireless had been providing him with daily updates from Ottawa.

As he stepped into the dimly lit empty corridor, he closed his cabin door behind him then headed to the smoking room. He hoped reading the reports his bureaucrats had prepared for him would put him to sleep. If they didn't, the chairs in the smoking room were very comfortable. And at this hour of the night, the quiet might help him get some much-needed sleep.

MARCH 8, 1917
NEVSKY PROSPECT, PETROGRAD

"I don't think we should've come this way?" said Christine, who was walking beside Samantha Lonsdale.

"I think you're right," Samantha replied. She didn't like the mood of the crowd on the street, and it was making her nervous. Petrograd was always a tense city, but if you kept your wits about you and knew which parts were best to avoid, you would be relatively safe. However, ever since the workers at the Putilov steel mill held a strike for higher wages on February 18th (based on the Russian calendar), the tension in the city had become unsettled. It had become especially worrisome after the mill had locked out twenty thousand workers. From there, the unrest had spread with nearly half the city being on strike for one reason or another.

"I really don't like this," Christine complained again as she and Samantha picked up the pace to clear the side street that connected to Nevsky Prospect. They were heading to the Passage department store on Nevsky Avenue for some desperately needed toiletries. Samantha's eyes darted at the shops lining the street to see which ones were open in case they needed to duck in for safety. Most were closed and boarded up to protect the display windows from the strikers and looters. Some, she suspected, had gone out of business. Getting merchandise to sell was next to impossible. Even if they did manage to get goods, many of the citizens of Petrograd could not afford them.

"Neither do I," replied Samantha. She suddenly clutched Christine's arm as the crowd started unfurling several banners. Her Russian was limited, so she couldn't read the slogans on them. Most likely about high prices and low wages.

"Oh, shit!" Samantha blurted. "We've better get off the street."

"Ouch, that hurts," Christine complained. "Why? Oh?" She gulped when she finally saw what Samantha had spotted. A cavalry troop of Cossacks was now blocking the way to Nevsky Prospect. Turning their heads to look behind them, they saw a similar troop blocking the other end. They were dressed in khaki uniforms with bandoliers criss-crossing their chest and rifles slung on their backs. The Cossacks were not a good sign.

"Do you see any shops that are open?" Samantha asked as she and Christine scanned the stores again.

"I'm not seeing any. Do you think we'll be okay? The Cossacks at last week's demonstration were peaceful."

"I heard the same," replied Samantha. From the stories, she had been told the Cossacks had been quite friendly to the demonstrators. They had even played with the kids.

"There!" Samantha shouted as they ran to the dress shop that looked open. Just before they got there, the door slammed shut. When Christine had gotten there, she started rattling, then pounding on the door. Through the glass window, Samantha could see the clerk inside shaking in fear. She backed away and then hurried to the back of the shop. Samantha glanced at Christine. "Let's stay here. We'll be off the street at least." She hoped that the door frame's deep inset and the shop's bay windows would make them less visible.

She watched as the banners continued to move toward the Cossacks. An officer kicked his horse forward out of the cavalry troop then shouted out commands. From his tone, there was no doubt that he wanted the crowd to disperse. They ignored him, refusing to stop. Some yelled defiantly at the lined-up Cossacks.

He must have given a command, by voice or gesture, because suddenly there were the sounds and the flash of sabres being drawn from their scabbards. The crowd trembled for a moment but continued forward. The officer made a motion with his hand. The Cossacks' horses stepped toward the crowd at a steady pace with steel sabres resting on the troopers' shoulders. The horses, the sabres, and the blank faces on the Cossacks scared the hell out of her. Samantha hadn't felt this way since Ypres. The crowd started to splinter into smaller groups as they flowed around the horses when the troopers hit the protesters' front line.

Suddenly, Samantha heard the familiar sounds of rifle fire, then one of the horses reared up, throwing its rider. Not waiting to see whether their comrade had been shot or not, the Cossacks started slashing at the crowd with their sabres. Samantha saw a couple of the troopers being dragged off their horses. Once on the ground, the protestors started punching and kicking the downed men.

As men and women started yelling and screaming, they started to back away to avoid the slashing sabres. There were cries of shock and pain when a blade or rifle bullet struck home.

In less than a minute, the street was cleared. Ten or so bodies were lying on the cobblestone. Samantha left the safety of the shop door when saw them.

Christine yelled at her, "What the hell are you doing?"

"They need help," she shouted back as she headed to the nearest body. Samantha noticed several others in the crowd stop to help some of the wounded.

The first one she reached was a young woman in her mid-twenties. Samantha couldn't help noting that she had lost a shoe, but she was more concerned about the blood that was seeping from a cut on her shoulder. She tried to calm the woman as she examined the wound. Fortunately, it was a shallow six-inch cut. Her heavy coat and sweater had taken the brunt of the sabre. All she needed was a bandage and few stitches. When a man hurried over to help, her husband, she presumed, she motioned him to keep pressure on the wound to stop the flow. The man nodded but then helped the woman to her feet so they could get off the street.

The other man wasn't so lucky. He had a deep gash that ran down his back. She guessed that he was running away when he was struck. He was groaning in pain as he tried to rise to his knees, but he then collapsed. She used the remnants of his dirty jacket, all that she had, to put pressure on his back.

"*Nyet!*" said a voice. When she looked up, she saw a Cossack officer pointing a sabre at her.

She pushed the point aside and said, "*Ya medoesta*," Russian for *I'm a nurse*.

"You English," he said with a thick accent.

"Canadian. This man needs help," she replied as she stared at the officer. The Cossack pressed his lips together, then grunted. He waved at two men with a wheeled cart nearby. They were nervous when they rolled the cart over to Samantha. They helped her put the man in it, then they started to wheel him away, to a hospital, she hoped. She didn't have time to worry about it as she went to the next patient.

MARCH 9, 1917
85TH BATTALION, GOUY-SERVINS

Stepping out of his staff car, Sir Robert Borden smiled as his cousin gave him a smart salute. "Good afternoon, Colonel," he said as he shook his cousin's hand.

"Prime Minister," replied Lieutenant-Colonel Allison Hart Borden. They were rather formal with each other, which was to be expected, especially since Major-General David Watson, the GOC of the 4th Division, was accompanying him on this part of the tour of the Canadian Corps' front.

"You're looking well," Sir Robert said as he took a good look at Allison. His cousin was thirty-eight years old and was two inches shy of six feet. He did look a bit thin. His moustache and hair had turned greyer since he had last seen him.

"I'm fine," Allison replied warmly.

"I'm glad to hear that," Borden said. Still, there was a touch of concern in his voice. The weather was cold enough that the dusting of snow on the parade ground hadn't melted. His cousin was in his battle dress with his steel helmet, while the top button of his trench coat was digging slightly into his throat. He had buttoned it as protection against the brisk wind. Instead of a helmet, he was wearing a black wool fedora to keep his head warm, since the weather was Canada-like.

Borden had been busy ever since he had arrived safely in London on the 22nd. He hadn't wasted any time before he was in meetings with the king and Lloyd George. His meetings with the British prime minister were to discuss the Allied war effort and the details of the upcoming Imperial War Conference. He also had long discussions with Perley concerning the new Canadian Overseas Ministry. He had made suggestions to George to hire aides to help relieve him of some of his workload and to find confidential sources to keep him informed on what was not in the reports he was receiving from his general staff. When he wasn't in meetings, he was visiting hospitals to see the wounded. A sad case was one of his fellow Nova Scotians suffering from shell shock. He seemed to be cheerful and good-natured, but he couldn't stop trembling. Yesterday, he had inspected the

Moore Barracks Hospital and the Canadian units training at Folkestone before taking the ferry to Boulogne-sur-Mer. There, he had visited the 3rd Canadian General Hospital, where one of the nursing sisters, after working there for two years, mentioned that she was desperately homesick.

He had spent the night at Hesdin before heading to the Canadian Corps HQ at the Château de Ranchicourt, where he was greeted by Major-General Currie and his staff. Before having lunch with Currie, he had been taken to an observation tower to view the St. Eloi battlefield. He guessed the Germans must have heard he was in the vicinity, because the duelling German and Canadian artillery had given him a show. On the drive to back to Corps HQ, he had been informed that the day before, the Germans had targeted the road they were using and that several men had been killed.

The two companies arrayed before him were dressed similarly to his cousin. Major-General Watson had informed him on the drive to Gouy-Servins that only A and D companies were available for his inspection. The B and C companies had been assigned as work parties to the front trenches.

Allison had been on light duty with the Royal Canadian Regiment the month before the war started. In his second year of study at the staff college in England, he had fallen ill. It had been severe enough that he had to drop out; it meant he was no longer on the promotion path. After a year, he had sufficiently recovered that he had been given command of the newly created 85th Battalion in September of 1915. It had been his job to fill the new battalion's ranks. He had been so energetic and successful at it that by the end of the month the 85th was up to full strength.

This had been noticed by the Woods Building, who then authorized the formation of the Nova Scotia Highland brigade with his cousin in command. Until the brigade had reached its full strength, it had delayed the 85th sailing for France until September of last year, when the Highland Brigade had finally arrived in England to join the 4th Division. The irony was that now only the 85th remained. He had gotten an earful from his fellow Nova Scotians when they found out the Corps had broken up the Highland Brigade to supply the front line units with much-needed reinforcements to replace the losses they had suffered at the Somme.

"They're a fine-looking group of men," Sir Robert stated.

"Yes, they are," Allison said with pride as he led Sir Robert to the first row of Nova Scotians. "They're looking forward to meeting you."

Borden couldn't help but glance at his cousin. Part of him wished that Allison had stuck with the law. Instead, he had decided to join the Royal Canadian Regiment, stationed in Halifax, after spending only a year articling. He had already lost one cousin to the war, Jessie Jaggard in September of 1915. She had volunteered as a matron with the Canadian Nursing Service and died of dysentery at Lemnos during the Gallipoli campaign.

There was very little that he could do for Allison directly. He doubted he would have appreciated Borden's intervention. He hoped that the war would be over soon, but then he recalled his conversation with General Byng, in London on sick leave, and Lady Byng at a dinner last Sunday. Byng thought that the war might end this year but then qualified his statement by saying he was no expert on the matter.

CHAPTER 6

"I'm sorry, Lieutenant," said Masterley in a sympathetic tone. The lieutenant-colonel was standing with a group of senior officers near the finish line. "You'll have to run it again."

"Why? Sir?" Ryan asked as he drank water from a white-enamelled tin cup.

"I'm afraid that Major Craig, Captain Kindle, and you were given the wrong orders at the second checkpoint," said Masterley. "You'll have to do the course again."

"How did this happen?" Ryan asked after he stifled his urge to swear. He didn't really want to run eight and half miles again. His legs ached and started to stiffen. And he still felt clammy. The morning had started off with dull grey cloud cover with the look of rain. He did get wet a couple of times when it showered. His body heat had dried his clothes somewhat. He hadn't worn much, just boots, slacks, a khaki sweater over his shirt, and his forge cap. On his hip, his satchel contained his compass, the standard Verner MK VII model, and a map.

His time wasn't that bad, but it wasn't great. He had done the course in fifty-eight minutes and thirty-eight seconds. He had pushed himself hard, but he doubted it would improve by much the second time around unless the corrected orders shaved some of it off. He was pretty sure that he wasn't in the running for the first-place prize, a silver cigarette case.

The race he had just run had been a map-reading point-to-point competition. You were issued a compass, a map, and four checkpoints to find. The first one was given at the start line, then as you reached each checkpoint you were given the location of the next one. There wasn't a specific route to follow. You had to use the compass and the topographical map to find and navigate the fastest route between the checkpoints.

From the start line, he had headed east to Houdain for about a mile and a half, then south for two miles, and then west for another two and a quarter miles. The final checkpoint had been less than a mile from the plateau at Maisnil-lès-Ruitz, where the 65th had been billeted for the last four days after a route march from Grenay. While the countryside had been pretty, the rolling terrain had been tiring.

"It just happened," Masterley replied. Ryan noticed he didn't want to get into it. It was somewhat embarrassing, since he was the one responsible for organizing the race.

"Who had the best time?" Ryan asked. There had been fourteen officers in the race. They left the start line in five-minute intervals. The senior officers had decided the race would be a good training exercise, as well as some entertainment for the other ranks who were gathered at the finish line to watch the competitors stagger in.

"It was Major Craig. He did the course in forty-seven minutes," Masterley stated.

"You're kidding," Ryan blurted. That was impressive. Point-to-point racing was demanding, mentally and physically. A simple mistake such as a misreading of the map or the compass would cost you valuable time. One degree off course could mean you'd miss the checkpoint by a couple of hundred yards.

He was tempted to refuse, but the recent reorganization of the 65th from four guns to six, mandated by Corps HQ, gave him pause. He had been told that the new organization meant that each battery would have a single major, captain, and six subalterns. Competition for the slots was fierce. While Masterley liked him, he still had to display some eagerness if he wanted to keep his slot. The alternative was that he could be sent to the surplus officer pool, or worse, to the mortar trench batteries. "Yes, sir. I'll do my best."

"That's good Lieutenant. That's very good," said Masterley as he went back to the start line.

MARCH 15, 1917
THE LABYRINTH SECTION, VIMY RIDGE

"We didn't capture any prisoners," was the first thing Captain Lowry said to Lieutenant-Colonel Llewellyn when he slid through the gap in the wire and down the wet bank into the trench. He wasn't surprised to find him waiting for him. Lowry would have preferred the lieutenant-colonel stay in his advanced command post dugout, where it was somewhat safer than in the front-line trenches. Lowry was well aware that ever since Llewellyn got buried last October at Albert, his CO didn't like being underground. Still, it would have given him time to see to his men, brush some of the mud off his battle dress, and fancy up a report, such as it was, for him.

The men were sullen as they plodded past him and Llewellyn as they headed to the waiting hot food, coffee, and rum. Some would pour their rum ration into their coffee to make it last. Pressed against the trench wall, Lowry saw that Llewellyn had read the message from the men that the raid hadn't gone as planned.

"We didn't capture a single one," Lowry repeated.

"How many did we lose?" Llewellyn asked, giving some of the passing men a word of encouragement as he patted some on the shoulder.

"At least four are unaccounted for. More once I get the rest of the reports in," he replied.

"Killed or captured?"

"I don't know," the captain admitted. "They were ready for us when we launched our raid."

"Shit!" Llewellyn spat as he sent a glare toward the German trenches. His view was blocked by the wet sandbags.

The 2nd Brigade had taken over the Labyrinth section of the line. Whoever had called it the Labyrinth had named it well. The series of communications and front-line trenches was such a tangle, it wasn't uncommon for units to get lost, in some cases swallowed whole. The French and Germans had suffered losses of nearly a hundred and sixty thousand men here. Half of them were still out there. His men regularly stumbled across their skeletons during their nightly raids. In the dark, they couldn't tell if they were French or German. It didn't help much that it had rained recently and that No Man's Land was soft.

"Yeah, they opened up on us when we got to their front wire. We got pinned, and we couldn't move forward. Then the mortars started landing on top of us."

"No German patrols?" Llewellyn asked.

"Not for the last two nights. Our listening posts didn't hear anything unusual or that the Boche were on the alert."

"Hmm, that's two in a row," Llewellyn stated. "This and B Company's raid two nights ago."

Lowry nodded in agreement. B Company's raid had been a dud. The trench they had raided was empty. If they had known, they might have been able to exploit it to open a gap. However, the Stokes mortar teams, machine guns, and the 65th's 18-pounders, who were providing them with fire support, were following a strict timetable based on the Fusiliers' raid plan. Llewellyn was trying to build flexibility into the Fusiliers so they could deal with unexpected problems as they came up. The empty trench had been an opportunity, but exploiting it meant calling on the reserves and then getting Major-General Loomis to bring in the rest of the brigade. It might have even required calling on the entire 1st Division's resources. Sadly, by the time everyone would have gotten their act together, it would have slipped away. The Huns weren't fools. Once they had realized what had happened, their mortars and artillery started hammering the empty trench. Luckily, by then B Company was back in their start line and hadn't suffered any losses.

Actually, the Huns weren't the ones they were afraid of. They were more afraid of Major-General Currie's reactions when he found out. He already had shown his displeasure with his brigade commanders who didn't come back with prisoners. Everyone knew he wanted them to gather intelligence for the Corps' upcoming operations. He had made it perfectly clear that failure was not an option.

"See to your men," Llewellyn finally said. "Once you've done that, come to my dugout. We need to discuss what we need to do next."

"Yes, sir," replied Lowry.

★ ★ ★

The Richmond Fusiliers' advanced command post had been dug out of the soft chalk by the mining section. There was the ever-present risk of banging one's head on an outcrop or a hanging light, since the tunnels were not that tall. The passage leading to Lieutenant-Colonel Llewellyn's HQ was dripping water from the support beams. The electric lights brightened the gloom, but the drips sometimes shorted the power lines, tossing everyone into darkness until the torches were lit and the power restored.

When he entered the cave that served as Llewellyn's office and sleeping quarters he found captains Hastings and Marshall, the B Company and the C Company COs, already sitting on overturned empty mortar ammo crates in front of Llewellyn. One had been left empty for him.

Llewellyn motioned for him to take a seat. As he crouched down on one of the crates, Llewellyn asked him, "Did you get your men settled in?"

"Yes, sir," Lowry replied. "The final tally is that I'm missing six men."

Llewellyn grimaced. "Killed or prisoners?"

"I'm hoping that they are prisoners," he replied.

Llewellyn grunted an acknowledgement, followed by a flash of concern. One of the lieutenant-colonel's practices was to keep the men informed of operations so they could do their jobs better. Also, the men weren't stupid, for the most part. They inevitably picked up scraps of information here and there concerning future operations that would interest German intelligence.

"We'll find out soon enough from the Red Cross," replied Llewellyn. "Now, I called you in because of tonight's raid. It's the second one without results."

All three men looked grim. Brigade and Division HQs weren't going to be happy. "When I passed the info up the line, I want to also propose a plan to fill in the gaps that we have about the Huns."

Llewellyn tossed his head at the large map hanging on the wall and the panoramic view of the Hun trenches hanging below it. The view was created by stitching together pencil drawings of the enemy positions. The map showed the current dispositions of the Richmond Fusiliers and the 2nd Brigade. But, more importantly, above the German trench lines Llewellyn had written *1st Bavarian Reserve Division, Group Vimy.* Below it showed that the German 1st and 3rd Infantry Regiments were holding the front trenches with the 2nd in reserve. Scattered among the German infantry were markings where the 1st, 3rd, and 17th German Pioneers were working to improve their trenches and where they were building machine gun nests. Squares indicated where each German unit's HQ was located. Along with the unit names, the names of their COs were written. The most prominent name on the map was General Karl Ritter von Fassbender, the GOC of the 1st Bavarian Reserve Division. Not much was known about the Bavarian general, just that he had come out of retirement when the war started and had proven to be a good general.

"We still have too many gaps that we need to fill," Llewellyn said as he glanced at the sketches before returning his gaze back to them. When Llewellyn sighed, Lowry knew, having spent enough time with the lieutenant-colonel, he was going to give orders he didn't particularly like but that he felt were necessary to get the job done. "We have to capture some prisoners, and we need to do it tonight. The Boche are probably going to be waiting for us, but what I want you three to do is to select a platoon each. Then, at three-hour intervals, we're going to raid the German trenches and keep raiding until we come back with prisoners. Do I make myself clear?"

"Yes, sir," Lowry and the other two officers answered.

MARCH 16, 1917
DRAWING ROOM, SOLTYKOFF PALACE, PETROGRAD

"So, what happens now?" Samantha asked.

Meriel Buchanan gave her a slight *I have no idea* shrug as they sat in the small drawing room in the British consulate. Through the window that faced the Neva, Samantha could see the grey skies above the Saints Peter and Paul Cathedral's gold-painted spire on the other side of the river. It had been cold when they came to the embassy, but at least there was little wind. It was usually bitter at this time of year, or so she had been told. She skipped over the paintings of aristocrats and former British ambassadors that covered the walls when she returned her eyes to Meriel sitting in a deep brown leather wing chair. She and Dorothy were sitting directly across from her in a similar coloured settee. In front of them was a pot with hot tea steaming from the porcelain cups.

The room was peaceful, considering the embassy's tense turmoil when they had come to pay Meriel a visit. Meriel looked a little drawn, with her hair neatly combed and put up. Her dress was more for warmth and comfort instead of for style. Samantha and Dorothy were wearing their nurses' dresses, since they didn't have time to change after they had completed their shifts at the Anglo-Russian Hospital. Meriel had been happy to see them. Samantha knew, ever since she had arrived back from visiting a friend in the Baltics, that her father had insisted she not leave the embassy. Ambassador Buchanan was extremely concerned about her safety. Samantha sympathized. It had been risky for her and Dorothy to come to the embassy, although it was only a half-hour walk from the hospital. They had hoped that nursing uniforms would provide them with some protection as they made their way here on foot.

"No one is certain at the moment," Meriel replied. "When I arrived at the train station, it was the first that I learned about the riots. At the station, one of my father's officers was waiting to escort me home. The trams weren't running, and the cabs were on strike. My friends and I, and our luggage, all had to get into one motor."

"Some of the trams and wires still aren't working," Dorothy said as she picked up her teacup.

Samantha nodded in agreement. "I tried to call you about the rumours that Czar Nicholas had abdicated, but the lines were dead. On our way here we saw why; the telephone boxes were wrecked."

"My father warned him in January that he needed to make concessions. It was up to him to lead Russia to victory or to a revolution or to a disaster."

"It looks like a disaster at the moment," Samantha said.

"Why didn't he listen to your father?" Dorothy asked after taking a sip of tea.

Meriel frowned when she said, "He's under the influence of the czarina, and she wasn't in any mood to make concessions, especially after what happened to Rasputin. It didn't help that Protopov supported her." When Meriel saw their blank looks she said, "As the minister of interior, he was responsible for the police and Russia's food supplies. According to my father, he was slowly going insane."

"So, he's the one responsible for this mess then?" Samantha stated.

Before Meriel could reply, Dorothy asked, "Who's going to be the next czar?"

"We don't know. He had abdicated in favour of his brother, the Grand Duke Michael. But the Duke refused. He said he would only accept becoming the czar if he was unanimously elected by the people."

"Is there any likelihood that is going to happen?" Dorothy asked.

"I don't know," Meriel replied. "The Duma has picked Prince Lvov as the prime minister, and he also shall be the minister of the interior. Milyukov shall be the minister of foreign affairs."

"Do you think they'll pull out of the war?" Samantha asked.

Meriel sighed. "I don't think so. My father says Lvov is competent. He was chairman of the Russian Union of Zemstvos and Towns. They're the ones who have been keeping the Russian army supplied with what little they have.

"As for Milyukov, he seems to be favourable to continuing the war."

Samantha glanced at Dorothy then chewed on the corner of her mouth in thought. If the Russians pulled out of the war, it would mean that she wouldn't have to deal with the broken bodies of Russian peasants that came in daily at the hospital. But it would also mean that the German armies facing Russia would be freed to be sent to the Western Front to face James and the rest of the Canadians.

"How are things at the hospital?" Meriel asked. "Father hasn't allowed me out of the embassy in days." She had worked shifts at the hospital, since she had some basic training as a nurse.

"The riots and the strikes have put a strain on all of us," Samantha said. "We've all pulled extra-long shifts."

"It was days before we could leave the hospital. We had to wait until it became quiet or at least quieter," Dorothy stated. "But we're short on medical supplies and food. Not only for our regular patients but also those who were hurt in the riots. We couldn't turn them away when they showed up at our doors."

"If it's bad for us at the hospital, I don't know what it's like for the refugees," Samantha pointed out. Dorothy grimaced in agreement.

"We did lose our guards for a few days, but they're back now," Samantha said. "What concerns me is that the Imperial coats of arms that used to hang above the shops have been torn down and burnt. We had to cover the Imperial seal in front of the hospital. We may need to remove the placards in the wards. As you know, they name the aristocrats who have subscribed to the hospital fund."

"I did hear at the Winter Palace they've replaced the czar's yellow flag with a red one," Meriel stated.

"At the Winter Palace?" Dorothy blurted.

Meriel nodded an acknowledgement.

"What's going to happen to the czar and his family? Are they staying in Russia?" asked Samantha.

Meriel shook her head. "My father is looking to make arrangements for them to come to England."

"Where's he now?" Dorothy asked.

"He's still in the palace," Meriel replied.

"I wonder what he'll be doing since he's out of a job?" Dorothy asked.

"Well, if he's looking for work, he can help out at the hospital," Samantha suggested. "We have plenty of bedpans that need emptying."

They all chuckled at the thought of the czar cleaning bedpans.

MARCH 20, 1917
ANGLO-RUSSIAN HOSPITAL, PETROGRAD

Samantha squeezed her eyes shut when a bright light fell directly on her face as the door to the former grand duchess's wardrobe was pulled opened. It took her a couple of tries before her eyes adjusted. The other nurses who had been sleeping in the wardrobe shouted out at whoever the damn person was who had opened the door to shut it. While shadows hid her face and turned her blue uniform to a dark grey shade, Samantha had recognized the figure who was partially blocking the light.

"Is it time already?" Samantha croaked as she sat up. She had tossed and turned for the few hours that she managed to doze off. It hadn't helped that she had slept in her uniform. She wanted more sleep, but she knew she wouldn't get it; her night shift was starting soon.

"I'm afraid so," Dorothy replied. The nurses continued to complain as Samantha rolled off the mattress lying on the plank flooring to rise to her feet. She brushed at her dress to smooth out some of the wrinkles as she glanced around the closet with an ironic smile. The wardrobe that once had been filled with a duchess's shoes, coats, and dresses was easily large enough to accommodate five sleeping nurses. Thin mattresses and pillows had been spread out to make it somewhat more comfortable.

"How are things outside?" Samantha asked Dorothy as she stepped into the hallway. The door closing behind them cut the complaints.

"Last time I looked, it was pretty quiet. There're some soldiers on the corner who have a fire lit to keep warm. It's freezing outside," she answered.

"Glad to hear it's quiet. What I wouldn't do for a hot bath," Samantha said with a sigh. The last time she and Dorothy had been out of their clothes was four days ago when they had visited Meriel. Afterward, she and Dorothy had first tried to get something to eat at the Astoria, which sadly was in ruins because of the fighting. Then they went to the Europe Restaurant, but it had been closed because of the lack of food. They were forced to go to the Club, a former men's club converted into a nurses' residence by the Anglo-Russian Hospital when they first opened. The Club didn't have much, just boiled turnips, but when she and Dorothy had discovered they had warm water, the baths they had taken had been wonderful.

"Anything to eat?" Samantha asked. Her stomach growled as she followed Dorothy to the nurse's station in the main ward. The ward's lights were low to help the patients get some sleep. Still, she could hear some of the patients snoring and the squeaking of beds as others tossed and turned.

"Just tea and rye bread," Dorothy replied.

"Tea it is," Samantha stated as she took her chair behind the table with the nurse's logbook lying open. She gave it a quick glance then looked up at Dorothy to ask, "Do you think with the new Duma that things will return to normal?"

"You're asking me?" Dorothy replied. "I was surprised like everyone else when the czar and the czarina abdicated. Who knows what's going to happen next?"

Samantha had to agree. From the hospital windows, they'd seen some of the marches dissolve into riots on the Nevsky Prospect. There was no love lost between the locals, the police, and the Okhrana, the Russian Secret Police. The locals hated the Okhrana so much so that they had ransacked their headquarters on the Fontanka Quai. Others had looted the local arsenals, so now everyone had a weapon of some sort. Motor cars regularly drove past the hospital handing out ammo boxes to whoever asked. It was the soldiers now, instead of the police or the Cossacks, patrolling the streets, trying to keep the peace.

Both Samantha and Dorothy turned to the windows when they heard machine-gun fire, a now familiar sound. They suspected that there was one on top of the buildings across the street. They heard ragged rifle fire respond then the thud of bullets hitting the hospital walls. There was the twinkle of glass as bullets struck the windows then smacked into the ceiling. Plaster dust swirled from the holes they had made. Samantha wondered why they were firing at their building. Didn't they know this was a hospital? Those patients who could rolled to the floor with harsh thuds. Samantha and Dorothy scanned the ward checking for broken glass, but it appeared the bullets hadn't actually shattered the windows, just made holes in it.

"Here we go again," Samantha said as she and Dorothy headed to the patients so they could move them away from the windows. The sanitors were also checking to see whether anyone was hurt or had their wounds reopened when they fell out of their cots. Since it seemed the firing had stopped, the sanitors started to clean up the damage.

They had barely moved one of the cots when they heard angry voices and the pounding of feet coming up the stairs that led to their ward. Samantha headed for the ward's entrance with Dorothy on her heels. She glanced at the walls to check that all the insignia and plaques had been removed. With the abdication, they had removed, like most of the stores on Nevsky Prospect, all traces of royal patronage.

When they had reached the doors, they were confronted by a squad of soldiers who were levelling rifles at her and Dorothy. Samantha paused for a moment then raised her hands up before asking, "What's going on?"

The leader, a man of medium height, black hair, and moustache, and dressed in a uniform with a red button on his breast, barked at her in Russian.

"What's he saying?" Dorothy asked beside her. Her arms were raised as well.

Captain Krushchev appeared from behind the soldiers in civilian dress. One of the startled soldiers fired a shot that echoed in the staircase. Everyone froze for a moment, then the officer started berating the soldier that had fired. Luckily, no one was hurt. Then he started yelling at Captain Krushchev.

"Captain. What does he want?" Samantha asked as she kept her hands up.

"He wants to go to roof. Says machine gun on roof," he replied.

"What makes him think there's a machine gun on our roof? Doesn't he know we're a hospital?" Samantha said.

"He does, but his men insist the machine-gun fire came from our roof. He wants to check it."

"Well, show him the roof," Dorothy ordered.

The captain slithered between the soldiers and then led them down the hallway to a set of stairs that led to the roof.

"Do you believe that?" Samantha said, exasperated, as she put her hands down. "A machine gun on a hospital?"

"I know," Dorothy replied as she lowered hers as well.

A few minutes later, the soldiers returned. Samantha wasn't sure if they were mollified or angry because they couldn't find the machine gun. The Russian officer berated Captain Krushchev before they left.

"What was that all about?" Dorothy demanded.

Captain Krushchev sighed. "He says if we hospital, we should fly Red Cross flag."

"Where are we going to get a Red Cross flag at this hour?" Samantha asked.

Dorothy opened her mouth then closed it. "We do have white sheets. All we need is something red."

Samantha crinkled her nose in thought. "Do we still have that Santa suit?"

"I think so. It's in a box somewhere," Dorothy replied. Suddenly, she realized where Samantha was going with it, she said, "Oh, I see. If we sewed it on the sheet, from the street it will look like a Red Cross flag."

"I don't know if it will help much, but it couldn't hurt," stated Samantha.

CHAPTER 7

"So, what do you think?" Major Gavin asked Lieutenant-Colonel Llewellyn.

"I don't know," Llewellyn replied as he inspected Private Andrew Gilschrist. The young man, with eyes looking much older than his nineteen years, had been in a lot of action since he had joined the Richmond Fusiliers last August.

"I suggest the lad get on the scale," Sergeant Duval said. He was standing nearby with his arms crossed.

"Hop on, Private," ordered Llewellyn as he motioned him to mount the scale that was set up in the middle of the shed. They had borrowed the scale from the quartermaster, who had been using it to check the supplies they were buying from the locals weren't short-weighted. The scale, sitting on four steel wheels, could easily handle Gilschrist's weight, since six hundred pounds was its max. Dressed in his regulation uniform, without his helmet and kit, he came in at a hundred and sixty pounds.

Gilschrist stepped gingerly on the scale. He had to use his Lee-Enfield for balance as the metal place dipped slightly under his weight. He was dressed in fighting order: a steel helmet, a small box respirator sitting on his chest, ammo pouches filled with the standard 150-round load, and four Mills bombs attached to his ammo pouches.

Llewellyn had begun handing out grenades to all the men in his battalion. He was starting to question the need for a bombing section as tactics were starting to dictate the advantages of each man being equipped with grenades. Some of the bombers were carping about it. They didn't want to lose their special status. Besides, anyone could easily be taught to throw a grenade. It wasn't that difficult.

On Gilschrist's left hip hung a bayonet and a truncheon for the entrenching tool. On his right hip, he had a filled water bottle. His pants were neatly folded under the puttees that were tightly wrapped around his calves and covered the ankles of his hob-nailed boots. The private's shoulder sagged slightly under the weight of the load he was carrying on his back: a heavy haversack with a folded rubber ground sheet underneath, a mess tin held in place by a strap with the buckle on the lid sat on top, and the canvas carrier for the steel plate entrenching tool dangled two inches below his waist belt.

Once the private was settled, Major Gavin slid the weight on the beam that jutted out from the scale back and forth until it was level, then read the weight. "He comes in at two hundred and twenty-eight."

"Damn, that's still too much," Llewellyn muttered.

"Yeah," Gavin agreed.

Llewellyn pursed his lips. They had weighed the private earlier in full marching order, and he had come in nearly twenty pounds heavier. To reduce his load, they had removed inessentials such as the greatcoat that weighed eight pounds dry but twenty when wet; the small toiletry kit was a pound; the sewing kit, the clasp knife, and the oil bottle and pull through, which were several pounds; and other items the men had taken a fancy to. That was one thing about the 1908 Webbing kit. It was a modular system that allowed you to add or remove parts based on operational needs.

"It's going to be worse for the bombers and the Lewis gunners," the major pointed out. Llewellyn grunted an acknowledgement. Corps HQ had ordered that he reduce as much as possible the weight the men carried into battle. Llewellyn snorted in derision when he read the order. The men were already quite adept at getting rid of anything in their gear they thought was useless. The Lewis gunners had to carry more weight than the bayonet men. The Lewis gun was twenty-eight pounds, and the two spare ammunition pans the gunners carried were nearly four and a half pounds each. The rest of the three-man Lewis gun team carried five pans to keep the Lewises supplied. The bombers with their vests and buckets carried similar weights.

At the beginning of the war, the total weight of a full kit was sixty-eight pounds, while in fighting order it was reduced to fifty-eight pounds. The addition of new equipment such as steel helmets, Mills bombs, wire cutters, and small box respirators had increased the weight he and his men had to carry. It presented a huge problem. Ideally, the men shouldn't have to carry more than forty percent of their body weight, which was a nice balance of endurance and speed. A couple of pounds didn't seem like much, but Llewellyn knew from experience how exhausting it was carrying that load crossing six hundred yards of rough terrain before entering a German trench. His legs always felt watery, and he didn't have much energy to fight more than a few minutes. The forced marches were great at building the men's endurance, but it wasn't the same as when they were in the attack. Reducing his men's carry loads could mean the difference between gaining or losing ground.

"I know. We have to see what we can do to lose a couple of pounds here and there."

"We could reduce the ammo load from one fifty to a hundred maybe even ninety rounds. We can save some weight that way," suggested Gavin.

"Now, hold on!" exclaimed the corporal. "What are they going to use when they run out?"

"That's what the SAA carts are for," replied Major Gavin.

"Colonel!" Duval implored when he turned to him for support.

Llewellyn was about to agree then paused. "How much do we carry in a raid?"

"Well, that's different. We're in and out right quick," Duval replied. "When you have captured a trench it's different. We need ammo, food, water, and the supplies to consolidate the trenches."

"We have the fourth wave. They can carry most of those supplies," Llewellyn stated. He paused then said, "I have a question. How often have the men used all their rounds?"

It was Duval's turn to think, as did the major. "I really don't know. We never thought about that."

"I know the one fifty is the standard load. Do a head count and see how often our men used all of them in a fight. If they haven't, then we can reduce what we need to carry. We may need to push the SAA carts to the third wave." Llewellyn didn't say anything, but he knew, based on the current plans, that Byng was planning to capture the Vimy Ridge in under four hours. "Now that's a possibility. I'm not saying yes or no."

"Yes, sir," replied Gavin.

"Now let's see what we can do to lose a few pounds," Llewellyn said as he reexamined Gilschrist's kit.

CABINET ROOM, 10 DOWNING STREET, LONDON

As Big Ben struck four o'clock, Lloyd George paused for a moment then continued, "It's a mistake for us to assume we can beat the Germans in 1917."

Sir Robert Borden, who was directly sitting across from the British prime minister, glanced at George Perley, who was next to him. Borden could hear the creaking of leather chairs arranged around the massive table that dominated the cabinet room on the second floor of 10 Downing

Street. Some of the noises were from restlessness; it was nearly teatime, and they needed a break. They'd been there since eleven o'clock, as attested by the stack of classified reports and papers covering the green tablecloth. The nib pens in front of the clear crystal glass inkwells were dripping black ink onto notepaper from the wooden box organizers arrayed on the table. The air was thick with grey smoke from cigarettes, cigars, and pipes. The light was beginning to fade from the large windows at Sir Robert's back.

Borden returned his gaze back to Lloyd George, who was sitting in the only chair with arms in the room. Directly behind the PM was a white marble fireplace, above which hung the only painting in the room. It was of Sir Robert Walpole, the first prime minister of Great Britain. "So there is no hope of victory by the end of the year?"

"We can only hope," Lloyd George replied to Borden's question. The British prime minister was in his mid-fifties and of medium height. His grey hair and bushy moustache were in a need of a slight trim. Borden was familiar with Lloyd George, since he had been the minister of munitions during his previous visits to England to discuss shell contracts. He had shaken up the bureaucracy and had been responsible for the increase in production.

Since he became the prime minister last December, he had shown a willingness to do things differently. One of them was forming the first Imperial War Cabinet. "Germany is still in a powerful position, and she is stronger than she has ever been. She has more men, more powerful weapons, interior lines of communications, and enormous resources. It is true; our civilian army has become a veteran one. Its amateur officers are now becoming trained skilled leaders of men. But as the struggle goes on, we have to depend more and more on the resources of the British Empire. For us to succeed in our aims, we need more men!"

Sir Robert kept his silence, as did the prime ministers of New Zealand, William Massey, and Newfoundland, Edward Morris. Lieutenant-General Smuts, the South African defence minister, acknowledged with a grunt. Borden had met with both Massey and Smuts before the cabinet meeting to discuss several issues they had in common. He was also interested in how the New Zealand prime minister had managed to form a coalition government between his Reform Party and his opposition Liberals. He was seriously considering the same thing with his Liberals, if he could convince Laurier of the benefits of a coalition government for the country. His government's term was running out, and the *BNA Act* would require him to call a general election. He wanted to avoid that if he could. It was for the same reason that Billy Hughes, the Australian prime minister, had decided not to attend the first ever Imperial War Cabinet meeting. Hughes couldn't afford to be away from Australia for six months when a writ for general election was dropping soon. The Empire's dominions and colonies were all grappling with the thorny issue of conscription. Borden was well aware that the growing French-Canadian opposition to the war made the issue even more complicated.

Everyone was feeling their way, since this was the first ever Imperial War Cabinet meeting, and no one was quite sure how it would work. Borden, however, was pleased that after so many years of pushing, Canada finally had a voice in the highest councils of the British Empire. The Imperial War Cabinet included the five new members of the British War Cabinet Lloyd George had formed in December. They were sitting across from him. Besides Lloyd George, there was Lord Curzon of Kedleston, Bonar Law, the chancellor of the exchequer, and ministers without portfolio Arthur Henderson and Lord Milner. On the wings of the five sat Arthur Balfour, the secretary of state for foreign affairs, William Long, the secretary of state for the colonies, and Arthur Chamberlain, secretary of state for India. On Borden's side of the table, besides George Perley, his minister of the overseas military forces of Canada, also sat Joseph Ward, the minister of finance and posts for New Zealand.

At the beginning of the meeting, Lloyd George had set out the goals of the Imperial War Cabinet, which were distinct from the British War Cabinet's. The British one was responsible for setting policy for Great Britain alone. The Imperial one would set policy and direction for the Empire as a whole. At the beginning of the meeting, Lloyd George had indicated what his aims were: peace terms when the war was finally won, creating a league of peace to avoid future wars, democratization of Europe, disrupting the Turkish Empire, and the peacetime reconstruction of Great Britain.

Lloyd George continued, "Germany has put every available man in their army. They don't believe that we can continue past 1917. If the war continues into the next year, France will have nothing to spare. She already has put one in six men in her armies. Next year she'll have at most 300,000 men aged seventeen available for service.

"Then there is Russia," he said with a sigh. "She could put a million men into the field. But she has major problems with poor lines of communication and transportation. That means winning the war, in the real sense of the word, will depend on the full resources of the British Empire."

Borden pursed his lips. *If the Americans came into the war, it would make a difference*, he thought. He glanced at Balfour, who had informed him about the Zimmerman telegram British agents had stolen from the German embassy in Mexico City. A copy had been delivered to Walter Page, the American ambassador, who had promptly given it to President Wilson. The Americans then released it to the newspapers with the resultant hue and cry. The US Senate however, had balked at giving the president full authority to prosecute the war. Many felt the telegram was a fake.

It was sad to contemplate that it might take the sinking of an American ship by a U-Boat to push them into the war.

"Since it's time for tea, we should adjourn for the day," Lloyd George said as he pushed back his chair and rose to his feet. "We'll continue our discussions at our next meetings. We've agreed that they will be held here Tuesday and Thursday mornings and Friday afternoons. And we have a photographer in the garden to record this momentous occasion."

Everyone followed the prime minister to the white painted double doors set behind twin Corinthian columns. Borden knew the discussions would continue during tea. He glanced at the Newfoundland prime minister, who fell in beside him. He and Morris had much to discuss, especially about the fishery. However, he wasn't about to bring up Confederation. For now, that was a dead issue for Newfoundland.

MARCH 24, 1917
TRAINING GROUND, ESTRÉE-CAUCHY

Lieutenant-Colonel Llewellyn was crouched in the mock Black Line trench, watching the cavalry troop canter at a sedate pace to the Richmond Fusiliers' next objective, the mock Red Line. The cavalry was pretending to be the 65th Artillery's creeping barrage they had planned for during their actual assault. At timed intervals, the evenly spaced troopers carrying lances tipped with yellow flags held high would move forward. His men were following them at the appropriate pace and distance.

Behind him, he could see squads mopping up machine gun nests and strong points that had been bypassed during their assault. The plan called for speed and forward momentum. They had strict orders that the first waves were not stalled. It was up to the last waves to secure No Man's Land behind them.

"What's the time?" Major Gavin asked.

"We're at zero-thirty-five," Llewellyn replied as he watched some of the men go through the motions of consolidating the captured trench to defend it against possible German counterattacks. The major had command of the day's training exercise. Llewellyn was just along as an observer. During the actual assault, one of them would be left behind if they needed to reconstitute the regiment.

Gavin was watching the A and C company commanders reorganize the platoons for the next assault. They had forty minutes to get ready to stroll across the two hundred yards from the Black Line to the Red Line. They were on a strict timetable. The artillery would be pounding the Red Line until zero hour plus seventy-five minutes, after which the barrage would move forward to the Blue and Brown Lines.

"Where the fuck are the Vickers and Stokes mortars?" the major shouted.

"They're still at the Bonnal Trench, sir," replied Corporal Biggins, the signaller standing beside him.

Llewellyn looked behind him as guards escorted fake captured German prisoners across the dusty plain back to the Bonnal Trench for fake interrogations. Stretcher bearers were evacuating the wounded. Some were actually casualties. There were always a few that got hurt during these exercises with cuts and bruises, sprained ankles, strained backs, and heat exhaustion.

The training ground at Estrée-Cauchy, just twelve miles north of Écurie, had been transformed into a mock-up of Vimy Ridge. Today, it had been configured to conform to the ground that the 2nd Brigade would be tasked to capture. It had been laid out based on the regular intelligence reports being fed to the Canadian Corps and the recent aerial photos provided by the Royal Flying Corps. All the craters, machine-gun nests, and strong points had been taped out, numbered, and the depth indicated. The deeper craters were being avoided during their rush because they would have slowed their assault.

Today, they were practising a battalion assault. Tomorrow, Brigadier-General Loomis had ordered the 2nd Brigade to run through the course. Next week, the entire 1st Division was scheduled to conduct the same exercise.

He had already briefed the Fusiliers on the plan and what their objectives were so everyone knew what their role was to make it work. No one knew what the actual Z-date was, although everyone suspected it would be in early April, the start of the fighting season. By then the weather would be warmer and the ground firm enough to support the men's weight.

An out-of-breath Vickers machine-gun team finally arrived hauling their gun, tripod, and ammo boxes. They found a suitable spot in the trench and began setting up the gun. Farther down the trench, he could see a Stokes mortar was ready to support the third and fourth wave.

At Z plus seventy-five minutes, the horses cantered over the Red Line as the assault teams began to cross the two hundred yards to the Red Line. Once they had dropped into the Red Line trench, they went through the motions of consolidating it.

"What do you think?" asked Major Gavin as he lowered his binoculars. "If we can do this in the actual attack, we'll be done by noon."

"That's the plan. I have to admit the rehearsals have been looking good," replied Llewellyn. It was true that it had gone quite smoothly. Oh, sure, there were some problems that needed to be corrected once they sat down and did a debriefing. But still, something was bothering him. Major Gavin caught it in Llewellyn's tone. "What's the problem? Did you spot something that I missed?"

"Not that," replied Llewellyn as he continued to watch the assault on the Red Line trench. "Something is just gnawing at me."

"If you don't mind my saying so, but you have been working pretty hard. And, you haven't had leave in a quite a while…" Gavin paused as he watched an Emma Gee gunner trip and fall. It took the man a while to get up. "And you haven't received a letter from your girl in a while." Gavin had noticed his mood improve when he got mail from Samantha.

Llewellyn shook his head. He hadn't received anything recently from Samantha, and he was a bit worried about her. He had been reading the newspaper reports and the daily intelligence briefings as well that included a summary on the Petrograd situation. It did not look good, not good at all.

"At least you didn't get killed today," Major Gavin said with a grin.

Lieutenant-Colonel Llewellyn burst out laughing. It was true that during the training exercise, he usually ended up dead, to the amusement of his men. They were a suspicious lot. They couldn't help noticing that when he died during rehearsals, the operations he led afterward were usually successful. He hoped that his not dying today didn't foretell bad luck.

Vimy Ridge was already a tough enough nut to crack.

APRIL 1, 1917
DMITRI PALACE, PETROGRAD

"Do we have any more bandages?" Claire asked after she had checked one of the patients.

"Only what the night shift had," Samantha said as she looked up from the entries the night shift had entered in the logbook. Ten new patients had come in last night. She had been wondering where the supplies for them would come from and who would pay.

Claire turned toward the window when she heard singing. "They're singing the 'La Marseillaise' again."

"I'm afraid so," Samantha replied. She could hear the song quite clearly through the nearby open window. The night shift had opened them just as their shift ended to air out the ward. Some of the patients were enjoying the fresh air, such as it was. Others were clutching their blankets against the crisp temperature and were demanding that someone close the windows. Samantha rose from her nurse's station to close one of the windows. As she did, she spotted the procession with red banners fluttering in the wind marching up Nevsky Prospect.

"What are they protesting today?" Claire asked when she came to stand beside Samantha.

"I have no clue," replied Samantha. She didn't bother trying to decipher the Russian script. The citizens of Petrograd had taken to protesting for the slightest slight or complaint.

Yuri, one of the sanitors, came over from the patients he was attending to look out of the window. "Bolsheviks," he muttered.

"Bolsheviks," spat out the patient he had been looking after.

Samantha raised an eyebrow and then stepped over to the soldier who had spoken. She placed her hand on the young man's forehead to check his temperature. He was in his early twenties, with blue-grey eyes and close-cropped blonde hair. He had come in several weeks earlier, feverish with a bullet wound in his chest. She had been surprised he managed to survive this long. It must've been a good surgeon at the front who had patched him up well enough for transport. Most of the soldiers with chest wounds died. She noted he was cool to her touch. When she glanced at Yuri, he informed her, "Fever is down to thirty-eight."

"Good," she said with a smile. "Let's check your bandages."

The man's eyes shifted to the sanitor who translated her instructions. He moved his blanket down so she could examine the bandage on his left chest. The standard treatment for chest wounds was a loose bandage soaked with iodine and ice to keep the area cool. Ice they had plenty of; it was Petrograd, after all, but bandages and iodine were in short supply.

"You don't like the Bolsheviks?" she asked him. The patients gave Yuri a quizzical glance. When he finished translating, the patient shook his head, causing him to grimace in pain. Whatever morphine they had, went to the more severe cases.

"Where are you from?" she asked.

"He's from a village near Siberian border," Yuri translated.

"Did he volunteer?" asked Samantha.

"No."

"Does he like the army?" she asked. She had a fairly good idea what the man's opinion was when he snorted.

"Are the conditions bad at the front?"

"Yes, they very bad. In his regiment men threw out officers. The men voted new officers," the sanitor translated.

"The men voted their own officers?" Samantha asked in surprise.

Yuri nodded yes. "Officers elected by soldiers. Men refuse to fight."

The patient poured out a long stream of Russian. He then indicated that Yuri should translate what he said. He stared at the sanitor and Samantha, waiting for their reactions.

"He said many men leave the army to go home. Bolsheviks say war is over. They lie. Government still wants war. Men don't want to fight. Czar gone. No reason to fight. Soldiers at the front agree not to shoot."

Samantha looked startled. She had heard about the Christmas truce two years ago on the Western Front. She hadn't heard the same thing had happened on the Russian front, especially with the anti-German feelings most Russians had. "Soldiers? You mean German and Russian soldiers agreed not to shoot at each other?"

"Yes," replied the sanitor.

Samantha nodded absentmindedly. She finally understood the gossip that she had been hearing. When some of the ministers of the provisional government had gone to the front, there were rumours that they needed the Russian army's support to remain in power. In Petrograd, most of the regiments, such as the Cossacks, had sided with the revolutionaries and were supporting the provisional government. No one was sure where the Russian army outside Petrograd stood. Many were fearful that the army might decide to march onto the capital to reinstall the czar.

If what the soldier was saying was true, it meant that the Russian army was in worse shape than anyone knew. She had already seen the slovenly appearance of some of the regiments that were garrisoning Petrograd. And she had seen soldiers disobeying their superior officers' direct orders. Discipline was collapsing.

"What does he want to do when he gets well enough to travel?" she asked.

"He wants go back to farm. To wife. To *deti*," Yuri replied.

"Yes," Samantha agreed. "I think we all want to go home."

CHAPTER 8

"Then there is the question of shell shock," said Brigadier-General Arthur Edward Ross, the deputy director for medical services for the Canadian Corps. He was forty-six, with a fair complexion, and had light brown hair and grey eyes. He had contributed to finding solutions for trench foot and for mustard gas. "We demand certificates from the commanding officers to help my MOs diagnosing men claiming to be suffering from shell shock. My officers won't authorize the evacuation of such cases beyond the special medical units without the COs signing off on them.

"I know that there has been some difficulty in striking these men off strength, but my hands are tied."

Lieutenant-General Byng frowned. Shell shock cases were a problem for the Canadian Corps. He had seen the figures from the Somme. In some units up to forty percent had suffered from it in one form or another.

"We'll have to refer it to GHQ for them to develop a policy," he replied.

"Yes, sir," the brigadier-general replied.

"Next on today's agenda…" Byng said as he glanced at the twenty or so officers who were attending the day-long conference he had called to hammer out the last-minute details of the operation they'd been planning for the last few months. He had been holding the meetings in what was formerly the garden room of the Château Camblain-l'Abbé, his current headquarters. The room's plants had long since been removed by the previous units who had used the château as their HQ.

A large clay model of Vimy Ridge was set in the middle of the room with tables surrounding it. For the last ten days or so, his Corps' artillery, along with the guns loaned from the Imperials, were pounding the Black, Red, Blue, and Brown Lines, the Corps' objectives on Vimy Ridge. He had ordered that only half the 245 heavies and the 480 18-pounders were to be used to soften the German defences. He didn't want General Ludwig von Falkenhausen, the commander of the German 6th Army, to know how many guns he had at his disposal. Byng couldn't help glancing at the marker on the clay model where the German commander had set up his HQ.

He was responsible for seven thousand yards, nearly four miles, of trenches from the Arras-Lens Road on the right to the Brisson Communications Trench on his left. Flag pins of his four divisions were placed in numerical order from left to right. Each pin matched their division's colours.

Red pins for the 2nd and 3rd Brigades of Currie's 1st Division were placed between the Arras-Lens Road and the Aux Rietz Communications Trench. They were facing the 1st Bavarian Reserve Division. The 1st Brigade's pin, as the reserve, was placed between Major-General Loomis's HQ and the two assault brigades.

The 2nd, Major-General Burstall's division and the 3rd, Major-General Lipsett's division, were arranged against the 79th Reserve Division. The 2nd Division's 4th and 5th Brigades' dark blue pins were between the Aux Rietz and the de la Fourche Communication Trenches with the 6th Brigade and the British 13th Brigade in support.

The 3rd Division's light blue pins for the 8th and 7th Brigade were positioned to cover from de la Fourche to the la Salle Avenue with the 9th in reserve.

The green pins were for the 4th Division, who were covering from la Salle Avenue to Brisson. They would be contending with the 79th Reserve Division and the 16th Bavarian Division.

He noticed that a few changes had been made to the model. It was updated regularly with the latest intelligence reports from captured German prisoners, the overnight patrols and raids into No Man's Land, and aerial photos. He glanced out of the large wall of rain-splattered windows to the circular driveway filled with staff cars. It was the grey-black clouds that concerned him. It meant he wasn't going to get any photos today, since the Flying Corps' 16th Squadron, attached to his Corps, couldn't put their reconnaissance planes in the air.

Major-General Currie noticed his glance. "The weather hasn't been cooperating."

"I'm aware. We may have to delay the Z-date if the weather doesn't improve," replied Byng. He turned to Lieutenant-Colonel Sessions, his GS-02 for Intelligence. "What are the latest forecasts?"

Sessions, a thin man who barely met the height requirements, sitting along the wall, coughed as he flipped through his papers in a black leather folio. When he finally found it he said, "The latest forecast we've received from London indicates we can expect winds ten to fifteen miles per hour. It may increase to gale force winds with the strong probability of rain or snow."

"We can tell that by just looking out the window," someone muttered rather loudly.

Sessions glared at the offending officers, cutting off the men's chuckles before he continued, "The winds will become steady, after which the weather is expected to be milder."

Some of the divisional commanders wore skeptical looks. The weather forecasts they've received from the London meteorologists were accurate for a day or two at most. Any further out than that, their guesses would be just as accurate.

Byng gave a resigned shrug. There wasn't much you could do about the weather. His attack on the Vimy escarpment was a diversion for the French Army's attack along the Aisne and their attempt to break through between Reims and Soissons. While Vimy Ridge was of tactical importance, the Canadian Corps' main job was to tie down as many German divisions as they could to help weaken the German defences for French General Robert Nivelle's assault.

"We'll keep our patrols out to make sure the Huns are actually where we think they are," Byng said as he glanced at Currie, Burstall, Lipsett, and Watson. They were sitting with their aides at the tables in divisional seniority.

Major-General Lipsett stated, "The orders have already been issued." The other three nodded in agreement.

"We'll keep an eye on the weather. The Z-date has been fixed, and the marching orders will be sent out for the W, X, and Y dates," Byng stated. The British practice was to designate the attack date with a Z for the zero date, while W, X, and Y dates were those that preceded the attack date. He had insisted, and made sure it had been carried out, that the men down to the lowly private had been briefed on the plan and their role in it. As for the actual date, it hadn't yet been divulged. "Now, about the loads our men have to carry?"

Currie shifted his pear-shaped body in his chair before he answered, "We've submitted reports on the loads the men need to carry. The basic load, a rifle, two Mills, two sandbags, 150 rounds, his basic kit, is seventy pounds. If you add a spade, it's seventy-five. A pick adds eight pounds.

"A bomber comes in at seventy if he's carrying five Mills and fifty rounds. The bomb carrier, loaded with ten bombs and fifty rounds, comes in at seventy-seven. The rifle grenadier, who is required to carry ten bombs, rods, and fifty 303s, has to carry eighty-two pounds.

"The Lewis gunner carrying only his weapon comes in at eighty-four. His number two with his service weapon, fifty rounds, two Mills, and eight pans for the Lewis weigh in at a hundred pounds."

"It'll be tough for them to keep up," remarked Major-General Lipsett. He, like most of his commanders, had spent considerable time in the front lines and had an appreciation for the difficulties the men had.

"It also depends on how far they have to carry," Currie added. "For short distances it shouldn't be a problem. For longer distances, it'll exhaust the men. We've been looking at reducing the loads further. One suggestion has been to leave the blankets behind. But everyone agreed that the men will need them after they capture the trenches. They will need them to sleep on and to keep warm at night."

The equipment loads were a concern to the 1st and 2nd Divisions, since they had to penetrate as far as the Brown Line, nearly four thousand yards, slightly over two miles. The 3rd and 4th Divisions were to capture and consolidate the Black and Red Lines. "Continue looking at what we can do to lighten the men's loads. I have a feeling we might not be able to make major adjustments at this stage," Byng said.

He then turned to Brigadier-General Lindsay, his chief engineer. "What about the water situation?"

"We're in good shape. We've laid forty-five miles of pipe, field pumping stations, and reservoirs to keep our horses happy. We can now pump up to 600,000 gallons of water per day," the chief engineer said. He had been handed the task of providing sufficient water to satisfy the thirst of the Corps' fifty thousand horses that were needed to support the Vimy operation. "It gives us sufficient capacity for our own men. In hot weather, though, the men should be issued two canteens and should be trained in water economy.

"Also, we have fully replenished our dumps and are ready to supply the men with what they'll need."

"Good, very good," Byng acknowledged, pleased.

"If I may?" asked Major-General Watson, the 4th Division commander. He was in his early fifties, with grey hair and grey eyes. "Has any further consideration been made to deal with possible enemy tanks? We have eight of them to support us. If we encounter German ones, an antitank gun would be useful."

"I'm afraid we'll have to rely on the 18-pounders or the Stokes to deal with them. I've been informed that most of our light artillery pieces, and any suitable artillery we capture will be going to arm our merchant ships. They'll use them to protect themselves from German submarines," stated Major-General Morrison, the GOC of the Corps' artillery.

"That does bring up an important point," continues Watson. "How can we transmit the information back to the brigade HQs and the artillery, if we encounter tanks? For that matter, how about the latest intelligence coming from the battalions to the brigades and orders being sent from the brigades to the battalions? I know we've buried miles of cables in the communications trenches. Also, the new wireless sets we've been issued have proven useful. But is there anything else we can do?"

"Don't forget the pigeons and the Airedales for messages," said Lieutenant-Colonel Session, who had signal flashes on his shoulders. He was in his early forties, with a fringe of hair surrounding his bald head.

"I haven't," replied Watson.

"I still think the Signal Service should control communications up to the front lines," stated Session.

"No!" was Currie's emphatic response. "Communications should remain with the front-line units. It's not a good idea, nor is it efficient. If it were transferred to the Signal Service, the service would need to be enlarged. As far as I'm aware, we don't have sufficiently trained men for the work."

Byng interjected, "I believe the matter has been dealt with. Let's move on to the next item, the shortage of NCOs."

"Agreed," said Major-General Lipsett. "We need to increase the number of our NCOs by at least twenty percent."

"I concur," replied Currie. "Our major problem is getting rid of NCOs that aren't suitable. It's extremely difficult to remove those with a substantive rank. We have to refer them to GHQ." He stabbed at the table to emphasize his point. "If we have to add more NCOs, and we do need them, I suggest they be given actings until they have demonstrated they are efficient."

Byng acknowledged Lipsett and Currie with a nod. "I've brought the issue to GHQ's attention, and I'm waiting for their response. I've also contacted General Turner and have expressed my concerns on the training and the preparedness of the reinforcements for our fighting units. He's informed me he's aware of the problems, and he's made some substantial headway concerning improvements. Unfortunately, we aren't likely to see the results for a few months."

"Thank you, General Byng. I appreciate that," Major-General Lipsett replied.

"It's nearly noon," said Byng. "I think that we're ready to break for lunch. Does anyone have anything to discuss before we do?"

"Yes, sir, I have something, and I hope it's a quick one," said Lieutenant-Colonel Aides. He was sitting near the glass windows with his face slightly hidden by the shadows.

Byng nearly sighed. He was well aware what the man wanted to discuss. "I assume this is about biscuits."

"Yes, sir. I've been getting a lot of complaints about the iron rations biscuits." Byng was quite familiar with the 7" x 11" cotton canvas pouches the men had been issued to carry their rations in. "In these damp conditions, the biscuits get wet then crumble. I know … I know … they're supposedly hard tack. By the time that the men sit down to eat, all they have left is a handful of dust. And the bags are sometimes not the most sanitary, as the medical officers can attest." He glanced at Major-General Ross, who nodded in acknowledgement.

"This matter has been brought up to GHQ," Byng stated.

"Yes, sir. I understand," Aides continued. "I would still like to suggest a cover or a tin be issued to help protect the biscuits. We've been instructed to economize, and it would be quite useful and efficient in that regard."

"That has been brought to GHQ's attention," Byng repeated.

Aides's eyes flirted around the room as he realized that he might have been pushing it to hard. "Thank you, sir. I appreciate it."

"Let's retire to the mess for lunch," Byng said as he rose to his feet.

"Let's hope they're not serving biscuits," someone muttered as they headed out.

APRIL 3, 1917
65TH ARTILLERY, NEUVILLE-SAINT-VAAST

"Sir, when do you think we'll be getting our rum rations?" implored Corporal Higgins.

"You'll be the first to know when I do," Ryan replied, trying to keep the irritated tone from his voice. It was all that the men could talk about since yesterday.

"A bit of rum helps warm the bones," said the corporal as he shivered in his greatcoat. Higgins had a scarf around his neck, a wool cap under his Brodie helmet, and woollen gloves with the fingertips missing. Ryan was similarly attired, but his gloves had fingertips.

They were standing in the 65th's camouflaged battery position just southwest of the small village of Neuville-Saint-Vaast in the A10 quadrant. They were about a mile and a half from the German front lines. The weather had been miserable and continued to be. They had to speak louder than normal to be heard over the strong winds that were buffeting their camouflage nettings. At least they managed so far to keep the gun pit dry. From his position he could see his friend, Sergeant Reggie Ramus, unpacking one of the neatly stacked fuse boxes.

"I know,' replied Ryan. The rum the British army issued was strong stuff. He had to take it in sips. He had tried once tried to down his portion in one shot, but the coughing fit nearly cracked one of his ribs. He had to admit, though, once it hit his stomach, the warm glow was something to look forward to.

The men were grumbling because of the weather and the work they needed to do for the second phase of Major-General Morrison's artillery plan. The first phase had been completed. The Corps' guns had been hammering Fritz's support trenches and artillery pieces to make the Huns miserable. For the last twenty days they had been dropping shells on Thélus, Les Tilleuls, Farbus, Givenchy, Vimy and Petit Vimy, La Chadieyre, and Willerval. The 65th had, until now, only used half their allotment. The fierce winds were making hitting the targets they had been assigned in the A7 map square difficult.

"The horses and mules are having a tough go. I've spoken with Colonel Masterley this morning. We've lost twelve last night," Ryan stated. Their battery wasn't on one of the tramlines that supplied the heavies. They were reliant on the horses to supply them with the nearly 1,300 shells per day that they needed to feed his hungry 18-pounders during phase two. The animals didn't have much protection from the vicious wind, the cold rain, and the snow. His experience with Captain Fuller, the 65th's vet, didn't help much when the stressed and overworked horses started to collapse. All that he could do then was to put them out of their misery.

Higgins grimaced. "Six men were on sick parade this morning."

"I know," Ryan replied as he glanced at the stack of green boxes with *Fuse Igniter 106* lettering on their sides. Reggie was examining the safety cap on one of the new graze fuses. His 18-pounders used two fuse types: time and percussion. They used the time fuses for shrapnel, and for the high explosives they used percussions. On the HE shells they had been using the number 44 fuse, but there had been problems with the 44s. The delay between the shell striking its target and detonating was too long to be effective in cutting barbed wire, especially in muddy conditions when the shell burrowed too deep. The new 106 fuse was designed to solve this problem. The fuse's mechanism was so sensitive that when the shell touched the ground or barbed wire, it detonated. From the reports his FOOs had been sending him, the new fuses had been quite effective in cutting the German wire.

"Now, about..." Higgins snapped his mouth closed when Ryan gave him a glare. The men hadn't received their rum rations for about a month because of shortages. They'd been having similar problems with their regulation rations. They had been receiving the bare minimum, but some of his larger men were starting to lose weight.

Ryan couldn't blame Higgins. He was pissed off at the bastard who got the brilliant idea of starting a rumour, on April Fool's Day, that a trainload of rum had arrived. And that everyone would be getting a double ration to make up for what they had missed. Ever since then, all the officers had been fielding questions from the men about when they would get their share of the rum.

The problem was Ryan had squirrelled away a couple of rum jars. He had intended to break them out to reward his men for their hard work. Now, he was in a quandary how to do it without starting a riot.

APRIL 8, 1917
MAISON BLANCHE SOUTERRAINE, NEUVILLE-SAINT-VAAST

"Gentlemen, Z day is tomorrow," Lieutenant-Colonel Masterley stated to the assembled senior officers. "And zero hour is set at dawn, five thirty."

"It's about time!" acting Captain Paul Ryan overheard Major Ashwith from the 3rd Battery say.

"Things too dull for you?" asked Major Freeson, the CO of the 2nd Battery as he poked him with an elbow. Ashwith was new to the 65th. He had arrived from England a few weeks ago and was still getting a handle on running his new battery. The 65th had been pounding the Huns for several weeks now, but Ashwith's first baptism of fire, so to speak, would be tomorrow. Ryan suspected the major's frustration partially stemmed from the twenty-four-hour delay in the assault on Vimy Ridge.

Ryan glanced at the rest of the senior officers seated in the large cave in the Maison Blanche chalk quarry. Chalk had been used for centuries as building material until red bricks replaced it for home construction. This section hadn't been modified from its original state, except for the overhead lights and the carvings some of the CEF's stone masons had etched into the cave walls. Other parts of the quarry's caves had been expanded with additional tunnels and spaces for command posts, billets, and warehousing by the tunnelling companies.

The major opened his mouth to make a retort then closed it when he thought better of it.

"We've been testing our communications for the last several weeks, and so far it seems to be working fairly well. We've been making some last-minute adjustments, though, and I've decided to assign Lieutenant Murden to the Bentata Tunnel as our man on the spot, so to speak." Masterley indicated the lieutenant with his chin sitting several chairs away from Ryan in the 1st Battery's section. Ryan was pleased that it wasn't him for a change. "The observers will be sending their reports to battery HQ via the buried cables or wireless. The battalions will also have eight pigeons with them in case their cables get cut or they lose their wireless when they go over the top.

"The SOS signal will be continuous red Very lights. If they send up white ones, it means they've taken the Black, Red, and Blue objectives. When Thélus and Hill 140 are captured, they'll send up silver, and gold rockets.

"Also, two men in each platoon will be carrying blue and yellow battle flags. Keep an eye out for them. They'll be in the leading edge of the assault, and they will be waving them."

"If they don't?" asked Lieutenant Murden.

"What do you think?" Masterley retorted sharply. He then continued when Murden dropped his eyes, "If the observers report hearing heavy rifle fire or machine gun at the Brown Line, you are to treat it as if it's an SOS."

Ryan made a note with a pencil in the black leather notebook he held in his hand.

"After eight tonight, no one is to use the road from Écoivres to Fond de Vase except for the infantry. After midnight, the XVII Corps will be then using the roads. So, get whatever supplies and equipment you need before then. Make sure you have sufficient water and oil to help keep the guns cool. Individual sections will fire in sequence to allow the 18-pounders to rest and cool between barrages. You all have been assigned targets.

"Aeroplane calls will be transmitted to Brigade HQ and then sent to the batteries via cable. If you get a tank call, use HE.

"Before I forget, everyone is to wear box respirators in the alert position." Masterley pointed to his box respirator lying on the corner of the table he was sitting at. "We'll be using plenty of smoke, and our heavies will be firing gas shells at the Boche. We can also count on the Boche to use gas.

"Check your barrage maps, since they've been revised. Timing for the creeping barrage has been changed from ninety one twenty to ninety two twenty. Rate of fire will be four rounds per minute per gun. As for the protective barrage, during the pause the first ten minutes will be three rounds per minute. Each ten-minute interval, reduce your rate of fire by one round. At thirty minutes, I'll leave it at your discretion whether to fire one or two rounds per minute."

Ryan spoke up, taking a glance from his CO. "What about our ammunition supply? What I heard is that Z day was delayed twenty-four hours because of that."

Masterley grimaced. "I know we had problems several days ago, but they have been resolved. We've been getting adequate supplies from the tramlines and the pack horses. According to the returns I've received, each of our batteries have their allotment for the task at hand."

"Thanks, sir," replied Ryan.

"Now, where was I?" muttered Masterley as he scanned his notes. "Ah yes, it's important when walking the shells to the Hun trenches that you try to keep two hundred yards ahead of the leading wave.

"Once the Black and Blue Lines have been captured, we will start moving some of our 18-pounders forward to support the infantry. You should have sufficient material to construct new pits. If not, you'll have to make do. If there's captured German supplies available, use that," Masterley said. "Anyone have any questions?"

Ryan glanced around the room then spoke. "How's the wire-cutting been?"

Masterley cracked a smile. "Actually, not that bad. The new 106 graze fuse has been effective. The raid by the 10th has reported that the wire has been severely damaged but is still an obstacle. We'll have to concentrate some 18-pounders on that section.

"We're to continue our normal program for the rest of the day. It's important that everything we do is part of our regular routine we've established for the last few weeks. We don't want the Huns to get any ideas we're going to hit them hard tomorrow morning. Is that understood?" stated the lieutenant-colonel.

"Yes, sir," replied Ryan with the rest of the officers.

"Good, we have a lot of work ahead of us. Let's get at it," Masterley ordered as he dismissed them.

BENTATA TUNNEL, ÉCOIVRES

"Have the armbands been issued to the men?" asked Lieutenant-Colonel Llewellyn. He, Major Gavin, and his three company commanders were crammed into his command post for a meeting to discuss last-minute details. They were to go over the top this morning at five thirty, the Z-hour. The command post wasn't much. A single bulb above the curtain door was illuminating the rough-hewn chalk walls he was resting his back against. It had been dug by the tunnellers of the British 172 Tunnelling Company. Over the past months they had dug a number of similar cubicles off the main subway tunnel.

It was noisy in the various tunnels and corridors of the underground Bentata Complex as units of the 2nd Brigade made their way to their designated rest areas. There, they would wait until they moved above ground to their jumping-off trenches. The 1st Brigade would then replace them as they waited for their orders.

"The scouts have been given green armbands, the runners red, signallers blue, moppers white, and the salvagers khaki. I don't know why we bothered with the khaki ones," Major Gavin said with a shrug. "The traffic controllers are black. And we've given the wire cutters white tape for their right shoulders."

"Any word on the wire?" asked Captain Marshall, who was the C Company's commander.

Llewellyn replied, "The 10th did a raid this morning. They hit the Boche trenches behind the Argyll Group of craters. They took two prisoners, killed a couple of Huns, and bombed several dugouts. They reported that the wire on the right was well cut. I guess the new fuses that the artillery is using are working. There's still some wire two feet high and four deep. It's going to cause us some headaches. They also said the wire behind the number 2 crater is going to be a problem."

"I've been looking at the notes on the craters again," said the major. "Not much has changed. We can cross Craters 14 to 17, since they're shallow. Craters 19 to 27 are steep. We can use their front lips as defensive positions."

Llewellyn nodded. "Our patrols haven't found anything yet. Let's hope it stays that way. The reports from the 10th, our own scouts, and the prisoners who have crossed over to us to surrender all tell us that Fritz is in bad shape from our bombardments. They haven't eaten in days.

"You must keep up with the creeping barrage. If you run into a strong point, go around like we rehearsed. Let the second and third waves take care of them."

"Yes, sir," replied the major.

"The 10th also said they found the German trenches in good shape. They're six feet deep, bath-matted, and dry."

"That's a relief. I hate getting my feet wet," said Captain Marshall, which solicited chuckles from everyone.

"They said they didn't encounter machine-gun fire, but the snipers were a nuisance," Gavin stated.

"Let's hope the winds are favourable for our Stokes. We'll need it for the smoke bombs. If it isn't, we'll have to do without it," said Llewellyn.

"Shit!" muttered Captain Hastings the CO of B Company.

Llewellyn agreed with the captain. The smoke would help hide his men when they followed the creeping barrage.

"Have you made a decision yet?" asked Major Gavin. There was a hint of eagerness in his eyes.

Llewellyn winced. The orders from HQ were quite specific. Either the commander or the second-in-command had to be left behind. And it detailed the number of officers, NCOs, and other ranks that were to be left out of the assault in case they needed to rebuild the regiment. He knew why he was being chicken-livered about the decision. He suspected his men knew why.

Ever since he had gotten buried by a shell that had collapsed a trench on him last September at Albert, he disliked being underground. It always brought back the feeling of the dirt pressing on his chest, suffocating him. They'd all seen his hesitation, his paleness, and momentary hyperventilation whenever he entered the tunnels and the subways.

He stared at the major for a few moments and then made his decision. "You'll be leading the regiment, and I'll be the one staying behind. You're as familiar as I am with the march tables. The men did good time entering the tunnels and passing through the Clear Road junction tonight. Make sure the men stay on schedule when they are ordered to the jumping-off points at the Bonnal Trench."

The last thing anyone wanted was a traffic jam that could stall the brigade and take hours to sort out underground. The brigade had three thousand men to get to their positions in time for the attack. For this reason, the tunnels had been designated as one-ways. One flowed to the front lines while the other handled traffic coming from the trenches. Each unit in the attack force had been assigned a starting point, a start time, and given a specific amount of time to clear the tunnels for the units coming behind them.

"We will. We'll have to stop at the Ariane dump, though, to pick up some Mills bombs, aeroplane flares, and other supplies we'll need," replied the major.

"Just make sure the men don't get overloaded. They'll need all their strength for the attack. And make sure they check their gas masks. I don't want any gas casualties if we can help it."

"Will do," replied the major.

"Good, I don't think we've forgotten anything," Llewellyn stated. "We're as well prepared as we can be for tomorrow, God willing. Everyone get some rest. We'll need it. We're to be in position by three in the a.m."

"Yes, sir," said the three company commanders as they rose to their feet.

"Tell majors Moore and Stoats to come in on your way out," Llewellyn ordered.

A few moments later, majors Moore and Stoats entered and took their seats on the bunk bed.

"Doc, I wanted to talk to you about the medical arrangement for tomorrow. How happy are you with them?" Llewellyn asked.

Major Moore placed his hands on his belly and leaned against the stone wall as he pursed his lips. The light bounced off his collar's medical insignia. "I think we're in good shape, but it will all depend on how accurate our casualty estimates are. We've set up the RAPs at Lillie Post, Sutherland Avenue, Mine Gallery, and the Old Mine Rescue Chamber. Anniversaire Avenue will be our collection point to send them onto the

CAMC. Then we have the APS at the Ariane Dump, where we'll have plenty of supplies."

Stoats jumped in to add, "I've also made sure our men will have plenty of coffee and tea before they go over the top."

Llewellyn noticed the slight twitch at the corner of Major Gavin's mouth. As the morale officer for the Richmond Fusiliers, Stoats did wonders for the men's morale with a simple cup of hot coffee. Today, Father Stoats had held Easter mass in the training field near the Woodland Camp where they had been billeted. He had stood on a raised platform that the fitness instructors used to take the men through their morning calisthenics. His men had stood in company and platoon formation, stumbling through the mass's hymns. It had been bittersweet for Llewellyn watching them lined up for the Eucharist and a blessing from the chaplain. He couldn't help wondering how many would be gone by tomorrow night. He also knew Stoats wouldn't be getting much sleep tonight. He would be visiting the men to see how they were holding up and be available for any last-minute confessions or messages for loved ones.

"As well, any Germans we capture will be tasked as stretcher bearers until we lose the light. After that, they will be sent to Sunken Road. We'll assign men to keep an eye on them," Llewellyn stated.

"That will be fine," replied Moore. "Once the major sends up a white flare, we'll move some of the regimental aid posts to the Black Line. We'll be using the Mule Trail to evacuate the wounded to the tramlines. They will be then sent to the APS at Ariane. If the trams are down, we'll send them to Ariane via Anniversaire."

Llewellyn nodded grimly. "I hope that you'll have a light workload."

"So do I, Colonel. So do I," Moore prayed.

APRIL 9, 1917
ZWOLFER GRABEN TRENCH, VIMY RIDGE

"Have the sappers cleared all the trenches yet?" Lieutenant-Colonel Llewellyn asked as he followed the guide through the captured German trench to his new headquarters on Vimy Ridge. He had to make way for German prisoners being escorted to the New Bailey that had been temporarily setup at Anniversaire and Sunken Road to hold them for interrogation before they were sent farther behind the front lines. On their faces, he could see the effects the last several weeks of the Canadian bombardment had on them. Their uniforms seemed to be more oversized than usual for their frames. Their faces were strained, and most had vacant eyes as they helped their wounded comrades. Many sported bandages wrapped around their heads, arms, or legs. The basket cases, those with missing limbs, were being carried by stretcher bearers. The prisoners were mainly riflemen; he hadn't seen any machine gun or sniper insignia among them. They didn't lift their gazes as they passed him.

"Yes, Colonel," said Captain Ritz. "They found contact mines attached to the usual souvenirs the men like to pick up. You know bayonets, cap badges, and such."

"Did we lose anyone?" he asked as he skirted a stack of discarded Mauser rifles that he hoped had been emptied.

"Nope," replied the captain. "At least not from them."

"Glad to hear it. Once I've settled in, I want to visit Major Moore to see how our wounded are doing."

"Yes, sir," replied Ritz.

As the guide led Llewellyn, he couldn't help noticing how the trench, despite the damage, had been well constructed. He nodded in approval when he passed a squad working to convert the trench. The fire steps had been torn away from the left side, and the men were digging and hammering them into the right side so they could face the direction the Huns were likely to counterattack from.

They finally arrived at a heavy wood-framed dugout with sandbags on top layered five deep. The support beams must have been quite stout, since he didn't see any signs of sagging. Llewellyn raised an eyebrow when he read the street sign *Champs-Elysées*. Below it, in German, was another sign that read *Hauptquarter*.

"It's the former CO's headquarters. I don't think he'll be complaining too much if we use it," said Captain Ritz.

Llewellyn couldn't help chuckling. "I guess not."

He glanced up when he heard the drone of an aeroplane engine. A twin-wing, double-seater circling overhead had the colours of the 16th Squadron. The B.E.2 reconnaissance plane also had two black bands painted on the right wing and streamers fluttering from its wind spars. There were no streamers on the rudder, which indicated that the plane was flying missions for the 1st and 2nd Division.

"Where's Major Gavin?" he asked.

"He's in the Red Line, reorganizing and consolidating the trench.

The third and fourth wave are setting in artillery formation assaulting the Blue Line."

Llewellyn grunted in acknowledgement. Artillery formation was designed to reduce vulnerability to artillery fire. The assault companies were split into four platoons two hundred yards apart, with two in front and two bringing up the rear. Each platoon would be rushing the enemy trenches in columns of four with the company CO in the last wave. The idea was by the time the German artillery started firing, they would be hammering the empty space between the two assault lines.

So far, the German artillery had been ineffective. Llewellyn had to admit the Corps artillery had done a superb job. They had opened their barrage at Z-hour at five thirty on the dot, a half-hour before sunrise. His men had been ready in the jumping off trenches after they had emerged from the underground galleries to the Bonnal Trench. Raider discipline had held. There was no indication that the Germans knew they were there.

The patrols he had sent out the previous night had reported most of the German wire was still in disarray, but the Huns were trying to repair it. It also appeared the previous day's raid by the 10th Battalion had been effective in confusing the Germans about their real intentions.

While he hadn't been with his men to see it, the OPs at Claudot and Nourie reported that his Fusiliers had fixed bayonets and were following the creeping barrage laid out by the 65th Artillery in good order. As soon as the shelling started, the Huns had sent up a steady stream of red and green SOS flares.

Llewellyn had followed the assault from his HQ near the Bonnal Trench. Listening and reading the incoming reports flooding his headquarters was tough, especially when the Ops reported at six o'clock white Very flares indicating they had captured the Black Line. After they had breached the Black Line, it had taken Major Gavin forty-five minutes to reorganize the men for the assault on the Red Line being hammered by the 65th's 18-pounders. At nine o'clock, more white Very flares went up to say that the Red Line had been taken. Still, the feeling to take charge and to issue orders was nearly overwhelming, but he had to let Major Gavin do his job. His was to provide him with support if he needed it.

The company COs had informed him the German infantrymen had surrendered easily enough. It was the machine gunners and the snipers who had refused to give up. The machine gunners had given the Fusiliers the most trouble and had caused most of the casualties. But as they had been trained and rehearsed, it hadn't slowed down their assault as they moved around the strong points, leaving them for the Lewis gunners and the bombers. They didn't take many of them as prisoners.

He had concerns when the Richmond Fusiliers encountered stiff opposition at Wittelesbacher and Swischen Stellung junction. C Company had suffered so many casualties that he had to release B Company from the reserve to carry on the assault. Once the Red Line had been captured, reports came in that the work parties were consolidating the captured trenches. He had also seen the orders releasing the 1st Brigade to begin their assault on the Blue and Brown Lines.

"Captain, send two runners to Brigade HQ at Sunken Road to let them know I've moved my HQ to the Black Line," he ordered.

"Yes, sir," replied the captain.

"Once they've reached Brigade HQ, they are to stay there under their orders."

"Yes, Colonel," acknowledged Ritz.

"How are we doing with resupply?" Llewellyn asked.

"The 8th and the 2nd Field Company are connecting the New Trench, Sutherland, Dick, and Victoria avenues to the German lines we've captured. The Stokes teams are now in position in the Black Line. The 8th Battalion is halfway through bringing up two hundred shells for them," he informed Llewellyn.

Llewellyn nodded. The 8th Battalion had designated four teams of twenty-five men to haul the ten-pound mortar shells from the dumps that had been prepositioned to resupply the Fusiliers with ammo, rations, and materials to repair and wire the trenches they had captured. The Huns had left plenty of supplies and material behind, which meant they didn't have to draw or carry much from their start lines.

"Make sure the men get ammo, rations, and water," the lieutenant-colonel stated. "Don't forget the water." Llewellyn knew they had a hundred petrol tins of water in their dumps, and at the brigade dump they had two hundred more. If they ran out, he could access two storage tanks filled with nearly 3,500 gallons of water.

The captain nodded in agreement.

"I want to check our communications," Llewellyn said. He wondered if his team had managed to splice into the German telephone system. If they were lucky, they might still be able to intercept German traffic. If they'd cut their lines, they might still be able use the German equipment and exchanges to contact his own HQs.

"Understood, sir. I'll let Major Moore know you'll be dropping by," replied the Captain, making an about-face as Llewellyn entered his new command post.

NO MAN'S LAND, VIMY RIDGE

Major Stoats watched as the German soldier took his last breath. The tourniquets tied around what remained of his left arm and leg hadn't been enough to stem the blood loss. He had tried to make the young man's last moments as comfortable as he could, but the Hun who barely looked eighteen had borne his agony stoically.

When he had passed, Stoats closed the German soldier's eyes, said a prayer for the departed, then removed his ID disks. He picked up the nearby dirt-covered Mauser, pointed the muzzle to the ground, then jammed it in. Once he was certain it was firmly fixed, he placed a nearby German helmet on the rifle's butt so that moppers could find the body for burial. The man's ID disks would be sent to the Red Cross for them to inform the German authorities what had happened.

Stoats closed his eyes for a moment. He hadn't slept since his meeting with Doctor Moore and Lieutenant-Colonel Llewellyn. That night he had made himself available for anyone who wanted to see him. Quite a few had dropped by his small cell. Some had letters already prepared, while others needed some pen and paper to write a last note for a wife, a girlfriend, or a parent in case they didn't make it.

When it was time to man his coffee stand, he had to wait until the German 5.9s and 4.1s shells stopped pounding the Bonnal Trench and the Ariane Dump. He was ready with the coffee and tea as the men exited the Bontata Subway to head to the Bonnal Trench. He knew the men liked it strong and black. He had a tin of evaporated milk for those who liked a touch of colour.

The men had been grateful for the bit of warmth. It was a cold night, and they had to maintain raider silence as they made their way to their jumping-off points.

When the last men had left the tunnels, he had joined them as they waited for the zero-hour. At five thirty, a torrent of shells rained on Vimy Ridge. Then the whistles sounded, calling the gas-masked men to go over the top. Above the German lines, red and green SOS flares blossomed, calling artillery support. He had been surprised how weak the German artillery response was.

Exactly on time, the creeping barrage started, and he tried to watch the Richmond Fusiliers march close behind. Through the thick smoke, he occasionally saw gaps in the line as men fell. He had to wait until the second wave started before he could climb out of the trench and search No Man's Land for survivors and the dead.

"Padre, Padre!" he heard a voice yelling, forcing him to open his eyes.

"Yes," he replied as he scanned the terrain to find who had called him. He didn't bother glancing at the captured German trench a hundred yards away. He focused on the two stretcher bearers with their gas masks dangling from their chests near one of the large craters that pocketed the terrain. He gave the German a final glance before he made his way over to them. For the life of him he couldn't recall their names, although their faces were familiar. Being a stretcher bearer was just as dangerous as assaulting the trenches, and the casualty rate was just as high. Their helmets had the scars and dings to prove it. It paid to keep one's eyes open while in No Man's Land.

"Padre, we found another one," said the taller of the two, pointing into the crater. Finding all the casualties was difficult, since the men's khaki uniforms tended to blend into the terrain. It always bothered him finding men's boots in the middle of nowhere. It meant the man's body parts were scattered in No Man's Land. The only way to collect them was with a basket.

When Stoats looked into the crater, he could see several bodies; most were German, with a few Fusiliers mixed in. He didn't see any movement. For the stretcher bearers, the living took priority; the dead could wait. He knew they just wanted him to say a prayer over them.

"I'll take a look," Stoats said as he carefully stepped over the lip. When his foot slipped, he slid down into the trench, landing beside the half-buried bodies. Luckily, he hadn't suffered any damage. When he rolled over the nearest Fusilier, he recognized Michael Marks. Marks had been one of those who handed him a letter for his father, a seaman on the Great Lakes out of Sault Ste. Marie, in case something happened to him. He had been twenty-six and originally came from Liverpool. His family had emigrated to Canada when he was twelve.

Amazingly, he was still alive but unconscious. Stoats saw he was bleeding from a number of shrapnel wounds, but none appeared serious. He used his field dressing to cover them. He carried plenty of spares in his haversack and backpack.

"I'll bring him up," he said as he lifted Marks in a fireman's carry. When he stumbled a couple of times as he tried to climb to the lip, the smaller of the two came down to help. The two of them placed the wounded soldier gently on their stretcher.

"Get him to the regimental aid station," he ordered. "And take care of the lad."

"Sure, Padre," replied the taller one. "But you look done-in."

Stoats waved away his concern. "God will give me strength," he replied as he turned to go searching for more souls to save.

APRIL 13, 1917
THE BONNAL TRENCH, VIMY RIDGE

"We won't be getting up the hill until tonight," said Major Cranston, with CRE flashes on his sleeves. The brim of his steel helmet was pushed back above his forehead, and the engineer had a cigarette dangling from the corner of his mouth below the moustache. With his back against the ridge, the shadows deepened the lines and ridges on his face.

"Tonight?" Lieutenant Ryan asked more sharply than he had intended. The engineer had been nothing but helpful. However, he had orders to move his composite battery to the top of Vimy as soon as possible. They were to provide additional support to the Richmond Fusiliers, who might be facing counterattacks from the Arleux Loop and Fresnoy.

"The ground needs to dry out a bit," the major stated. His chin pointed at one of Ryan's 18-pounders and its limber being pushed and pulled by its gun crew across a wooden bridge the major's men had built above the trench. There were five more waiting their turn with mules and pack horses, his ammunition train, behind them.

Ryan glanced at the nearby communication trench that was filled with men moving up the ridge carrying supplies and materials to create dumps at the designated locations. While the trenches had been planked and bath-matted to keep one's feet dry, he couldn't use them to move his guns, so they had to go over top, through No Man's Land, to reach Farbus and the railroad tracks.

"At least the horses will get some rest," the Cranston said as he looked at the draft horses with a critical eye. "They look like they need it."

Ryan winced. They had taken the ones in the best shape to move the battery he had been given to command. Some of the guns and the gun crews had been lightly worked during the Vimy assaults, since each battery had kept one gun out of action. They were only to engage if they received an SOS signal. Since they were relatively fresh, they had been pulled to create his composite battery. Some of the men he didn't know very well, since he had only met them the previous day. He was still getting a handle on them.

"I'll let brigade know we're going to be delayed," Ryan said as he waved a runner over from the second gun crew.

"General Loomis's HQ is now at the Bontata Tunnel," the engineer said helpfully.

"I know. We were warned not to drop any shells on his HQ," Ryan said with a straight face after he had sent the runner off with his status report.

The major chuckled. The 2nd Brigade had moved their HQ to Bontata Tunnel after they were informed their objectives had been captured.

"Have you considered using motors for your guns?" suggested Cranston. "It'll save on the horses."

"Yeah, someone has already made that suggestion. It makes sense. It's gone up the line, but what I heard was some general doesn't like the idea of motors pulling the guns," Ryan replied with a shrug that said *you know what generals are like*. "But they think it's a good idea to use them for the ammunition train."

"Makes sense. A motor can carry a greater load and faster than the pack horses can," sighed the major as he looked at the tired horses.

Ryan nodded. One of his pack horses could carry roughly 250 pounds, which amounted to nearly fourteen 18-pounder shells. "Yeah, the motors can carry about six hundred unboxed shells. Until they get stuck in the mud."

"Yeah," the major acknowledged.

"Then I'll need my horses to pull the truck out of the mud," Ryan said.

"You've got a point there," agreed Cranston.

APRIL 20, 1917
NO MAN'S LAND, VIMY RIDGE

"How the hell are we going to move the damn thing?" asked Lieutenant-Colonel Llewellyn. "It's a beast."

He was starting at the long barrel for a 15-cm German gun his men had captured. It was one of five the 2nd Brigade had captured during their assault on the ridge. The gunners from the 65th had taken a look at it and had said it was a coastal gun the Germans had repurposed for trench warfare by installing it on an improvised gun carriage. The gun was heavy. It weighed 12,000 pounds, including the carriage. Its length was another problem as it was nearly twenty-five feet long.

"We'll get her out," replied Captain Mawby as he waved a stubby cigar. As part of the men's rations, they received two cigarettes per day. As usual, the British used the cheapest tobacco, so they weren't satisfying. The cigarettes that arrived in the care packages from home were prized and commanded a high price for trading. The Germans tended to be cigar smokers, so the German army issued two cigars with their cigarette rations. When they had overrun the Huns, they found boxes of *Batavia* and *Heer & Flotte* cigars, which were quickly salvaged. "We'll need a team of horses, but she'll come out."

"What are we going to do with it once it's out?" asked Major Gavin, who was standing beside them at the edge of the gun pit. It had suffered damage from artillery and rifle fire. The gun crews were notorious for refusing to give up their guns. In the pit, Llewellyn could see scattered shells forming once neat stacks and wires dangling from where the telephone sets had been pulled out. The gun itself showed scarring from shrapnel and machine gun and rifle bullets. The gunners had examined the damage done to the breech block and declared it unsafe to fire. He guessed it was their way to spike the gun.

"Once she's out, she'll go to Croydon," the captain said out of the corner of his clean-shaven face as he puffed on his cigar. "They're giving her a look-see. If she can be repaired and converted to fire our ammo, they'll put her back in action. If she can't, they'll scrap her, or one of the museum folks'll grab her as a war trophy."

"Let them know we're the ones who took the damn thing," Major Gavin said. "We want credit."

The captain grinned. "Got orders to record the serial numbers of everything we salvage." He stared at his cigar for a moment then said, "Well, almost everything. The same was being done with the MG 08s and the *minenwerfers*. Once they get to Croydon it will be up to the Imperials to decide."

"Yeah, they'll keep the best ones for themselves," Gavin muttered.

Llewellyn shrugged. "At least they aren't firing at us."

"The Huns don't seem to be short of them," Mawby said as he pointed his cigar in the general direction of the Lens-Arras Road. They could hear German shrapnel targeting the road, trying to cut supply lines. The previous night, they had targeted Thélus with incendiaries. They could still see black smoke being blown by the wind in a northeasterly direction.

Llewellyn gave Gavin a glance. They had work parties assigned to making improvements to the road. They had sent orders to recall them, and the other work parties salvaging the battlefield, back to their assigned trenches. They were preparing the final instructions for their attack on the Arleux Loop in the next few days. The Arleux Loop was heavily protected by barbed wire, and they needed to take it to give Vimy Ridge a deeper protective zone. He hoped that his work parties weren't hit. He needed every man he could get, since he hadn't received any reinforcements.

"When things quiet down, start pulling it out," Llewellyn ordered.

"Yes, Colonel," replied Mawby as he puffed on his cigar. Llewellyn could see he was calculating what he needed to do to get the gun out and down the ridge. He left him to it as he and Gavin headed to his headquarters. He had some figures he had to calculate as well.

APRIL 28, 1917
ARLEUX-EN-GOHELLE

"Fuck!" said Lieutenant-Colonel Llewellyn. He hit the cobblestone pavement as a machine gun peppered the red-brick rubble that remained of a one-storey house. There was a black gate, threatening to fall off its hinges, protecting a niche containing a six-foot Jesus on the Cross statute. He didn't like the statue's reproachful eyes staring at him.

"Anyone hit!" he yelled out. He was relieved that all the men in his squad called out their names, indicating they weren't hit.

He raised his helmeted head to take a quick look above the one foot of brick that remained of the house. He ducked when he saw muzzle flashes. The German MG 08 was holding them up. The Fusiliers were on the outskirts of Arleux-en-Gohelle, a tiny village of forty homes or so. They were about half-hour behind schedule in the 1st Division's plan to straighten out their lines by capturing the Arleux Loop and the village. One of the other objectives of the plan was to relieve some of the pressure on the French army attacking a plateau north of Asine.

This time he had left Major Gavin out of the attack on the Loop. The Arleux Loop, part of the Hindenburg Line, was a formidable trench system protected by miles of thick, looped barbed wire. They knew it would be a tough nut to crack. Last night, his scouts had told him the wire had been only partially cut, despite the 65th's and the 1st Division artillery's attempt to destroy it. The newfangled fuse didn't seem to be working as well here as it had on Vimy Ridge. What made it worse was he had to assault the wire half-blind. The scouts couldn't get close enough to tell him how much of it had actually been cut.

They had launched their assault at four thirty this morning on a 2,500-yard front. They, along with the 10th, got tied up in the barbed wire when the machine guns opened on them. His Richmond Fusiliers and the 10th had suffered severe losses, with most of the officers being taken out of action. Still, they managed to capture the front line trench, but now they were trying to get to the other side, their final objective. Once they did, they could consolidate their positions. Just the Huns were being stubborn about it. He was surprised by how many machine guns they had.

"Sir," said a runner who dropped beside him, breathing hard. "The Emma Gee is in position."

"What about No 1?" he asked.

"They're ready. They're waiting for the Emma Gees to open up."

"Let's get it done. We're late," Llewellyn stated. This particular machine gun was proving to be a real nuisance. The Boche had done a good job when they created it. It was located in the cellar of a house on the main road into the village, and they had used the collapsed walls for overhead protection. From this angle, he couldn't tell if the Boche were connected by escape tunnels to other cellars in the town.

Suddenly, Llewellyn heard the familiar sound of a Lewis firing at the machine gun's position. He watched as the German machine-gun muzzle tracked to the right to engage the Emma Gee. On his left, a Fusilier popped up and flung two Mills at the nest. One hit the brickwork and fell to the ground while the other ricocheted toward the Lewis machine gunners. When both detonated, the Germans stopped firing. He hoped the blasts got it. But they were dashed when it started up again.

"Shit!" muttered Llewellyn.

"Colonel!" said a familiar voice that dropped beside him. Llewellyn turned his head to see Sergeant Duval beside him.

"Sergeant?"

"The FOOs report the Germans are assembling for a counterattack."

"How much time do we have?"

"Half-hour, forty-five minutes at most," he replied.

"Do you think you can get that machine gun?" he asked, indicating the German MG with his head.

"I can try," Duval said over the sound of the Lewis firing again. Llewellyn saw the bomber throw a couple more grenades before he spun around after being hit. He fell, bent over a short brick wall exposed to enemy fire. Hands grabbed the downed man and pulled him to safety.

"Give me a couple of grenades," Llewellyn demanded.

"Colonel?" Duval said in surprise.

"Give them to me," Llewellyn ordered.

Suddenly, the bomber's carrier popped up, and threw two more. Finally, one went through the slit dead centre and then detonated. Smoke started pouring out of the nest's openings. The Lewis gunner stood up and started marching toward the smoke, firing from the hip. When he finally reached the nest, he emptied the magazine into the slit. A bomber ran up and tossed another grenade in for good measure.

Now sure that the nest was secured, Llewellyn rose to his feet. "Let's get moving. We have a lot to do."

From the sounds of the battle, he knew the Germans were retreating to their secondary lines. There, they would regroup and then counterattack with all they had to regain their lost territory, especially after their artillery had softened up his Fusiliers and the 10th. It was the latest tactics they were using to defend their trenches.

Llewellyn made his way to the injured bomber. He recognized the man as Kevin Haines from the A Company's 2nd Platoon. He was groaning in pain as his partner slapped a dressing on the wound. "You did a good job. Mr. Haines."

"Thank you, sir!" he replied with gritted teeth.

"The stretcher bearers will take care of you," Llewellyn said as they appeared. "I'll drop by and check on you when we're done here."

"Yes, sir."

Llewellyn returned his attention back to the task at hand. He still needed to clear the rest of the village. He shook his head. It looked like they'd have to do it one house at a time.

CHAPTER 9

Dear James,

I haven't received any letters from you for nearly a month and a half now. My heart hopes you are well when you receive this letter. We don't get much news here about the war in Europe. What news we do get comes from the British consulate or the American embassy. They did say the Americans are finally in the war. The news of the Russian armies' victories in Persia seems to improve the morale here a bit. But I haven't seen anything about what's happening back home or how our boys are doing in France.

I'm doing fine. I have the usual complaints about the food here, and from time to time I pine for some awful iron rations. For a while, after the czar abdicated, it improved. Some warehouses were broken into by the crowds to loot. They found them filled with hoarded food that the bureaucrats had been selling on the black markets. For a week or so there was plenty, and it was cheap. Now the bread lines are longer than ever. We permanently have to station one of our kitchen staff to a bread line so we can get a couple of loaves. We even had to hire guards to protect the lorries bringing provisions to the hospital. Even with the red crosses painted on them, they've been stopped and looted.

Things are little bit better now. But you have to be careful what you say and how you say it. We've seen arguments break out, then they start shooting each other. There are some streets you want to avoid because they've placed the cut-off heads of policemen on spikes. It's quite gruesome.

But life still goes on. Before heading out, we have to check with the cooks, who always seem to know where there is trouble in the city. The other evening, a group of us nurses needed to get away from the hospital. We all went to the opera to see a musical. It was quite pleasant to be able to forget everything for a few hours.

Today was a difficult day. All the invalid soldiers in Petrograd held an End of the War parade. Nearly all our patients marched from the hospital to the Tauride Palace, where the new provisional government, their Duma they call it, is set up. It's about an hour's walk from the Anglo-Russian hospital. It was hard seeing so many bandaged soldiers in one place with missing arms and legs marching up Nevsky Prospect. Those who couldn't march were transported on lorries.

Whether the new government will end the war, I have no idea. I've heard rumours that the war minister wants to continue the fighting, but the other side disagrees. I don't understand the Russian government, since there seems to be so many factions with contradictory positions. A few weeks ago some of the hospital's staff vanished. When I had asked where they went; they said they had gone to the Finland Station to see someone called Lenin who had just arrived. He's supposed to be some politician that the czar banned a while back.

At least there was no violence in today's parade. A couple of weeks ago they held a mass funeral at the Mars field for those who were killed during the March riots. I didn't attend it, but I was told they had buried nearly two hundred souls that day.

I'm hoping things will improve in Petrograd and that food becomes more plentiful, since spring is nearly here. Time will tell.

I must admit that when I get back to England, I'm going to find the nearest tea shop and stuff myself full of crumpets smeared with real butter.

Take care of yourself as best you can.

Love,

Samantha

P.S. We still have snow here.

MAY 13, 1917
PARADE GROUND, HAILLICOURT

"We do mourn for those gallant lads who lie yonder because we know they have fought and given their lives for the greatest cause in world history," said General Horne, the GOC of the First Army, as he stood on the raised platform.

Lieutenant-Colonel Llewellyn, positioned in front of the Richmond Fusiliers, had an unobstructed view of the First Army's GOC, flanked by Major-General Currie and Brigadier-General Loomis. He hadn't had a chance to speak with Loomis since he had been in London on a much-needed eight-day leave. He had arrived the previous night just in time for today's inspection. Standing slightly behind the moustached Horne, he could see the assistant chaplain general for the First Army in his vestments. Major Stoats, beside him, had assisted the chaplain general during his thanksgiving service for the Canadian victory at Vimy Ridge. The ADCs who had accompanied their COs were clustered unobtrusively behind them.

Llewellyn felt the light breeze from the northwest helping to relieve some of the late-morning heat. It would be hotter in the afternoon. He didn't need to look behind him to feel his men's contained restlessness. He glanced at Major Gavin, who was lined up beside him. It was the third time this week they had to parade.

Last Wednesday, Currie had inspected the entire brigade on the plateau at Maisnil-les-Ritz, about two miles south of Haillicourt. He had arrived at eleven o'clock riding his horse Brock, with his ADCs trotting behind him, to the plateau from his headquarters in Bruay. After the general salute, Currie had dismounted and walked the ranks kitted in fighting order without steel helmets. He had even paused to chat with Llewellyn for a few minutes, asking how he and his men were doing. He mentioned in passing that he needed to provide men for an honour guard for the Belgian king, Albert 1, who was visiting the Corps next Tuesday, and he might be in touch. Currie also said, before moving on, that he had read Llewellyn's reports with great interest.

To hear Currie's speech, the entire brigade had closed to the centre of the plateau, where he said they might not fully appreciate their achievements. He had made a point of praising the NCOs and had expressed regret for the losses they had suffered. He had finished by reading the congratulatory message from Lieutenant-General Byng. Then the 2nd Brigade marched past Currie in columns of four with fixed bayonets.

Then on Friday it had been Lieutenant-General Byng's turn. He had arrived at the Haillicourt parade ground in a motor and had been greeted by Currie. The 2nd Brigade had been arrayed in an open square formation, like they were now, with the 10th Battalion on the left wing, the 2nd Trench Mortar Battery, the 8th, the 7th, the Richmond Fusiliers, and the 2nd Machine Gun Coy in the centre facing the raised platform. Beside it, the 5th and 7th's regimental bands were stationed. On the left wing, they had placed the 5th Battalion.

After he had inspected the brigade, Byng gave a speech, which was basically the same one Currie had given them two days before, about the magnificent work they had done in the past month. It would form a glorious page in the history of the Dominion. After the march past in route order led by the 10th with the 8th, 7th, 5th, the Richmond Fusiliers, the 2nd Machine Gun Coy, and the 2nd Trench Mortar Battery, he said he had never seen a smarter and finer unit than the 2nd.

When today's march past General Horne had been completed, Llewellyn watched as he had a brief conversation with several of the Corps' generals, then shook their hands before heading to his motor car. Llewellyn and Major Gavin then led the Fusiliers back to their billets in the Haillicourt Camp. Once the men were dismissed, Llewellyn asked Major Gavin, "Are we all set for the soccer game?"

"You mean football," he replied.

"Good God, let's not start that again," Llewellyn stated. There had been too much time spent arguing over whether it should be called soccer or football. He really didn't care. "The men aren't tired from yesterday's Brigade Challenge Cup." The 8th Battalion had retained the cup, again. He found it irritating that they kept winning. Major-General Currie and the other division's GOCs and brigade commanders had been in attendance to watch the track and field and the horse events. As usual, everyone enjoyed the horse wrestling.

"Good God, no," replied Gavin. "Once they're changed their kit, they'll be out on the field rehearsing."

Llewellyn nodded. "By the way, Currie reminded me that we haven't submitted names for the honour guard for the Belgian king. We'll have to send them to HQ by the end of day."

"Sure, I know who to pick," replied Gavin.

"So, what are our odds us winning this afternoon?"

Gavin shrugged. "We've lost some of our best players."

"Yeah, but so have the seventh," Llewellyn said with a sigh of regret.

MAY 15, 1917
CAFFE RUSSO, CHAMPS-ÉLYSÉES, PARIS

"Hey, the woman over at the next table seems to like you," Lieutenant Simmons whispered to Furnell and Ryan. Lieutenant Furnell whistled after he craned his head to look around Ryan. "She has a nice pair."

"What makes you think she's looking at me?" Ryan whispered back as he discreetly tried to look in the direction Simmons had indicated. He quickly glanced away when a pretty brunette caught his eye and held it. Her long hair was pulled up in a high hairstyle hidden by an earth-tone beret with a centred jewelled brooch. She was wearing a dark brown worsted suit, open-lapel jacket, and shirt. Her crème blouse was open slightly and two buttons were undone, so he had a glimpse of a couple of inches of white skin near the neckline. There were two other ladies sitting at the table with her; they looked around his age. One had black hair, while the other's hair was a soft chestnut.

"You speak frog," said Lieutenant Simmons. "Go over and talk with them."

"What would I say?" asked Ryan.

"I don't know, *Comment tu t'appelles*, for starters. Don't be shy. We only have six days left in our leave, and I haven't even gotten a sniff of tail yet," urged Simmons. Furnell shook his head at Simmons's crudeness.

"But CO warned us…" Ryan protested.

Furnell cut him off, "Kevin is right about that."

"Okay," Ryan agreed reluctantly. He would have preferred to have gone to Paris by himself; he wanted to visit the museums, but Masterley had insisted no one went on leave to the City of Lights alone. Therefore, Kevin Simmons, Peter Furnell, and he had been granted a ten-day leave. He also had been warned of the dangers of picking up women in the French capital to one's health and pocketbook. Lieutenant Simmons had recently joined the 65th and was currently in charge of the gun batteries' wagon trains. Although he was from Laval, on the outskirts of Montreal, he didn't speak French. He was in his late twenties, with black hair and brown eyes, and was married with two kids. Marriage didn't seem to bother him very much when it came to chasing women. Furnell, who was single and was also in his late twenties, had similar colour hair and eyes. He had a thick body with a blacksmith's arms and chest. He commanded the No. 2 Battery of the 65th.

Simmons and Furnell were sharing a hotel room, while Ryan had somehow managed to get a single room at their hotel. The train trip to Paris had been rather uneventful. While they had to switch trains, the YMCA canteens at the stations where they had to disembark had provided them with sandwiches, tea, and coffee. He had been hoping to stay at one of the hotels the Canadian YMCA had set up in Paris. However, Simmons and Furnell thought they would be rather straight-laced for their tastes. They had found a small hotel, a boarding house really, on rue Bonaparte in the 6th Arrondissement. They were within walking distance of the Notre Dame cathedral and the Louvre. It was run by ex-French soldiers who had served in Algeria and had bought the place when they retired. It was clean and the food was good, though they really hadn't eaten there much. They were close enough to the YMCA's Hotel d'Ostende, where they could take advantage of the tours they offered. Today, they had visited Bonaparte's tomb. Tomorrow, they were scheduled to visit Versailles. Yesterday, they had visited the Eiffel Tower, although they couldn't enter or climb to the top, since access was restricted. It was being used as a military communications centre.

It was a bit of a shock arriving in Paris to see the crowded streets filled with people, carriages, trucks, and trams going about their business as if there wasn't a war. There were a few signs here or there of the war's impact. There were a fair number of men in uniform, French blue and British khaki on the streets. They'd seen a few American khaki uniforms with the arrival of the first American troops.

They quickly discovered how expensive things were in Paris, but the pastry shops caused his mouth to water with their various confections. The French baguettes loaded with camembert cheese made a tasty cheap meal.

It had been made quite clear to Ryan, though, that Simmons and Furnell were only interested in getting hammered and chasing women. Simmons had shown him the French postcards that depicted naked women and couples in the midst of coitus. He had been shocked that such things existed and were easily available. Still, it would be nice to spend a few hours with a young pretty woman who smelled fresh and clean compared to his two companions.

He rose to his feet, set his forge hat at a jaunty angle, then approached the three women. He could finally get a good look at them. The dresses they wore were of the latest styles but of modest cost. He had been dragged through enough dress shops by his mother and sister in Montreal that he could tell how much women's dresses cost. The black-haired woman was wearing a dark green suit, jacket, and skirt, with a white blouse buttoned to her neck. She had on a brimmed hat with a white ostrich feather. The auburn-haired girl was dressed in tan, with an open-necked crème blouse. The hat she sported was silk and floppy, embroidered with colourful flowers.

The girl that had caught his eye earlier was looking at him in amusement. "*Bonjour, mademoiselles. Comme allez-vous?*" Ryan asked.

"*Bien,*" the brunette answered. "*Vous êtes Canadienne?*"

"*Oui,*" he replied. "*Mes amis voulez parle avec vous?*"

The three women glanced over at his companions, then huddled together for a moment. "*Mais oui,*" said the black-haired woman. "We speak English."

Ryan gave a sigh of relief. He turned his head and motioned Simmons and Furnell over. They rose quickly to their feet with grins on their faces.

★ ★ ★

Clarisse quietly picked Ryan's pocket. She opened his wallet, pulled out the francs she found, then slid it back into place. She was tempted to count the money but thought she would be pushing her luck. She wanted to be as far away as possible once he discovered his money was gone.

She hadn't planned to sleep with him, but unlike most of the men she had rolled, he had been *très agréable*. He had bought the story she and her friends worked in a dress shop. If he remembered the dress shop's name and tried to find her, he would be disappointed.

Clarisse, Odette, and Marguerite had shown the Canadians parts of Paris they normally wouldn't have visited. They had steered them to some of the nightclubs that gave them commissions to bring soldiers in then charged them double for watered drinks.

He hadn't been grabby, like most of the other *cochons* she had picked up. She avoided the French soldiers, since they had no money, and she had a switchblade in her dress to discourage those who got aggressive. It had been easy to separate him from his friends by telling him she wanted to go somewhere private. He had been rather hesitant until she undid the top button of her dress. When he mentioned where he was staying, she had agreed, since she was familiar with the hotel. The old witch at the front desk had given her a glare when the *Canadienne* had asked for his key. She knew she would have to give her a cut. They had to be careful how often they cleaned out the soldiers to avoid having the hotel declare them off-limits.

She had planned to pick his pocket then find an excuse to leave, but he had been cute. When he entered his room, he had been so nervous that she realized that he was new at this. Even a virgin. She didn't get many of those. He was relieved when she took charge undressing him. She had to be careful with the first-timers, but she had to admit that she had enjoyed herself. However, it had taken some time for the alcohol to make him fall asleep.

For a brief moment, a very brief moment, she felt a touch of sympathy for the boy. She knew his friends would tease him mercilessly in the morning. But she had two babes to feed, and her mother. Francs were francs.

CHAPTER 10

MAY 18, 1917
APARTMENT, NESVKY PROSPECT, PETROGRAD

"Where did you find the potatoes?" Samantha Lonsdale asked as she eyed the six medium-sized ones. They weren't fresh, since the eyes were starting to sprout. If she had a garden, she would have planted them instead.

Christine pouted as she moved a blonde strand from her eyes. "They're pitiful, but they cost me a pretty kopek."

"With the onions and mushrooms that Alice brought, we should have enough for everyone," Samantha said as she gave Alice a glance.

"I guess," Christine said wistfully.

"Aye, I was lucking to get the last ones. I had to tussle some of the *babushkas* to keep them," Alice said. Samantha glanced at her freckled face. Alice would have given the tough *babushkas* a run for their money.

"I have some butter," Samantha said as she felt the heat from the cooking stove behind her. She then went to the cupboard to get some dishes. "At least, that was what they told me it was. I can fry the potatoes with onions and mushrooms. We can soft-boil the eggs I managed to get. For dessert, I got some apples."

"Oh my," sighed Christine as her stomach rumbled. She kept staring at the three red-skinned apples in the bowl. Samantha knew how she felt. They were constantly hungry, and tonight they were pot-lucking to extend what food they could scrounge.

They were interrupted by a knock at the door. "That must be Fran; she was supposed to get the bread," Samantha said as she headed out of the kitchen.

When she had come back, Fran greeted them in her Irish lilt, "Sorry I'm late. There was quite a crowd at the Nevsky Prospect."

"I would have thought most of them have gone home," Samantha stated. There had been a huge May Day parade held earlier by the Petrograd workers. While the Gregorian said today was the 18th, according to the Julian calendar it was May 1st.

"It was the largest I've ever seen," Fran said as she put a bag on the table then removed the scarf that covered her raven hair. "The bread lines were extra long, but I've managed to get us two loaves of bread. My nursing uniform helped." From her bag, she took out the loaves of black bread and placed them on the table, then she took out a bottle from it. "I also snagged a bottle of vodka. It's the good stuff."

Samantha, Alice, and Christine looked at the bottle dubiously. The czar had banned the sale of vodka at the start of the war, which resulted in *somagen* being brewed in people's apartments. One had to be careful with the moonshine. If it had not been distilled properly, it caused blindness.

"I got this from an aristocrat; it was made before the war. At least, that's what's on the label," Fran said as she glanced at the label. She didn't bother to say how she got a Russian aristocrat to give her a bottle. "Where are your glasses?"

"In the cupboard. A small one for me," Samantha replied. She didn't drink much, just to be social. When she took a sip of the vodka Fran had poured, she started coughing as it burned down her throat. "Oh God," Samantha said as she made a face and shuddered, to the amusement of Alice and Fran. It had left a bad taste in her mouth as she placed the glass on the counter. She sliced the potatoes, then tossed them into the cast-iron pan, followed by the butter. The mushrooms and the onions were next. Into a pot filled with cold water she dropped the eggs to be boiled.

As the food cooked, Christine said, "It smells heavenly."

"Anything exciting happening at the hospital today?" asked Fran after she emptied her glass and sighed contentedly.

"More patients are coming in from the front," Samantha replied. "Most of them are suffering from scurvy."

"Easy cases," Fran said, waving her glass.

"True," replied Samantha. "Some of the patients aren't. The doctors ordered a sauerkraut diet for them."

"Pickled cabbage," Alice corrected her with a grin.

"Yeah, pickled cabbage," Samantha said. Sauerkraut sounded too German. It was the current cure for scurvy. They weren't exactly sure why it worked. Most of the men who came into the hospital had bleeding gums, loose teeth, muscle pain, and night blindness. Night blindness was not a good thing for a soldier at the front. She had seen mild cases in the CEF before she came to the Anglo-Russian Hospital. It was the Royal Navy that had found lemon or lime juice seemed to have curative properties for scurvy, since their seamen, on their long sea voyages, were usually the ones that suffered the most from the disease because of the lack of fresh fruits, vegetables, and meats.

"At least the May Day parade was pretty quiet," Christine said.

"This is the first one I've seen. Was it this large last year?" Samantha asked as she stirred the potatoes.

Fran shook her head. "It was smaller last year. They had more Cossacks than people in the parade."

"The provisional government doesn't want to antagonize the people," Alice said.

"If they can get the food shortage sorted out, it would go a long way," stated Fran.

"I hope so," Alice agreed. "One good thing the new government did was get rid of capital punishment."

"And give women the vote. Don't forget that," Fran said.

"We can vote?" Christine asked. "Why do we want to vote?"

"So we can change things," an exasperated Alice retorted.

Fran, ignoring Alice and Christine, said, "Considering that it was the women who started the riots last February, I hope so."

Samantha shook her head. "If the garrison hadn't disobeyed orders, we wouldn't have the new government. And we wouldn't be in the mess we are now."

"What's done is done," Fran replied. "I'm for one glad we can now vote."

"I agree. The women in England have been fighting for the franchise for a long time," Alice added.

"The same in Canada, but it hasn't happened yet. Considering how stick-in-the-mud the government is back home, I doubt they'll ever give women the vote," Samantha said as she glanced at her frying pan. "The potatoes are nearly done."

"So which party do we vote for?" Christine asked, looking at Fran and Alice. "How do you decide?"

"You have to read up on the issues and decide which party you like best. Back home you vote for the Liberals, the Tories, or Labour," Alice said.

"The same in Canada, except we don't have a Labour party, as far as I know," replied Samantha.

"In Ireland, you're Sinn Féin, Unionist, or IPP," Fran said.

"Sounds complicated," Christine said.

"Complicated is Russian politics," snorted Alice as she set the plates on the kitchen table.

Samantha removed the eggs from the boiling pot with a fork and set them aside in a bowl. "I haven't bothered keeping up with Russian politics. It hurts my head."

"I have," Fran said. "The Kedat party wants a constitutional monarchy, like we have in England. They're mainly supported by the intellectuals and the professional elites. The Octobrist wants something similar based on some kind of October manifesto the czar issued to create the Duma, their parliament. They are mainly centrist right. On the left you have the worker parties such as the Socialist Revolutionary Party, Mensheviks, and the Bolsheviks."

"What's the difference? Aren't they socialists?" asked Christine. "What's a socialist anyway?"

"I wouldn't ask them that. They'll put you to sleep explaining what a socialist is and what the differences are between them," Fran replied. "I made that mistake once."

"You've been following politics?" Alice asked in surprise.

"That's all the men talk about besides where they can find food and vodka," Fran said. "It's sometimes wise to know what direction the wind is blowing. The hospital was being supported by the aristocrats. Some of the socialists want to get rid of them."

"That's why we had to remove all the plaques of the subscribers to the hospital from the wards," Samantha explained. "Some of our patients who are Bolsheviks have been giving us some trouble of late."

"The hospital committee won't let that happen?" Christine asked. "We do try to stay out of politics."

"I do hope so," replied Samantha with a sigh. "The food is ready. Let's eat."

HOUSE OF COMMONS, VICTORIA MEMORIAL MUSEUM,
OTTAWA

Sir Robert paused to take the glass that the page handed to him. He needed the cool water to soothe his throat, since he had been talking for two hours. The House would be recessing shortly — it was nearly six o'clock — to get something to eat and rest before they reconvened at eight. The press gallery above the speaker's chair was still full, no surprise, but the spectators' galleries had thinned out a bit.

He glanced at the remaining pages of his speech. It was a summary of the briefing he had given to his cabinet and caucus on the decisions made at the Imperial War Conference and his meetings with Lloyd George's Imperial Cabinet. His voyage back on the SS *Grampion* had been mostly uneventful, but they did get delayed by fog when they neared Quebec City. During the voyage, he had spent time with the three hundred soldiers on board in third class and had gotten to know them quite well. He had been pleased when they cheered him off. Laura had been waiting for him on the dock when the ship finally lowered its gangplank. He had been happy to see her and how well she looked.

When he handed the empty glass back to the page, his eyes fell on the new mace. It was set on brackets at the far end of the Hansard clerk's table and was pointing toward the government side of the House, as per protocol. He had escorted the mace back to Canada after it was presented to him by the Lord Mayor of London, Sir Charles Wakefield, and London's two sheriffs, Sir Alexander Touche and Sir Samuel George Shead. He had been relieved when it was finally delivered to the House. During the voyage, he had feared, for a moment, he had lost the mace when someone had broken into his cabin to steal his tobacco. They never did find the culprit. With nearly 1,500 passengers on board, it had proven difficult. After that, a man had been posted to guard his cabin.

They had a ceremony two days ago when the sergeant-at-arms was presented with the new silver and gold mace to replace the wooden mace they had been using. The wooden one had been in use ever since they had returned the Ontario government's mace to Queen's Park. They had borrowed it for several weeks after the fire. The new one was a replica of the original one destroyed by last year's fire, with a few modifications. One was the inclusion of an engraving of a beaver on one of the panels. Some had opposed the idea, since they felt the beaver looked like a rat. Borden had been pleased by the work the Goldsmiths and Silversmiths Company had done.

When he lifted his eyes from the mace, they fell on Sir Wilfrid Laurier, sitting across from him. He had briefed him yesterday on his trip to London, but he hadn't hinted at what he was about to spring on the House. There would never be a good time for his announcement, but the recent magnificent victory at Vimy Ridge would help blunt much of the opposition's criticisms of his new policies. His Quebec ministers had warned him they might lose Quebec because of it.

"Mister Speaker," Sir Robert Borden said. "It's my duty to announce to the House that early proposals will be made on the part of the government to provide compulsory military enlistment on a selective basis such as reinforcement, as it may be necessary to maintain the Canadian army in the field as one of the finest fighting forces in the Empire." He had to pause as MPs on both sides of the House rose to their feet, cheering and applauding. Some of the Liberals were conspicuous for remaining seated. When the MPs finally took their seats, he continued, "The number of men will not be less than 50,000 and probably will be 100,000."

He finally took his seat and waited for Sir Wilfrid Laurier to be recognized by the speaker so he could launch a fierce rebuttal and attack him and his government.

MAY 25, 2017
PRIME MINISTER'S HOME, GLENSMERE, OTTAWA

"So that's the political and military situation as discussed at the Imperial War Conference I attended in London," Sir Robert Borden said to Laurier. His briefing of Sir Wilfrid was a repeat of what he had given to the House. In addition, he had given the Liberal leader his views and impressions on the British, Commonwealth, and French leaders he had met while in France and England.

Sir Wilfrid, dressed in his usual elegant style, was sitting across from him on his patio, enjoying the warm spring day. The vegetation in his garden was starting to fill in. It was still cool in the early morning, but it had warmed sufficiently by the time Sir Wilfrid had arrived for their eleven o'clock meeting that they could sit comfortably outside. He had invited the opposition leader to an informal meeting at his home because he didn't want the wagging tongues in the East Block to speculate on what he and Sir Wilfrid would be discussing. "And Balfour will be visiting Ottawa next week on his way to the States. If you wish, I can arrange for you to speak with him."

"I would like that very much," replied Sir Wilfrid.

"Are sure you don't want more coffee?" Borden suggested as he made a motion to the table next to him, where a silver coffee pot rested on a tray.

"Thank you, but no," replied Laurier as he waved the offer away.

Borden set his cup down and locked eyes on Laurier. "I've made a vow to the men of the Canadian Corps who are giving their lives for a just cause that it will not be in vain. I would do everything within my power to provide them with what they need. That is the reason I've announced my government's intention to introduce compulsory military service."

"I see," replied Laurier as he eyed Borden thoughtfully, "and you want to ask me not to oppose quick passage?"

"In a way," Borden replied. He leaned forward in his chair then said, "What I want is your support in forming a coalition government."

Laurier gave him a startled look. "A coalition government?"

"Yes," Borden said. "My party and yours. Half the caucus will consist of Liberal members, the other half Conservatives. Of course, I would remain as prime minister."

"Have you discussed this with your cabinet?" Laurier asked as he studied Borden to see if he was serious.

"No, I have not," replied Borden tersely. Borden knew, as did Laurier, that while there was enormous public support for a coalition government, there was considerable resistance to one on both sides of the House. Many in his party thought it was a Liberal stratagem. "When I do, I will tell them it is my judgement that a coalition government is necessary for the good of the country. If they don't agree, they can find another leader."

"I wish you would've spoken with me before you announced it," Laurier replied with a touch of irritation.

"I felt it would be more appropriate to make the announcement prior to us entering negotiations to form a coalition government," Borden replied. He knew Laurier was adamantly opposed to conscription. If he hadn't announced it, he was certain that one of Laurier's conditions would have been killing the conscription bill.

"I'm afraid that my position remains unchanged. I do fear the consequences of such a policy in Quebec. Especially if it is passed by the current Parliament without a referendum," Laurier replied in a sour tone.

"What do you propose?" Borden asked.

Laurier leaned toward Borden then said, "Call an election. Put it to the people. If the government is returned, I have no doubt that Quebec would obey the law."

That is exactly what I wanted to avoid, Borden thought with a grimace.

"I'm not in favour of calling an election. First, my ministers are heavily involved in their war duties. It would be a distraction and a disruption to replace them, since they have extensive experience and knowledge in their department's tasks. Second, I fear the controversy with the Military Service Act would sow discord and disunion."

Borden put up his hand when he saw Laurier starting to speak. "I'm well aware of the political conditions in Quebec. That is why I want to talk to you about this."

Henri Bourassa, Borden knew, was a political thorn in Laurier's side. If he called an election now, he would be handing Bourassa a gift to hammer Laurier and the Liberals. Laurier looked away for a moment as he clenched his jaw.

"Would it help if I make a pledge that compulsory military service would not be enforced until an election is called?"

Laurier paused to consider Borden's offer. "I cannot commit now. I need to consult with Gouin and several others to consider the matter more fully. Before I do, I will need a clear statement, in writing, that you're proposing a coalition, that the Military Service Act will be passed, and your pledge not to enforce the act until an election is called."

Borden wasn't surprised. He hadn't expected Laurier to give him an answer today. What he was hoping was that there were sufficient Liberals who would agree that the conscription was necessary and they would put pressure on Laurier to enter into an agreement. The really tough part, Borden knew, if they settled on mutually acceptable terms, would be convincing his own party that it was best for the country.

"Agreed," Borden said, offering his hand to Laurier.

MAY 29, 2017
CHÂTEAU LAURIER BALLROOM, OTTAWA

Sir Robert was a touch concerned when he entered the ballroom and saw that the place was packed. The Centre Block fire was still fresh in his memory. All the tables were occupied, and there were people standing along the back wall, with more overflowing into the corridor.

There had been such a demand for tickets, people were willing to pay outrageous sums to get a seat for today's Canadian Club luncheon. They hadn't come to hear him speak. He was seated beside the man everyone had come to hear: Arthur Balfour. He had gotten to know the secretary of state for the colonies well during his stay in London and was pleased that he had decided to spend a week in Ottawa before heading to Washington. Balfour was heading a British mission to the United States, and his visit to the States was precedent-setting. The Americans and the British had diplomatic relations for decades, but the senior members of both governments had never met. There had been some talk of President

Wilson visiting England, but the war had killed that idea. Great Britain felt it was important that it show its appreciation for the Americans' entry in the war. Face-to-face meetings were thought best to discuss the war's aims and how they could cooperate.

The Americans had already requested permission to use some of the Canadian bases to train their officers and men. Gwatkin was already sending to the US War Department the latest training manuals used by the Canadian army. He was slightly irate when he found out they had asked for several thousand Ross rifles for training purposes. Until the Americans ramped up production of their Springfield rifle, the standard American service weapon, they had barely enough to equip the units being sent overseas.

He frowned slightly when he saw Admiral de Chair sitting on the other side of Balfour. Borden had been briefed on the meeting that Balfour and de Chair had with Admiral Kingsmill, the director of the Canadian navy. He was well aware of Kingsmill's concerns that his opposite number was attempting to undermine Ottawa's authority over the Halifax harbour. They had made some complaints about the work being done on repair and outfitting of Royal Navy ships at Halifax's dry dock. And they had expressed concerns about the harbour's submarine defences.

Borden had been raised on the majesty of the Royal Navy, especially during the years when he had been a lawyer in Halifax. In the last several years some of the mystique had worn off. He hadn't forgotten their refusal to give him a few of the submarines that had been built at the Vickers shipyard in Montreal. He had made his position quite clear to Admiral Kingsmill that Halifax belonged to Canada.

Borden was looking forward to hearing Balfour speak today. Yesterday afternoon, Balfour had been given the honour of speaking to a combined session of the House of Commons and the Senate. He was certain Balfour's speech today would be just as elegant as the one he had given yesterday.

He had taken the time to brief the secretary on the political situation in Canada and in the United States. He had informed Balfour of his intention to form a coalition government with the Liberals and to pass conscription legislation. He hadn't bothered to mention the death threats that he had been receiving ever since he had made his announcement concerning conscription. The threats were serious enough that Commissioner Sherwood had assigned a man to protect him and Laura. He was also certain Ambassador Spring-Rice would be giving him a fuller briefing before Balfour met with senior U.S. government officials.

When the waiter had taken away his plate and asked whether he wanted tea or coffee, Sir Borden knew that it was time for him to introduce Balfour. He rose to his feet and took the few steps to the podium. He also knew he had to keep it short, or the crowd would start booing him if he went on too long. For everyone in the room, it was a once-in-a-lifetime opportunity to hear one of the giants in British politics give a lecture.

CHAPTER 11

"There are three types of gases, lachrymatory, suffocating, and asphyxiating," stated Lieutenant-Colonel Mitchell. Lieutenant Ryan had a somewhat clear view of the fifty-year-old officer with his grey-black hair and moustache. On his shoulders were the flashes of the Canadian Corps' Gas Services unit.

He glanced at the other men attending the lieutenant-colonel's lecture on the offensive use of gas. About half the men in the room were artillerists, while the rest were infantry with a sprinkling of cavalry and engineers. He spotted Major Gavin from the Richmond Fusiliers sitting in front of him.

"Lachrymatory gas is used mainly in our gas shells," stated Michell as he tapped the 18-pounder shell standing upright on the lecture table in front of him. It was painted a light grey and with several red bands and one white band. For the past year or so, they had been painted for easy identification, black for shrapnel, yellow for HE, and light grey for gas. Beside the 18-pounder, there were a small box respirator and a German gas mask. "They're usually filled with benzol and acetone chemicals that contain chlorine, bromine, and other acids. We've been finding the 5.9 shells work best, since they hold nearly seven litres of fluid. One advantage of the gas shell is that our artillery can place a gas barrage exactly where one is needed. This is useful when conducting counterbattery work. The other is that the gas presents very little danger to our own men."

Ryan couldn't help touching his right eye. He had been hit by a German gas shell, and he was lucky that his blindness had been temporary.

"We've been experimenting with gas hand grenades and mortar bombs to test their effectiveness. And our chemists have also been experimenting with various chemical combinations to find ones that are most effective," said the lieutenant-colonel.

"Colonel," Gavin interrupted. "Will our gas masks work against the new chemicals you're developing and against any new German gases?"

Ryan noted the lieutenant-colonel didn't like being interrupted and took a moment before he replied, "Our chemists are constantly testing any new gases that the enemy uses. When the Huns gas your area, notify your gas officer. He'll be responsible for retrieving them and sending them to our chemists for analysis. Once they've been analyzed, they can develop effective filters for our gas masks."

Mitchell continued to stare at Major Gavin when he said, "It is important that the men are drilled regularly on the use and maintenance of their gas masks. Also, once a gas alert has been sounded, they must have their gas masks in place in less than six seconds."

Ryan saw that Gavin was clinching his jaw. He was well aware the Richmond Fusiliers weren't lax in their gas drills, unlike some other units he had worked with. The Gas Services section had officers and NCOs embedded in each unit to train the men on how to deal with a gas attack. They were at times a pain in the butt.

"Sir?" Ryan said, raising his hand.

"Yes," Mitchell demanded.

"Is there a time set for the horses?" he asked. "We need to put gas masks on them to protect them as well."

Mitchell looked stumped for a moment then replied, "I think six seconds would be sufficient for the horses as well."

"But…" Ryan blurted.

Before he could ask how the grooms would be able to get masks on all the horses in a unit under six seconds, Mitchell said, "I have a lot of material to cover today. If you have any questions, ask me after my lecture is done. Where was I…? Ah, yes.

"It's equally important that the Germans are aware you drill regularly and are alert. A case in point, a German regiment from Russia had recently entered the Huns' front line. When intelligence had reported, they had not been well drilled putting their gas masks on, we launched a gas cloud attack against them. It was estimated that nearly a third of the Boche were killed or wounded.

"Now, the next part of my lecture is gas clouds. Gas clouds use asphyxiation and suffocation to attack your respiratory track, causing difficulty in breathing, and you may vomit blood. There is a disadvantage in using a gas cloud in the attack. If the enemy is alert, they can easily spot the gas cloud forming. They may hear the whistling sound of gas being emitted from our gas cylinders, and the smell of gas. You all know the smell of chlorine and bromine. Phosgene gas smells like cut grass or hay. So if you smell that in the trenches, sound a gas alert immediately. The cloud does give them ample time to don their gas masks," Mitchell said as he picked up the German gas mask.

"The German gas mask is like our small box respirator. But here at the bottom," he said as he pointed to a metal ring, "is where they screw in their gas filter."

Ryan wasn't so sure. The German design seemed to be simpler to him than the small box respirator. He knew the gas mask routine quite well, since he had to take his men through it daily. First, he had to remove his steel helmet. Second, extract the mask from the satchel strapped to his chest. Third, bring the mask to his face as he slipped the hood over his head. Fourth, push the rubber mouthpiece into his mouth. Fifth, adjust the nose clip on his nose, forcing him to breathe through the mouthpiece. Then he had to drill his men laying the guns, setting fuses, and firing the 18-pounders while wearing them. At least his men didn't have to do the standard drills that Major Gavin had his men routinely practiced. They had to run two hundred yards wearing them. Then they had to do the same during musketry, bayonet fighting, and bombing drills.

"Is that what happened last March?" Gavin asked.

"That was an unfortunate set of circumstances," the lieutenant-colonel replied tersely.

"Can you tell us exactly what happened when the 4th Division launched their reconnaissance in force on Vimy Ridge? I heard they suffered significant casualties," Gavin asked.

Ryan could see Mitchell's eyes scan the room, not liking what he saw. He took his time forming his response before speaking. "We learned valuable lessons from the 4th Division's operation. The Imperials had provided us with nearly a thousand cylinders of gas, and they had loaned us men from their Special Gas Company. They were responsible for deciding when the weather conditions were right to release the gas."

"What went wrong?" asked Ryan. He suspected he knew the answer.

"We needed a stiff wind for the gas cloud to move up the slope. Gas tends to settle in low areas such as trenches and shell holes. We wanted a strong wind so our men wouldn't have to move through the gas cloud themselves. We didn't discover until after that some of the men had not been well trained in conducting an assault supported by gas.

"When the Boche spotted the gas cloud, they launched SOS flares. The German artillery responded by shelling the gas cloud and our front lines. Some of the gas canisters were hit, and we suffered casualties because of the released gas. Then the wind died before the second cloud could be released. The raid still went ahead, and by the time the raiders reached the Hun trenches, the Germans were on their firing steps, waiting for them."

Mitchell glanced at his watch and then said, "It looks like it's lunch time, so we'll take a break. This afternoon we'll continue with the general regulations that you as officers are required to be familiar with. And we'll discuss methods on how to construct gas-proof dugouts. Dismissed!"

"Joy," muttered Major Gavin when he rose to his feet.

"So, what do you think?" Ryan asked as he rose with him.

"Gas shells might be all right, but I doubt Colonel Llewellyn would ever approve an attack being supported only by a gas cloud. You know how he is about artillery support or lack thereof," replied Gavin.

Ryan made a face. He knew the reasons to well. "We're still working on improving communications with the Fusiliers," he replied. Then to show he had no hard feelings, he said, "I'll buy you lunch."

"Sure," Gavin replied. "What are they serving?"

"Knowing the army cooks, probably baked beans," Ryan replied with a straight face.

It took a moment, then the major chuckled. "You're an evil man."

"It would be a good test for our gas masks," Ryan pointed out with a grin.

JUNE 1, 1917
DMITRI PALACE, PETROGRAD

Samantha lifted her head sharply from the ward's inventory report she was writing at her nurse's station set in the middle of one of the wards. Her eyes went immediately to the bed in the far corner and fell on the soldier sitting on the edge of his bed. She wasn't surprised he was the reason that Fran was furiously stomping to her.

"That man!" Fran spat. "That man thinks we're a bloody hotel and we're his servants!"

Samantha quickly glanced at the patient to see whether he was listening. She had to admit he was good-looking. He had close-cropped blonde hair and blue eyes. His teeth had improved ever since he had been placed on a pickled cabbage diet to treat his scurvy. When he stood up, he filled the loose brown *gymnastyorka* tunic nicely, since he had well-toned muscles. A battered brown leather belt was wrapped around his flat stomach. Green britches were loosely tucked into calf-length black leather hobnail boots with horseshoe heels.

What put her off was the chip on his shoulder and the air of malevolence he carried. His eyes were cold and suspicious, especially when he thought you were an aristocrat. While he never admitted it, or at least the sanitors never said anything, she was fairly certain that he was a Bolshevik.

"Let's speak outside." Samantha indicated the corridor with her head. She had noticed some of the patients were keenly watching their drama. She wasn't certain if he understood English, but some of the others did, which meant their conversation would get back to him.

"I know. The man's an ass," Samantha told Fran.

"Can't we get rid of him?" Fran snapped.

"You know we tried. He's been officially discharged, but he won't leave," Samantha reminded her. "And we don't know what unit he belongs to."

Which was true. Generally, when a patient was discharged, their units would send an officer to pick the man up, or they would be sent to the nearest barracks. There, they would wait for orders to rejoin their units. With the abdication of the czar, many units had gone over to support the provisional government, causing confusion among the ranks. Add to that the burning and ransacking of government offices and military barracks, it had left many Russian soldiers lost in the system. Some liked it that way. Why leave the hospital if you were being kept warm, clothed, fed, and had pretty nurses to look after you?

"Why don't we get the guards to throw him out and let the Russian authorities deal with him?" Fran asked. "He's disturbing the other patients."

"I wish that was all he's doing," Samantha replied. "He's encouraging them to refuse our orders. You know men; they won't accept orders from us women. But they're refusing the doctor's instructions."

"But still..."

"Don't forget Order 1," Samantha stated.

Fran grimaced. She had heard about the order issued by the Petrograd Soviet that all orders issued by the military should be carried out except those that ran counter to those issued by the Soviets. They heard rumours that the Soviets were sorting out which officers were pro-czarist or anti-revolutionary.

"So he could be an informant then," whispered Fran.

"Yeah, I think he might be," replied Samantha. "If the doctors could

FRANK ROCKLAND

have discharged him before the note the foreign minister sent, we might have gotten rid of him."

"I doubt that," replied Fran. "He's become too comfortable here."

Samantha had to agree. When Foreign Minister Pavel Milykov's telegram had been leaked, Petrograd exploded. Everyone was incensed that the provisional government's foreign minister had assured the allies they would be continuing the war policies of the disposed czar. The anti-war Soviets had ordered the workers to strike, and some of the soldiers had joined them. Under pressure, Milykov had resigned, as did the war minister, to quell the city's street fighting. It seemed that the socialists had used the crisis to more firmly entrench themselves into the government.

"What about the Red Cross?" asked Fran. "Surely they can do something."

"The hospital committee has already spoken with them. They said they don't have the authority to force patients out."

"So there's nothing much we can do then," Fran said, frustrated.

"I'm afraid so," replied Samantha. "The Red Cross is meeting in a couple of weeks. We've received word the Russians are preparing an offensive in the next few weeks. The Russian Red Cross and the other hospitals are preparing to accept casualties. I guess the hospital committee can bring it up again. But with the socialists being anti-aristocrats, they aren't likely to change things."

"Damn," Fran muttered. "Do we have any Laudanum left?"

"I guess," replied Samantha. Then asked suspiciously, "Why?"

"We could douse him," she said with a straight face. "When he wakes up, he could find himself in one of the less savoury parts of Petrograd."

Samantha chuckled. "Now, now. We don't want to violate our oaths, but we'll keep that in mind as a last resort."

"Okay," replied Fran. "Nothing is going to stop me next time from accidentally pouring hot soup in his lap."

Samantha shook her head. She knew that Fran didn't let insults go easily.

JUNE 6, 1917
1ST DIVISION HEADQUARTERS, CHÂTEAU D'ACQ,
VILLERS-AU-BOIS

Lieutenant-General Byng's staff car drove slowly up the road lined by the men of the 2nd Battalion. The khaki line extended from the Chaussée

Brunehaut crossroad to the entrance of the château. Château D'Acq was a modest two-storey Renaissance-style country home with a salmon-coloured brick exterior topped by a grey slate roof. As the car stopped, the honour guard snapped to attention and the brass band struck up the 1st Division's marching song. When he stepped out of his car, Byng's eyes swept the château's front lawn, filled with the 1st Division's senior officers. He pursed his lips when he saw officers from all three brigades, plus those from the CRA and CRE, in attendance. He straightened his shoulders then turned to face Major-General Currie, who was waiting for him on the front steps.

He had grown rather fond of the pear-shaped Canadian general. Byng knew Currie would never strike anyone as a heroic figure, but he had proven himself to be a most capable officer. He had very nearly lost him last Sunday when a German aeroplane dropped bombs on Currie's advance headquarters at F.10 Central. Currie had a habit of being as close to the front lines as possible. It was sheer luck that he had just stepped outside to bring a telegram to his signal station when one of the bombs landed on top of his HQ. Currie had been close enough to the blast that he had been hit by debris. He had somehow managed to emerge unscathed, although bomb fragments had whined past his head. However, two of his men were killed and sixteen were wounded.

It had been a close call, but Byng thought it was unlikely it would ever happen again, since Currie would now be moving to the Canadian Corps' headquarters in the château at Camblain-L'Abbé, about three miles north of Villers-au-Bois.

He had been avoiding it for several months now, but he no longer had a choice in the matter. In the year since he had been given command of the Canadians, he had grown quite attached to them. They had their faults. They hated digging trenches, but they would fight to the last man defending the damn trench once he got them to dig it. Last Saturday, when he came to visit, Field Marshal Haig had put his foot down. Haig was promoting him and was ordering him to take command of the British 3rd Army. He would not take no for an answer.

After Haig had congratulated him on his promotion, the field marshal asked him, "Do you have anyone in mind to replace you?"

"Currie," was his immediate response.

Haig had given him a startled look. "Are you certain?"

"Yes. He's available and has all the necessary qualifications. The Canadian 1st Division is one of the best in the army."

"No doubt, no doubt," Haig replied. "But there are political considerations."

"Sadly, true," he had answered. In choosing a senior field commander, politics was always a factor. He was well aware Ottawa was pushing for more Canadian officers to be given command positions in the Canadian Corps, especially the Corps' GOC. He also knew Major-General Turner had stipulated, before he became the GOC of the Canadian forces in England, that he be considered for the command of the Corps when it became available. He was certain Turner would be lobbying hard for the position. He had done an excellent job in England, but Byng had serious doubts that Haig would ever accept Turner. Haig did have a good opinion of Currie, despite, on occasion, the Canadian giving the field marshal rather blunt and earthy assessments of his plans. If Haig couldn't get Currie, he would have no choice but to assign a British officer to command the Canadians. The Canadian government would have a fit if that happened.

"General Byng," said Major-General Currie when he saluted him.

"Sir Currie," he replied. Currie flashed a brief smile. The same day Currie was nearly killed, his name appeared on the King's Honour List. He was being knighted. It was quite a month for him, going from nearly being killed to being knighted, then becoming commander of the Canadian Corps. It didn't hurt that a lieutenant-generalcy went with it. It would be temporary until it was confirmed by the Canadian government. Byng had already put in a good word with Perley. If he was not mistaken, Perley would pass on a strong recommendation to Sir Robert Borden. It was Borden who would be making the final decision.

One of the thorny questions had been who would replace Currie as the GOC of the 1st Division. Brigadier-General Archibald Macdonell, who had commanded the 3rd Division's 7th Brigade, had been selected. He would be installed tomorrow.

"Would you like to have a word with the men before we have lunch?" Currie asked.

Byng glanced up at the sky. It was nice weather at the moment, but in the distance he could see grey clouds starting to move in. "Of course," he replied. His voice cracked for a moment. It was going to be tougher than he thought.

He marched with Currie to the front row of the officers. Using his parade voice to make sure that the men in the back could hear him, he said, "The past year has been the happiest of my life, if one could say that during a war. My promotion is the result of the hard work, dedication, and the sacrifices you have made. It is something that I will never forget. I wish you all well, good luck, and a quick end to this war. I just want to say thank-you and goodbye."

When he had finished, he dropped his eyes to the ground for a moment. When he collected himself, he started his review of the assembled officers and men of the 1st Division.

PRIME MINISTER'S OFFICE, EAST BLOCK, PARLIAMENT HILL,
OTTAWA

Sir Robert Borden sat dejected in his office chair, staring at the papers on his desk. "It is fortunate you have a great serenity of soul," Arthur Balfour had told him after he had gotten his impression of Canadian politics. He would need every ounce of it after his meeting with Sir Wilfrid.

Laurier had called him yesterday to request an interview, and he had been happy to meet with him at noon today. He had been somewhat hopeful that Laurier would join him in forming a coalition government, especially after he had offered not to pass the *Military Service Act* until after the country had gone to the polls. In one sense, he was somewhat relieved that Sir Wilfrid had said no to his proposal. As an enticement, he had also offered the Liberal leader a say in the Conservative membership in the new cabinet. It could have been perceived as making Laurier the de facto prime minister.

After the Liberal leader had left, George Buskard, his private secretary, entered his office. From the look on Borden's face, he knew Laurier had delivered bad news. "Sir Wilfrid didn't agree to come in?"

"That's correct," Borden replied sourly. "He said he couldn't support conscription, and he was fearful of Henri Bourassa's influence in Quebec."

"Sir Wilfrid's decision not to support a coalition will increase discord in Quebec," Buskard stated.

"I know, and that's why I wanted a coalition government to pass the bill," Borden replied. "Laurier and I agreed to publish letters to explain our negotiations and the reasons why we couldn't reach an agreement. We're hoping that it will reduce the discord somewhat."

"The Ginger Group will be happy with the news," his secretary stated.

Borden gave him a sharp look. The Conservative party always had its cliques and cabals. One of them was the Ginger Group led by Lieutenant-Colonel Currie, whom, thank God, was not related to Lieutenant-General

Currie. While his military record had been spotty, he had been sent home under a cloud after the Ypres battle in 1915, his service at the front had gotten him elected to the Simcoe riding and had given him a certain amount of influence. The group was dissatisfied with Borden's war policies, arguing that they hadn't gone far enough, and they felt that their voices were not being heard by his cabinet. He had felt the sting of their attacks and criticism in the House.

"They want conscription as an election plank," Buskard pointed out.

"True, I know I've lost Quebec. The Quebec Liberals will definitely not support conscription. My Quebec MPs will probably lose their seats when we go to the polls. If I allowed them the freedom to vote as they wished, they would vote against the bill." The Conservatives, as well as the Liberals, rigidly enforced party discipline and kept a tight rein on their members.

"Rogers thinks we will be hurt badly," Borden said. "I told him yesterday that the country is entitled to elect a new government. I would be happy to be relieved of the responsibility.

"I know some of the Western Liberals would support conscription. We might be able to convince them to cross the floor."

"The Ginger Group has been agitating to strip the franchise from aliens born in enemy countries. They are saying they tend to vote Liberal," Buskard said.

Borden grimaced. "I know. It's not only the Ginger Group. I've getting pressure from our western members. We'll have to consider that carefully, since they're Canadian citizens and they have the right to vote. However, we've been discussing extending the franchise to women. At least to women who have a family member in the service."

"That will go over well with the Liberals." Buskard chuckled.

"True." Borden cracked a smile. "Now, I'm going to have to prepare the letters that Sir Wilfrid and I agreed to publish."

"Yes, Prime Minister," Buskard said. "Would you like me to order lunch?"

"I've lost my appetite, but it would be best, since I still have a long day ahead of me," Borden replied. Buskard acknowledged with a nod before leaving Borden's office.

CHAPTER 12

JUNE 11, 1917
1ST DIVISION TRAINING SCHOOL, BURBURE

Lieutenant-Colonel Llewellyn watched as Sergeant Duval marched across the range, tearing up paper targets through his binoculars. Puffs of dirt spurted from the stop-butts behind the targets. He was certain Duval was enjoying himself, though his technique firing a Lewis machine gun from the hip was sloppy.

"So, what do you think?" he asked Captain Devenish, who was standing beside him in the slit trench. Special precautions had to be taken when the men were being trained on fire-on-the-move tactics.

"Well, he's enthusiastic," the captain said politely. The training school's commandant was in his late twenties, lean and clean-shaven.

Llewellyn grunted as he glanced at the rest of the class in the trench awaiting their turn. "That he is."

He noticed that Duval tended to fire low, a natural reaction, since the sergeant's instincts were to keep the Huns' heads down. But on the range there was a risk that a .303 would ricochet off the hard pan. As Duval stepped forward, the slung machine gun's muzzle lifted, sending slugs above the paper targets. He noticed there was no impacts of the bullets hitting the stop-butt. It didn't take long for a buzzer near the captain to ring. Devenish listened for a moment then pressed the stop signal. Llewellyn assumed the call was from the range officer stationed behind the stop-butt. It took a moment before Duval heard the alarm and stopped firing. Llewellyn knew the sergeant would be pissed. At least the range officer would be pleased that bullets were no longer whistling over his head.

"He's not doing very well, is he?" asked a voice with a Scottish lilt to Llewellyn's left. When Llewellyn turned his head, his eyes were drawn to the red tabs and the general's stars. When he looked up, he saw the blue eyes and the iron-grey moustache and hair below the forge cap of Major-General Macdonell.

"General," both he and Devenish said as they snapped sharp salutes. Llewellyn's quick glance at Devenish saw that he was surprised as he was to see the GOC of the 1st Division here.

"My apologies, sir. I wasn't expecting you till tomorrow," the captain blurted.

"No harm done," replied the major-general. He then indicated Duval with his chin. "He's not doing well."

"Not with the Lewis, I'm afraid," replied Llewellyn. "But he's an excellent sniper, nearly a hundred and fifty kills."

"Is he now," he replied with a wry smile. Everyone had heard the story about the German sniper who had wounded the major-general in the arm. Instead of taking cover, he had stood up, raised a fist with his good arm, and cursed the Huns in Gaelic. It was only when the sniper had put a second bullet into his good arm that his men were finally able to drag him out of No Man's Land.

When he heard that Macdonell had been appointed as the GOC of the 1st Division, he had gone and spoken with some of the officers of the 3rd Division's 7th Brigade, the major-general's former command. They had told him they were sorry to see him leave the 7th, but then he hadn't been in command of the brigade since last December because he had been on sick leave, suffering from stomach gastritis. They had informed him his new GOC was a front-line soldier who had spent as much time in the trenches as the privates had. They also said Macdonell could get somewhat batty when he was under fire.

"He's trying to catch up to Peggy," Llewellyn informed the major-general.

"Indeed," the major-general murmured in approval.

Everyone knew who Peggy was. It was the nickname of the 1st Canadian Infantry Battalion's sniper, Francis Pegahmagabow. He had run up quite a number of kills and was the top sniper in the Corps. The snipers were a competitive lot, and they were all trying to catch up with the Ojibwe's tally.

Llewellyn was particularly surprised by the major-general's approval. He had gotten a good read on him when they met yesterday for his inspection of the Richmond Fusiliers. He had mentioned in passing that some of his men would be at the training grounds near the village of Burbure, two and half miles southwest of Lillers. In the distance, Llewellyn could see the roofs of the one-storey houses through the sparse treetops, where most of the platoon COs and NCOs were being billeted during their ten-day course.

But Macdonell wasn't here to see him or his men. Rather, he was here to inspect Captain Devenish and his training staff. It was the usual standard protocol, the incoming GOC making the rounds inspecting the units under his command and for the men to get a look at him. Llewellyn did wonder what changes he might make. The incoming GOCs always eventually liked to put their personal stamp on things.

"How's the training coming along?" Macdonell asked the captain.

"General, sir, it's their first day. They'll improve by the time we finish with them," replied the captain as he motioned with his hand at the trainees. "The colonel's men know the basics very well, so I don't foresee any problems."

The major-general raised an eyebrow. "That's good to hear."

Llewellyn was pleased by the captain's compliment. The men he had selected for the course had already been through the refresher course at the Brigade's training school. The Divisional school was intended to train the company COs and NCOs the advance tactics for the bomber, Lewis machine gun, and Stokes mortar teams.

"I see that you are training the men to fire from the hip?" Macdonell stated.

"Yes, general," replied the captain. "I saw the memo asking for opinions as to whether or not we should continue this type of training. We're continuing it until we receive instructions to do otherwise."

"What're your views, Colonel?" the major-general asked Llewellyn.

Llewellyn glanced at Captain Devenish, then asserted, "I think we should continue to train the men in firing from the hip. You can fire the Lewis gun from the shoulder, but from the hip it can be more effective in keeping the Huns' heads down. The sling helps a lot. It's a heavy gun. For the riflemen equipped with the Lee-Enfield, it is more effective in the trench getting a quick shot off. At the ranges we are talking about, they are not going to miss. And it saves a few seconds in the man's reaction time."

"Hmm," the major-general replied, nodding in agreement. Llewellyn felt like he had passed a test.

"Very well, carry on," Macdonell ordered. He then turned to Captain Devenish. "If you would please introduce me to your staff now?"

"Yes, sir. Of course, sir," replied the captain as he led the major-general out of the slit trench. "Our main administration office is this way."

JUNE 12, 1917
PRIME MINISTER'S OFFICE, EAST BLOCK, PARLIAMENT HILL,
OTTAWA

"I've just been informed that General Byng is being promoted and is being given a higher command," Sir Robert said when Kemp and White took their seats in front of his desk. He had called them into his office to discuss some of the agenda items for the day's cabinet meeting.

"When is this going to take place?" the finance minister asked Borden as he gave the minister of militia and defence a glance.

"It's happening as we speak. George sent me a telegram last Friday informing me of Byng's promotion. He said it was temporary appointment," Borden informed them as he leaned back in his chair.

"General Byng is being given command of the Third Army," Kemp added.

White looked thoughtful for the moment. "So it's unlikely he's coming back to the Corps then."

"That's what George thinks," Sir Robert said.

"Who's in command at the moment?" asked White.

"Currie's in temporary command," replied Kemp.

"Temporary! Does that mean the War Office will be appointing another British officer? Are we going to have any say in it?" White blurted. He knew Borden had been chafing at the War Office.

"George says that Byng wants a Canadian officer given command of the Corps," Borden replied.

"It's about bloody time," White said as a grin broke out on his face. When he saw Borden's disapproval of his outburst, White said, "You've been complaining about the War Office's habit of appointing and promoting British officers to the Corps without consulting us."

"You're right," Borden replied sourly. "It will be popular with the electorate that a Canadian is commanded the Corps. Very few would object to that."

"Who does George have in mind?" Kemp asked.

White cocked his head at Kemp's tone. He got the impression he already knew who George was going to suggest. While his colleague was the minister of militia and defense, the CEF actually reported to the Canadian Overseas Ministry.

"Currie," replied Sir Robert.

"Makes sense. Byng and the War Office think highly of him," Kemp said.

"What about General Turner?" asked White.

"Not so much," Kemp replied.

Borden nodded. He had met both when he attended the Imperial War Conference in London. "George indicated in his telegram that Turner was senior to Currie, but George doesn't want to let General Turner go. George says he's been invaluable as his GOC in England.

"George also says that Turner's temperament is that of a fighting soldier, but he's been away from the front for over six months now. He thinks he might be out of touch with the current conditions at the front. Currie is considered more suitable by the senior officers in the Corps, most of the men, and the War Office."

"Do we still have to report to the damn War Office!" complained White grumpily. He then asked, "Will there be friction between Turner and Currie if Turner is passed over?"

"George says he'll accept it," answered Borden. "Both of them have strong support in the Corps. He did suggest that we promote both men to lieutenant-general so that Turner remains senior to Currie. That should reduce some of the friction."

White swayed his head gently as he rested his hands on his stomach. "Let's hope that it helps. We don't want to have any more friction between them than we need to."

"I agree," replied Kemp.

"That raises the question. If we're promoting Currie, who's replacing him as the GOC of the 1st Division? Garnet Hughes?"

There was a moment of silence, then Kemp said, "That's one of the names being considered, even though he's currently the GOC of the 5th Division. As you are aware, they are currently in England being readied for France."

"And the other?" asked White.

"General Archibald Macdonell. He's currently the GOC of the 3rd Division's 7th Brigade. He was wounded at the Somme last fall. Before the war, he was a North-West Mounted Police Inspector."

"If George likes him, I don't have any objections," replied White.

"I think it is more of the case whether Currie likes it or not. Currie is rather prickly about political interference in the Corps. That's one of the reasons he turned down the job Turner is performing so well."

"I can see Garnet and Sam kicking up a fuss. I suspect they really want the 1st Division," White pointed out.

"That may be," replied Borden. "I'll send word to Perley that Currie is acceptable to us, and we'll leave it in his capable hands."

"That sounds good," replied White. He noticed that Kemp nodded in agreement.

"If Currie accepts it, I would like him to mention in his acceptance announcement the need for reinforcements," Borden added.

"I saw that story from Quebec," White added.

"They continue to insist that the *Military Service Act* isn't necessary. The CEF has all the men they need," Borden said sourly.

"The bill is in second reading," Kemp said. "We'll get it passed soon."

"I know. I want to discuss it at today's council meeting, along with the Byng announcement," Borden stated.

"Well, I better let you get to it," White said as he got to his feet.

"I'll see you at the caucus room before Question Period," Borden said.

"Of course, Prime Minister," he replied as he ambled out of the office.

JUNE 15, 1917
WOODS BUILDING, SLATER STREET, OTTAWA

"We are in agreement?" asked Major-General Gwatkin as he polled the members of the Militia Council sitting at the table.

He made a mental count as he saw Major-General Fiset, Major-General Mewburn, Major-General Macdonald, and Brigadier-General Elliot nod. John Borden, a civilian member of the council, nodded as well, even though technically it was a military matter. There would be some savings that he would be pleased with. However, Gwatkin doubted the senior officers in England would be as happy with their decision as Borden, their chief accountant, would be. The policy they decided to implement required the senior officers to choose reverting to a lower rank or be shipped home on the next available transport.

"I think it will go a long way to solving our surplus officer problem," stated Major-General Mewburn, who was the adjutant-general responsible for personnel.

"The real question is how many of them are willing to accept reverting to the rank and pay of a lieutenant? I know I wouldn't like it," said Fiset.

"I suspect it will be a small percentage," Macdonald said, who was the quarter-master general. "I think it will be mainly captains and majors. I doubt lieutenant-colonels will be willing. We'll need to find berths for unhappy men for their return home."

"Those arriving on the latest transports will not be pleased when they arrive in England and are informed," added Mewburn.

"It can't be helped," Gwatkin said with a slight shrug. "If we can't use them in France, they'll have to come home. We have lieutenants who have said they were willing to give up their commissions and join the ranks to serve in the Corps."

"We need more of those," Fiset agreed. "We all hope the *Military Service Act* will start bringing in more reinforcements. The Corps needs them."

"I agree," Gwatkin stated. "With the Americans having just landed in France, the Allied manpower situation will see significant improvements." The American 1st Division had just landed at Saint-Nazire in France, the same port that the Canadian 1st Division had landed at nearly two years ago. "It will take them several months of training before they'll be ready to enter the trenches. The Americans will be green, but with the training from us and the French they'll be a welcome addition. At least they'll have several years of experience to draw on."

"Our training officers have reported the training has been progressing well," said Macdonald. They had lent some of their training officers to the Americans to help prepare them for what they would be facing in France.

"Sounds good. That clears most of the items on today's agenda," Fiset said. Looking uncomfortable, he coughed softly to clear his throat then said, "Unfortunately, I've a rather delicate matter I need to bring to everyone's attention concerning an unpaid tailor's bill."

Gwatkin noticed several of the officers who were not yet privy to the details raised their eyebrows in amusement while those in the know frowned.

"*That* tailor's bill," said Major-General Macdonald. He was one of those in the know, since he was the quartermaster general. He had been pushing for a court of inquiry into the matter for some time now.

"Yes, $10,883.34 plus interest," John Borden stated. Since he was the department's senior accountant, he was expected to be exact. He had also been asked by Minister Kemp to prepare a memo on the subject.

"Mr. Borden is correct. When the 50th Battalion was authorized in 1913, we had allocated nearly $17,000 for their uniforms. Since Highlander uniforms had not been available in our quartermaster stores, they had contracted with the Moore, Taggart & Company in Glasgow, Scotland, to supply them. The 50th had made the first payment, but they never made the second payment."

"Why not?" asked Brigadier-General Elliot, a British officer seconded to the Canadian army, responsible for ordnance. "Didn't the department send the second payment?"

"We did," replied Fiset. "However, General Currie deposited the cheque then used the funds intended for the 50th Battalion to pay personal obligations."

There was a stunned silence in the room. The officers understood the implications. Embezzlement was a court-martial offence.

"Has he made any attempt for restitution?" asked Macdonald quietly.

"No, he has not!" replied John Borden.

"Moore and Taggert have been quite patient, especially considering the affair has been ongoing for the last three years. They have been hesitant to take legal action because there is a war on. But their patience is wearing thin and they have been pressing to be paid," Fiset stated. "Minister Kemp has put the matter in our hands to find a solution to such a delicate matter. He has concerns about public confidence if the affair become common knowledge."

"Does the prime minister know?" asked Elliot.

"Not that I'm aware," Fiset replied.

"Has Minister Perley been informed?" Gwatkin asked.

"Not as yet," replied Fiset.

"I would suggest we put it in front of Minister Perley for his views and what he thinks are the next steps that need to be taken," Gwatkin suggested. "Especially since Lieutenant-General Currie officially reports to him."

"I understand. I'll prepare all the pertinent information, and I'll then forward it to Minister Kemp," Fiset said. "Let's hope that a discreet solution can be found."

The officers at the table nodded in agreement. The last thing they wanted was a public scandal, especially after it was announced that Currie was being knighted and promoted to command the Canadian Corps.

JUNE 18, 1917
FIELD OF MARS, PETROGRAD

Samantha felt some trepidation as they drove past the Field of Mars. There was still a considerable crowd milling at the square. About half were in civilian clothes while the rest were in uniform. She couldn't help noticing the red banners planted predominately around the twenty-two-acre large park near the Neva River. In the middle of the park, people had gathered around the spot where nearly two hundred of those who had been killed during the February riots were buried. They had held a mass funeral about a month or so in their honour, and now the park was being turned into a shrine by the socialists. It was turning into a favourite spot for them to hold demonstrations. They had held a massive one today, around nine o'clock, when they had called the people out to show support for the soldiers refusing to go to the front. It was estimated nearly four hundred thousand had shown up.

It was one of the reasons why the embassy had offered them a motor to drive back to their apartment. Even using the car was risky because people liked hitching rides by jumping onto the car's running boards.

It was a fine sunny day for the demonstration, she thought. This was to be her first summer in Petrograd. So far, she had only experienced the winter. Spring she had missed when she blinked. It had sped by so fast.

"Look," Christine said as she tried to point out of the car window, but Fran quickly pushed her hand down. Christine glared at her. "I just wanted to point out the women are carrying rifles and are wearing military uniforms."

"Even more reason not to point," Fran said sharply. "I heard about them. I think they're from the 1st Petrograd Women's Battalion."

Samantha had heard about a number of women's battalion being formed as combat units to be sent to the front.

"I wonder why they're here?" Fran said as she glanced over and watched as the squad of women marched off the Field of Mars in formation. "I didn't think they were Bolsheviks."

"I guess they wanted to show their support," Samantha stated.

"I don't blame them," Alice said. "I heard the latest offensive isn't going well."

"That's the rumours we've been hearing," Samantha said sourly, watching the women disappear as they marched in the direction of the Tauride Palace, where the Duma was currently in session. "I don't like the idea of leaving."

"That's not certain yet," Fran replied.

"You know things are not looking good at the hospital," Samantha said. "You know as well as I do that it's getting worse there."

The Bolsheviks seemed to be gaining more and more influence. *Pravda* was the most popular newspaper at the hospital, especially since their troublemaker had made a point of delivering it to every patient. That was one of the reasons they had gone to the British embassy earlier this afternoon to see what could be done. The news wasn't good. Meriel had explained that the hospital committee had spoken with the Russian Red Cross; unfortunately, they wouldn't be of much help because they were in disarray. Most of the key officials had been from the aristocracy who now had either resigned or had gone into hiding. Those who had remained had little authority. It didn't help matters that the socialists were pushing to set up worker committees to handle many of the Red Cross functions.

This meant the future of the Anglo-Russian Hospital was now in doubt.

"I don't understand why the Russians are launching an offensive. Didn't they say they would only be defending their territory?" Alice stated.

Samantha shrugged. "The new war minister wanted it."

Meriel had explained Kerensky had launched the assault to strengthen his political position. Samantha had actually seen Kerensky once when she attended the Russian ballet with Meriel at the opera house. When he was escorted to his box, the entire theatre had turned their heads to watch him. Some even rushed for a closer look.

Fran said with a frown, "I heard it hasn't been going well."

"Those are the latest rumours," Samantha agreed.

"Congratulations, by the way," Fran said. "They told us at the embassy your Canadians had won a great victory at Vimy Ridge."

"Thanks," Samantha replied with a tinge of worry. The three women seated across from her heard it.

"I'm sure that James is okay," Fran said.

That didn't seem to help Samantha much. She knew he would be in the thick of it. Like her, he seemed to be caught up in events that were dragging them along, willing or not.

"I'm sure that he's written to you. You know how the mail service is of late," Christine said, trying to ease her concerns. She became silent when Alice and Fran gave her quick glances. Samantha hadn't received a letter or a telegram from him in the last few weeks. She wasn't sure if he simply couldn't write or if it was just the terrible Russian mail service.

Trying to change the subject, Christine asked, "If we're forced to leave, who'll replace us?"

"There are plenty of Russian nurses," Samantha replied. Which was true. Much-needed nurses were being trained by the Russians for their stationary and field hospitals. Some of the women she had seen were from the upper classes. Quite a few had been struggling with some of the basic nursing tasks such as washing and cleaning wounds. However, they had heard rumours that some of the nurses in the field hospitals had been badly treated by patients and, in some cases, by hospital staff. They hadn't seen much of that behaviour at the Dmitri Palace. Lately, there had been a few incidents at the hospital instigated by their troublemaker that were starting to disquiet her.

Samantha stared at the Field of Mars. In one sense, she hated the idea of leaving the job half-done. Over the motor's engine, she heard voices in the park singing "La Marseillaise." It sent a foreboding shiver down her spine. Every time she heard that song, she couldn't help thinking about the fate of Marie Antoinette.

JUNE 25, 1917
FIRST ARMY HORSE SHOW, CHÂTEAU DE LA HAIE

"Easy, Brock," Lieutenant-General Currie murmured as he sat deeply in his saddle. He held the reins lightly as he slackened his leg pressure on his horse's flanks. Brock — his full name was Brockleband — had tensed up when the marching bands signalled the start of the opening ceremony for the First Army Horse Show. "Easy, easy."

"He seems to be rather nervous," stated the Duke of Connaught, who was sitting on a white charger beside him. The former governor general was on a visit to the front to help keep the troops' morale up. A couple days prior, the duke had lunched with him and his senior commanders at his Corps HQ. It wasn't his first visit. He had been here in early March, when Sir Robert Borden had visited the Canadian Corps. It was a few weeks before his wife, Princess Louise, the Duchess of Connaught, passed away.

"No, Your Excellency, you would think he would be used to this by now," he replied as he felt Brock relax beneath him. Currie knew he didn't strike a heroic figure on the red hackney. And the horse hadn't complained very much about the extra weight he had put on around his middle. Still, Brock was his favourite and the one he used most frequently for parades, reviews, and horse shows such as today's First Army Horse Show. He had come with him in 1914, and for the last three years he had proven to be a healthy, reliable steed. Occasionally, though, something would enter his head and he would be off for fifteen minutes or so, but he never was a sulky horse.

Currie's grey eyes noted General Horne on the other side of the duke. His face showed some satisfaction at the units of his First Army on display before them. Currie gazed at the competitors for today's events from the I,

XI, XIII, the Canadian, and the Portuguese Corps as they marched pass. The Portuguese Expeditionary Force Currie knew, totalling 55,000 men, had been assigned to Horne's First Army shortly after Germany declared war on Portugal earlier in the year. On their heels were the troops assigned to the First Army HQ and the Cavalry Division.

Currie's eyes were fixed on the Canadian contingent. For the past two weeks, all the Canadian divisions had held competitions to select the contestants for the day's events. There were thirty-two events scheduled on three rings that had been built on the grounds of the Château de la Haie. The château was about fifteen miles west of Vimy Ridge. The events ranged from turnouts for chargers, GS wagons, limbers, and lorries. There were the usual horse events such as tent-pegging and horse jumping, as well as tug-of-war and cross-country racing.

He knew the competition would be stiff today, but he had high hopes his men would do well. Unit pride was involved. He suspected Brock had picked up on his nervousness. He hadn't been pleased when he had read the divisional reports on the Canadian divisions' recent competitions. The reports had indicated the men's uniforms, leggings, small box respirators, and boots had grease spots. What was most disappointing was that their uniforms hadn't been properly pressed and the buckles on the Sam Browne's hadn't been polished. Also, the horses' leather strappings were disgraceful. He had sent word down they were representing the Canadian Corps, and he expected only the very best from them.

First thing this morning, he had inspected the committee tent the Corps erected on the château's grounds. He had been satisfied that his officers and men were dressed per regulation, were wearing clean, pressed uniforms, and their Sam Brownes had been polished to a glossy gleam. He had done a few spot checks on some of the chargers' fittings. The saddles had been cleaned and well oiled, as had the reins and bits. When he had turned over the horses' buckles, he saw that they had been polished as well. The judges were notorious for checking both sides.

He had been pleased. They all had the night to make sure that everything was spotless for his inspection. His men had spent the night crowded in one of billets in the four camps, the Canada, the Niagara, the St. Lawrence, and the Vancouver that surrounded the château. Some of the men had to be billeted as far as two miles away at Gouy-Servins. The French château was humming with all the horses, equipment, and spectators.

"General Currie," said the duke as the last of the units marched pass.

"I just want to offer my congratulations on Canada's golden jubilee."

"Thank you, Your Highness," replied Lieutenant-General Currie as he nudged Brock to stay pace with the duke, who was following General Horne.

"Do you have any plans to commemorate the event?" asked the duke.

"We do have a few for July 1st. Special meals for the men, masses, and a warm celebration for the Huns," Currie replied.

"Hmm, yes that does sound rather festive," replied the duke.

CHAPTER 13

The Ford had to make way as the tram disgorged passengers. Samantha couldn't help noticing that they were carrying rolled-up bedrolls on their shoulders, carpetbags, and luggage cases of various sizes. Most were securely tied with twine. Like her, they were heading to the train station's main entrance. The Finland Train Station didn't appear to Samantha to be particularly attractive. The two entrances on the left and right had grey slate canopies to provide some protection from the elements. One of them, she didn't know which one, was the entrance to the czar's pavilion. She didn't think he would be using it anytime soon. It was the same station Lenin had arrived at several months earlier.

"That didn't take long," said Alice as the car slowly pushed forward through the horse-drawn carts and other motors to the main entrance. The large clock above the doors read six o'clock. It had only taken them about half an hour to drive from their apartment to the station. They had plenty of time to catch the six forty train to Helsinki, and they had arrived without incident.

"Yes, let's hope the train isn't delayed," said Christine, who was seated beside Samantha.

"I hope not," answered Samantha as she pushed the car's door open. The moment she stepped out, a porter appeared to take care of her luggage. She was travelling light with only a kit bag. Christine, Alice, and Fran each had a couple of carpetbags. Samantha clutched her handbag firmly, since it contained her passport, tickets, and exit papers the British embassy had arranged for her. It was the exit papers that were critical. It seemed rather strange to her that the Russians demanded exit visas to leave. In Canada, if you wanted to leave, you simply left. It was entry into Canada that was the hassle.

With several porters in tow, they entered the station's main hall. It was packed with people standing in line at the ticket windows. From their clothing, she could tell most of them were aristocrats, with some wealthy merchants mixed in. The rest were peasants trying to get into third class or the luggage cars. They all probably suspected their future in Petrograd would not be good. Samantha headed for the doors that led to the train platforms, where a green-painted train was waiting on the tracks. Once they got onto the train and the porters had stored their luggage securely, she, Christine, Alice, and Fran started to relax slightly.

"How long will it take the train to get to Helsinki?" Christine asked.

"I was told five hours or so," replied Samantha as she watched an elderly couple arguing with one of the armed guards as more passengers scurried for the train.

"Then a steamer for England," Alice said.

"We might need to wait a day or two for a Royal Navy ship to escort us," Samantha pointed out.

"Really?" Christine said as she perked up. "You mean we might have a day or two to see the sights?"

"I guess," replied Samantha with a sigh. Part of her was sad to leave the hospital, but only a part. She had made some good friends during her stay here. But with the political unrest and the loss of the czar's support, the Anglo-Russian Hospital's position was becoming untenable. It made raising money to pay the staff and for medical supplies and food extremely difficult. They were among the first being sent home. She knew that Matron Cotton would be returning to England in the next several months, she hoped, but she didn't know the exact date.

"By the way happy birthday," Alice said.

Samantha blinked in surprise. "It isn't my birthday."

"Isn't July 1st Dominion Day?"

"Oh my God, I forgot," Samantha exclaimed.

RICHMOND FUSILIERS' HEADQUARTERS, PAYNSLEY AREA

"Colonel," said Major Gavin. "I just received a message from the training school Brigade HQ set up at St. Eloi last month."

"So, what do they want?" asked Llewellyn as he rose. He picked up his helmet lying on the table that he was using as a desk.

"They are ordering 180 men from our battalion to attend their courses," the major replied. "Forty machine gunners must go, plus thirty from our trench mortar company."

"For how long?" Llewellyn asked as he put on his helmet and fastened the chin strap.

"Eight days," the major replied. "They'll be put through four courses. General Loomis wants everyone to take them."

"That should be all right," Llewellyn replied. "We'll be relieved on the 4th."

His clerks were already preparing to move his HQ, and they'd already been assigned huts at the Ottawa Camp. His battalion was being assigned to the reserve. The Fusiliers were currently in the support trenches in the Paynsley area, about a thousand yards northeast of what remained of the small village of Neuville-Saint-Vaast. Major-General Loomis had his HQ in the Paynsley Dugouts, about five hundred yards from his position. The dugouts were quite deep. After Vimy, though, many of the men preferred to be above ground, so huts had been built for the senior staff officers.

"Have the work parties returned safely?" Llewellyn asked. The Fusiliers had been supplying working parties to improve the front-line trenches. From the intelligence summaries he had been getting, the Huns had been pretty quiet. Of course, there were the usual German work parties improving their trenches and German snipers taking their daily toll. There was some concern about the considerable amount of movement on the Douai Road and that Hun aircraft were more active than usual. They might have some suspicions about what the Canadian Corps was planning for today.

"Yes, sir. Everyone was accounted for."

"Good," Llewellyn said with relief. At least he wouldn't have to write condolence letters today. "Was anyone hurt by the artillery shell?" A German 4.1 shell had landed in a field near his HQ.

"No sir," replied Gavin.

"Anything else?" Llewellyn asked.

"Yes, I'm afraid so. Corps HQ has requested a return for our rockets and Very lights," the major stated.

Llewellyn frowned. "I saw a report from our quartermaster. He said we were running low, and he'd been having trouble requisitioning more." He knew they went through a couple of hundred a month, and they were usually handled by the signallers assigned to each company.

They used them when the telephone lines were cut and when there were no other means of communicating. If there was a suspected German patrol out in No Man's Land, the sentries would send up a flare to light them up so they could be hammered by the riflemen, machine gunners, and the artillery. They tended to rotate the colours between red, green, and gold to confuse the Germans, but they found it also confused their men. It seemed they couldn't remember which colour flare was for which signal.

They finally settled on using three quick red flares to signal an SOS; they were under attack. When they were attacking, the unit would only send up red, if they were being held up or they were being counterattacked and needed artillery support. Three green flares meant stop firing or to lift the barrage; the company was advancing. Three white flares announced they had captured their objectives.

They used a mixture of signal rifle grenades, hand grenades, rockets, and Very pistols. The signal grenades were starting to be issued, but they didn't have a large supply. The one-pound signal rockets they used flew to nearly two thousand feet then released a parachute that held a flare aloft until it burned out after sixty seconds. Mostly, his men used Very pistols that were easily carried in a hip holster with the one-inch shells carried in bandoliers across a man's chest. The flares, similar to shotgun shells, had brass rims at the base with cardboard tubing that contained the propellant and the illuminating charge. A colour band was painted at the base to indicate the flare's colour. The flares flew about six hundred feet or so and burned for thirty seconds.

"What I heard was we need to economize and build up our inventory during our quiet times."

Llewellyn snorted. "For how long?" He seemed to be asking that question a lot lately.

"I don't know. The usual, I guess. Demand is exceeding what they are producing. It'll be a while before we start getting anything in quantity."

"Great!" Llewellyn muttered. "Pass the word. Use them only if necessary. And let Pete know so he can scrounge some for his usual sources." Pete, his quartermaster, had some sources he wasn't supposed to know about.

"Of course. I should have thought of that," replied Gavin with a grin.

"I guess it's time," Llewellyn said as he glanced at his wristwatch. It was five minutes to twelve. He picked up his Lee-Enfield mounted near the dugout's entrance. He checked to see whether the magazine was full. He saw the major pick up his rifle as well.

Outside, he saw a platoon lined up in the nearby communication trench with their rifles in the port position. Llewellyn and the major lined up next to them.

When the minute hand of his watch swept past twelve o'clock, he ordered, "Ready, aim, fire!"

The synchronization was a bit ragged, but they all fired five rounds in the general direction of the German trenches. Nearby, his mortar teams also fired five rounds. Overhead, he heard the salvos from the 65th Artillery heading in the same direction. Llewellyn knew at twelve o'clock, every artillery piece, mortar, and rifle in the Canadian Corps had been ordered to fire salvos to celebrate Canada's fiftieth anniversary.

65TH ARTILLERY, BOIS DE LA VILLE

Lieutenant Ryan had his right arm raised ready to slash forward as he stared at his wristwatch. His eyes flickered from the minute hand that was sweeping across the dial and the barrage balloon floating above Vimy Ridge, two miles north of his position at Bois de la Ville. There wasn't much left of Farbus, the small village facing east, and the woods.

He had synchronized his watch just before he had gone to the divine service, held at nine thirty this morning at the 48th Howitzers' wagon lines. The CO had ordered as many men as possible to attend the service to commemorate Confederation's fiftieth anniversary.

The mass had ended around ten thirty, so they had ample time for him and his gun crews to man their 18-pounders. The guns had been well oiled and cleaned for the occasion. Below the camouflage netting, the stacked shells had a polished sheen.

Based on the scouts' and forward observers' reports, the Huns had taken precautions. The Germans were well aware that the Canadians were there, and they knew, or should have by now, the Canadian Corps habit of firing three salvos at their trenches on Dominion Day. It was actually turning into a tradition. So, at exactly 12:00, 12:02, and 12:04, the Canadians Corps' artillery would fire a barrage at the German positions. The balloon, floating above Vimy, had been sent up to help synchronize the Corps' barrage.

His 18-pounders were targeting the Boche front line trenches while the 48th's howitzers would be bombarding an enemy battery, a trench junction, and a mortar emplacement in the rear trenches.

To be honest, he never gave Confederation much thought. It hadn't been a major holiday in Canada. It had crept up on him, kind of. He had to admit he did feel pride in the *Canada* flash sewn on his upper sleeves.

He flashed his arm down when the minute hand had swept past noon, and the signal flares started bursting above the barrage balloon. The nearest gunner then pulled the lanyard. The timing had been so perfect that the battery sounded as if only one gun had fired.

JULY 2, 1917
CENTRE BLOCK, PARLIAMENT HILL, OTTAWA

"Nothing is to be feared if the Canadian people hold sacred the principles of justice, tolerance, and broad human sympathy. And if they always maintain their ideals at the forefront, and use them as beacons to guide the nation in its vicissitudes. There will be storms, it is folly to hope otherwise, but they will be equal to all emergencies," said Sir Wilfrid Laurier as he finished his speech.

The crowd, filling the expansive lawn in front of the Centre Block, applauded enthusiastically. Borden could see some of those on the fringes were already heading for the gates. They didn't want to wait for the assembled troops to march pass the dais to be reviewed by the assembled dignitaries. They wanted to enjoy the rest of the day's leisure time. Since July 1st fell on a Sunday, the commemorative events for the fiftieth anniversary of Canada's confederation had been pushed to the Monday. The country's citizens had been encouraged to take the day off.

Borden had been pleased by Foster's arrangements. The ceremony had been simple and impressive. Because of the war, they had to thread a fine line between being celebratory for Canada's fiftieth birthday and commemorative for the men that had given their lives in France and who were still fighting. The slate today had been restricted to three speakers: the governor general, himself, and Sir Wilfrid Laurier.

A temporary raised dais, covered with Union Jacks and bunting, had been built in front of the steps that led to the Centre Block. Flags from the Allied countries hung from the East and West Block, along with other festive decorations. Directly in front of the stage, a swathe of the lawn had been left empty to give space for the troops marching pass. To his left, a very large chorus and a military band was providing the musical accompaniment. Directly across from him, on the lawn, chairs had been arranged to seat MPs and senators, as well as for senior civil servants and the military staff from the Woods Building. The six Supreme Court justices were prominent in their white fur-trimmed red robes. Sitting beside the justices was a small group of foreign consul generals. The rest of the lawn was filled by the large crowd overflowing onto Wellington Street that had come to witness the historic event.

Why not? It was a perfect summer day. The temperature was comfortable, and even Ottawa's notorious humidity had given them a break.

The duke had given his speech at noon, and when he was finished, he had pressed a button to raise a Union Jack to reveal a bilingual tablet. It was to be attached to one of the pillars in the Centre Block's Hall of Fame to commemorate the dedication of the building and the men fighting in France. When the governor general had finished reading the tablet's inscription to the crowd, the choir started singing "O Canada." Borden had followed the governor general. The choir sang "The Maple Leaf Forever" when he ended his speech.

Borden glanced behind him at the Centre Block. Construction seemed to be going well — for a government project, that is. Two storeys were already up, and the steel beams were being set for the third floor. The current estimate was that the Centre Block would be completed in two years' time. Whether he would still be prime minister by then was an open question. His party was putting enormous pressure on him to call a snap election with the collapse of talks with Sir Wilfrid on a coalition government.

At least neither Laurier nor he had mentioned that in their speeches. In his, he had made reference to the old Centre Block and how beautiful it had been. He also said he could see that the new Centre Block, once it was completed, would be a magnificent edifice. He had emphasized the great debates, now forgotten, in its chambers that had helped shape the Dominion. He stated his hope the new building would foreshadow the country's future of great national purpose and duty. When he finished his speech, he said, "On the fiftieth anniversary of her natal day, Canada, in proud sorrow for those who have fallen, with solemn pride in what they have achieved, with firm confidence in her sons who hold humanity's battle line beyond the seas, sends to them a renewed assurance that their sacrifice shall not be in vain, and that their country will sustain them in the final issue of peace through victory."

JULY 12, 1917
PLACE D'ARMES, ALBERT

Lieutenant-General Currie glanced up at the golden statue of the Virgin Mary threatening to fall off the Basilica Notre-Dame de Brebières' spire. He was well aware of the story circulating among the men that the statue, damaged by bombs, wouldn't fall until the war was over. The Roman Catholic cathedral dominated Albert's Place D'Armes, where today's ceremonies were to take place. Most of the two-storey buildings that surrounded the square had been similarly damaged, much of it during the first year of the war. Through the telephone wires being supported by ten wooden braces, he could see a squadron of British aeroplanes providing overhead cover. Considering the number of dignitaries and senior officers standing in the open-faced marquee set up in the square, it was a prudent precaution. A fair number of the officers wearing red and white armbands belonged to corps headquarters staff. His eyes fell on the spectators, made up of the locals and off duty soldiers, being held back by two-foot white pillars strung with cord. The French and Australians in the crowd were easily identified by their headgear.

As the line moved forward, he nearly bumped into Major-General Edward Fanshawe, the commander of the British V Corps. He was dressed like he was in a freshly pressed khaki uniform, polished Sam Browne belt, riding breeches, and polished cavalry boots with gleaming spurs. Fanshawe was in line for the same reason as he was. They were both being knighted by King George V. They had just watched the king knight General Pètain, the French commander-in-chief, as a Knight Grand Cross of the Order of the Bath. He and Fanshawe were to be knighted one grade below as Knight Commander of the Order of the Bath.

Earlier in the afternoon, he had lunched with the king at General Byng's new headquarters here in Albert. Byng had been officially appointed as the Third Army's commander on July 1st, Dominion Day. As the newly appointed Canadian Corps commander, he had been pleased to have escorted the king yesterday when he visited his men at Camblain-l'Abbé. He, Prince Arthur of Connaught, and his senior division commanders, had met King George and General Byng at the junction of Bethune-Arras Road and Plank Road. He had led them from the junction to a special observation post he had ordered built for the King on Hill 145. The hill gave King George a very good view of the German defences on the Douai Plain below. He also had escorted him when he toured some of the captured German trenches. He was amused when the king picked up a couple of German cartridges that he found to keep as souvenirs.

Currie had been pleased the visit had gone without a hitch. He had some concerns when he had noticed German activity was below normal, wondering what they might have planned. While security was tight, he wouldn't have been surprised if the Germans had found out that King George was visiting the Canadian Corps.

Currie had to wait as several French officers had medals pinned to their chests before it was Major-General Fanshawe's turn. He watched as the King tapped Fanshawe once on each shoulder with a cavalry sabre, then drape a ribbon with a dangling star on the man's chest. Then it was his turn to march in front of the king. After he saluted, he kneeled with his right knee on the small stool set on the oriental rug in front of King George. From the corner of his eye, he could see General Byng beaming as he knelt. King George tapped him on his left shoulder then his right shoulder with the cavalry sabre that one of his aides had handed to him. Even kneeling, he was taller than the king who was of medium height and slight of build. When he rose, he leaned his chest forward so the king could pin the insignia to his chest. Then he had removed his cap and bent from the waist as the king draped the Knight Commander star, hanging from a ribbon, over his neck. After the king had shaken his hand, he saluted and moved away, since there were more men behind him, waiting for their awards. He couldn't help the broad smile that appeared on his face as he marched to the next marquee tent for the customary refreshments.

CHAPTER 14

Llewellyn took a few deep breaths to calm his nerves as he stepped out of his cab in front of the Thackeray Hotel. He gave the British Museum a glance as he handed the driver a shilling for the fare. Most of the visitors on the museum's front steps were dressed in khaki, since it was a popular tourist attraction for those on leave. He, however, didn't have any intention of spending any of his seven-day leave there; he had other plans.

It had been a short ride from Charing Cross train station to the hotel. If he had known how short, he would have walked because it was, for London, a warm, comfortable July day. Then again, a long walk would have given him more time to fret. He was surprised at how nervous he was as he stood before the five-storey grey cement building with red brick accents. There were bay windows alternating with square panes of glass running from the bottom floor to the top. He then hefted his haversack and headed for the Thackeray Hotel's entrance. When he stepped through the arched oak door into a small foyer, an elderly clerk at the concierge desk raised his eyes. He studied first Llewellyn's haversack draped with his greatcoat, then his officer's stars on his shoulder boards, and then the Canada, the 1st Division, and 2nd Brigade flashes on his field jacket.

"How may I help you, Colonel?" he asked.

"I'm here to see Matron Lonsdale. I've been informed she is residing here?"

"Of course, sir. If you would give me a moment," replied the clerk as he flipped through the hotel's register. He paused when he found Samantha's name. "Yes, she is staying at this establishment. What is this in regard to?"

Llewellyn quirked a brief smile. He knew the man was being protective of his hotel's guests. "It is a personal matter. If you would send her a message that I'm here, I would greatly appreciate it."

"Of course. Who would I say is waiting for her?"

"James. She'll know who it is."

"If you take a chair, I'll inform her of your presence," the concierge said, pointing to the small waiting area to his left, which had rattan chairs and a table covered with tourist pamphlets that sat on a dark oriental rug.

"Thank you," replied Llewellyn. "By the way, would you have a room available for the next seven days?"

"Do you have a reservation at our establishment?"

"I did send a 'gram before I left on leave. Your hotel's reply was that you were booked solid. I was wondering, might there be a cancellation?" asked Llewellyn. According to the hotel's ad he had read, it had two hundred rooms with the tariff starting at $2.00 per day. It boasted it had a passenger lift, electric lights in every room, and bathrooms on every floor. It had the usual dining, reading, writing, drawing, billiard, and smoking rooms. The one thing it didn't have was a bar. After all, it was a temperance hotel.

"I'm afraid nothing has become available," he stated after checking the register again.

"No matter, thank you," replied Llewellyn as he made way for the guest behind him to take a seat in the waiting area. Though he was disappointed, he wasn't concerned because he already had a reservation at the Toksowa House in Dulwich. When he had asked the driver how far away it was, he was told it was a half-hour drive from Charing Cross.

He was browsing through the Thackeray House's brochure when something made him look up into Samantha's smiling face. He snapped up to his feet, and despite the askance looks of the nearby guests, he enfolded her in his arms. When he looked into her blue eyes he said, "I've missed you."

* * *

Through the bay window, Samantha glanced at the traffic in front of the British Museum before returning her gaze back to James. The maître d' of the quaint and comfortable dining room had seated them at a table for two that faced the street. She was fairly certain that he had done so after James's display of affection in the foyer. One rarely saw a khaki-clad officer embracing a woman, dressed in a nursing sister's uniform, no less, in such a familiar manner in public.

"So how was your voyage from Petrograd?" he asked. She felt his hand graze her left hand.

"It was quite boring," she replied. "I spent most of it sleeping in my cabin."

"Seasickness?"

"No, just tired," Samantha replied. James nodded. When you were in the midst of it, you didn't feel it because you were so focused on getting your job done. It was only when you were out of it that the exhaustion hit you, and then you barely had the energy to get out of bed.

"Petrograd was pretty rough?" he asked.

"It's pretty rough everywhere," Samantha replied. She could see the tension on the streets resulting from the recent air raids by German aeroplanes and Zeppelins. The casualty lists in the newspapers didn't help.

He gazed at her for a moment. She was happy when he didn't press the matter. Instead, he changed the subject by motioning one of the waitresses to bring them menus. "We better order lunch. I think you'll need all your energy."

"What do you mean energy? Don't bother with the menu. They only have one item on it. Table d'hôte for two shillings. It's fish, I'm afraid. Beef is scarce," Samantha said.

"I'm not surprised," James replied with a grin. "Better than iron rations, though."

Samantha pursed her lips. "Quite. What do you mean by energy?"

"I didn't want to say anything, but you do look a bit thin," James replied as his eyes, studying her figure, caused Samantha to blush. "I do have a seven-day pass, and I was thinking of the various attractions we can visit. We can go to some of the musical entertainments in the evenings. I heard the Pell Mell show at the Ambassador Theatre is quite good."

Samantha, with a slight tinge of pink still on her cheeks, raised an eyebrow. "Didn't a general complain the scantily dressed girls and songs of doubtful character were bad for morale? It's been my experience the higher up you're promoted, the less a sense of humour you possess," she murmured as she stared at the lieutenant-colonel's stars on James's shoulder boards.

James glanced at what she was staring at, then said, "There are exceptions."

"Of course." Samantha smiled.

"My men's morale improved after they saw the show."

"Why am I not surprised?"

"Have you been given your new assignment yet?"

"Not yet," Samantha replied. "I've been waiting for orders from Matron Macdonald. There's a bunch of us on the third floor waiting."

"Third floor?"

"The Nursing Service has booked rooms at this hotel permanently for nurses arriving from Canada and for those being transferred between posts. I'm sharing a room with a nurse who just came from Vancouver."

"I see," replied James. There was a hint of disappointment in his voice.

"Do you have a room here?" she asked.

James shook his head. "I did manage to find a room at the Toksowa Hotel."

"Have you checked in yet?" she asked.

"No," James replied. "I came here first."

"Well, then, I'll help you check in after our lunch," Samantha said.

"I would like that," James replied. "I'm hoping they have comfortable beds."

"I think I can help you find out," Samantha replied as she placed her napkin in her lap when the waitress delivered their lunch order.

JULY 17, 1917
WESTMINSTER PALACE HOTEL, VICTORIA STREET, LONDON

"So how was your interview with Matron Macdonald?" asked Leslie Andrew.

"Pish posh, I don't want to know about that," Carmen Landry interjected. "What I want to know is what happened when you saw James?" Samantha's face warmed as she blushed. Carmen's eyes widen as she leaned toward Samantha. "My, my, my. Tell us everything."

Leslie gave Samantha a scandalous look. "You didn't."

They were sitting in the Westminster Palace Hotel's dining room. It was a convenient place to have tea to catch up with Carmen and Leslie after her interview with Matron Macdonald. She always liked the dining room, with its elegant decor and furnishings, though it was expensive. Tea and a slice of cake was a shilling. She had occasionally indulged, since CAMC headquarters in the Victoria Chambers was just down the street. The maître d' had recognized her and seated her at a small table near the window that faced Victoria Street. There were people lingering over their tea from the lunch session that ended at three.

Samantha tried to change the subject. "My interview with the matron went well."

"Now, now," Leslie replied. "You and your colonel are more interesting. Has he asked you to marry him yet?"

"No, not yet," Samantha said reluctantly. Truthfully, she had considered marriage with James, but if she married, she might have to leave the service. Some of the regulations had changed since she had been in Petrograd.

"So, what have you two been doing for the last few days?" Leslie asked as she took a sip of her tea.

"The usual, visiting the museums, walking in the gardens, shows in the East End. Oh, we did see a Chaplin moving picture — *The Vagabond*," she answered.

"I haven't seen that one yet," said Leslie.

"From what I heard, you don't spend much time at the Thackeray," Carmen said.

Leslie raised an eyebrow when Samantha's flush deepened, then she said wryly, "I'm assuming he's been sleeping on the floor."

"Of course," Samantha replied with a straight face.

"But how much actual sleep has he been getting?" Carmen remarked with a wink.

"Not much," Samantha acknowledged. She paused then added, "The neighbours have been quite noisy."

Carmen nearly spat out her tea when she started laughing. "I missed you. I'm glad that you're back." Leslie nodded in agreement.

"I'm glad to be back," she replied as she fiddled with her teacup. She was still savouring the touch of honey and cream that she had been missing for so long.

"Was it pretty bad in Russia?" asked Leslie.

Samantha sighed. "It was difficult when I arrived in Petrograd. But I met some really nice people there. And some not so nice, especially near the end. Food was never plentiful, but after Rasputin was killed and the czar's abdication, things went from bad to worst. I feel sorry for the people there. They don't have much, and things are going to be harder for them. I told all this to Matron Macdonald when I met with her earlier to discuss my new posting.

"By the way, I ran into General Jones when I was leaving. I was surprised to see him. I thought he had been relieved."

"He was. But he came back in December," replied Carmen.

"He did?"

"You didn't hear the story?" asked Leslie.

Samantha shook her head. "We didn't get much Canadian news."

"When the general was relieved, they had appointed Colonel Bruce as the surgeon-general," Leslie informed her.

"Why am I not surprised?" Samantha remarked dryly.

"His report caused quite a stir back home," Carmen stated.

"That I remembered," replied Samantha.

"After you left, the government wasn't happy with Colonel Bruce's report. Especially when it was being used to attack the government. So they created the Babtie Board to study his report," Carmen informed her.

Samantha shook her head in disbelief. "What did they find?"

"They disagreed with Colonel Bruce's conclusion. They said he didn't understand the Medical Service. Considering how much our army had expanded, the service had done a remarkably good job. The men had been very taken care of. Of course, there was a need for improvements and the service was always open to suggestions. They even said it was impractical to confine our medical services to only our men."

Leslie jumped in, "He lasted until December. The entire time he complained about the same things General Jones had complained about. Minister Hughes and his subcouncil weren't of much help either. When Borden got rid of Hughes, the subcouncil disappeared."

"Don't forget he didn't like paperwork," Carmen said.

"Dear God!" Samantha exclaimed. Anyone who had joined the army to escape paperwork was in for a rude awakening.

"So when he left, General Jones came back for a couple of months," Carmen said.

"So things haven't improved then?" Samantha asked as she glanced at her two friends.

"Oh no," Leslie said. "When they set up the Overseas Ministry, things started to change."

Carmen nodded vigorously. "They set up a fourteen hundred-bed hospital at Liverpool for our casualties who are being sent home. We now have a regular hospital service from Liverpool to Halifax. They've increased the inspections of our wounded in the Imperial hospitals. And they've centralized food service to save money, and the food is much better now."

Leslie agreed, "Things are running much smoother as well."

"I'm glad to hear that," Samantha replied. It sounded to her that they had implemented most of the recommendations in Colonel Bruce's report. At least some good came out of the fiasco.

"So where are you being transferred to? France?" asked Carmen.

Samantha shook her head. "Matron Macdonald informed me I'm being assigned as an acting matron to the Bromley Hospital."

"Really!" exclaimed Carmen. "That's wonderful! Now we can get together more often. The hospital is in Kent. It's only half an hour from here by train.

"It will be a bit of rest for you after Petrograd," Leslie stated.

"I hope so. At the very least I'll be avoiding bombs and machine guns for a while," answered Samantha.

JULY 18, 1917
TOKSOWA HOTEL, DULWICH COMMON, LONDON

Samantha tried to stifle her moan. The hotel walls were rather thin, and she didn't want to confirm to the other hotel residents what she and James had been up to most of the morning.

She rested on James for a moment to catch her breath, then rolled off him to lie on the comfortable bed. The glow that covered her naked body started to cool, even though there was a warm breeze from the slightly open window. It was promising to be a comfortable July day. She slid under the sheet for warmth as James rolled toward her, his left arm cradling his head while his right draped across his chest. She couldn't help noticing he had gathered a few more nicks and scars in the months she'd been away.

As she ran a finger across his five o'clock shadow, which felt like sandpaper, he asked, "Too rough for you?"

"You need a shave," she replied.

"If I'm getting up out of bed to go out, I'll shave. Don't want to be brought up on charges," James replied. "What will my men think of me?"

"We can't have that." She grinned. She then became more serious as she tugged the sheet higher. "Tomorrow's your last day?"

"I'm afraid so. I've to report back on Monday," he answered.

"So we only have a day left then," she said.

"Do you have any suggestions how we should spend our time?" James asked as he caressed the sheet that covered her left breast, causing her to quiver slightly.

"I have a few ideas," she replied with a crooked grin. "But we still have to get out of bed to get something to eat." Samantha sighed. "I'm a bit disappointed with the hotel."

"Oh."

"Yes, I expected it to be a bit more oriental," she said.

"I was expecting the same thing," replied James as Samantha watched him glance around the hotel room. The rooms didn't contain a single oriental item to go with its name. It was decorated with typical English furniture and landscape paintings. The styling even extended to the brickwork that surrounded the gas fireplace. It was a white three-storey building covered by green vines that contained some fifty bedrooms. It had been styled more like a typical English country home to make the residents feel as if they hadn't left the countryside. The Toksowa included a nine-hole golf course, although the fifty ambulances parked on the fairways marred the illusion a bit.

"I kept meaning to ask. How was your tea with Leslie and Carmen?"

Samantha raised her head and placed it in the palm of her right hand. Her cheeks dimpled as she pushed a blond lock from her face and gazed into James's eyes. "I had a lot of fun, and it was good to catch up with all the gossip I missed."

"Anything interesting?"

"You can say that. Did I ever mention Colonel Bruce?" she asked in a chilly tone.

"Vaguely."

"His report last year got General Jones fired as the director of the CAMC. Colonel Bruce was then appointed as his replacement," she said with a snort. "When he had tried to implement his policy of having Canadian soldiers treated only at Canadian hospitals, it didn't go well. It seems the colonel's report caused quite a kerfuffle in Parliament, so they created a committee to investigate his findings. They didn't agree with most of Colonel Bruce's findings and recommendations. After that, the colonel lasted only a couple of months before he was relieved of his command and then was transferred to the Imperials. Jones was brought back to replace him, but he didn't last long either and was replaced by General Foster. Leslie and Carmen's feelings were that the Bruce report raised too many questions about his efficiency."

James rolled his eyes. "Now I understand why you wanted out."

A shadow crossed Samantha's face. "If I had an inkling what was going to happen, I would have stayed here."

"I don't think anyone could have predicted that the czar would abdicate," he replied. He then nodded at the newspaper that was lying on the night table. "I read about the riot on Nevski…"

"Nevsky Prospect," she corrected him.

"Do you know where that is?"

"Yes, the hospital was just off it. There have been a number of riots on that street."

"Close to the hospital?"

"Yes."

"Did you get caught up in any of them?"

"Yes," she replied curtly. She saw James looked startled.

He stared at her for a long moment then said, "In this war there are no safe places, are there?"

"No," Samantha said. "You saw the shell holes as we came into the hotel."

It was true; both she and James had seen the damage from the bombs that the German planes and Zeppelins had dropped on London. The civilian casualties were a drop in a bucket compared with those on the Western Front, but still, the British government was outraged by the civilian deaths.

After a moment he asked, "Have you heard about your next assignment?"

Samantha shook her head. "Yes I have. Before having tea with the girls yesterday, I met with Matron Macdonald. After she told me about some administrative changes at the CAMC she did ask me where I would like to be posted."

"What did you say?" Samantha noticed touch of concern in James's tone.

"I told her I would like a posting in France, if one were available," she replied.

"Samantha!" James protested.

"What?" she replied tartly as she pulled the sheet higher. "What do you want me to do? Teach at the CAMC training school? Or become a matron at the new Liverpool hospital they've set up to prepare the patients for their return to Canada?" Matron Macdonald had informed her about the new hospital, where 18,000 patients were waiting to be sent back home.

"Well, yes, some of them are my own men," retorted James. "I would prefer you stay on this side of the channel."

"Orders are orders," Samantha said simply. She stared at him for a moment, then said, "She told me that she had a posting for me as an acting matron at the convalescent hospital in Bromley."

"Why didn't you say that in the first place!" Llewellyn exclaimed.

"Just wanted to see how you would react," replied Samantha.

Llewellyn snorted.

"So what are your orders for the rest of day?" James asked as he surrendered. His eyes travelled down her body outlined by the sheet.

"Carmen yesterday told me that the Toronto Hospital has come back from Salonika. They're now at Basingstoke. So I'm going to drop in and see Emily. I haven't seen her in ages."

"Now!"

"Well, not right this minute. For the next half-hour or so I'm ordering some exercise," she said as she pushed him onto his back. She then moved so her chest was touching his. His hand reached down and gently tugged the bed sheet away until she felt his warm skin.

"Orders are orders," James said as he kissed her.

JULY 23, 1917
CANADIAN CONVALESCENT HOSPITAL, BROMLEY HILL, KENT

"Single file, fall in," shouted the drill instructor.

Samantha watched as twenty patients fell into a column of fours five rows deep. They were dressed in hospital blues, white shirts with red ties, blue pants, and polished boots. Their blue jackets had been left in the nearby Indian tents until they finished their Swedish drill. Her Sudbury gymnastic teacher, when she was a teen, had taken her and her classmates through the movements a Swedish fencing instructor had developed. He had wanted to promote health and mental concentration on a more scientific basis. The system they used at the hospital was a militarized version.

"Distance sideways, place!" the instructor ordered. Each man raised his right arm to touch the shoulder next to him then shuffled to get the correct distance.

When they dropped their arms, he commanded, "Attention!"

After they snapped to, he yelled, "Dismissed!"

"So, what do you think?" added Major Creighton, who was standing beside her. Samantha smiled at the thirty-eight-year-old from Windsor. She had been surprised and very happy to run into him at the hospital. She hadn't seen him for a few years since they had come to England as part of the first contingent. She noticed he had lost some of the earnestness he had when she first met him. The war and his marriage to one of her best friends, Emily, may have accounted for that. He did tell her he was anxious to see his wife again, since her unit was arriving soon from the Mediterranean. For the last few years, Emily had seen service at the

Greek island of Lemnos, and she had been transferred to Salonika when the Gallipoli campaign ended.

"Are you sure they are ready to be discharged tomorrow?" she asked. "Some of them were struggling towards the end." The instructor had been exercising the men for the past hour.

"They're ready," Creighton assured her. "At least, ready to be discharged from the hospital. Some of the patients you're seeing are class Ds. While they've been drilling for several weeks now, they'll need a couple of months at a command depot before they can be reassessed and recategorized as A or B men."

Samantha cocked her head as she listened to Creighton. The Medical Services had standardized the categories assigned to the men during the recovery of their wounds. The A-class man had to be able to march, shoot, hear, and withstand service conditions. They would be sent directly back to their units to refresh their training and further physical hardening. The B-class were those could walk up to five miles and could see and hear for ordinary purposes. They would be assigned to line of communications, office duties, labour, or a forestry unit. The E-class men were deemed medically unfit and would be discharged and released from the service.

When the major stiffened, Samantha turned her head and spotted one of the patients heading toward them. He was of medium height, with a walrus moustache and close-cropped hair. He seemed to be dragging his left foot slightly.

"Matron," he acknowledged with a nod. He then turned to Creighton and said, "Doc, I've been told I'm being discharged tomorrow."

"That's correct, Sergeant Wilson," replied the major.

During her brief orientation, she had learned the hospital discharged patients on Tuesdays and Thursdays. She knew the Canadian Convalescent Hospital had been the first of its kind when it was established in early 1915 on a two-acre estate that once belonged to Lord Farnborough. The mansion that had been built on Bromley Hill had been converted into a hotel in 1904, and the latest owner of the hotel, a Quebec financier, had offered it to the CAMC for their use at the start of the war. She was familiar with the facility. She and Matron Macdonald had regularly visited the hospital to inspect the nursing staff.

Currently, they were treating nearly a hundred and forty patients. Half were in the three-storey grey sandstone building behind them, while the other half, who were ambulatory, in the bell tents that dotted the field behind the hotel. It was felt the fresh air would be beneficial for their recovery. It also helped lightened the load somewhat for the nursing staff, since they could focus on those who needed electrical treatments, massages, and therapy for those with missing limbs, and their bandages checked regularly.

"But I'm not being sent back to my unit," the sergeant demanded. "Why?"

"I'm afraid you have been categorized as class D," replied Creighton.

"I've recovered from my wounds, and I'm in fine shape," Wilson argued.

The major shook his head. "No, you're not. The travelling medical board has looked into your case, and they've agreed with me. You'll need at least three more months of training and hardening at the command depot. After three months, you'll be reassessed. If you become an A or B, you'll then be returned to your unit. Until then be a good chap and get your things. You'll be discharged with the rest of the men."

Samantha winced when the sergeant retorted, "Thanks a lot, Doc."

He then stomped toward the bell tents. She was surprised Creighton hadn't charged him with insolence.

The major noticed her look and gave her a wry smile. "He's being discharged tomorrow, then he'll be the command depot's responsibility."

"If you say so," she replied.

"How have your first few days been?" he asked as he led her to the main building.

"Exhausting," Samantha replied.

"Are you ready for the forced march tomorrow?" he asked with a grin.

"You had to remind me," Samantha replied with a shake of her head. She wasn't looking forward to it, but it was standard hospital routine to help the patients recover and for the hospital staff to maintain their fitness. She knew she had lost some of her breath while in Petrograd. While she had taken long walks with James, it wasn't the same as a forced march. She knew she would be extremely sore afterward. *At least they have massage therapy here,* she thought.

"How did the board of inquiry go yesterday?" she asked.

"Eh, no real surprises," he muttered. A board of inquiry had been called to investigate an accident where an ASC truck had collided with the estate's gates and had severely damaged them. "The driver said his brakes failed, and the mechanic agreed. He said the truck's brakes should have been replaced long ago."

"Is the driver okay?"

"Minor cuts and scrapes," he replied. "The truck's front end is bashed in. His load of white flour and vegetable cans spilled all over the road. It was a mess cleaning it up."

"Snow in July."

Creighton laughed. "You can say that. We better go in for the ceremony."

"Have you met our new CO yet?" asked Samantha. The hospital's new CO was taking command today, and they were required to attend the transfer ceremony.

"No, I haven't," he replied. "I hope he doesn't make too many changes."

"There's bound to be," she replied. She had only been here for a few days, so she hadn't adapted completely to the new routine. For her staff it would be a different matter. She would have to deal with the uncertainty as they adjusted to any changes their new CO might have in mind.

CHAPTER 15

Sir George Perley read the headlines, and they weren't good. He was in his office with the *Times* open to the second page. Its front page was dominated by adverts. He was reading the story that the Russian army's morale was collapsing and Premier Kerensky had been given unlimited powers to reorganize the army and restore discipline. Whether he would be able to do so remained to be seen. With various factions attempting to overthrow the government, the political situation in Russia was confusing and perilous. The paper also reported that Kerensky's government was attempting to arrest Lenin and Trotsky, the more prominent socialist agitators, if they could find them.

Perley shook his head. While they had limited CEF personnel in Russia, a couple of nurses still in Petrograd, and a medical unit in Salonika, he knew that British policy was to keep the Russians in the war. They were key to tying down German divisions on the Eastern Front that couldn't be used on the Western Front. A frown appeared on his face when he recalled the predictions made at the War Conference several months ago suggesting that the war wouldn't end this year. Lieutenant-General Byng had expressed the same opinion when they met go over some of the policies being proposed and discussed at the conference. Byng also said he could be wrong, since he wasn't an expert in such matters.

At least, General Pershing and his 1st Division, currently training in the Gondrecourt area of Lorraine, were providing a ray of hope. And, the latest reports indicated the Americans were sending men to expand the numbers they had in Europe. One of the tasks he had assigned to Turner was to prepare a return on the number of Americans presently in the CEF and how many wanted to transfer to the American Expeditionary Force.

His eyes fell on the news article that was being broadcast over the wireless announcing the successful raid by the 116th Battalion of the Canadian 3rd Division at Avion. During the raid, they had penetrated five hundred yards into the German trenches and had captured fifty-three prisoners before they had to withdraw. Naturally, the story didn't mention the seventy-four casualties.

"Sir, here's the latest dispatches from Ottawa," stated George MacInnes when he entered his office. His tone caught Perley's attention. He stared at the manila envelope with the red stripe across it. "I think you need to read this one," he stated as he handed him the envelope.

Perley took the envelope and unravelled the string that kept the flap closed and removed the folder he found inside. He read the covering letter from Major-General Fiset, then he sat up in his chair. He flipped through the supporting documentation quickly then he reread the covering letter. He looked up at George when he was done. "How many have seen this?"

"It was addressed to you as personal and confidential," George replied.

"That's good," Perley replied. It had reduced his apprehension somewhat. At least the information could be contained for now. The ministry had become smaller in the last few months as its operations had become smoother and more efficient. He could sense the War Office had been pleased with the improvements he and Major-General Turner had made in the Canadian organization.

Turner would be a problem if he learned about Currie's embezzlement. He may already be aware of it, but he had never mentioned it when he was passed over for GOC of the CEF by Currie. He did now understand what Garnet Hughes meant when he had threatened to get back at Currie when he didn't get command of the 1st Division. It also could be one of Sam Hughes's cronies stirring the pot out of spite and malice.

All he could think of now was how he could minimize the damage this would cause if it became public knowledge to Currie and to the CEF. And the damage it would cause Sir Robert Borden and his current efforts to form a coalition government. It would be especially damaging when Borden was on record about his strong desire to stamp out corruption. There was no indication in the file that Borden had been made aware of Currie's embezzlement.

The matter was too important to move on until he got clear instructions from Borden. He pulled a clean sheet of paper from one of the trays on his desk and quickly wrote a note with his fountain pen. "George, have this message put in cypher and have it sent to the prime minister's office, high priority."

"Yes, sir," replied George as he read the telegram Perley had written.

"And no one is to discuss the matter with anyone!" Perley ordered.

"Of course, sir," replied George as he turned and headed back to his desk to encipher the text.

"We wasted an hour this morning," stated Minister Kemp as he followed Prime Minister Borden into his office. Even with the windows open, the office was stifling. It was a typical Ottawa day in July with the temperature in the mid-nineties, but it felt hotter because of the high humidity.

"Sir Roblin visited me last Friday. He was quite incessant on Kelly's release," replied Borden. Kemp knew he was referring to the former premier of Manitoba, Sir Rodmond Roblin. Roblin's political machine in Manitoba had helped Borden win his majority in the last election.

"I've been hearing Kelley's medical situation at the Stony Mountain Penitentiary is not very good," Kemp stated as he stroked his walrus moustache.

"Doherty has asked the hospital's doctors to give him a fuller report," Borden replied.

"That should help confirm whether he is as sick as he claimed," said Kemp.

"There's that. His flight to the United States, and then fighting extradition in the US courts, certainly didn't help his cause," Borden pointed out. As a lawyer, Borden was well aware how the courts dealt with such defendants. "And with the reconstruction of the Centre Block, I don't know if it would be politically prudent."

Kemp winced at the comment. The former Winnipeg contractor was facing kickback charges related to the construction of Manitoba's new provincial legislative building. While the investigation hadn't found any evidence linking the then Premier Roblin to the scheme, members of his cabinet had been implicated. The scandal sparked Roblin's resignation, and in the subsequent election the Liberals won by a landslide.

Kemp suspected that Borden didn't want a whiff of scandal during the Centre Block's reconstruction, especially when there were already cost overruns. When he had walked over to the East Block from the Woods Building on Slater, he couldn't help pause for a brief moment to watch sweating workers lifting heavy sandstone blocks into place on top of the Centre Block's third storey.

As Borden sat behind his desk, he removed a handkerchief from his pocket to wipe the sweat from the back of his neck. Then from a pitcher of iced water set on a nearby table he poured two glasses of water. He handed one of them to Kemp.

"Well, at least the military service bill passed third reading," Kemp said as he drew a long drink of the cool water from his glass.

"That's a bit of good news," Borden replied. The bill was carried 102 to 44. He had been pleased how Arthur Meighen responded to Laurier's speech against it in the House. He had been surprised by how weak Laurier's speech was. He had expected a much stronger attack.

"Have you heard anything from Sifton?" Kemp asked.

"I haven't as yet," replied Borden. He had enlisted the aid of Sir Clifford Sifton, owner of the *Winnipeg Free Press*, to help him form a union government with disaffected Liberals. He had deep connections with the Liberals, since he had been Sir Wilfrid's former minister of the interior, responsible for Indian Affairs and Immigration. It had been Sifton's immigration policies that had expanded and settled Western Canada. The fact that Sifton's brother, Arthur, was currently the Liberal premier of Alberta, didn't hurt.

Sifton had a falling out with Laurier in 1905 over the education clauses in the bill creating the provinces of Alberta and Saskatchewan. Still, in 1909, Laurier had appointed him chairman of the Committee of Conservation. In retrospect, it had been one of Borden's wiser decisions not to replace him after the Conservative government had come to power in 1911.

Borden knew Sifton was deeply committed to Canada's war effort. Four of his five sons were in France with the CEF.

"I heard he was really depressed after the Liberal convention in Toronto," Kemp said.

"He was," replied Borden. "Before he went to the Liberal convention in Winnipeg, I told him the Western Liberals shouldn't let their views be obscured by the insignificant creatures in Toronto."

Kemp snorted an agreement.

Borden's eyes fell on a red-striped folder on his desk. He flipped open the cover as he took a long sip of water. From the upside-down letterhead, Kemp could tell it was a CP telegram. "I received this from George yesterday evening. He made a reference to a folder General Fiset had sent him regarding a senior officer."

Kemp grimaced as he eyed Sir Robert Borden. "Yes, Prime Minister General Fiset did send him a folder. On my instructions. The reasons I asked him to send it to him…" Borden became more and more distressed as Kemp laid out the case against Lieutenant-General Currie. "That is why I had asked General Fiset to send the file to George in London. I wanted his opinion on how best to approach General Currie on how we can resolve the matter of the outstanding tailor's bill with the minimal amount of fuss."

"Why wasn't I informed earlier?" demanded Borden.

Kemp did not want to correct the prime minister by telling him the COs of the 50th Battalion had requested help from his office on a number of occasions, but it had fallen through the cracks or other priorities had taken precedence. "Never mind," Borden said sourly.

"I've sent a telegram to George suggesting if he were willing to pay half, I would pay the other half." Both George Perley and Alfred Kemp were among the wealthiest members of his government. They could easily afford it. "If that is what you want done, Prime Minister."

Borden looked at him steadily and then shook his head. "No, I don't think that it would be wise if this becomes public knowledge. The situation is bad enough as it is. Let's not compound it," he stated flatly. Kemp had to agree. The public would get the wrong impression if Canada's two war ministers paid for Currie's indiscretion. "Have the department pay the outstanding bill. We'll recover the funds from General Currie when the war is over."

"Would that be wise?" asked Kemp. "The amount exceeds ten thousand dollars. We'll be required to prepare an order-in-council and have the cabinet approve it. We'll have to give them some kind of explanation for the expenditure."

Borden's frown deepened. While the cabinet was sworn to secrecy, it didn't mean there wasn't an occasional leak. Not everyone was happy to see that Currie had been given command. "Have one prepared, and I'll have the cabinet sign off," Borden ordered.

"Of course, Prime Minister," replied Kemp. He paused for a moment and then asked, "Are you still planning to go to the Thousand Islands this weekend?"

Borden nodded, appearing to be glad he had changed the subject. Kemp was certain he had enough bad news for the day. Borden's top priorities were to get the *Military Service Act* and the *Soldier's Voting Act* passed. Following that, he knew Borden would be focused on forming a Union government. "John invited Laura and me to stay at his cottage in the Thousand Islands. Labatt and Green are coming down as well. Laura's planning to stay for the week. The weather there should be cooler than what we've been having here in Ottawa. I'll be travelling down next week to pick her up when she's ready to come home."

"Good, I'll have an order-in-council ready for you by next week," Kemp stated as he rose to his feet.

"Meanwhile, I'll send a 'gram to George telling him not to discuss the matter with General Currie, and we'll be resolving the matter on our end. We'll need to inform Currie he'll be required to make payments on the outstanding debt," said Borden.

"Prime Minister, I have no idea how he'll pay us back the ten thousand, even on a lieutenant-general's salary," Kemp remarked.

It would take quite a number of years for Currie to repay what he owed, since his current salary was only $41 a day.

CHAPTER 16

Shells detonated around the observation post, showering Lieutenant-Colonel Masterley and Lieutenant Ryan with debris. Ryan shook his head to scatter some of the dirt off his helmet. He thought the shelling had been rather perfunctory, more of a warning from the Huns they suspected they were there, and not to get any ideas. It was rather late for that. They already had plenty. That was what he and the lieutenant-colonel were doing in the Village Line Trench, refining their part in the upcoming operation to take Hill 70.

"Seven-point-sevens," said Masterley as he ran a hand across his helmet to brush off some dust.

"That's about right," Ryan whispered back at him. So far they'd seen 7.7- and 10.5-cm shells being fired at them. He turned his notebook over to shake out grains of sand that had fallen between the pages. He unfolded a small map attached to one of them. The map was a pencil sketch of the German trenches, strong points, and possible artillery positions he had drawn. The sketch wouldn't have won any artistic prizes, but it was done well enough that it was comprehensible. None of the Canadian trenches were on it in case it fell into enemy hands.

He put a pencil mark where he thought the 7.7s and the 10.5s were firing from. The 7.7 was the equivalent to his 18-pounder. At the beginning of the war, the 7.7-cm Feldkanone 16 had a much shorter range then the 18-pounder, but by lengthening the barrel and putting it on a 10.5-cm gun carriage to give it more elevation, it now had an effective range of ten thousand yards. The 10.5-cm Feldhaubitze 98/09 were their field howitzers that had a range of nearly twenty thousand yards and were the equivalent to their 4.5-inch howitzers. "We'll have to deal with them."

Masterley shook his head and then replied cryptically, "It's like we talked about yesterday."

Ryan understood. They couldn't discuss in the trenches the details of the Corps' plan. One never knew where there would be a listening post set up to overhear their conversations. Masterley had held a conference yesterday with all the 65th's officers to go over the proposed operation. The 18-pounders and the medium trench mortars had been tasked to cut the

German wire. The plan also called for the 48th and 2nd howitzer batteries to destroy the reinforced strong points and to engage the enemy batteries.

He had already sketched the German wire in his notebook, and it seemed to be the typical German wire system; caltrops in front of the wire to pierce boots, and *chevaux de frise* barbed wire, two crossed wooden posts with a beam connecting them with wire draped overtop. In addition, some of the trenches had the extensible post system where metal pots were hammered into the ground with pull rings to extend the wire upwards and sideways.

There would be plenty of work for the forward observers during the operation. It would be important to move with the infantry and establish OPs as each objective was captured to relay critical information back to the CFA's brigade HQs. The observer teams would be led by a lieutenant supported by a team of signallers and linesmen. The way that the lieutenant-colonel was looking at him, he suspected he would be one of them.

The Richmond Fusiliers were already in the line, getting familiar with their new trench system and the terrain. The 1st Division had picked the 2nd and 3rd Brigades to lead the assault, with the 2nd on the right flank and the 3rd on the left. They were going to be pulled out in a week or two to train on the mock-up of Hill 70.

Ryan glanced at his watch and saw that the second practice barrage was ten minutes away. It was scheduled for six fifteen. He then studied the pencil marks he had made indicating where the first trial barrage had struck earlier in the afternoon at one fifteen, when the batteries had fired three rounds per minute for two minutes. They had reported the results back to the 65th HQ and now were waiting to see the results.

He tapped the lieutenant-colonel's shoulder then pointed skyward. It was a clear, sunny day, muggy, with a few clouds. In the distance, they could see some specks in the sky moving back and forth above the lines, but they were too high to tell whether they were Allied or German planes. They had orders to halt the practice barrage if there were any German spotter planes in the vicinity.

The 65th had moved from the Bois de la Ville to the Les Brebis area just two days earlier, and they needed to register their guns to make sure there weren't any gaps in their barrage. Their men were busy being resupplied with shells and were currently sorting them out by lot numbers. Certain manufacturers and lots were more reliable than others. They had seen some issues with the first practice, and they had sent corrections back to brigade HQ by runner, since they couldn't yet trust the telephone lines and cables. There was plenty of buried German cable in the area; therefore, their messages were at risk of being intercepted by the Boche. After the practice shoot, their batteries would remain silent, except for SOS calls. They didn't want to expose themselves to the Huns and provide them with any more info than they had to. The less they knew, the better.

Ryan was glad the day was coming to an end. He and Masterley had been in the OP since early dawn. They were under strict orders that there was to be no movement during the daytime. The Boche on the hill above had an excellent view of their trenches, and the German snipers were quite bothersome, as usual. At dusk, guides would arrive to lead them out of the trenches to the tramlines.

"Is your watch synchronized?" asked Masterley as he glanced at his.

"Yes, sir," replied Ryan. He had synchronized his watch with the brigade HQ before he came into the trench. "It's coming on to six fifteen, sir."

Masterley frowned at his watch just as the first shells started to land.

CHAPTER 17

Lieutenant-Colonel Llewellyn was pleasantly surprised when he took a spoonful of bread pudding. It was a simple dish made from leftover stale bread soaked in condensed milk with a dash of plum and apple jam for sweetness. Whoever the cook was, he had a light touch.

The meal had been on the whole a pleasant one. It had started off with slices of veal loaf covered by a light brown sauce, boiled potatoes still in their jackets, and green peas. The red wine, — Llewellyn would have preferred a beer — had been a passable local vintage.

The dining room was of modest size in the château, more of a manor house than a palace, which had once been the former residence of the local mine manager. Bracquemont, once a fashionable suburb of Noeux-les-Mines, was now dotted with Nissen huts to billet the units passing through. He wondered how fashionable it had been, since Fosse 1 was close by. If the wind blew in the right direction, you could hear the coal miners during their shift changes.

He glanced down the table at Major-General Macdonell, who was sitting at its head. To his right was Brigadier-General Loomis. Both he and the general had driven to Macdonell's HQs from the 2nd Brigade's HQ at Les Brebis, about two miles south of Bracquemont. Across from Loomis was Major-General William Griesbach, the GOC of the 1st Brigade. He was nearly forty, with short-cropped black hair, a Charlie Chaplin moustache, and blue eyes. He had raised and commanded the 49th Battalion before he was given command of the 1st. Llewellyn had heard the story going around that when Griesbach volunteered for the Boer War, he couldn't meet the weight requirement without hiding a lump of coal in the back of his shirt. Next to him was Brigadier-General Tuxford the GOC of the 3rd Brigade. Llewellyn was familiar with him, since he had led the 5th Battalion at Ypres. He was forty-five years old, with a light complexion.

"Has the relief been completed?" Macdonell asked in his Scottish lilt as one of the servers removed his plate and refilled his cup with coffee.

"Yes, the 10th has replaced my 5th in the line. They've confirmed A and D companies are in the front trenches and B and C are in support," replied Tuxford.

"Very good," Macdonell said.

"Have we received word yet when the next Z date will be?" asked Llewellyn. August 1st had been the Z-date for the operation to capture Hill 70.

"I'm afraid not," replied the major-general. "We've been waiting for the weather to improve. The rain for the last few days has played havoc with the schedule."

"It would have been a great anniversary gift," Llewellyn stated with a wry smile. The men at the table chuckled in agreement. It was true today marked the third anniversary of the war. This year, there had been few commemorative events, and those that did take place were sober affairs. Some of the units in the Corps had been given a half-day's leave. The 1st Division hadn't been so lucky, since they were in the line. While they had made some progress this year, reality had set in, especially after the losses they suffered in April and June. And the losses they would likely suffer when they took Hill 70.

"It gives us more time to soften the Hun defences," Major-General Macdonell stated.

"True," replied Griesbach. He was well known for having an analytical mind. "But the Boche have changed their tactics. They are now defending shell holes and have placed isolated strong points in front of their trenches. We've had to clear them, or else they'll be a serious threat in our rear."

"We've been sending out patrols to scout them out," replied Llewellyn as he lit his pipe. "And I think the new platoon organization will be effective against the strong points. Our Emma Gees, rifle grenades, bombers, and our riflemen should make short work of any strong points they encounter."

"I still have some concerns about our frontage," Loomis stated as he took a sip of his coffee.

"It can't be helped I'm afraid," Macdonell said. "General Currie has assigned us Hill 70, so we'll have to make do with what we have."

"What worries me is mopping up and carrying and evacuating the wounded," replied the brigadier-general.

"If we assigned special parties to those jobs, we wouldn't have enough men to do the fighting."

"I know," replied Loomis. It was clear that he didn't like it.

Llewellyn understood his CO's concerns. It had been decided the best way to deal with the problem was to have the last line of the attack wave mop up after the first wave had captured it. Once they had completed their mopping-up operations, they would start carrying forward the needed supplies to continue the assault and to consolidate the captured German trenches. Then they would turn around and act as stretcher bearers for the wounded.

It all depended on the first wave's success. If things went wrong, it would be a mess.

"So far, from what I've observed at the Houchin Training ground, it should be sufficient," stated Griesbach. The 1st Brigade had been assigned as the reserve.

"I agree," replied Tuxford. "My men have gone through the taped course in mock attacks, and they have studied the plaster of Paris model of Hill 70 that the First Army provided to us. I'm confident we'll be in fine shape. I really wish the weather would clear up soon. The photos the Flying Corps has been providing us are invaluable."

Everyone at the table nodded in agreement.

"It also gives us more time lying cable," Griesbach said. "I've read the work party summaries. The 2nd has laid nearly 11,300 yards of cable in No Man's Land."

"My men have done an excellent job in the last few weeks. I lost a few men when the Hun shells landed on top of them. The night after that, the Boche hit us with gas shells. They had to stop working when they put on their box respirators."

Llewellyn could attest to how uncomfortable it was working wearing gas masks, especially in the dark. It really cut down the men's efficiency. Laying cable was a tough job. The cables needed to be buried and disguised so that they wouldn't be spotted by the Germans. And the ends of the cables needed to be easily found so that they could be extended or connected to the telephones during the attack to allow them to send reports back to the advanced command posts.

"That's one of the reasons our artillery is continuing to shell the German rear and support positions," stated Macdonell. "And we want to keep them guessing when we'll actually launch our attack."

"Yes, sir," replied Llewellyn. "I'm well aware we'll need every advantage we can get. They're not going to give up that hill easily."

"What's the date today?" asked Lieutenant Felix Hayward as his pencil hovered above a field report pad he was using to record his observations.

"August 4th," replied Lieutenant Ryan as he adjusted his steel helmet so it sat more comfortably as he stared over the trench using a box periscope. "I think."

Hayward turned his clean-shaven face toward him in surprise. "The 4th?"

"Yeah, I'm pretty sure it is."

"Shit!" replied Hayward. "How long has it been for you?"

"Three years," Ryan answered as he turned his attention to the Richmond Fusiliers officer.

"A year and half for me," he replied as he put the date into the blank field at the top of the standardized form the Corps was now using to record the FOO's observations.

"It reminds me," Ryan said. "You'd better call in to synchro your watch."

"Crap, I know my watch can be slow at times, but three times a day?" muttered Hayward as he lifted the Fuller phone receiver to buzz Brigade HQ.

"Welcome to my world," Ryan chuckled as he peered through the periscope. They had orders to sync their timepieces three times a day.

"MAISE here requesting time check," he stated as he lifted his wrist to check his time piece, "7:05. Righto."

Ryan checked his left wrist, and it read 7:05 as well.

"You want coffee?" asked Hayward as he handed him a canvas-covered canteen. "I don't have any rum to celebrate."

"That's okay. There ain't much to celebrate," Ryan replied as he took the canteen and poured some into a white tin cup that he had nearby. He was surprised by how strong the black coffee was and how good it tasted. "Where did you get this?"

"At the YMCA hut on our way in. They have great coffee, and it's free," Hayward replied as he took the canteen back and took a sip. "They must have some Frenchie making it. Coffee in our mess tastes like tea."

"You don't like the petrol taste?" Ryan teased. Empty petrol cans were used to haul water up to the front lines. No matter how well they were cleaned, a slight taste of petrol always seemed to linger. When he saw Hayward's grimace, Ryan added, "You get used to it."

"At least the coffee hides it better than the tea does," Hayward said as he took another sip from his canteen. Most of the men preferred coffee over tea, even though tea was a standard part of the men's rations. The supply people were allowed to substitute an ounce of coffee for 5/8 of an ounce of tea.

Ryan liked the Richmond Fusiliers officer who hailed from Orillia. He was in his mid-twenties, with hazel eyes, of medium height, and stocky. Llewellyn had designated him to be a liaison officer between the 65th and the Fusiliers. The word had come down from Corps HQ that cooperation between the artillery and the infantry needed improvement. One of the suggestions was to train an infantry officer as an artillery specialist.

Ryan had already spent a considerable amount of time in the front lines. As an FOO, he was already quite as familiar with the current infantry tactics as Hayward. Also, Llewellyn didn't say anything, but he got the impression that the lieutenant-colonel thought Hayward had potential to grow into a higher command.

"Here we go," said Hayward as shells started landing on the German barbed wire about five hundred yards distant. Behind the wire, they could see what remained of the mine pitheads on the outskirts of Lens. The city had once been a major mining hub in France.

The 1st Division wasn't planning to attack Lens directly. It was to well defended by the German IV Corps. Lens lay in a basin formed by the Souchez Valley. It was dominated by the high ground on the north, west, and the southwest, all under German control. The pitheads at Lens were constructed with masonry walls three to four feet thick and foundations that sank twelve feet down. Behind the pitheads were the workers' houses the locals called *corons*. The houses were mainly one- or two-storey redbrick buildings. Most had cellars that provided protection from men of the German 7th and 8th divisions from their 18-pounders and 4.5 howitzers.

"So, what do you think?" Ryan asked as they watched the explosions walk along the barbed wire through the periscope.

"They're the 2-inch mortars," he stated. "It looks like they are doing a pretty good job."

Ryan nodded. The 1st Division's plan was to use the 2-inch mortars to cut the wire. He moved his periscope to his left to view the seventy-foot-high hill they called Hill 70.

The 65th, along with the 2nd artillery Brigade of the CFA, was located in dips in the ground just south of Loos, hiding them from the Germans' direct view. The Corps didn't want the Germans to know how many guns were pointing at them. There were nearly a hundred 18-pounders hidden along the 1st Division's front. Nor did they want them to see the tramlines they had built to bring shells to the forward supply dumps. The 18-pounders' allotment was eight hundred shells per gun, and they had only fired enough rounds to register their targets based on Brigadier-General Thacker's artillery plans. It also helped with the wear and tear on their gun barrels. The 2-inch mortars were proving to be adequate for cutting the wire, since they could launch a forty-two-pound spherical high explosive shell nearly six hundred yards.

A couple of minutes later, the German artillery started to retaliate. Both Ryan and Hayward scanned the hill, looking for gun plumes. There was supposed to be an active 10.5-cm Hun howitzer opposite them. They wanted to confirm it hadn't been recently moved. Both of them had read the two-page counterbattery report before entering their OP, listing the map reference, calibre, the area that they were shelling, the information source, confirmation date, and the ID number of the aerial photo, if available.

"Looks like it's still there," stated Hayward as he drew a mark on his map at H.4.C.88.45.

"What do you think?" asked Hayward, "18s or the 4.5s?"

"More likely the 4.5," Ryan replied. "We're saving the 18s for the creeping barrage. Once we capture Hill 70, we'll have to move them up there. It's going to be a bitch, but we'll get it done."

"Yeah," Hayward replied as he continued to study Hill 70. It really was going to be a bitch to take. Ryan could see in his eyes that he was wondering how many of his men he would lose.

CANADIAN CONVALESCENT HOSPITAL, BROMLEY HILL, KENT

"Matron, may I have a moment?" asked Ida Norgrove, her assistant matron. She was standing in the door of her office, which was formerly the hotel's Ladies Reading Room. The walls had been papered with blue violets. The room's furniture, a desk with mismatched chairs and a four-drawer filing cabinet, all had seen better days. The window behind her opened to the vegetable garden, where patients could be seen weeding with spades and hoes.

Samantha waved her in. Her assistant seemed to be somewhat tense when she took a chair. Ida was a big-busted woman in her late thirties, of medium height with hazel eyes. White strands hidden under her nurse's veil were starting to appear in her short chestnut hair.

"Has the roll call been completed?"

"Yes, all the patients are here and accounted for," Ida replied.

Samantha chuckled. "And no one tried to escape?"

Ida snorted. "Not today at least." She was responsible for the roll calls that the hospital conducted three times a day, at eight in the morning, at two in the afternoon, and at nine in the evening. It was part of the hospital's routine. Reveille was at five thirty, meals at seven, noon, and five o'clock. The doctors made their rounds at nine in the morning. Lights-out was at quarter to ten.

Ida wrinkled her nose when she added, "The last couple of men who did found themselves assigned to the VD ward."

Samantha nodded. There were always a few of the patients, mainly the newer ones, that liked to wander off, especially with London only a half-hour away. It caused headaches for the staff, since every patient needed to be accounted for. Some of the patients were easily found in the pubs in and around Bromley. Others managed to make their way into some of the less respectable areas of London.

"So, what's on today's schedule?" Samantha asked as she pulled a brown leather-bound calendar from under a stack of reports. She was startled when she realized it was August 4th and surprised she hadn't received any notifications or orders to commemorate the date.

"The usual. We're having some of the patients out weeding," Ida stated as she indicated the garden behind Samantha with her chin. "The cooks are happy. They're getting some fresh fruit and vegetables."

"The men will like that, although they would prefer meat," Samantha replied.

"That would be all they would eat if they had the choice."

With rationing, the garden helped stretch the hospital's food supply. It was considerably better than what she had in Petrograd, but they still had orders to economize as much as possible. When fall came, the excess would be canned. It would be good if they could become self-sufficient, but that wasn't realistic. At least it kept the men occupied.

"The baseball team is set to practice for the upcoming game with Massey-Harris," Ida stated. The Massey-Harris Convalescent Hospital was one of their sister hospitals in Kingswood. All the Canadian hospitals in the area were part of the very competitive Pill-Slinger baseball league, where a mixture of staff and patient teams played against each other for bragging rights.

"We did well at the last game," Samantha remarked.

"We did. Potterfield had a no-hitter," Ida replied. "It's too bad that the travelling medical board had invalided him out to Canada." Potterfield had been with the Richmond Fusiliers when he lost his left arm last June. As a right-hander, he had a wicked spitball.

"Captain Little has a good arm," Samantha pointed out.

"That he has," remarked Ida. "A nice brawny one."

Samantha raised an eyebrow when Ida blushed. She hadn't realized Ida was seeing the captain. She wondered what else she might have missed. Samantha knew the captain was four years younger than Ida and wondered if that was the reason she was nervous.

Changing the subject, Samantha handed Ida a sheet of paper. "Colonel Spier has notified me that General Turner has indicated he wants to visit the hospital in a day or so to present medals to some of the men. His office has sent over this list of the men who need to be made available when the general comes."

Ida glanced at the list and then said, "Some of these men are on the planned trip to the House of Commons."

Samantha grimaced. "I forgot about that. I would hate to cancel the trip. Especially when MP Mitchell went through all the effort to accommodate us." The hospital arranged day trips for their patients to keep their minds occupied, mostly to concerts, shows, moving picture theatres, and tourist attractions in the London area. One was a tour of the Houses of Parliament.

"It's planned for the afternoon. The tour needs to be finished before Question Period," Ida pointed out.

"And if the general is late, it will upset the schedule," Samantha said, frowning. "I'll talk with the colonel. We'll see what General Turner's schedule is like. We might be able to work around it."

"Good, have you taken the tour?"

"I'm afraid not."

"I have. Several times. I never get tired of it," Ida stated then added with a touch of pride, "I voted for the first time last June."

"You did?" Samantha said in surprise. "When did this happen?" She'd been trying, with limited success, to avoid any news about politics. She'd had enough of it in Russia.

"We got the vote in Alberta last spring. The women in BC got the vote last December. The rumours are Prime Minister Borden is going to give women the vote in the next election."

"That would be something," replied Samantha. "I've never voted before."

Ida leaned forward and whispered conspiratorially, "If you are interested, some of the girls meet at the Village Tea Rooms to discuss politics."

Samantha pursed her lips and then replied, "I'll have to consider it." Regulations prohibited political activity on a military base or station. Off-base, on their own time, they were allowed to have meetings and discussions. She was in a delicate position as a matron. Reading political material and discussing the political issues with close friends was one thing. Attending public political discussion groups was a whole different matter because it could impact her authority and position.

When Ida leaned back in her chair, she fidgeted nervously. Samantha suspected she might be reconsidering what she had said about the political meeting.

"Matron," Ida finally said in a formal tone, "I would like to request a week's leave."

Samantha gave her a surprised look. Matrons were granted twenty-one days leave every six months by the Nursing Service, while the sisters were entitled to only seventeen days leave for the same period. "Where are you planning to take your leave?" she asked. She was required to know in order to prepare the necessary paperwork and passes.

"Paris," replied Ida with a nervous smile.

"Paris!" Samantha exclaimed, finally understanding her nervousness. When she had left for Russia, leave for Paris had been prohibited. Now it was allowed as long it was approved by the Canadian Overseas Forces command in London.

"Will someone be going with you?"

Ida blushed and then finally admitted, "Captain Little."

"I think we can spare you for a week," Samantha said brightly. "What date are you looking at?"

"The first week of September," Ida said anxiously. "That should be enough time to get all the approvals."

Samantha chuckled. "We hope so." She knew Ida had been through the process before.

"Paris in the fall," Samantha said with a smile. "Sounds wonderful."

I wonder if James can get leave, she thought. *Oh yes, taking leave in Paris is a wonderful idea.*

OLD UNION BRIDGE, OTTAWA

Sir Robert was pleasantly tired as his driver drove him over the Old Union Bridge that spanned the narrowest point of the Chaudière Falls. The cauldron-shaped falls was about two hundred feet at its widest and had a drop of forty-nine feet. From his seat in the car, he couldn't see the water's turbulence below. At this time of year, it would be mild. In the spring, with the snow melt, the water would be a fierce turbulence of grey and white. He could see the lights from the dam that had been built at the falls to generate electric power for the lumber mills and other industrial plants that hugged both sides of the river.

There was a fair amount of traffic on the bridge. Most of it was workers heading home to Hull for supper after a long day's work. He had just finished eating at the Royal Ottawa Golf Club. It had been a perfect day for a round of golf. The temperature had been a touch cool for August, and without much humidity. He recalled with satisfaction that he had made a clean sweep of Hugh Clark. It had been only a nine-hole match, but he had won it by the fifth hole. They had continued playing, and he had won the remaining four.

Through the bridge's rusting metal trusses, he could see the evening sun striking the Parliamentary Library on the hill. It threw shadows onto the new Centre Block that was slowly continuing to rise. He had wanted to get away from the office for a couple of hours for some exercise. The fact it was the war's third anniversary and they were entering its fourth year weighed on him. He had said as much in his annual statement sent to the press yesterday to be published today. In it, he had said the people had to steel themselves for another year of war. That her sons were fighting for liberty and justice and were not giving their lives in vain. Canada, as well as the rest of the British Commonwealth, reaffirmed their invincible determination to a victorious issue. And Canada had vindicated her place as one of the world's greatest and truest democracies.

That was one of the things he had to explain to the Win-the-War delegates. The Win-the-War movement had started a few weeks ago, and branches had quickly been set up in every province in the Dominion. They had just had their first convention in the Toronto Arena with nearly five thousand delegates. A delegation from the convention had arrived at his East Block office this morning with the resolutions they had hammered out last Thursday and Friday.

One of the first things he had to tell them was while he sympathized with their goals, the *BNA Act* specified that the House of Commons cannot sit longer than five years. By tradition, elections were called every four years upon the advice of the prime minister. He already had an amendment to the *BNA Act* passed the year prior by the British Parliament to extend the Canadian Parliament to a sixth year. He had hoped that he would be able to get unanimous consent for another extension, but sadly that had not been possible. As for their major demand for conscription, he pointed out to them that the *Military Service Act* was currently being voted on in the Senate. He had been ecstatic to learn after they had left that the final vote came down. It had been passed by a substantial margin, fifty-four to twenty-five.

As for union government and the women's delegation's demand for the franchise, he had explained his thoughts on both topics to them. He had been pleased the meeting had gone fairly well. He frowned slightly when he thought of Sifton, who had already sent him a telegram stating all the western Liberal governments were in favour of a union. It was the federal Liberals he needed to convince that it was best for the country. He hoped Sifton's efforts at the Winnipeg Liberal convention, starting on Tuesday, would bear fruit. He was running out of time.

CHAPTER 18

Lieutenant-Colonel Llewellyn was breathing hard through his small box respirator strapped to his chest. He hated the damn thing, but the Huns had decided to fire an artillery barrage of gas shells at him and his men just as they made their way to the assembly point for their assault. Zero hour was less than two hours away, at four thirty.

He tried to appear calm as he waited for his company commanders to report their status and whether they had suffered any casualties. Corps HQ was anxious the 2nd Brigade made it to the assembly area intact, and he felt more than the normal pressure. It was Currie's first major operation since he had become the Corps GOC two months ago.

Currie had demanded detailed plans of the assault for his review and approval. Woe to a commander if he had submitted one that had been slapped together without much thought. Llewellyn had felt Currie's displeasure before. He winced as he recalled his dressing-down.

As he watched the gas cloud dissipate through the lens of his gas mask, it distracted him for a moment from the mental checklist he was reviewing in case he had missed something. He turned his head to confirm the curtains were down to prevent the gas seeping into his command post the 4th Australian Tunnelling Company had dug for him. The Huns had been using a new type of gas shells for the past month. The chemists had said it had a high boiling point and was a sulphur derivative that highly irritated the mouth, nose, eyes, and caused skin blisters. The men had orders to cover as much of their bare skin as possible.

His men were facing the 26th, 165th, and 363rd regiments of the German 7th Division. They were good, very good. His scouts had reported they were well trained, disciplined, and with high morale. Despite the artillery, Stokes, and machine-gun barrages, the 7th had not only repaired the damage, they also had built new defences. They'd been digging dugouts connecting two or three shell holes and had been converting them into machine-gun strong points. It allowed the defenders to move easily from one shell hole to another without becoming a target. And during one of the Fusiliers raids, his men had come back with a Lewis gun modified to fire Mauser ammunition. Fritz liked the Lewis and was happy to get their hands on them. They probably had plenty of captured .303 ammunition, but Llewellyn was sure the Mauser supply was more reliable. That wasn't the only captured machine gun they were using. The scouts had reported one strong point had a Vickers.

All he could do was to prepare his men as best he could. Each of his companies had gone over the taped course on the east side of Aix-Noulette and Bully-Grenay. He had work parties bury hundreds of yards of cable so he could keep in touch with brigade HQ, and he had confirmation, just after noon, that the advance brigade headquarters had been activated after their move to the mines at Le Bris. He was having linesmen follow the first waves of attack to repair any cut cables. They would have the usual allotment of signal lamps, flares, rockets, and pigeons. If they met the schedule, he doubted the pigeons would be of much use. They wouldn't probably arrive to their home coops until the attack was over.

Senior officers from the Corps, the 1st Division, and the 2nd Brigade had all come to inspect his front lines and to take a personal look at Hill 70. He had been pleased how complimentary they were concerning the Fusiliers' sharpness and efficiency and had passed that along to his men.

But efficiency wasn't going to be enough. He had sat with the 65th Artillery, the mortar teams, and the 2nd Machine Gun Company to select targets, barrage plans, and schedules. The heavies had been assigned to destroy the trench lines. The 18-pounders would provide a rolling barrage seventy-five yards in front of his men. The 2nd Machine Gun Company would be providing harassing fire until his men reached the front lines. For the past few weeks, they had been firing twenty thousand rounds of indirect fire per day. The mortars were to take out machine guns and mortar emplacements. Once they captured the Blue Line, the artillery and the machine guns would move to designated positions for covering fire.

The Royal Engineers had positioned nearly three thousand oil drums that once ignited would create a smokescreen for them. With the prevailing wind, it should provide cover for his men. It was one of the reasons they had spent the time practising attacking wearing gas masks. The thick smoke from the oil drums would make breathing difficult.

His companies' initial rush would be in artillery formation, and when they got near the German trenches, they would form into two waves for the final assault.

He also had sat down with Major Moore to estimate the casualties his regiment would suffer. He and the doctor had far too much experience because they had both agreed that they would be looking at a twenty percent casualty rate. He didn't like it. Once translated into actual numbers, he would likely suffer two hundred men killed or wounded by the end of the day. He had left the details for the medical planning and the arrangements for burials in the nearby cemetery to the good doctor.

He had seen Father Stoats earlier hearing confessions and giving blessings to the men as he headed out. The tension was always unbearable as you waited for the zero hour. It was almost a relief when you finally had to go over the top.

The faint sound of feet on the trench's floorboards made him turn his head toward it. The runner came to a halt when, despite Llewellyn's gas mask, he recognized him.

"Captain Henry ordered me to tell you we're in position," he said. The gas mask muffled his voice, and he didn't bother to salute him. No one did in the trenches to avoid telling the German snipers who the officers were.

"Casualties?"

"Only five wounded. Nothing serious."

"Good," grunted Llewellyn. "Stay close by. I'll be needing you shortly."

"Yes, sir," the runner acknowledged.

Llewellyn pulled the black curtain aside and pulled it closed quickly behind him to keep the seal. However, he still kept his mask on just in case.

"Send the word to Brigade. We're in position," he told the telephone operator.

"Yes, sir," the operator replied, his voice muffled by his gas mask. He only had to use one word to tell HQ they were ready. The word was "Ypres."

DYNAMITE ROAD, HILL 70, LOOS SECTOR

"Shit!" whispered Danny Weber in his Liverpool accent.

Sergeant Duval glanced over at his spotter lying beside him, trying to scan the terrain with the lens of his gas mask pressed against a pair of binoculars. He wasn't doing much better. The lens in his gas mask made viewing through the Winchester scope on his Ross rifle difficult. "What did you see?"

"I thought I saw movement from the shell hole seventy-five yards out," was Danny's muffled reply.

Duval adjusted the scope as he swept the shell hole, but nothing stood out.

Greg March, lying beside him on his left, whispered, "I don't see anything?"

Duval grunted. Greg was the third man on his three-man team. He was wearing, as they all were, a sniper smock coated with grey-white dust to blend into Hill 70. Greg's rifle and scope were wrapped, as were his and Danny's, with a spare pair of puttees to prevent the sun reflecting off the metal. Greg was a recent addition, since the Fusiliers were experimenting with three-man teams. Duval hadn't been completely sold on the idea. He and Danny had been working together for well over a year now as a two-man sniper team, and he trusted Danny implicitly. However, Corps and Brigade HQs thought a spare would be useful for odd jobs and would give much-needed experience to those who had passed the sniper course.

The shell hole they were studying was some hundred and fifty yards to the left of Dynamite Road. Not that there was much traffic on the road with all the artillery, mortar, and machine guns tossing lead and steel around. Near the shell hole, he could see several half-buried German soldiers. Its neighbour, twenty yards to the left, was well positioned to give the B and C companies some trouble as they made their way through the Blue Line to capture the next objective, the Red Line. The Blue Line had been the Hurdle Trench system that ran from the top of the hill to Cité St. Laurent. The A and D companies had exhausted themselves when they pushed through the five hundred or so yards from their trenches to the Hun lines. The B and C companies then had to cross to the Nizam and the Nun's Alley Trenches. Once they had secured the Red Line, they would have to regroup before making the final push to the Green Line a farther five hundred yards just in front of the small suburb of Cité St. Auguste.

He and the other sniper teams had been pushing ahead of the companies with orders to take care of the strong points and any targets of opportunity. Up to now, he had killed fourteen Boche, mainly machine gunners. Duval had taken the time to study the maps and had made notes on points of interest during his previous sorties into No Man's Land. He also had to rely on the observations from the artillery OPs, intelligence reports from other scouts, and on the aerial photos the lieutenant-colonel had given him on what he would find on this side of the Blue Line. There was supposed to be a strong point, a couple of large shell holes connected by a dugout, near the Dynamite Road on their right. The aerial photos he had taken a look at didn't show much detail, but it looked like they had dug a firing step on the inside of them. So far, they hadn't seen any activity. Duval suspected Fritz was waiting for the two assault waves to pass them so they could shoot them in the back. It wasn't very sporting, but nothing very much was in this war.

Duval was glad he had brought his scope, even though Brigade HQ had ordered they were to be left behind. The lieutenant-colonel hadn't said anything when he saw him the previous night as he filled his mess tin with hot soup from the Soyer soup kitchens. He and his team had gotten through without a scratch since the artillery had done a fine job cutting the wire.

"It's getting a bit lively," said Greg as he clutched his Lee-Enfield. Duval was the only member of his team equipped with the Ross.

"Patience, patience," Duval said as he peered through his scope again. He finally saw movement at the edge of the shell hole. Through the scope, he could see it was grey-white that blended well with the dirt, but the shape was too smooth to be other than the top of a German helmet. When it rose another half-inch, he fired.

"Someone just popped out of the shell hole on the left," Danny said as Duval pulled the bolt back, ejecting a casing, and then pushed it forward to load the next round. He quickly focused on the next shell hole and saw two heads appear. He got one, but the other was to quick and missed him.

"Let's go," Duval ordered as he rose to his feet. In a crouching run, he made his way to the shell hole. He hit the dirt at its lip, then pulled out a Mills grenade out of the satchel he had strapped to his waist. Duval pulled the pin and dropped them into the shell hole. A couple of Huns jumped out before they detonated. Danny and Greg shot them. After they had dropped, he peered over the lip. What he saw was a firing step and a shadowed opening to a dugout.

"I'm going to toss some more Mills into the gopher hole," he said as he took out the last of his hand grenades. After he had pulled the pins, he tossed them into the dugout's opening. He heard the faint sound of German cursing just before the grenades went off. He must have gotten lucky. A few seconds later, he heard secondary explosions, then some of the Huns' ammo started cooking off.

Huns started spilling out from a shell hole on their right. When Duval saw the first Fritz raised his Mauser, he shot him from the hip. After the man tumbled down the slope, Duval started yelling, "*Hände hoch! Hände hoch!*"

In shock, after seeing their comrade killed, the remaining Germans reluctantly raised their hands. "Greg, get their gear while we cover you," Duval ordered.

Once they had been stripped of their weapons, Greg asked, "What do you want to do with them?"

"Take them back to our lines for interrogation," stated Duval. "Me and Danny will stay out here for a while. Don't want Smiley beating us." Smiley was the second-best sniper in the Fusiliers. He was number one. He wasn't about to give up his title today.

"You think you can handle them?" Duval asked.

Greg did a quick count. "There's only ten of them. Piece of cake."

"Good, when you bring them in, make sure we get credit," Duval said.

"Sure, Sergeant. I'll let them know it was us," Greg said as he motioned with his rifle for the Boche to start marching.

AUGUST 16, 1917
THE RED LINE, HILL 70, LOOS SECTOR

Brigadier-General Loomis grunted after he lowered the box periscope he had been using to view No Man's Land as it sloped downward from the Red Line, on the crest of Hill 70 to the Green Line near its base.

It was nearly eleven o'clock, and the sun was nearly at its apex. Sweat stained Lieutenant-Colonel Llewellyn's battle dress. He knew he reeked, since he hadn't been out of his clothes for the last three days. He felt the usual tiredness, but the black coffee he and Loomis shared earlier had dispelled some of that.

The 107th Canadian Pioneers had just connected the Nun's Alley trench to the Netly Trench that crossed the former No Man's Land behind them. Already, supplies were starting to pile up. Boxes of S.A.A. ammunition, petrol tins filled with water, bundles of shovels and picks, canvas buckets filled with Mills and rifle grenades, and crates of Stokes mortar bombs. A and D companies had carried them all forward from the Blue Line after they had finished their mopping-up operations. They had found a considerable number of Germans lying dead and wounded. The artillery had cut many of them as they tried to retreat to the Red Line.

Llewellyn nodded to the bombers, with green armbands on their upper left arms, that they could fill their satchels with the standard twelve Mills. A runner with a red armband and signallers with blue armbands hovered nearby in case he or the general needed to send a message.

"So, what do you think?" asked Llewellyn as the brigadier-general handed the periscope to Major Burnham, the Brigade's intelligence officer. Both men had come to see for themselves the terrain they needed to cross to capture the Green Line. The 2nd Brigade CO cocked an ear as German shells started landing in No Man's Land between the Red and Green Lines. The Fusiliers had spent most of the night trying to reorganize for a final push, but they had spent most of it fending off German counterattacks.

"I think the plan we discussed is practicable," Loomis stated. The brigadier-general, pleased with their success so far, had called a conference earlier this morning to work out the details for the next phrase of the operation. The Germans were continuing to put up very stiff resistance, but they still had managed to overcome the Boche's defences. What had been of great interest was the map Captain Saunders had brought to brigade HQ that the 3rd Australian Tunnelling Company had found in one of the German dugouts they had cleared. There were standing orders that no one was to enter a German dugout until the Australians had cleared them from the usual German booby traps. The German map showed the location of all their strong points. Their coordinates had been sent to the artillery and mortar teams, who were setting up to rain shells on them.

"The 10th and the 5th will lead the assault," the brigadier-general said. "You'll be in the reserve, and you'll continue with the consolidation of the Blue and Red Lines."

"Yes, sir," Llewellyn replied. The plan was for the 10th, on the left, and the 5th, on the right, to assault the Green Line at four o'clock this afternoon.

Loomis gave him a slight grin. "What I've seen so far is your men are fit and ready."

"Yes, sir, they're rather keen on making the assault," replied Llewellyn.

"Private Combe made that quite clear," Loomis said. He had seen Major Moore at the regimental aid post. The doctor had taken over a German dugout and had arranged for three tiers of stretchers to be set up to accommodate the incoming casualties. One of the casualties had been Private Combe, barely nineteen, who had been shot in the thigh. It had been a clean wound; no bones or arteries had been hit. He was having a smoke when the general popped in. When the private saw him, he tried to stand to attention.

The general ordered him to relax, but the private replied, "If you need me, I can still fire a rifle."

Brigadier-General Loomis replied, "I'll let you know. In the meantime, I would suggest you try to rest and recover."

Llewellyn was about to ask about artillery support when he spotted Sergeant Duval and privates Danny and Greg prodding a group of German prisoners along, carrying three stretchers. From the looks on their faces, they weren't happy to see him or the general. It was more likely the general, since the men tried hard not to be noticed by the red caps. As scouts, they should have heard the general was in the trenches. Llewellyn did notice the string of German IDs that hung around Duval's neck. It was standard practice to retrieve them from dead they found on the battlefield. Eventually, the ID numbers would be forwarded to the Germans as part of the information exchange on captured prisoners so they could notify families that their loved ones had been killed.

The prisoners couldn't help but stare at the officer stars on their collars. Llewellyn could see what they were thinking, but the nearby men who appeared to be casually pointing their Lee-Enfields in their direction gave them no second thoughts.

"We were taking a dump in a shell hole when a couple of them popped up," explained Duval. "Scared the shit out of me."

"Must have been the smell," remarked a man nearby who was refilling his satchel with grenades.

Duval gave the man a knifing glare before returning his attention back to Llewellyn and the brigadier-general. Llewellyn noticed Loomis was trying hard not to laugh.

"I thought A and B companies should had mopped up No Man's Land," Duval complained.

Llewellyn frowned. "They did. Obviously, some got missed."

"Did you go into the dugouts?" Loomis asked.

"No, sir," Duval replied. "After I've dropped off the prisoners at the field ambulance, I was going to send word to the Australians to check them out."

"Good," replied Loomis. "We're moving some of the 18-pounders to the Blue Line to provide support when we attack the Green Line. I don't want any unpleasant surprises."

The artillery had been quite effective against the Blue and Red Lines, but not very much against the Green Line. The range had been to great, so they decided to implement part of the plan requiring the batteries to move forward once the trenches had been consolidated. Also, he had been creating OPs to give more accurate information to the 65th.

"When will we be going over?" Duval asked.

Loomis glanced at Llewellyn and then replied, "We'll have to see. I suspect it will be soon, very soon."

BLUE LINE, HILL 70, LOOS SECTOR

"Put your fucking mask back on!" Lieutenant Ryan shouted at Bombardier Warren through his gas mask. He should have been used to it by now with all the rehearsals, training, and gas alerts. Still, he had to keep a constant eye on his men to make sure they kept their masks on. Sometimes, the lens fogged up and they would slip the masks down so they could see the settings on the 18-pounders to lay the guns properly or to set the time on the fuses. It was tempting to remove his as well, but he didn't want to end up in the RDA.

He had ordered his men to put on their masks when the reports started coming from the FOOs assigned to the Richmond Fusiliers. His suspicions that he would be picked had proven to be fortuitously false. Lieutenant Simmons didn't even get out of the Fusiliers trench before he was killed. Lieutenant Furnell had taken his place and command of the eight-man squad.

Furnell had reported the 77s the Germans were using to bombard No Man's Land between the Blue and the Red Lines were detonating strangely. They would explode with a plopping sound and spray liquid in an eight- to ten-yard radius. He had recalled the recent reports the Huns had been using a new gas shell at Ypres. When they exploded, they didn't seem to have any immediate effect. It was hours later that the men would start sneezing and coughing, vomiting, blisters appearing on exposed skin, and have eyes so inflamed they were practically blind. It seemed that the wind hadn't dissipated the gas as normally expected; instead, it had sunk into low-lying areas such as the trenches. When they had recovered one of the unexploded shells, it had a yellow cross painted on its casing. It looked as if they were using the same type of shells here.

When Ryan had been satisfied Warren had put on his mask and had set to work setting the fuses on the shrapnel shells, he glanced at his barrage map. He put his finger on the barrage lifts N to X. The barrage was to cover the 2nd Brigade's assault on the Green Line.

"Did we get the latest wind and barometer readings?" he asked Sergeant Collins.

"We did, and we're all set."

Ryan glanced at the stacks of 18-pounder shells that had been recently replenished. All things considered, their resupply had been running smoothly with the tramlines bringing them from the dumps to where the horses could then haul them to the gun pits. He caught a glimpse of a horse wearing a gas mask being led away.

He checked his watch. A barrage had been set for three o'clock to cover the Fusiliers' assault on the Green Line. So far, the Fusiliers had been pleased with the curtain of steel that they had been providing. They, along with the 5th and 10th Battalions, had captured the Blue Line two hours after they had gone over the top yesterday. The Red Line objective had fallen into their hands four hours later. While the casualties had been light when they captured the Blue objective, the Huns had put up a fierce fight for the Red Line. The casualties there had been significant.

"Has Lieutenant Furnell sent any more messages?" he asked the sergeant.

"Not for the last hour or so," the sergeant replied. "Things are pretty quiet on the hill."

Even through the gas mask he caught the sergeant's tone. The Germans had been pounding their former lines until they stopped at eight o'clock this morning. That was not a good sign.

"The lines could be down again," Ryan remarked.

"They've been pretty good bringing them up again," the sergeant replied. "The line to Brigade HQ is good. They sent us those strong points they got off that German map they found."

"That they did," Ryan replied. He had seen the diagram of the communications system created for the operation. With the FOOs on the ground and with the 16th Squadron flying above Hill 70, they had been providing them with good targeting information via cable and over the wireless to the base stations near Brigade HQ. While the FOOs had also been supplied with pigeons, they had been totally useless. It had taken the birds over an hour before their messages could be processed and delivered.

He then pursed his lips. Yesterday's barrages between the Red and Green lines hadn't been as effective as they had hoped. Part of the problem had been that they didn't have any OPs in position to provide them with the info they needed to make corrections. During the night, the

2nd Brigade had put up SOS flares when they needed artillery support to fend off counterattacks. He hadn't responded to some of them because the Germans had been mimicking the Fusiliers' SOS flares to deplete his ammunition supply and to pinpoint his battery's position.

What was also worrisome was that the chalk quarries opposite Loos were still in German hands and had been giving the Fusiliers fits.

Ryan glanced at his wristwatch and saw that it was nearly time to start their barrage. He jerked his head up when he heard Warren remove his gas mask and started throwing up.

"Goddamn," swore Sergeant Collins.

"Better get him to the RDA," Ryan ordered. Warren must have gotten a whiff of the new German gas. "And get Bombardier Sean to replace him. We have ten minutes for zero hour."

"Yes, sir," replied the sergeant.

AUGUST 19, 1917
RICHMOND FUSILIER'S BILLETS, BRUAY

"You and your men did a good job on Hill 70," said Lieutenant-General Currie.

"Thank you, sir," replied Llewellyn. He, Major Gavin, and his four company commanders were clustered around Currie and his ADC, Lieutenant-Colonel Henderson, in the field near the Richmond Fusiliers' billets in Bruay. Llewellyn had wished he could have occupied his former digs, but they had been occupied by a British unit.

"General Haig has also sent his appreciation," Currie informed them.

"General Loomis has forwarded his message to us, and we shared it with our men. They were pleased General Haig was happy with our efforts."

"I'm glad." Currie gave him a wry smile. "My staff is preparing the usual reports on our operations on Hill 70. I would appreciate any comments or observations you may have."

Llewellyn glanced at Major Gavin and Lieutenants Fuller, Darwin, and Candace. They had been invited to a brief meeting with Currie after he inspected the Richmond Fusiliers. Earlier in the day Currie had visited Brigadier-General Loomis at his headquarters in the School House in Ruitz. They had been moved into the Corps reserve after they'd been relieved by the 4th Division on Hill 70. "We've been discussing among ourselves what we did right and what we could improve," replied Llewellyn.

Llewellyn could tell from the quirk in Currie's jowls and the way that Currie's hands played with his swagger stick that he was interested in his opinions."

"One of the things that worked well were the artillery and machine gun barrages. We had selected the possible positions from where the Germans would assemble for a counterattack. Once we've sent up an SOS, they were quick on concentrating their fire on them."

"We had worked with the 65th and the Machine Gun Corps and the heavies beforehand," Major Gavin added. "It helped quite a bit when we had to call on them. They did a very good job on the wire."

Currie gave the major a thoughtful nod as Henderson made a note in a leather notebook.

"The new platoon organization you requested implemented was quite effective in dealing with the isolated machine gun and strong points we've encountered." Currie flashed a brief smile. He and Currie had discussed the new platoon structure after they visited the French Army at Verdun last January. Much of what they had seen and discussed was now bearing fruit.

From the corner of his eye, he could see that Lieutenant Fuller was dying to say something. Lieutenants normally don't speak directly with the Corps Commander, but Llewellyn decided to take the risk. He nodded at Fuller that he had his permission to speak. "Having the Stokes keep up with us was really helpful during the counterattack."

"How bad was it?" asked Currie.

"Nearly as bad as Vimy," replied Fuller.

"Hmm," murmured Currie as he glanced at the rest of Llewellyn's officers. He could tell they hadn't fully recovered from their ordeal.

"What did the men think about the forward dumps?' Currie asked.

The look on Llewellyn's men's faces was his answer. "They did prove useful," Llewellyn said.

"But," Major Gavin added, "we did make mistakes in mopping up. We didn't get a good handle on the new German tactics. Remember when Sergeant Duval and his team captured that German strong point in No Man's Land behind the Blue Line? If he hadn't captured them, we would have lost a company."

Currie gave him a quizzical look. Llewellyn informed him. "Sergeant Duval is one of my top snipers."

"Why wasn't he in front of the Blue Line?" Currie demanded. "That's where he's supposed to be."

"It's one of the problems we encountered during the attack," Llewellyn replied to placate the general. "We hadn't selected positions beforehand after we took over objectives. I have to admit it took us too long getting ourselves sorted out and for my scouts to identify good positions for our sniper teams. It was a good thing Duval got stuck behind us. He captured what, a platoon of Germans."

"Two, actually," Major Gavin corrected Llewellyn.

"I see," replied Currie. "I hope you've put him up for an award?"

"I've put him up for a Military Medal," Llewellyn answered.

"Good, I'm looking forward to reading your recommendation," Currie replied.

"Thank you, General."

"Good," said Currie as he glanced at Lieutenant-Colonel Henderson. "My ADC is anxious to get moving. Who's next on our list?"

"The 10th Battalion, sir," replied Henderson.

"The 10th it is."

"Thank you for coming, General. I know my men appreciated it."

"We can't win without them," replied Currie.

"Yes, sir."

"Take some time to rest and work up your men. We'll need you soon," Currie ordered.

"Of course, General," replied Llewellyn.

"Good, on the QT," Currie said. "Field Marshal Haig has expressed an interest in inspecting the 2nd Brigade."

"I'm looking forward to it, sir," replied Llewellyn. Currie gave him another wry smile. He knew how much the men enjoyed inspections.

CHAPTER 19

"I received a message nearly a week ago from the Western Liberals. They're in favour of creating a national government and a six-man war council. The council would include myself. But they think a change of leadership is needed. They suggested four names under whom they're willing to serve. At the top of the list is Sir George Foster," stated Prime Minister Borden.

The senators and MPs crowded in the East Block's reception room erupted with yells of Liberal buggers and bastards, catcalls, and curses. Dagger glares were thrown at Sir George Foster, his minister of trade and commerce, sitting in the front row beside Sam Donaldson, his MP for Prince Albert.

Borden saw Foster's face turn pale and his Van Dyke beard shake slightly. Being suggested to replace him as prime minister by the Liberals was not a good thing. However, under normal circumstances, every man jack in the room would have jumped at the chance.

"Order! Order!" shouted J.E. Armstrong as he rapped his gavel on the polished walnut table. The MP for Lambton East was chairing the Conservative caucus meeting Borden had called. He had been briefing them since eleven this morning on his efforts to form a union government.

Once the crowd had subsided into a low murmur of indignation, Borden continued, "I have stated before, and I continue to assert the question of forming a union government must be based on the support of all elements of the Canadian population. They must all join in an earnest effort to win the war, which must be above personal and party considerations.

"It is my conviction my personal status and political fortune is insignificant. I'm quite willing to retire or to serve under Sir Foster if it will unite the population to support a union government," Borden said.

As Borden took his seat, the senators and MPs yelled, "No! No!"

"Mr. Chairman, may I have the floor?" Foster demanded as he rose to his feet and adjusted his wire-frame glasses.

Armstrong nodded. "You may."

Foster turned to face the murmuring, hostile crowd. "I have known and worked with Prime Minister Borden more years that I can count. I hope I'm permitted to say that we have a warm relationship, and we work well together. Ever since the war began, I've appreciated the enormity of the task that has confronted Sir Robert. I've seen for myself his untiring patience and devotion to his duties as the prime minister of this great Dominion. As he stated, he is willing to serve in any capacity. But I believe with his vast knowledge of the conditions and requirements not only in Canada and overseas that Sir Robert should remain the leader of our government. He will make sure the full strength of the country will be made available to help win the war."

The applause slowly started, then the room vibrated with the noise. Armstrong let the applause continue for a few moments before bringing the meeting back to order.

"Mr. Chairman! Mr. Chairman! May I have the floor?"

"The chair recognizes Senator Taylor," Armstrong said as he rapped his gavel again. Taylor had represented the Leeds riding until Borden appointed him to the Senate.

"I propose we declare that we, wholeheartedly, approve the government's policy and achievements during the last three years of the war. We endorse the earnest and patient efforts by the prime minister to bring a union of all the forces in Canada to speak to the world that we will see this war to victory," Taylor said, emphasizing his statement with his arms.

"Hear! Hear!" the crowd agreed.

"We must declare unanimously our personal admiration for the great work and leadership of Sir Robert. There is no other man who can discharge the tremendous task the prime minister has during this crisis and that he remain as prime minister is indispensable to the nation," Taylor declared.

"Borden! Borden! Borden!" the crowd chanted. Taylor used his hands to encourage them to chant louder.

Borden rose shakily to his feet. He was so overwhelmed by the senators' and MPs' support he couldn't speak. His lips trembled as he fought back tears.

"For he is a jolly good fellow," Sam Donaldson started singing as he rose to his feet. The rest of the men in the room soon followed.

Lieutenant-Colonel's Llewellyn's stomach sank as the plane rose into the sky and then banked to the right. His body was pressed against the side of the nacelle. He was grateful that he had tightened the seatbelt as he stared at the green ground below. It was disconcerting, terrifying, and exhilarating.

Once the aeroplane levelled off, Llewellyn remembered to start breathing. The air whistling through the wires was cool and crisp. He was surprised how cold it was as the plane flew higher. He was grateful that he was dressed warmly in a fleece leather jacket. His leather helmet and goggles helped with the buffeting from the propeller's backwash. He could see it spinning through the sites of the Lewis gun. He wondered if firing the machine gun would shoot its blades off. He didn't want to find out.

Llewellyn turned his head to look at the moustached pilot who was seated behind him. Lieutenant Leek grinned at him as he chewed his gum and gave him a thumbs-up. Leek was dressed in a dark brown leather jacket, a black silk scarf, a leather helmet, and goggles.

When he had arrived at the aerodrome, he had seen a flight lift off the grass runway into the blue sky. The pilots had said it was a good day for flying. There were a few clouds in, and the winds were light. The 16th Squadron's commander had invited members of the 2nd Brigade to tour the aerodrome to get a better sense of the work they did. And, for those brave enough, had offered them a chance to fly in one of the squadron's aeroplanes.

He had been pleasantly surprised to find out the pilot assigned to take him up was a Canadian. "So, you want to take a jaunt, sir," Lieutenant Leek said as he led him to a plane that was sitting in front of the nearest Bessonneau hangar. The hangar had wooden walls and a canvas roof secured by ropes. It looked as though it could be easily dismantled and reassembled if the aerodrome needed to move to a new location. He had seen several mechanics working on a couple of the machines housed inside.

"Yes," answered Llewellyn as he eyed the airplane. It was painted with the blue and white roundels on the nacelle, and there were blue, white, and red stripes on the tail rudder. "Where are you from?"

"Kawartha Lakes," Leek replied as he unwrapped a stick of Wrigley's gum and started chewing. "Volunteered last year. Did my initial flight training at Camp Borden before I shipped to England. In England, I was assigned to the 1 Squadron at Gosport. After I completed my advance training, got assigned to the 16th."

Llewellyn looked at him in surprise. "Didn't know we were training pilots in Canada."

"Oh yeah," Leek replied as he blew and popped a bubble. "It's run by the Munitions Board. At first they'd set it up to recruit and train aeroplane mechanics, then they expanded to pilot training. Quite a few of us joined up."

"Same kind of planes?" Llewellyn asked.

"Naw, I was trained on the Canuck. It's essentially a Curtis Jenny with some modifications. That isn't what we're flying today," Leek replied, pointing to the plane with his chin. "This is a B.E.2c. It has a wingspan of nearly thirty-eight feet and is twenty-seven feet long. The engine can generate ninety horses. We can fly as fast as seventy-two miles per hour, and she has a range of two hundred and seventy miles. She can also climb to ten thousand feet."

Llewellyn looked rather skeptically at the aeroplane. It was made of wood, canvas, and wire.

"Climb into the front seat."

"The front seat?"

"Yes, sir, the pilot sits in the back."

"Okay, where's the camera?" Llewellyn asked. He had seen and used the aerial photographs the 16th Squadron's pilots regularly provided the Corps.

"It's usually mounted here between the pilot and the observer," the lieutenant replied.

"No camera today?"

"Not today no," replied Leek. "You better strap in."

"Okay," Llewellyn replied. He manoeuvred through some of the wires as he stepped onto the wing then swung into the tight seat. It was even tighter because of the clothing they had made him wear. He could feel his shirt starting to dampen, since it was a warm day.

"Comfy?" the lieutenant remarked. "Tighten the seat belt. We don't want you to fall out."

Llewellyn felt nervous. Fall out? He could barely move. He wondered how the observer could man the Lewis machine gun. The model attached to the mount had the cooling shroud removed. He then felt the plane sink slightly when the pilot got into the back seat.

The mechanic standing in front of the propeller yelled, "Switch off!"

"Switch off!" replied Leek.

"Petrol on!"

"Petrol on!"

"Air closed!"

"Suck in!"

"Suck in!"

The mechanic rotated the propeller a couple of times.

"Contact!" yelled the mechanic.

"Contact!" Leek yelled back.

The mechanic swung the propeller hard then ducked away. The propeller turned a couple of times until the engine started to sputter, and then it roared to life. After a minute, the engine settled down to a steady rumble. The mechanic then pulled the chucks from the wheels, and Leek started taxiing the plane onto the grass field.

The plane started to pick up speed as it bumped down the grass runway. At first, the plane didn't seem to want to get into the air. The trees at the far end seemed to be coming up fast. Then, she suddenly lifted into the air and slowly started climbing into the sky.

Above the tree line, the pilot banked the plane and headed to No Man's Land. From the height, all he could see was the grey scar that cut across green and tan squares. Llewellyn had to admit the view was spectacular. Eventually, Leek made a gentle turn and headed back to the aerodrome. Llewellyn wondered idly how Leek knew where he was and where the aerodrome was.

The landing was the scariest part. The pilot pointed the nose down, and the ground seemed to be coming up to him pretty fast. At the last minute, the nose lifted and the plane bounced a couple of times until they finally rolled on the bumpy field.

Llewellyn straight-armed the cockpit when he saw the water tower at the end of the runway. The plane didn't seem to be slowing down, nor did Leek make any effort to turn. It finally stopped a few feet short.

When Leek finally shut down the engine he asked, "So what do you think?"

"I think I shit my pants," Llewellyn replied.

SEPTEMBER 5, 1917
READING ROOM, CANADIAN CONVALESCENT HOSPITAL,
BROMLEY HILL, KENT

Lieutenant-Colonel Spier came into the reading room in a rush. He looked harried when he took his seat at the head of the small table. Samantha sympathized with Spier, since he had taken command of the hospital only two weeks ago. Obviously, he wanted to make a good impression during his second senior staff meeting.

Samantha didn't know much about the lieutenant-colonel. He was nearly six feet tall, with brown hair and eyes. He had been a surgeon in Royal Mount, Quebec before he had volunteered two years ago. For the last six months he had been on sick leave due to pneumococcus.

"I see we're all here," Spier said as he glanced at her and the rest of the department heads seated in a semicircle in front of him. Behind him, through the window, Samantha could see patients harvesting vegetables from the garden. "Let's begin. Captain Leeds, if you may."

Captain Leeds was sitting on the far end. He was in his late thirties, balding, with a thick, waxed moustache. He spoke crisply. "We currently have 137 patients. In August, we admitted 175 patients, and we discharged 181. About fifty-five of our patients are here due to illness while the rest are battle wounds. And, since July we've seen a significant number of mustard gas cases."

Everyone heard Major Creighton sigh. He flushed pink in embarrassment when he realized that everyone heard him. "We're going to get a significant number more cases. I've been reading the latest reports from the Medical Research Committee on mustard gas."

Samantha cocked her head as she listened to him. She had heard about the Medical Research Committee that the British government had created a year before the war. It was set up to dispense funds for medical research, and their first project had been on tuberculosis. Since then, the committee had been funding research on war wounds and diseases.

"What they found was eighty percent of the men didn't have their masks on. No surprise there. Symptoms start to manifest three hours after exposure. The top symptoms in France were conjunctivitis, coughing, vomiting, dyspnea, and burns. Once the patients arrive in England, the symptoms are chest pains, coughing, conjunctivitis, burns, and gastritis pain," the major said.

"Have any new treatments been recommended?" asked Samantha.

Most of the treatments would be handled by her nurses and orderlies.

"The symptom that has been the most troublesome is conjunctivitis. They have tried a variety of treatments, but the most effective is to irrigate the patients' eyes four times a day with a saline solution. After which, a warm drop of castor oil is applied to each eye.

"As for the burns, if they are extensive, we have to immerse them into a warm bath of soda bicarbonate for about ten minutes. When the bandages are soaking wet, they're removed. Multiple treatments may be needed until the wounds stop blistering."

"What about those with minor burns?" Samantha asked as she considered the number of baths available and how much soda bicarbonate the quartermaster would need to requisition.

Creighton cranked his head to look at her. "A simple soaking of the bandages in the same solution was found effective. At least three treatments were needed."

"I'll see to requisitioning an ample supply," Major Meadows said when he saw her concern. He was in his late twenties, trim, with sandy brown hair and hazel eyes. "I'll add it to my weekly quota.

"As you are aware, the quartermaster from HQ was here last week, and they were pleased with the building. They found only a few things that needed repair."

"One of the items they were looking at was our mess and how we economize. They studied the diet sheets and summaries and our conservation efforts. We've put pails on each floor for each food type, fruits and vegetables in one and the meat scraps in the other. We empty them daily. The fruits and vegetables go for composting in our gardens. The meat scraps are used for tallow. We've also installed grease traps in all the kitchen sinks."

"Isn't that additional work imposed on our staff?" asked Spier. Samantha knew the CO was worried about staff burnout.

She glanced at Major Almond, the head of personnel, sitting two chairs over. The Quebecer was of medium height, slender, with a pencil-thin moustache. His black hair was slicked back. He replied with his slight French-Canadian accent, "We've added orderlies and nursing staff to our complement. With personnel shortages, it's been difficult. We've taken on locals to do some of the work. We've recently hired Miss Wilson, Holt, and Janes as drivers for our ambulances."

"If I may," Samantha interjected. "Complaints have been made by my nurses and the patients concerning orderlies Malcombe and Crane."

Almond frowned at her interruption. "I've spoken with them about their conduct."

"What conduct?" asked Spier.

"Both orderlies had displayed attitudes that the work they are required to perform was below their station. I've indicated my displeasure, and I have informed them if it continues I will be docking their pay. If it does, I will take more drastic action," Samantha stated.

There was concern on Spier's face. The major answered, "We've had very few issues. On the whole, discipline has been very good."

Spier acknowledged with a nod as he gave Samantha a glance. Samantha frowned with concern. She had to admit that ever since she came back from Russia, she had little tolerance for some of her staff's poor attitude. She knew she was getting a reputation as a hard taskmaster. She was also aware of the less flattering names she was being called behind her back.

"One other item," she said. "As you are aware, there is talk about a fall election back home. I would urge that political discussions be toned down. There had been a few occasions already where some of the patients' disagreements became quite heated."

Some of the remarks she had overheard were regarding the government's efforts to give the women the vote.

Spier pursed his lips. "I agree. We'll do what we can." Changing the topic, he asked, "How are we doing on our budget?"

Lieutenant Michaels, sitting next to her, raised his hand. "We've dispensed to the patients nearly forty-four pounds. To the staff at the hospital, we paid out thirty-five pounds. With the civilian workers' pay and sundries, it makes a total of ninety-seven pounds for the month of August. And the dry canteen earned a profit of twelve pounds and five shillings."

Spier made a note in his pad. "What have we been doing to keep the men's morale up?"

Samantha spoke up, since it fell under her preview. "In August, we had nearly sixteen entertainments in the hospital. Local bands and choirs have come to give musical entertainments. We've been looking at having moving pictures brought in. Also, part of the profits from the dry canteen are being used to buy books, puzzles, and games. As well, we have daily outings to places of interest in London and to the theatre. Then there are the sporting events. The Pill-Slingers are quite popular with the patients as well."

Spier gave a quick a smile at the name Pill-Slinger League before moving on to the next items in his agenda.

SEPTEMBER 9, 1917
65TH ARTILLERY HEADQUARTERS, LIÉVIN

Paul Ryan was standing just outside the 65th Artillery's dugout when he saw Reggie leading a work party pushing wheelbarrows filled with red bricks. Ryan saw they were dumping them into the back of a GS wagon.

"Sergeant," he called out. "May I have a word?"

"Yes, Brigade-Major," replied Reggie as he strolled over to him.

"What are you doing?" Ryan asked.

"We need bricks for the No. 1 gun pit. There's plenty here, so why not," Reggie said as he waved at the battle-damaged buildings that surrounded the square. It had once been a green space that was replaced by a mound full of shell holes under which the 65th had placed its headquarters dugout. Liévin had been once a prosperous coal-mining town with a population of nearly twenty thousand.

"Those aren't from the church over there?" Paul asked as he pointed to a building with its cross still standing on the top of the church's front wall.

"Good God, no! I'm no philistine," Reggie replied quickly.

"I haven't spoken with the mayor yet. He might not like it if we strip the town bare," Ryan pointed out.

"There's a mayor?"

"Yes, there is. And we have to be respectful," Ryan replied. "Until I talk with him, don't take any more bricks." Currently, most of the people in the town were the CEF. However, some of the residents, the braver or stubborn ones, were returning.

"Yes, Brigade-Major," Reggie answered in a tone that caused Ryan to wince. "You'd think they would be thankful we're cleaning up this mess," he muttered as he went back to his men.

Ryan sighed. He would have to buy him a drink later to smooth things over. He turned and pushed back the cloth screen used to prevent gas entering the dugout. He stopped at the communication room on his way to his office and asked the clerk on duty to find the mayor for him. The clerk said he would try and then mentioned he was needed in Masterley's office.

Colonel Masterley's small office was already taken up by two men. The colonel sitting across from Masterley had flashes on his shoulders, indicating he was with the Corps artillery. Ryan was already familiar with the forty-year-old gunner from Montreal, since he had accompanied him on his inspection of the 65th Artillery's wagon lines several days before.

"Colonel Masterley, Colonel Ambrose," Ryan said as he greeted them with a quick salute.

"Ah Lieutenant Ryan, pleasure seeing you again," Ambrose replied, then turned his attention back to Masterley. Ryan didn't say anything, since he had already briefed Masterley on his impression of the colonel and the faults he had uncovered during his inspection.

Ambrose cleared his throat then said, "On the whole your unit's horses seem to be in pretty good shape, all things considering."

"Considering what?" asked Masterley.

"The Corps wants to avoid a repeat of what happened last winter and would like to take steps to reduce the wastage. I've been tasked to make inspections and recommendations. Our horses are essential for the artillery's efficiency."

"Go on," Masterley prompted.

"Like I mentioned, your horses are in good shape. I was quite pleased that your grooms were not timekeepers, like they are in other batteries."

Ryan spoke up. "It takes about ten to fifteen minutes to groom them if they need it. It depends on the weather conditions and whether the horse has been worked. When they're muddy, it takes longer. You know as well as I do how sensitive they are when you're grooming their legs." Ryan had groomed many of the 65th's horses. He would start with a hoof pick to clean the hooves. Then, he would use a currycomb to loosen the hair and dirt, followed by a hard brush on their shoulders, flanks, and haunches. A soft brush was used on the sensitive parts such as the face and the legs. A wire brush was needed to remove tangles in the mane and tail. Then, to finish off, a light spray of water.

"I know that. My concern is you only have about eighty NCOs or ORs working in the wagon trains. This might be sufficient for the current establishment, but I've been informed that another forty to fifty horses are expected as reinforcements?" the colonel said, looking at Masterley expectantly.

Masterley made a slight grimace. "We've been shifting some of our batteries to new positions, so we've been using men from the wagon trains for our work parties when we need them. Since the reinforcements aren't expected for the next day or so, it's a good idea keep them busy. Idle hands and all that."

Ryan interjected, "Our normal complement for the wagon lines is about a hundred and twenty men. But with men on sick parade, on course, or on leave we tend to have about a hundred or so available. We prefer to have one man per horse when they're taking them to water, exercising them to keep them fit, and when feeding."

Colonel Ambrose looked pensive then said, "The lines are well arranged. There's very little likelihood the horses will spread infectious diseases from one herd to another. However, I'm recommending to Corps HQ that the men attached to the wagon trains no longer be used for work parties except in emergencies or making improvements to the wagon trains."

Ryan glanced at Masterley, who gave the colonel a quick nod.

"I've glanced over the reports prepared by the previous officer in charge. I've noticed there was a discrepancy in the fodder that had been received," Ambrose continued as he glanced at a page in a folder he was holding.

"That particular officer was transferred to another unit," Masterley said flatly. "He was required to check the fodder daily and had failed to do so."

"I've noticed among the junior officers a dislike for being assigned to command the wagon lines…"

Ryan chuckled, interrupting Colonel Ambrose, who gave him a sharp look. "It's true, Colonel, that some of the subalterns don't like the duty. Some feel it denies them the opportunity for promotion."

"Then don't you think it would be better to have an officer who is not trained as a gunner be in charge? Naturally, they would need to know horse management, since it is the essence of the job," Ambrose stated.

Masterley shook his head as he considered the pros and cons, but Ryan wasn't surprised by his response. "Here at the 65th Artillery, all the subalterns do a stint as the CO of the wagon lines. It allows me to see how they deal with their men, manage the horses, and the paperwork to make the unit run smoothly. There's more to being an artillery officer than simply pointing and pulling a lanyard. If they don't meet my expectations, they're transferred out. If they can't handle the wagon lines, they can't handle a battery. It's as simple as that."

"I see," replied the colonel. "I wish that the other units were so efficient."

"As for the fodder, I'm a bit surprised you have a full complement of chaff cutters," Ambrose said. When he didn't get an immediate reply, he added, "I understand they're to be treated as trench stores. To be left behind when the battery moves to a new location."

Ryan didn't glance at Masterley because he didn't want to confirm Colonel Ambrose's suspicions. It had been his suggestion that they keep the cutters that they used to cut straw or hay to mix with the horse feed. When they moved, they had frequently found the chaff cutters missing at each new wagon line position.

After a few more moments of silence, the colonel finally said, "Some of your vehicles need repair. As for the horse standings, I found some of the stalls can blind a horse."

"I had them removed as soon as you mentioned it," Ryan said.

"The horses' shoeing was quite good. I didn't see any problems," the colonel said as he snapped his folio closed. "I have to admit the 65th is one of the better units that I had the pleasure to inspect."

"I'm glad to hear that," replied Masterley. "We'll take your suggestions to heart, and we'll be making changes."

"Very good," Ambrose replied as he rose to his feet. Masterley rose as well and saluted. Ryan followed suit.

Once the colonel had left, Masterley said with relief, "That went pretty well,"

"We can't fix some of the things he mentioned until we move again," replied Ryan.

"We might be."

"Passchendaele?" asked Ryan.

"That's what it looks like. Things aren't going well there," replied Masterley.

"Damn, why are we always the ones being called upon?" complained Ryan. When Masterley raised an eyebrow, Ryan sighed. "Yeah, I know. We're the best."

CHAPTER 20

Borden frowned at Arthur Meighen and Dr. John Reid, who were sitting in front of his desk. It was early Friday afternoon, and they had wanted to speak with him before Question Period at three. From the reports, his MPs had been pounding the Grits in the House quite thoroughly so far today.

"Do you want to wait for Clifford? I'm meeting with him before I go into the House," Borden suggested.

Meighen and Dr. Reid glanced at each other. Dr. Reid was a former medical doctor who had been educated at Queen's and at Trinity College. He had practiced medicine for a short time, but his principal interest had been politics. Sir John A. Macdonald had asked him to run in the Granville riding in 1906, and he had won. Borden had trusted him enough to appoint Reid as his minister of customs, especially since that department generated the bulk of the country's finances.

"We wanted to talk to you before our meeting with Sifton," Meighen replied tersely.

"Oh," Borden replied. He suspected one of the reasons they wanted to talk to him were the charges that Liberal MPs Power and Tobin had made that Sifton was against conscription. Borden knew Sifton was always a sly one, and a superb backroom operator. He suspected, when he had arrived in Ottawa last spring from England, that he had sounded out some of the Liberals on their stances concerning conscription. He might not have actually said he was anticonscription but left them with the impression he was on their side.

"We think further negotiations with the Liberals are useless," Meighen said flatly.

Borden glanced at each man in turn.

"I'm in agreement. I've been frustrated with my talks with Sifton's brother, Calder, and Crerar. They've been refusing to commit, and their demands keep changing," said Reid. Borden's frown deepened at the mention of Clifford Sifton's brother, the premier of Alberta. "And they fully expect to be made cabinet ministers," Reid added.

Borden snorted. "Clifford's been hinting at a Senate seat."

"No surprise. We knew the Liberals wouldn't come in while Bob was in the cabinet," Meighen stated, referring to Robert Rogers, his former minister of public works. The Liberals hated Rogers, and Rogers's feelings were mutual.

"Don't forget that after Rogers resigned, they then wanted you to resign," Reid said, recalling the Conservative caucus several weeks prior.

"Let's face it, Sifton hasn't much to show for all his effort in the last three months," Meighen said. "He went to the July Liberal convention that they held in Toronto. Before he went, he said they were likely to support our efforts on conscription and union government. He also said with Premier Rowat's support that it was practically a done deal.

"Look what happened. They voted against extending Parliament, against a coalition, and against conscription. And they called for an election running under Laurier's banner."

"Don't forget what the Liberal press has been writing about you," Reid said.

"I'm aware," Borden said curtly. To say they were unflattering was an understatement.

"In August, he then went to Winnipeg, where the western Liberals had their convention," Meighen continued. "They were supposed to be amenable to our positions. Look what came out of that."

"I know," replied Borden with a deep frown. "Considering the vicious debates in the House and the Senate, it makes me more convinced than ever that we need a union government. And it's one of the reasons I've made the decision to apply closure to get our bills through."

Reid interrupted, "My concern is that they're playing a deep game. Even if we manage to convince a sizeable number of Liberals to join us or at least intimate they'll join us, I fear they'll abandon us once you call an election. Especially if Laurier has a better chance of winning. If that happens, we'll be at a great disadvantage, your cabinet will be disorganized, our best men may not be available, and our election machine will be in disarray."

"I agree," Meighen stated. "It looks to me we lost Quebec. That means we need Ontario and the Western provinces to win. We may pick up a few seats in the East, but the Liberals have great strength there."

Borden's face was grim. "I understand. Things seem dire at the moment, but I still want you to continue your negotiations."

Both men eventually nodded. They had tried to change Borden's mind, but he had refused to change their marching orders for better or for worse.

SEPTEMBER 18, 1917
ABERDEEN PAVILION, LANSDOWNE PARK, OTTAWA

"Prime Minister, these are some German helmets and body armour our men found after they captured Vimy Ridge," said Arthur Doughty as he pointed to the display.

"I like the one with the white horsehair," said John Doherty, who was standing beside Borden as they examined the exhibit. Set on a table draped with a German flag, a spread-winged imperial eagle on a white background, were various Pickelhaube helmets, caps, and fur hats. One of the fur hats had a skull head insignia attached to its front. Behind the headgear, on stands, were two gleaming steel cuirasses. A number of sheathed German cavalry sabres were hanging on the wall behind the table.

"It's quite impressive. May I?" asked Borden as he glanced at the Dominion archivist and keeper of records. The man was in his late fifties, with a trim moustache and thinning dark hair. He didn't have many dealings with Arthur Doughty, who headed the National Archives on Sussex Street.

"Of course," Doughty replied as he picked up the helmet with the white horsehair and handed it to Borden.

Borden was impressed by its workmanship. The white plumage was held in place by a brass tube that protruded nearly five inches high from the boiled leather that had been dyed and lacquered to a deep glossy black. Brass buckles attached to a leather chinstrap sat on the front edge just below a brass imperial eagle fixed to the helmet's front.

"The spike is removable so they can insert the plumage for ceremonial purposes," Doughty said as he picked up one of the Pickelhaubes and unscrewed the spike to show how it came out.

"I see," said Borden as he handed the helmet to his justice minister so he could take a closer look. He wasn't surprised by Doughty's enthusiasm. In April, he had been given a lieutenant-colonelcy to lead a team of historians and archivists to England and France to conduct a survey of the Corps documents and records. The archivists wanted to make sure future historians could document Canada's war effort. And in July Doughty had hammered out an agreement with the War Office that the Canadians would have first pick of any war trophies captured by the Canadian Corps.

The war exhibit was divided into two themes. The Canadian side displayed recruitment posters, especially the prominent one with Lord Kitchener's image. He couldn't help the flare of anger as he recalled the pamphlet John Ewart had just published. In it, he had criticized him and the Canadians' devotion to the British Empire. Ewart had always been an ardent Canadian, but Borden felt he had gone too far this time. He had tried to call him, but Borden had refused to talk to him. The rest of the hall was filled with unit insignia, military equipment such as web gear, Ross and Lee-Enfield rifles, Vickers and Lewis machine guns, and photos of Canadians at the front. Doughty managed to obtain a Stokes mortar as well as 18-and 60-pounder shells.

The German half displayed the war trophies that the men of the Corps had captured. Along with German flags and insignias, there were German uniforms, Mauser rifles, an MG-08 machine gun, a *minenwerfer,* and steel masks the Germans used to protect their faces from flying bullets.

"Has attendance been good?" Borden asked.

"It has," replied Doughty. "We made nearly a hundred dollars yesterday." There was a twenty-five-cent entrance fee to the exhibit. "And we're having some of the students from the local schools come in to see the exhibit today."

Borden cracked a smile. While Doughty had been born in England and had studied at Eton, he had taken a great interest in the Dominion's National Archives and in promoting Canadian history.

"I'm glad to hear that. The students will certainly enjoy your exhibit," replied Borden.

"Thank you, sir," Doughty said. He paused then said, "I understand you have a meeting with Professor Shortt?"

"Yes, its later this morning. I want to discuss with him his duties as the head of the Historical Documents Publication," replied Borden.

"Of course, Prime Minister," replied Doughty. Borden knew he had been pushing to have Adam Shortt head the board, since it reported to the National Archives.

"Very well, carry on, my office will inform you what the professor and I have decided," stated Borden as he turned to leave the pavilion.

"I must say I enjoyed your exhibit very much," said Doherty with a smile, just before turning to follow Borden.

★ ★ ★

"The franchise bill has finally come back from the Senate," Borden said to Doherty as a squad of signallers was double-timing across the front of their car, heading to their classes. The Department of Militia and Defence was using Lansdowne as a signal training depot. Once the squad had past, Borden's driver put the car in gear and headed up Bank Street to the Hill.

It looked like it was going to be another gorgeous day. He would have loved to order his driver to skip the Hill and head for the Royal Ottawa across the river. There weren't going to be many days like this left. Golf season would be ending in a month's time, when the temperature became frosty.

Borden's thoughts were interrupted when Doherty asked, "Do you want to meet with Lougheed and Meighen to discuss the amendments?"

"Yes, the only time I can see them is just before Question Period. After my meeting with Professor Shortt, I have a two-hour meeting at ten with the Military Service Committee to discuss the military service bill, which I want strictly enforced. Colonel Ballantyne is coming up from Montreal to discuss the political situation in Quebec and our prospects, so I'll need to talk with him," Borden said. Ballantyne was a well-known Montreal businessman and a moderate Liberal. Then with a sigh, "Then there's the French-Canadian delegation that wants me to appoint the pope to my cabinet."

Doherty made a humorous snort.

Borden continued, "Have you seen the latest amendments the Senate made to the franchise bill?" The Liberals in the Senate had tried to gut it by removing the section disfranchising those born in enemy countries. And they had added text expanding the women's vote to include all women.

"Mostly corrections and clarifications of our intent. We had to clarify that officers cannot be discharged. They can only resign or be dismissed from the service."

"Good, send the latest draft so I can have it on hand when I meet with Lougheed and Meighen."

"I've also received the latest Senate amendments concerning the judges bill. I don't agree with their suggestions concerning the judges' pensions. I'm going to make a nonconcurrence motion and have it sent to committee for further work."

Borden frowned. "I was planning to prorogue Parliament after the franchise bill is given royal ascent.

Doherty sighed. When Parliament was prorogued, all legislation in the House and Senate died. When a new session started, bills could be reinstated at the same state before prorogation, if there was unanimous consent. Doherty knew once the current session was prorogued, Borden would dissolve Parliament and call an election. That meant all the current bills would have to be reintroduced and go through the entire legislative process again.

"The judges aren't going to be happy," Doherty pointed out. The bill concerned the salaries of the Superior Court judges in Saskatchewan and Ontario.

"We can't have that," Borden said. "But I can't overstate the importance of getting the franchise bill through third reading and royal assent."

"Understood," replied Doherty. "I'll see what I can do to push the judges' bill through over the next few days."

"Are you still planning to go to Echo Beach next week?"

"That's my plan. I'm tired. I need some rest before the election campaign starts in earnest," answered Borden as his car finally drove up to the East Block on Parliament Hill.

"Don't we all," replied Doherty.

CHAPTER 21

"Your men did well today," remarked Captain Armstrong as he shifted to make room for Lieutenant-Colonel Llewellyn at the table in the marquee being used as the mess tent. As Llewellyn set his tray on the table, he couldn't help noticing they had a clear view of the rifle range. He wasn't surprised. The captain was the chief range officer for the Canadian Corps Rifle meet.

Llewellyn had driven nearly two and a half hours from his headquarters at Liévin to Pernes with the squad he had picked for the four-day event. Nearly 1,800 men from the Corps were competing for medals and shields at the Canadian Corps' Training School's rifle range.

"I'm surprised Duval still has his stripes," Armstrong said with a London accent. He had been born there before emigrating to Canada. "I would've thought he'd lost them by now."

Llewellyn gave him a grin. The school's chief sniping instructor was nearly six feet, with a fair complexion, a moustache, blue eyes, and below his Glengarry cap, black hair. Armstrong was dressed in the kit of the 48th Battalion: a khaki jacket and a pleated kilt that fell above knee length black socks. "He hasn't exactly been working hard on keeping them as he has been on his sniping skills."

"He and his Ross are in third place behind privates Harris and Brierly. He's just two points off. They're tied at thirty-two," Armstrong pointed out.

"The weather's too good for him," replied Llewellyn. "He likes a wee bit of wind." It had been a beautiful day, with very little wind and plenty of sunshine. It looked like it would be the same tomorrow. The last of the competitions would be over by noon, after which the ceremony would be held to hand out medals and shields.

Armstrong chuckled in amusement. Llewellyn knew the calibre of the snipers at the meet was quite high. He glanced to where the snipers had been placed for the competition. Boxes of .303 ammunition were neatly stacked nearby. Each sniper team had brought their own to make sure it came from batches, from experience, that had proven reliable. They didn't trust the ammo provided by the school.

Both men looked up when they saw some of the men stiffen and rise to salute. They instinctively did the same before they saw Lieutenant-General Currie enter the mess tent. Currie waved them down as he started to stop at each table to chat with the officers. When he spotted Llewellyn, he gave him a smile as his pear-shaped body approached their table. "Colonel Llewellyn, Captain Armstrong," he greeted.

"Pleasure to see you again, General," Llewellyn said.

"General, sir," said Captain Armstrong.

"How are your men faring?" Currie asked.

"Not very well I'm afraid, sir," Llewellyn replied reluctantly.

"True," Currie answered with a shrug. "The 1st Canadian Light Horse has done extremely well in the Battalion and Company competitions. However, you're still in the running for the remaining meets."

"Yes, General. I'm sure that my men will distinguish themselves," Llewellyn replied confidently.

"I'm sure they will," Currie agreed. Llewellyn sighed. He had men entered, besides the sniping competition, in the snap shooting, the rapid fire, the revolver, the falling plates, the Lewis machine gun, and the rifle grenades events. Besides these there were also the team events: platoon, company, and battalion.

The platoon cup had been the most interesting. He had been impressed by the 1st Battalion. He had watched their lieutenant lead his four sections, one a Lewis gun, as they attacked the course. His men, led by Lieutenant Bainbridge, did well, but they couldn't match the practiced smoothness as they advanced with the Lewis providing covering fire. He knew his men weren't going to like him when they got back to base.

For now, he was leaving them to enjoy themselves at the local estaminets. The winners would be bragging, and the losers would be drowning their sorrows. He knew a few fights would break out, but he hoped none would be serious.

"I must say I'm most impressed how efficiently you've organized the range, Captain. My compliments," Currie said.

"Thank you, General," Armstrong replied, beaming.

After a quick nod, Currie headed to the next table.

"The range does look good," Llewellyn said as he took a bit of his stew. He was surprised at how good it tasted. He was also looking forward to the whiskey and the cigars the school had set aside for the officers. He wasn't about to ask where they got them from.

"Five hundred yards," Armstrong replied. "We've made improvements since the last time you were here."

"I've noticed. Everything looks more permanent now with the huts. No more tents," Llewellyn replied. Except for the temporary tents erected for the meet, most of the students were billeted in Pernes. There had been room for a hundred officers, twenty-four hundred other ranks, and three hundred horses.

Llewellyn remembered when Lieutenant-General Byng established the school last year. The school's first-year anniversary was coming up. It was something Llewellyn didn't want to think about. The school had syllabuses to train officers and NCOs in becoming instructors in drill, bayonet fighting, physical training, musketry, and trench warfare. However, one of the key purposes of the school was to get officers and men from the various units to meet, to talk, get to know each other, and to learn from each other. It was very easy for the men to get stuck in their own units and not talk with the regiment next to them. That was why all the classes had a mixture of officers and men from each of the divisions.

"Don't remind me," Armstrong replied. "I've spent quite a few nights in leaky tents. We've put up classrooms, mess halls, and a drill shed for wet weather. We even have a theatre now for concert parties like the one this evening."

"I hope it'll be a good show," replied Llewellyn. He wondered from which division the concert party was coming. Some of the singers and musicians in the concert parties rivalled some of the professional entertainment groups that toured the front areas. "It'll keep the men entertained."

Armstrong nodded. "We've nearly finished the 13th course and will be starting the 14th next week." He paused then asked, "How have you been finding the latest recruits?"

"Much improved, actually. It's taken Turner a while, but they've improved their knowledge of squad, section, and platoon drill. Their musketry is good, but they've been training on the Ross in England. We need a few days to get them used to the Lee-Enfield. Their bombing is good, and so is their trench work."

"I've been seeing the same thing," replied Armstrong. "Makes my job a little easier."

"They're an eager bunch that I like. Could use more of them," Llewellyn said.

"Don't we all. That new conscription bill the government is passing will help," said Armstrong.

"I hope so," Llewellyn replied, trying to keep his tone neutral. He was of two minds about Borden's conscription bill. Corps needed reinforcements, but he had seen some of the conscripts in the British and French armies. He preferred eager volunteers instead of sullen conscripts. Either way, he didn't expect them to start arriving until spring of next year at the earliest.

"I might be sending some students your way."

"Oh," Armstrong said as he glanced at Llewellyn.

"They don't seem to know how to salute properly," Llewellyn said. "The hand is not quite in the correct position when addressing an officer passing them on the street."

Armstrong chuckled. "It does seem to be a recurring problem. One we haven't quite been able to solve."

SEPTEMBER 30, 1917
CANADIAN CONVALESCENT HOSPITAL, BROMLEY HILL, KENT

"That wasn't properly cleaned," Samantha stated as she pointed to the offending spot. It was obvious only a cursory pass of the mop had been done in the corner.

"Yes, ma'am," replied Sergeant Powell with an embarrassed look. He had missed it when he did his inspection. Samantha was sure his squad would hear about it. "It will be done right away."

"Otherwise, everything looks good," Samantha said as she gave the room a final look. The smell of disinfectant was quite strong in the former hotel suite. It once had been an expensive one. While they had tried to cover them, she could see where the fixtures had been removed to protect them. It was now filled with ten white metal beds, five on each side, with fresh linen piled neatly on top of the bare mattresses. "Once the beds are made, the patients can be moved back in."

"Yes, ma'am," the sergeant repeated. "It'll be a bit crowded, but we'll manage."

"Some of the tents were in pretty bad shape," Samantha said. "I'm surprised that they lasted this long."

"The government likes to economize," replied the sergeant with a shrug of his burly shoulder. "We've been trying to get them replaced for months."

Samantha had to look up at the sergeant to acknowledge him. Powell was a foot taller than she was. He was useful in moving patients when needed.

"The weather was pretty good this September," Samantha said. "We didn't get too much rain."

"Sure," he answered, "but it was only sixty today, and it's dropping to at least forty tonight."

"I know," Samantha said. The hospital's CO had decided to transfer the patients in the worst tents to the main building. The rest of the patients would be moved in when the cold really started to bite. The hospital staff had taken advantage of the transfers to clean the wards. Some of them really needed a good top-to-bottom cleansing.

"I'm going downstairs to check to see whether the men in the tents have sufficient blankets for the night," Samantha said as she headed for the corridor. "I'll be back to do a final inspection once the patients have settled in."

"Yes, ma'am," he answered.

In the corridor she spotted Major Creighton exit the corridor that led to the VD ward. The ward was isolated and in the far wing of the hospital. Looking up from the notes he was reading, he said, "You're working late tonight."

"No sleep for the wicked," Samantha replied with a smile.

Creighton raised an eyebrow and glanced behind him. "Some of the men weren't happy with the medical board."

"I heard the ruckus," replied Samantha. The men in the venereal disease ward weren't the happiest patients to begin with. The medical officers had orders to randomly inspect the men for VD. The men hated those inspection parades. If they were diagnosed with a sexually transmitted disease, they were relieved of their duties and ordered to take treatment at an army hospital until they were cured. Treatments were injections of Salvarsan serum until a Wasserman blood test indicated negative results. What made it worse than their confinement to a VD ward was their pay was stopped. If they were sending family money, they would be suffering for several months until the soldier was cleared for duty.

"I'll have to put some men on guard duty to make sure they don't make a run for it," the doctor said with a frown.

"The last time one of them tried, he broke a leg in three places when he jumped out of the third-floor window," Samantha pointed out.

"Don't remind me," he replied sourly. "I don't really want to put bars on the windows and turn it into an actual prison ward."

Kind of late for that, thought Samantha. Most of her nurses didn't like working the VD ward. They felt the men eyeing them gave them the creeps. Samantha was sure there were a few. The rest, she suspected, just wanted some human contact, since there were severe restrictions on their activities and on visitors.

"I'll let my nurses know. I don't think it would be wise for them to be on the ward for the next day or two."

"Whatever you think best, Matron," Creighton replied crisply. "So where are you off to?"

"I was going out to check whether the men in the tents had sufficient blankets for the night. It's going to be chilly," she replied.

"I'll come down with you," said Creighton. "I want to see on how the transfer is coming along."

When they stepped out of the rear exit of the hospital near the cafeteria, they couldn't see much past the tents that glowed with electric light bulbs that had been strung inside them. It was a full moon, and the stars sparkled as the sparse clouds drifted past. In the distance, they could see the glow of London. Some of the men were ambling to the hotel carrying sheets and blankets. Others were sitting on lawn chairs chatting while having a smoke, some were playing cards, and a few were reading papers and letters in the dim light. They could hear two men arguing over a chessboard.

Suddenly, searchlights started piercing the night sky to the south. Pricks of light appeared as antiaircraft guns opened up. In the quiet stillness of the night, they heard the sound of the shells detonating and the roar of aeroplane engines. Samantha looked up, but she couldn't see anything yet in the night sky.

"Anyone have a torch?" shouted the doctor when the lights suddenly turned off.

"Here you go, Major," said a voice behind a flashlight that suddenly appeared.

When Creighton pointed his torch at the person that had given it to him, Samantha saw that it was Sergeant Powell. "We received word of a German air raid. Figured we'll need torches to get the patients inside where it will be safe," the sergeant said. After a pause, he muttered, "Relatively safe."

201

"Good man," Samantha said when he handed her a torch as well. Ever since she'd been back in London, everyone was terrified of the Gotha and Staaken aeroplane bomb raids. They had embarrassed the British government. To protect London, the government responded by creating an air defence system of observers, searchlights, antiaircraft guns, and a squadron of Sopwith Camels to intercept the German bombers before they could drop their loads.

"Let's start getting the men inside," ordered Creighton.

"We really don't want new patients," Samantha said. The bombers weren't especially accurate, although she didn't think they would be primary targets. Sometimes the Germans dropped their loads just to get rid of them.

"Matron!"

"Yes, Major."

"I want you to inspect the tents to make sure we haven't left anyone behind," Creighton ordered.

"Yes, sir," Samantha replied as she used her torch to light her way to the tents.

CHAPTER 22

"Gentlemen, I'm glad you could come," said Sir Robert Borden when he entered the small meeting room just off his office. Through the window he could see the Château Laurier's green copper roof lit by the late afternoon sun.

"It's our honour and pleasure, Prime Minister," replied Arthur Sifton as he rose from his chair. Unlike his younger brother, the Alberta Liberal premier was clean-shaven and had long since gone bald, with only a thin fringe of grey hair.

"I hope the train wasn't too tiring," Borden said as he shook hands with the three other men who had also risen to their feet. The first was James Calder, the Liberal premier of Saskatchewan. Calder was heavyset, in his early forties, bald with a thick fringe of hair and moustache. Next was the Manitoba attorney-general, Albert Hudson. He was in his early forties, bald with a thick fringe of hair and moustache. The odd man out, since he hadn't been elected to a public office, was Thomas Crerar, the leader of the powerful Manitoba Grain Growers Association. He was the youngest man in the room and the only one, besides Borden, with a full head of hair and a neatly trimmed moustache.

"It was pleasant enough with the trees changing colours," Calder replied.

Borden wondered if he were alluding to this afternoon's discussions. A few weeks ago, the prospects of having this meeting had been dim. Now, it seemed that his gamble was beginning to pay off.

He needed these four men and their political machines to solidify his prospects in the west. He had already made concessions in the *Military Service Act*; farm workers would not be conscripted, and in the *Wartime Elections Act*, alien-born voters would be disenfranchised to accommodate their demands.

"I didn't notice. I was getting work done." Sifton replied. The Siftons were well known as hard men and hard-working.

"Gentlemen, I asked you to meet with me to discuss appointments to my cabinet," stated Borden as he took a seat at the head of the rectangular table.

"Of course, Prime Minister," replied Sifton. "We have suggestions for good, solid men suitable for cabinet posts." The other three men nodded in agreement.

Borden knew picking cabinet ministers was not always about selecting the best man for the job, although he wished that really were the case. Selecting a cabinet was a delicate complex dance between rewarding party stalwarts and regional party interests. To this mix, he needed to add Liberal ministers to the cabinet. He had already heard complaints about the two Liberals he had appointed the week before. He had appointed Hugh Guthrie, who had crossed the floor as his solicitor-general, and he had made another Liberal, Lieutenant-Colonel Ballantyne, his public works minister.

Ballantyne's appointment was the one he got the most complaints on. Public Works was one of the most coveted ministries because of patronage. His caucus didn't want Ballantyne to load up the department with Liberals, especially since they had spent the last six years getting rid of them.

"We would like to suggest General Mewburn for militia and defence department. He would be running under a Liberal banner," said Sifton.

Borden raised an eyebrow. Major-General Mewburn was currently the adjutant-general for the army based in Canada. At the start of the war, as a lieutenant-colonel, he had commanded the Royal Regiment of Canada in Hamilton. Since then, he had been promoted twice. Borden was also aware the general had lost his second son, Lieutenant John Mewburn, in action the year prior. The prime minister suppressed a sigh. He personally knew too many families who had suffered a loss in this damn war.

The one thing he liked about Mewburn was that he was a quiet and efficient officer. He did have a concern how Gwatkin would react when he was informed his subordinate would become his boss.

"It's a possibility," said Borden reluctantly. "Kemp's been doing a fine job as the minister of militia and defence, and I don't want to lose his experience."

"What do you suggest?" asked Calder.

"I was thinking of moving Kemp to become the minister for the Overseas Force," Borden replied.

"What about Perley?" asked Hudson.

"He would remain as high commissioner," replied Borden. He was sure Perley would be pleased his workload would be cut in half, since he had been complaining how overworked he was. However, he would be unhappy that he would no longer be a cabinet minister. The Canadian High Commission in England was not a cabinet post, although Perley had been pushing to make it one.

Borden noticed that the four men didn't look at each other. While he had need of them, he did have the advantage that critical departments were still under his control. The question was which of the lesser departments would he be willing to trade for their support.

"That is a possibility," Crerar remarked. "As for the Agriculture Department, we were considering..."

Borden nodded and shifted in his chair to be more comfortable. He knew they would be at it for the rest of the evening as they hammered out who would get what.

OCTOBER 13, 1917
65TH ARTILLERY WAGON LINES, CITÉ DE CAUMONT

It wasn't difficult for Acting Captain Ryan to find the estaminet on the outskirts of Cité de Caumont. Actually, it was located on a crossroad that led to Liévin to the north and Angres to the west. It was his job to know, in case they received a SOS, and they would have to move the batteries into action. It also helped he could hear the music, the buzz of voices, and the laughter when he was a couple of hundred yards out.

Parked in the field next to the ancient farmhouse, constructed of thick stone, were a couple of lorries and GS wagon with draughts still tethered to them. There were also a couple of bicycles and motorcycles leaning against its walls.

For a moment, he thought he should've sent a runner instead of going himself. He had been working in his office all day, and he needed a break before he headed off to bed. The estaminet was designated for the lower ranks, and they didn't take kindly with senior officers when they interfered with their fun. He had seen the MPs hovering nearby in case the fun got out of hand. He knew, from experience, that several would need to be claimed by their COs in the morning.

When he pulled the door open, he was hit by a wall of grey smoke. His eyes watered, and he began coughing until his lungs stopped protesting. He glanced around the large, open room. A heavy, thick-necked man tended a makeshift bar in the back. In the middle, there was a scattering of mix-and-match tables and chairs that were all occupied. In the corner, there was a trio playing a fiddle, a harmonica, and a piano.

He wasn't surprised most of the men in the bar were gunners. The men tended to stick together. The 65th, along with the rest of the 2nd Brigade field artillery, was coming off their first real rest since January. They were going to be back at it soon. That was one of the reasons he was here.

He spotted Reggie sitting at a table playing poker with several other sergeants from the 65th. As he stepped farther into the room, he got stiff glances from the men.

"Sergeant, may I have a word?" he said when he reached Reggie's table.

"Yes, sir," Reggie said as he placed an empty beer glass on top of his cards.

As he rose, Ryan glanced at the blue ribbon with red and white strips pinned to his left chest. He had put Reggie's name in for the Military Medal in last August when he helped save an 18-pounder during the attack on Hill 70. He had been pleased that it finally came through.

Major-General Macdonell had pinned the ribbon on Reggie's chest at the ceremony held in a field near the wagon lines ten days ago. The entire artillery brigade had been assembled for a divine service, officiated by the Reverend Lieutenant-Colonel Scott, the 1st Division's most senior chaplain, to remember friends and comrades they had lost on Hill 70. The weather seemed appropriate for the service: dull and grey.

After the mass, ribbons had been pinned by the major-general on the chests of all the NCOs and ORs who had been awarded decorations in the past year. After they had been handed out, the brigade had marched past the general in columns of four as the Royal Canadian Regiment band played "The British Grenadier," one of the artillery's standard tunes. He was pleased his men had sung the official version when they marched past the 1st Division's GOC, not the unofficial version of the song with verses referring to dripping pricks.

Ryan was glad to get out of the smoke-filled room into the fresh air. "Sorry to interrupt your game, Reggie."

"Not a problem, I was down two francs. Hopefully, my luck will change," he replied. "What can I do you for?"

"I've gotten orders. We'll be moving," Ryan stated.

"I knew it couldn't last. Where are we heading?" Reggie replied as he ran his hand through his hair. "I hope the billets will be better?"

Ryan nodded. While the horse lines had been good when they took over, the billets had been in poor condition. At least Reggie wasn't complaining about the work they had done to bring them into shape so their replacements would enjoy them.

"North."

"Flanders! Shit!" muttered Reggie. The rumours floating around the brigade indicated things weren't going well up north.

"Looks like it," Ryan replied. "Let the men know they need to make good use of any remaining leave. We'll have to start preparing for the move."

"The usual?" asked Reggie.

"Yes, we'll need to reduce our baggage. We'll have to take a few days to harden the horses for the trip north," Ryan replied.

"We're marching instead of using the rails?" asked Reggie.

"So far as I know, we're marching. We both know we're going to have problems with transport, so we'll have to prepare for it. I know the men will grouse, but the colonel and I are depending on the NCOs to help maintain march discipline."

"The general's inspection still set?" asked Reggie.

"That's been cancelled," replied Ryan. Major-General Macdonell had been scheduled to inspect their wagon lines next Thursday.

Reggie sighed in relief. Ryan knew it would have been too much preparing for a move and inspection at the same time.

"Well, I better let you go back to your game."

"Okay, but I think I'm going to get drunk tonight. Whether I win or lose," Reggie answered as he turned to head back into the estaminet.

"Yeah, but don't get so drunk that I need to come and get you from the red caps," Ryan ordered.

"I'll do my best," Reggie replied as he pulled the door open, allowing grey smoke to swirl out.

Ryan wasn't too sure from Reggie's tone if he would comply.

OCTOBER 16, 1917
CANADIAN CONVALESCENT HOSPITAL, BROMLEY, KENT

"My hands are starting to cramp up," Samantha complained to Jody Boydell, her assistant matron. She was sitting beside her in the empty massage ward. It was nearly dusk, and the last rays of sun could be seen through the large bay windows behind them.

"Like I've been telling you. You need the right techniques. Less thumbs and fingers. More body weight to avoid becoming sore in the morning, like Gabrielle who today reported for sick parade."

"It's a bit more than that," replied Samantha. When Jody gave her a curious look, she said, "Haven't you noticed she's been snappish of late, and she's been showing signs of fatigue? When I checked her file, I found she hasn't taken much leave."

"She didn't say anything to me. I thought we were on good terms," replied Jody.

"The good ones usually don't," replied Samantha. "I was thinking of suggesting she take a two- or three-week leave to get some rest and to refresh. Otherwise, I worry if she doesn't, she might suffer a breakdown."

Jody frowned. The work in the wards took its toll on the nursing staff. "We're already short-staffed as it is," she replied as she flexed her stubby hands. Jody was short and stout, in her mid-thirties, with reddish-brown hair below her nursing veil.

"I know. I lost three nurses when they were transferred out last week," Samantha replied. "We're to take four nurses on strength next week."

"Any with massage and electrical therapy certificates?" she asked with a touch of hope in her eyes. Jody ran the massage and electrical therapy ward located on the second floor of the hospital. They were resting in front of the large bay windows that faced the gardens behind the hotel. It had been a long day of treating patients. During the day, the windows provided plenty of light for the ward. When she came in this morning, she had found Jody and three other nurses attending patients lying on one of the four massage tables set up in the room. A couple of the men had been fitted with Bristow coil machines that generated electrical currents to stimulate the leg muscles to avoid atrophy. One of the patients was rebuilding their muscle strength using a massage machine, a cross between an upright medieval rack and guillotine, set on the opposite wall. Waiting for their sessions to start or for one of the nurses to attend to them there had been another half-dozen or so patients in chairs near the windows.

Samantha had recognized the patient Jody had been massaging when she came in. The blue patient's jacket set on the stool next to the table didn't have any patches, but she knew Corporal Hasting was from the RCR regiment. He had been diagnosed with shell shock. He couldn't make it through the night without disturbing nightmares causing him to yell and scream. Massage therapy, they found, allowed him to fall into a peaceful sleep for a few hours.

Jody had put her to work on the patients who needed light massages to get the blood circulating, getting and setting heat pads, and unhooking the Bristow coil machines when the patient's time was up.

"I might have to put in for leave myself," Jody said.

Samantha tried to stifle the look of alarm she gave Jody. She didn't want to lose her, since finding a replacement for her was going to be very difficult. Jody was one of the few nurses who had a certificate in massage and electrical therapy. The CAMC had, like the Imperials, underestimated the number of casualties that needed convalescence. However, the Imperials had been able to draw on the therapists from the Almeric Paget Military Massage Corps. Almeric Paget, the 1st Baron Queenborough, industrialist and Conservative, MP had created and funded it until the War Office recognized its value and took it over. The Massage Corps provided massage therapists to all the British Hospitals. Where the CAMC shared facilities with them, the CAMC took advantage of their services.

At the Canadian hospitals, Matron Macdonald had insisted that all the massage therapists be certified as nurses first. Samantha had disagreed with that, since she had seen how valuable the therapy was. But until Matron Macdonald changed her mind, there wasn't much she could do.

"For how long?" asked Samantha.

"Only for a week," replied Jody. "I think that Janice can handle things while I'm gone."

"Okay," Samantha said with a sigh of relief. "Put in your request, and I'll approve it. Once you've come back, I'm going to ask you to train some of the nurses." She liked to rotate her nurses between wards and duties so they could gain experience and stay fresh.

"I heard a training course is starting up in December over in Buxton?" Jody stated.

"That's true. The Granville Hospital is putting on a three-week course," Samantha stated. When she heard Jody murmur a "hmm," Samantha glanced at her with concern. Jody could teach the course there.

"That's good news. We need more massage therapists," Jody replied and then grinned at Samantha. "You should consider taking the course."

"I haven't given it much thought," replied Samantha.

"You should."

"Oh why?"

"I don't think I'll be out of work," Jody said as she shrugged. "These men will still need my care when the war is over."

Samantha looked thoughtful for a moment. The last patients they had boarded and invalided to Canada would need more therapy when they arrived back home. She also hadn't given much thought to what she and James would do after the war. "It's something to consider," she replied.

CHAPTER 23

"Goddamn it! I can't fight the Boche with idents. I must have guns!" Lieutenant-General Currie exploded at Major-General Buckle.

There were shocked faces on the senior officers that crowded the long conference room in the Casino. General Plumer stared at Currie with his watery blue eyes for a moment then said sharply, "General Currie, don't lose your temper!"

Currie wrestled to contain his emotions as he leaned his bulk back into his chair. He wasn't pleased to be back in Flanders, especially since his impression was that the Flanders campaign had run its course. He would have been happier staying in the Lens Sector training and rebuilding his Corps.

This wasn't the first time he had lost his temper. He and General Horne got into a heated argument when the First Army's GOC had dropped by his headquarters in early October to inform him Haig wanted to move two of his divisions to Passchendaele and that they would be attached to General Gough's Fifth Army. Currie had made it quite clear he would never serve under Gough, since he didn't like Gough's style. Either the entire Corps went to Passchendaele or they would have to find someone else to lead the Corps.

He had been somewhat mollified when the orders came through that the Corps would be attached to General Plumer's Second Army in their old stomping grounds in Ypres. He had to admit he still had suspicions that the Imperials wanted to break up the Canadians. The Corps recent victories didn't seem to make much of a difference in their attitudes toward the colonials.

He did get along with Plumer, since they had worked together before and were similar in their approaches. Plumer, unlike Gough, who was a thruster, was a bite-and-hold man. Currie found Gough too aggressive for his taste, and he felt that Gough's staff didn't do enough detail planning. Plumer preferred setting limited objectives that were achievable: once they had been captured and consolidated, have the Germans break their backs trying to take them back.

Since early September, both Gough's Fifty Army and Plumer's Second Army had been launching assaults in the Ypres area, with limited success and heavy casualties. Fresh troops were needed, and that was why they had called on the Canadian Corps.

"My apologies, General Buckle, for my loss of temper," said Currie once he had calmed down. Buckle, the commander of the 2nd Army's artillery, accepted stiffly. The general was in his mid-fifties and sported a thick grey walrus moustache. He gave a glance at Major-General Morrison, who was sitting beside him, then continued, "General Morrison has informed me we have been debited with 306 18-pounders, but he has only been able to locate 162 of them. Those he could find; a fair number of them were out of action. Out of the 250 heavies, he found only 220, and nearly ninety of those are in need of repair at the workshops."

Plumber glanced at Buckle seated opposite Morrison, then back to Currie.

"If I'm going to commit my men, I need as many working guns as I can. My staff is estimating that my Corps will suffer nearly sixteen thousand casualties once we've done." From the reports he had read, both Gough and Plumer had already lost nearly two hundred thousand men so far in this campaign. "Men I can ill afford to lose."

Plumer glanced at Buckle again then stated, "I'm confident General Buckle will investigate the matter and will provide you with any assistance you need."

Buckle acknowledged with a nod. Before Currie could thank the general, Morrison interjected, "We're already starting our preliminary planning. We're currently looking at having six 6-inch batteries, two 60-pounder batteries, and three brigades of 18-pounders in the Southern Group. In the Northern group, four brigades of 18-pounders."

"We'll have to do some rearranging of the battery positions to provide better support for the infantry and counterbattery work."

"And your allotment?" asked Buckle.

Morrison replied, "We're estimating nine thousand tons of shells of all types. And we'll need priority on some of the roads to move the guns. I've been informed orders had been issued forbidding the guns using the roads because they could create logjams."

Buckle sighed. "The weather has been quite wet, so the roads are in poor shape. Much of the terrain has turned to mud, and it has been known to swallow shells whole."

Currie had a good idea how bad the terrain was in Flanders. The water table was close to the surface, and the artillery from both sides had destroyed much of the drainage system. The weather had been good of late, but no one knew how long it would last. "I'm having my engineers start to rebuild the roads and tramlines to get the supplies to the dumps and the guns. We'll need to use the motors and wagons to get everything in place. If we have to use horses and mules, it will delay us somewhat."

Buckle made a note on the pad in front of him. "I'll talk with my staff, and we'll modify the orders to accommodate you."

"When do you think you can begin operations?" Plumer asked. "Is the 20th and the 21st feasible?"

Currie glanced at Morrison, who gave him a slight shrug. Currie was aware Plumer was anxious to complete operations before the winter weather came. "Possible, but I'll have to talk with my staff. There are still some details we'll need to consider. We'll be able to give you a better answer by our next conference. It'll depend on the weather."

"It always does," replied Plumer.

OCTOBER 27, 1917
TRAINING FIELD, NIEPPE

Lieutenant-Colonel Llewellyn watched as the aeroplane made a low pass above him. He was standing in a six-foot-wide circular gun pit dug deep enough that only the muzzle of the Lewis gun could be seen about the pit. The Emma Gee team in with him was dressed in fighting order: back packs, gas masks, and steel helmets.

Sergeant Mackay, a twenty-five-year old with a swarthy face, was handling the Lewis gun. Private Harrison, the sergeant's ammo carrier, was loaded down with spare Lewis pans. The baby-faced private from Richmond, who claimed he was nineteen, had his Lee-Enfield pointing skyward.

Mackay turned his hazel eyes at Llewellyn and asked, "Can I put some holes in the bugger?"

Llewellyn started laughing. For some reason it had struck him as hilarious. As he wiped his eyes he replied, "I don't think the Flying Corps would appreciate us poking holes in one of their aeroplanes."

The plane banked over another training group near a copse of trees. If he recalled correctly, they were training using the latest rifle grenades they had been issued. Llewellyn's attention was drawn back to the R.E.8. It was emblazoned with the 21st Squadron insignia, a large A in front and dumb-bell behind the roundel on the fuselage. Under the wings were two black rectangles. To make sure that it wasn't fired upon by friendly forces, the men had a tough time telling the differences between Allied and German aeroplanes because the designs were so similar. It had its navigation lights turned on and from time to time sounded a Klaxon horn.

Mackay peered down the sights as the plane lined up for another training run across the field. As the R.E.8 flew past, Mackay lifted his head and said in surprise. "God, he's fast."

"He's that," Llewellyn agreed.

The Corps had ordered that in the forward areas they were to fire at any enemy aircraft below three thousand feet. Llewellyn needed to set up his Lewis gunners no more than five hundred yards apart to provide anti-aircraft cover. The 2nd Brigade was organizing a second line of defence fifteen hundred yards behind the front lines. Those machine guns were no more than eight hundred yards apart. A system of anti-aircraft guns was being developed to protect the various headquarters and billets in the rear areas as well.

It was needed. Yesterday, the PPCLI was strafed while on a forced march, and several days prior, Currie's HQ at the Ten Elms Camp was bombed. A brief grin appeared on his face. He had heard Currie was annoyed by the bombing because it had interrupted one of his conferences.

Llewellyn shook his head. Last year he hadn't worried too much about the aeroplanes overhead. Sure, he would have liked to have shot them down, only because they were the eyes for the German artillery. Now, they were an additional threat to his men.

When he thought about Currie he asked Mackay, "When are you scheduled to visit Ten Elms?"

"Tomorrow. We'll be bussed there and back," Mackay answered. Then, he said with a straight face, "I regret I'm going to miss the general's inspection tomorrow."

"A right shame, that," added Harrison.

Llewellyn stared at both of them for a moment, but he didn't say anything. Currie was scheduled to inspect the brigade tomorrow. He doubted Currie would object to some of the NCOs being missing, especially since they were all required to visit Corps HQ to study the Passchendaele plas-ticine model. They had already been briefed on the operational plan. The 3rd and 4th Divisions were to launch their assaults during the first phase to capture the Red Line that ran from Friesland to Vapour Farm to the Gouldberg Copse. After they had done their jobs, the 1st and the 2nd Divisions would assault the Passchendaele Ridge.

The Fusiliers were currently in the Corps reserve, but he was expecting orders in the next few days to move north.

"No stopping at Poperinghe to get a drink now," Llewellyn added.

"Fat chance of that, sir. By the time, we leave, the estaminets will be closed," replied Harrison.

Llewellyn nearly smiled. The estaminets in Poperinghe were open from eleven to one in the afternoon and in the evening from six to eight.

"Colonel," said Mackay, changing the subject, "I still have a problem; I can't tell if I'm firing high or low. At the speed they are passing, I'm going to only have a couple of bursts at them. I heard the flyboys are using tracer bullets in their machine guns. I think they might help us a mite."

"We did get five hundred rounds of tracer bullets a few days ago. I was wondering what we could use them for," replied Llewellyn.

The tracer bullets were a relatively new ammunition type that started to appear last January in quantities. The bullets contained a mixture of peroxide and magnesium. When they were fired, they left a burning trail for nearly eight hundred yards before they petered out. There was a major problem using them, though. While they were helpful to see whether you were on target, the enemy could also follow the trail back to the source, not a good thing for the machine gunners.

"We can test them on the range and see how they work out," he replied. "We might be able to use them for anti-aircraft work. But I don't think it's a good idea to use them when we're raiding or on an assault."

"Of course not, sir," replied the sergeant.

Harrison suggested, "We can mark each pan so we'd know which ones have the tracers."

"Sure," acknowledged Llewellyn in a slightly skeptical tone. In combat, it would be quite easy to make a mistake and load the wrong pan. "We'll give it a try."

Llewellyn was about to make an additional comment when he heard a rifle going off nearby. "What the fuck!"

He continued to swear when he spotted a grenade rise into the air. At six hundred feet, it exploded, releasing three flares, red, green, and yellow, suspended from a small parachute. The rifle grenade was one of the new SOS signal grenades. It was a good thing it was easy to spot. The bad thing was it was directly in the path of the plane making another training run. Llewellyn watched as the pilot jerked his machine in the air to avoid the flare.

Llewellyn jumped out of the pit and left behind a stream of swearing that impressed Sergeant Mackay and Private Harrison as he marched to the group that had fired the grenade. There was going to be hell to pay for the man who had broken the safety regulations. After which, he would have to get on the horn with the CO of the 21st Squadron to smooth out their ruffled feathers.

OCTOBER 28, 1917
SAINT CONSTANCE CHURCH, L'ABBÉ DE MONT DES CATS,
MONT DES CATS

Captain Ryan rode up to the abbey perched on a hill that dominated this part of Flanders. He had been told the church and the abbey had been built during the Middle Ages, but the two-storey neo-gothic buildings didn't look old to him, more as if they were only twenty or thirty years old. He wondered how many Trappist monks lived here as he passed through the red-brick archway with the statue of Saint Bernard, the founder of the Cistercian monks, set in a niche in the arch's apex.

In the busy courtyard, he saw a couple of staff cars with Corps insignia painted on their bonnets parked near the church's entrance. At the nearby water trough, there were several riders and heavy drafts quenching their thirst. He knew why everyone was here. All the 2nd Brigade Artillery's billet officers had been ordered to report to the Roman Catholic church, Saint Constance, for billet assignments and instructions.

The arrangements for billets had become pretty well standardized. He had to submit form AFW3401 to the town major, the officer assigned to liaison with local government officials, indicating the number of billets he would need for his officers and men. Once the town major had given him the billets, he had twenty-four hours to resubmit the form listing: the address of the house or building, the names and ranks of the men occupying it, and the number of horses and the stabling arrangements. He also had to inspect the billets and certify, like he had done at Boyeffles, that the billets were clean and in good condition. This had to be done to reduce damage claims to the quartermaster after they had vacated the premises.

As he led his horse to the trough, he recognized Lieutenant Avery from the 5th Battery and gave him a nod. Avery came over and said, "I see you made it in one piece."

"Yeah, did get a little wet, though," Ryan replied.

"I was talking to the horse," Avery grinned.

"Ha-ha," Ryan answered.

"He looks in pretty good shape," Avery said as he admired the riding horse. It was a brown quarter-horse that stood fifteen hands tall and was well muscled. He was named Pounder, and, because of his disposition, he was Ryan's choice when he needed a rider.

It was true Pounder was in good shape after the 65th had marched nearly forty miles, from Boyeffles to Godewaersvelde, during the last three days. The weather the first two days had been fine, but on the third day, when Major-General Macdonell was to inspect them on their march, they got soaked. The senior officers hadn't been too happy that they couldn't impress the general with the brigade's smartness.

Most of his men were under tarpaulins until they could be billeted. He wanted to get a roof over their heads as soon as possible.

"This must be old home week for you," Avery stated. Ryan knew that Avery, a lanky six-footer from Sault Ste. Marie with brown hair and eyes, had been with the Corps for only six months now.

"I can't say. I've never been here before. When I marched in with the brigade, I didn't recognize much," he replied. It was true. Many of the places he once knew intimately had been so bombarded, they were now unrecognizable.

"Has the town major arrived yet?" Ryan asked.

Avery shook his head. "He's supposed to be here by eight, but I haven't seen him."

"While we wait, we might be able to buy some beer and cheese from the monks," Ryan suggested.

"Cheese yes, beer no. The monks told me they haven't made beer for the last ten to fifteen years."

"I wonder if the beer was any good?"

"Who knows?" replied Avery. "What do monks know about making beer?"

Ryan snorted in agreement, then asked, "Did you have a chance to take a look at the wagon lines?" Avery had been with the advance party.

When he made a face, Ryan frowned. "That bad."

"Yup, you'll need your swimsuit. It's a sea of mud."

"For Christ's sakes?" muttered Ryan. When he realized he was standing in front of a church, he blushed. He glanced around to see if anyone had overheard him.

"Yeah, you better start requisitioning material. You gonna need it for the wagon lines and the gun pits. And packs for the horses and mules to carry the shells."

"Great," replied Ryan. "I thought we were going to take over the New Zealand batteries with their guns and wagon lines."

"That's what I heard," Avery replied. "But I got to tell you I saw a bunch of abandoned 18-pounders out there."

"What! You're kidding!" exclaimed Ryan. It was a mortal sin for a gunner to leave his gun behind. If he absolutely had to, he would spike the gun so that the enemy couldn't use it against them. Once the battle was over, most were retrieved. If an 18-pounder couldn't be made operable, they would strip out the usable parts and what remained would be sent to the salvage unit for recycling.

"Wish I was. They're up to their axles in mud. A couple I've checked didn't need much, just a good cleaning. Another one was badly damaged, but the barrel seemed okay. It's going to be a bitch to pull them out."

"I guess we're not going to get much rest for the next little while," said Ryan gloomily.

"Nope, I don't think so," Avery replied. Avery then noticed the officers stood to attention when the doors of the church started to open. "His Majesty the town major has finally arrived."

"Looks like," Ryan replied as he lined up to get his billet assignments.

GOVERNOR GENERAL'S STUDY, RIDEAU HALL

"Hazen has been an important member of my cabinet for the last three years. He's run our Marine and Fisheries and our Naval Service departments," Borden said after he read the memo the Duke of Devonshire handed to him.

The duke nodded, then said, "The colonial secretary agrees that a Canadian representative be appointed in Washington. He has brought the matter to the cabinet."

Sir Robert glanced at the memo, then back to the Lord Victor Cavendish. The governor general was in his study, sitting in a white paisley cloth chair. Cavendish was nearly fifty years old, with close-cropped grey hair. His handlebar moustache, a light brown, matched his eyes. He was dressed casually in a dark suit and tie overtop a white shirt.

Borden had been ushered into the study by one of the Governor General's Foot Guards stationed at the side entrance, a few steps away, that he used when he visited the governor general on political business. It saved him walking through the main hall and reception room to access the Monck Wing Corridor that led to the study in the back of Rideau Hall.

The oval-shaped, walnut-panelled study was lined with bookcases filled with leather volumes. To Borden's right, beside the large window overlooking the snow-covered gardens, was a white marble fireplace with a fire crackling. Above it, the Royal coat of arms was carved into the walnut panel. The twin lamps on the large desk, dating to the Napoleonic Wars, were lit to brighten the room from the gloom. It was cold and cloudy outside. Set on both sides of the desk was straight back chairs with massive legs and curved wooden armrests. The duke normally sat in its matching chair, favoured by the governors general because one could see the chair's tread marks in the green carpet that covered the floor.

Borden frowned then glanced at Sir Cecil Spring-Rice, the British ambassador to Washington, who was on one of his regular visits to Ottawa. Spring-Rice was nearly sixty, with thinning hair and a boxed beard streaked with grey. He was a career diplomat with postings to Persia and Sweden before replacing Ambassador Sir James Bryce four years earlier. Spring-Rice said, "Sir Bryce had mentioned more than once that nearly three quarters of the work at the Washington embassy was dealing with Canadian matters."

Spring-Rice glanced at the governor general through his wire-rimmed glasses then turned his gaze to Borden before saying, "Most of my work of late has been dealing with the War Office contracts for war supplies. Ever since the Americans have entered the war, the demands on my staff have increased substantially."

"Exactly!" exclaimed Borden. "Because of that, some files of vital interest to my government haven't been dealt with in a timely manner. Favelle from the War Munitions Board has been complaining to me that some of the issues could have been resolved by now if we had a Canadian representative in Washington." He raised his hand when he saw Spring-Rice was about to protest. "I'm well aware you and Pope have done tremendous work, but I'm uncomfortable with the delays." Both men knew the Pope he was referring to was Sir Joseph Pope, the under secretary of state for external affairs.

"At the moment, my food and fuel controllers and my grain supervisors are conferring directly with their US counterparts. In the past, we and the US have settled disputes between ourselves concerning the use of boundary waters and the fisheries. And our commercial and business relations are much closer to the United States than they are with the United Kingdom. Naturally, this has grown over the years and will continue to do so, especially with Canada's growing population."

"The Imperial government doesn't object to having a Canadian representative in Washington, as Lord Long indicated in his memo. He's recommending he be attached to the British embassy. Of course, he would under your control," the duke stated.

Borden shook his head. "If Hazen isn't given an appropriate title, he'd be insulted. That was why I've suggested he be given a title like high commissioner or the equivalent."

He noticed the duke's frown when he mentioned high commissioner. He knew the duke had been put out when his proposal for a Canadian representative had been sent to the Colonial Office; somehow, his staff had failed to keep him abreast of the matter. It was a shame, because he had grown to like Lord Cavendish, and they had developed a good working relationship. He had gotten over not being consulted by the British government when they appointed him.

Borden knew London's objections were the same ones Pope had raised. Pope felt that it would set a precedent and would loosen the ties that bound Canada to the Empire. London was also concerned that if the colonies were allowed to develop and manage their own external affairs, the British Empire would not be able to speak with a single voice.

"That might create a constitutional problem," the duke said, restating one of Long's objections.

Borden couldn't help snorting. "I don't see why. As far as I'm aware, there is no constitutional impediment to my government having a high commissioner in Washington."

There was a moment of silence, then Spring-Rice said, "I'm afraid it may require further consideration after the war has been won. Unfortunately, finding accommodation in Washington is extremely difficult and expensive. Renting a suitable home for your representative will cost about

$25,000 a month. A small home, $15,000. In fact, Lord Reading is currently paying $21,000 for three months."

Borden was startled by the outrageous sums. Before he could respond, there was a knock at the door. Lord Cavendish turned his grey head and said, "Enter!"

A Foot Guard sergeant opened the door and said, "I apologize for interrupting, Your Excellency, but Lady Borden has arrived."

"Thank you," replied the governor general. "We'll be joining the ladies for lunch in a moment."

"Of course, Your Excellency," he said as he retreated.

"Let's put aside our discussion for another day, shall we? We don't want to keep the ladies waiting," Lord Cavendish said.

"Of course, Your Excellency," Borden said as he and Spring-Rice rose to their feet. "It would be my pleasure to discuss it further at a more suitable time."

CHAPTER 24

"We'll have to keep an eye on how much weight the men will be carrying," Brigadier-General Loomis said.

Llewellyn glanced at the other battalion commanders the 2nd Brigade CO had called to a conference to discuss Order 246 they had received from divisional headquarters. Loomis was holding the meeting in his HQ at the Ridge Camp, a couple of miles east of the Belgian village of Brandhoek. Llewellyn's men were billeted in the Toronto Camp, located about a half-mile northwest of the brigade's HQ.

The 2nd Brigade had entrained at Ebblinghem, and they had arrived in Brandhoek yesterday. Since there was a light rail line near the camp, they didn't have far to march. The Ridge Camp seemed to be slightly more comfortable than the Toronto Camp. The huts at the Ridge Camp were made from wood, with the bottom half protected by sandbags from shrapnel. The weather today was fair, but the ground was so saturated with water, it felt soft underfoot and slick. Where possible, the engineers had placed wooden boardwalks to keep mud down.

"We've all been looking at what we can do to reduce what the men have to carry," replied Lieutenant-Colonel Ormand, the CO of the Bluffs, the 10th Battalion. Ormand was in his early thirties, with grey eyes and brown hair. A lawyer by trade, he hailed from Winnipeg.

"But it's tough," Llewellyn added. "Everything they're carrying is needed for one thing or another."

"With the current weather conditions, the ground soft and mud knee-deep, the men will be exhausted just getting to their objectives, let alone fighting," stated Lieutenant-Colonel Prower, the CO of the 90th Rifles, the 8th Battalion. Prower was a couple of inches short of six feet, with blue eyes and brown hair. Llewellyn was never clear what his trade had been before he signed up in 1914. Someone had told him Prower put down *Gentlemen* on his attestation papers, whatever that was. However, he had ten years of military service, seven with the Imperials and three with the Canadian militia. "We've been looking at replacing the overcoats with leather jerkins. The jerkins won't absorb as much water and mud. It'll weigh considerably less than the overcoats."

"The problem is, is there enough to supply our men?" asked Lieutenant-Colonel Tudor, the commander of the 5th Battalion. Tudor was in his early forties, six feet tall, with brown hair and blue eyes. He had been a rancher before the war.

Loomis sighed. "I don't think we have much of a choice. We may have to double the carrying parties to bring us the supplies we will need to consolidate our positions once we've captured our objectives."

"We'll have to make use of any Hun wire we can find until we get the supplies in," said Major David Philpot, who would lead the 7th Battalion, the 1st British Columbia, during the assault, instead of Lieutenant-Colonel Stanley Gardner, who was going sit out, being in command of the reserve company. Philpot was in his early thirties, with hazel eyes and brown hair. He had been a contractor before the war.

"Well, I think we've going to have another meeting to fully discuss what we will need to do. I don't know if the rear waves in artillery formation are going to be appropriate," said Loomis with a thin frown.

"My first waves are going in a three company assault, and I'm holding a company in reserve," replied Major Philpot. "Colonel Ormand will be going in with two companies, one company in support and another in reserve."

"The problem we're facing with the terrain is that the spurs are nearly impassable because of the mud and water."

The brigadier-general nodded grimly. "The Hun tactic here is to fire their machine guns directly down the slopes. The spurs are ideal for them. That's why we're directing the artillery to fire a slow barrage. They'll fire for six minutes on the German lines, then they'll lift one hundred yards every four minutes. The men will have to stay low and take advantage of any shell holes they'll find."

"They'll be crawling for most of the way," Llewellyn pointed out.

"I know," agreed Loomis. "That's why we're thinking of using the mortar company as carriers. And I want to issue every man the Mills 23 type and the 27s to every second man."

Llewellyn nearly sighed. The grenades would add a couple of pounds to the men's load. The Mills bomb type 23 could be used as a hand grenade or as a rifle grenade for greater range. There was a base plug into which you could screw a steel rod in then slide it into the barrel of a Lee-Enfield. A blank cartridge was then used to fire it. He made a mental note to check to see what his supply was. A live rifle could be used in a dire emergency, but it was not recommended. The results were sometimes unpleasant. The type 27 was a grenade they started to receive in quantities last January. It used phosphorus to create a thick white smoke to provide them with cover and to confuse the Huns. It had proven useful in smoking Boche out of their dugouts when they wanted prisoners.

"We're going to need them to take out these 'pill-boxes' that the Germans have built here," Llewellyn said with disgust.

"I'm not surprised," replied Ormand. "Considering the reports we're getting on the conditions of the trenches. They're wet and shallow."

Llewellyn grunted an acknowledgement. The pillboxes most people carried contained medicine that was supposed to be beneficial to one's health. These pillboxes were anything but. They were circular structures built out of thick concrete, usually camouflaged with dirt piled on top or in abandoned farmhouses with slits cut for the machine guns. They were difficult to spot and hit with the artillery. The German tactics were to anchor thinly held trenches with the pillboxes. The boxes would sweep the assaulting troops with machine-gun fire, then the German infantry would counterattack to recapture their trenches.

Everyone hated the machine guns. However, they were a necessary evil.

"Now we won't know the exact objectives or the jumping off point until the 1st Brigade completes their operations. The latest reports say they're on schedule, but we won't get confirmation until tomorrow." The 1st Brigade's battle plan had been distributed through the 1st Division.

"That doesn't give us a lot of time," Ormand replied with a touch of concern.

"Do you think the jumping-off point will be Green Line, and the Blue Line will be an objective?" asked Llewellyn.

"More than likely," replied Loomis. "So, keep that in mind when you're working out the details for your operations. I would like preliminary drafts submitted by nine tomorrow morning."

"Yes, sir," everyone acknowledged.

"Our medical staff has done a reconnaissance and has designated the casualty stations. They'll be alerting your MOs shortly," said the brigadier-general. "One more thing before I send you back to your units. When you've achieved your objectives, use your white flares and Watson fans to make contact with the Flying Corps aeroplanes. For certain, the Huns will be making reconnaissance flights, so use your Lewis guns and rifles to knock them down, or, at the very least, discourage them providing information for the Huns' counterattack. We want to disrupt them, if we can.

"Well, gentlemen, let's earn the King's shilling, shall we?" Loomis said as he rose to his feet, calling the meeting to a close.

CHRIST CHURCH CATHEDRAL, SPARKS STREET, OTTAWA

The bagpipe started the wedding march as the happy couple glided down the aisle to the cathedral's entrance. Lady Borden used the handkerchief she had tucked under the sleeve of her black georgette gown to wipe away a tear.

She craned her head around her husband to admire the gown that the beaming Lady Maude was wearing as she clutched her new husband's arm. Oh, to be twenty-one again. The dress was silver, with a long train falling from her shoulders. The bodice was made of lace with transparent sleeves. The veil floating behind her head had a thin bead of pearl through an orange blossom trim. The only jewellery she was wearing was an expensive rope of white pearls her father had given her.

The arm she clutched belonged to Captain Mackintosh, who was wearing the dark blue ceremonial uniform of the Royal Horse Guard. Gold braid crossed his chest, and the light flickered off his service medals on his left breast. He too was beaming as he escorted his bride to the waiting landau.

In their wake followed the bridesmaids and ushers. The bridesmaids were dressed in yellow georgette gowns and the ushers were dressed in their regiments' ceremonial uniforms. Behind them, the Duke and Duchess of Devonshire followed with their remaining five children, Blanche, Dorothy, Rachel, Charles, and Anne.

"It was a beautiful ceremony," Lady Borden said to her husband.

"It was quite pretty," Borden remarked in a slightly distracted tone.

Lady Borden glanced at Sir Wilfrid and Lady Laurier in the next pew as they rose to their feet to make their exit. Her husband had visited the governor general several days before to drop the writ for the election. The date had been set for December 17th. She knew all the politicians in the cathedral were thinking of the slate of candidates they would be running in the ridings. They would have to settle their slates by November 19th. She wouldn't be seeing much of Robert over the next few months.

Her eyes fell on Lady Sherwood and Commissioner Sherwood of the Dominion Police, sitting behind them. The last few weeks had been trying for her and her husband. Robert had been downplaying the anonymous threatening letters they had been receiving. But they were serious enough for the commissioner to assign them a bodyguard. There had been nights she couldn't sleep, and she would get up to check the doors and windows.

At least the wedding of the governor general's oldest daughter was a bright spot. The young couple had only met the year before when the young captain, after he had recovered from wounds he had suffered in France, had been assigned as the governor general's aide-de-camp.

It was the social event of the year. Robert's scheming and plotting was nothing compared with arranging the wedding. Competition for invitations to the church and the reception was fierce. She didn't envy the duchess's task of deciding who would be attending and who would be sitting with whom, especially when an election was in the air. The cathedral was packed with local city, provincial, and federal politicians.

Laura followed Robert as they made their way to the cathedral's entrance. She was in time to see the sabre archway formed by the general staff officers collapse except for the two that were blocking Lady Maude's path to her waiting covered landau. The sabre on the left of the couple gave Lady Maude a gentle swat with the flat of his blade on her behind, then said, "Welcome to the Royal Horse Guard, Ma'am."

The large crowd that had been waiting outside broke into warm laughter and cheers as Captain Mackintosh lifted Lady Maude's hand up to present her. When the couple waved at the crowd, the cheers became louder. Laura knew that from Sparks Street to Sussex it would be packed with people trying to get a glimpse of the happy couple as they returned to Rideau Hall for their reception.

After the reception, they would be spending a few days at Meech Lake before they headed out to California for their honeymoon. Afterward, they would be moving Washington to the captain's new assignment at the British embassy.

In the meantime, Laura had to keep an eye on her husband. It was going to be difficult for him not to worry about the upcoming election. She hoped they could find something else to talk about during the reception dinner.

NOVEMBER 10, 1917
VINDICTIVE CROSS ROADS, PASSCHENDAELE

"Fuck!" said Lieutenant-Colonel Llewellyn as German 4.9s rocked the dank and dimly lit pillbox he was using as his advance headquarters. The Germans knew exactly where it was, since it had once belonged to them. He had to admit they built it well. It had survived the shelling from the Corps' guns, and now it was shrugging off the Boche's own. "Lance-Corporal Hart is in command of A Company!"

"Yes, sir," replied Private Parks, who was crouching in front of him. The private had to, even though he was five foot six; the ceiling was only four feet high. The pillbox itself was ten by twelve, which included the four-by-six closet. Llewellyn's claustrophobia was bad enough in the larger chamber. "The Huns' machine guns and snipers had a direct line of fire down the Venison Trench. They got Captain Lowry, all three lieutenants, and the sergeants. Only the lance-corporal was left."

"Shit!" Llewellyn said as the pillbox rocked again. "Did they finally take care of the machine guns?"

The private shook his helmeted head. "An Emma Gee from the 7th Battalion hammered the bitch pretty good. They were able to rush the fuckers and take it out. They got themselves eighteen prisoners, and the machine guns."

"Good, good," Llewellyn muttered as he stared as his battle map, rubbing his chin. The Huns had known they were coming. When the Z-Hour for the 2nd Brigade assault approached, the Boche batteries and machine guns had targeted the most likely jumping-off point for their assaults. The Germans had been stunned by their loss of the village of Passchendaele. It was now the job of the 1st and 2nd Divisions to take the actual ridge. The 2nd Brigade had taken the Vindictive Cross Roads, which was nearly twelve hundred yards north of the captured city, relatively easily. The crossroads led to Westrozebeke to the north and Oostnieuwkerke to the northeast. Not that the Huns were inclined to let them tour the villages. "Did A Company get to their objectives?"

"Yes, sir, when the senior officers and NCOs went down, the corporal took command and led the assault. After we captured the Hun trenches, he sent me back to let you know," replied Private Park.

Llewellyn grunted his approval as he continued to study his battle map in the dim light. It wasn't unusual for companies to lose discipline and cohesion when the senior officers got killed. To prevent this, all the men had been briefed on the overall plan, their objectives, and their roles in the operation. The fact that A Company managed to continue their assault and capture their objectives was still impressive. If the lance-corporal survived, he would put him up for promotion and a medal. Meanwhile, he still had a battle to win.

"The lance-corporal wants the artillery to lengthen their bombardment," blurted Parks.

"Did he say why?" asked Llewellyn.

"Our shells are landing on top of us, but he told me the scouts were telling him the Boche were assembling for a counterattack. He says he doesn't think he can hold them off with what's left of the company. He wants to break them up before they get set," the runner replied.

"Where?" Llewellyn asked as he pushed the map to the runner.

The private looked at the map, then pointed to a map square. "They're coming in from Westrozebeke."

"How long ago was this?"

"About an hour or so," he replied. "In company strength."

Llewellyn grimaced. He had already released his reserve to support B and C Companies. Now all he had was a platoon at his headquarters. He would need to call on the 2nd Brigade's HQ to release some of their reserve to him. Llewellyn paused to think a bit more. "Did he send up SOSs?"

Parks shook his head. "We're out."

Llewellyn turned to Sergeant Hastings, his communication officer. He considered using the wireless, but the 65th wasn't on the direct circuit, so there would be a delay as the message was relayed. He hoped the landlines were working. "Can you get the 65th on the line?"

"Yes, sir," replied the sergeant. "Willow calling Dexter! Willow calling Dexter!" The sergeant pressed the receiver to his ear to block out the noise. Then he handed it to Llewellyn.

He took the receiver and pressed it to one ear. He plugged the other ear with a finger so he could hear over the 4.9s shaking the pillbox and forcing him to yell into the receiver. Despite the static, he recognized the voice of Captain Ryan. "Dexter, lengthen your shooting by two hundred. That's right. I've got a German company forming for a counterattack. Shrapnel's fine. When can you lay it on? Fifteen! Acknowledged."

Llewellyn turned to the runner. "The 65th will be firing a shrapnel barrage in fifteen minutes. Does Lance-Corporal Hart need supplies?"

"The usual, ammo, grenades, flares, and water," replied Parks. He shook his canteen to show it wasn't sloshing.

"Everything, but the water we can't do," replied Llewellyn. "We're out. I've put out a call for it, but the communications people tell me it will be a while."

Water was one of his biggest concerns. There was plenty of water. All that you had to do was to dig a hole, and it would fill quickly. The ground was saturated with all the rain that had fallen. That was why they had built and laid duckboard roads and paths. The problem was that none of it was drinkable. No Man's Land was a sewer filled with overflowing latrines and rotting corpses, both human and animal. If his men drank from the water-filled shell holes, he would lose half of them to dysentery and E.coli. They didn't have anything to disinfect the water. Sure, you could boil it, but that was impossible under the current conditions. Water, like the rest of the supplies, had to be transported on foot or by mule.

"I've raised hell with supply. They said they'll be sending up some water as soon as they can. In the meantime, guide me to the lance-corporal. I've got some men I can spare to shore him up," Llewellyn ordered as he reached for his Lee-Enfield.

65TH ARTILLERY GUN PITS, BERLIN, BELGIUM

Captain Ryan handed the receiver to Private Marcus after talking with Lieutenant-Colonel Llewellyn. He wondered for a moment why he hadn't used the wireless. Signals had setup a base station at Korek, about six hundred yards west of his position, with cables connecting to the FOOs and to the batteries. He was concerned about Lieutenant Quigley, who had been assigned to one of the FOOs teams. The 2nd Brigade artillery HQ requested each team be made up of two officers, two NCOs, six signallers, six linesmen, and four runners who would also act as carriers. The lieutenant had been assigned to Bellevue Heights. Not only had his team been equipped with a wireless transmitter, but he also had a Fuller phone, visual signalling equipment, pigeons, and runners. Ryan looked thoughtful for a moment when he realized it had been a while since he had received any reports from the lieutenant.

Ryan consulted the barrage map tacked to the plank table, then he motioned over Bombardier Sobey, who was today's runner. "Tell the number three and four to retarget two hundred yards past 406."

"Yes, sir," replied the Sobey as he rushed off to deliver his message.

Ryan glanced at the map again. The barrage had been arranged in eight-minute lifts that ran from 0 to 406. The eight minutes gave the assaulting troops adequate time, considering the soft terrain, to keep up with his barrage.

Ryan was about to ask Marcus to check on Lieutenant Quigley when the Lewises opened up. Under the overhead canvas, he followed the trail of tracers to a flight of V-strut Albatros with black iron crosses on their wings and fuselages diving for his gun pits. They had tried to camouflage as best as they could, but their position was an open secret. Overnight, they had suffered German counterbattery shelling. Mercifully, they hadn't suffered any casualties, but it did add to their misery.

After the tracers petered out, they had a limited supply; he knew they couldn't prevent them emptying their bomb racks. In the past year, the Albatrosses had been fitted with racks to carry four 10-kg carbonite bombs, two under each wing, The bombs were four pounds heavier than his 18-pounder shells. He followed the four bombs that the lead Albatros dropped. Three of the bombs detonated, spraying up geysers of mud and flooding the number 1 gun pit. The fourth bomb, swallowed by the mud, hadn't detonated. This wasn't unusual, since, in Ryan's experience, one in five shells didn't go off for one reason or another. The other Albatros' bombs sent up fountains of mud as they landed, but they had missed his guns by a wide mark.

Ryan swivelled his head as he watched them climb and bank. He knew they were coming back for a strafing run. "Yes," he muttered when a flight of Sopwith Camels jumped them, and they disappeared as the dogfight climbed into higher altitudes.

For a moment, he remembered the good old days when an aeroplane was a novelty. Men would stop their work and gaze up in wonder at the sight. And the pilots would lean out of their fuselages to hand-drop the bombs they carried. Those days were now long gone.

When he had turned his gaze to the number 2 gun, he saw its crew scrambling to clean the mud off what hadn't been protected by the overhead camouflage netting and canvas. He was trying to remember where the dud had landed. Not that he would ask any of his men to dig it up; there was no way of knowing how deep it was. And digging in sodden ground was an act of futility. At least, he could have it marked so everyone would know to keep away from it. When the ground dried up, it would be good and buried. They would likely be long gone by then.

After Ryan had sent another runner to check to see if anyone were injured, Private Marcus caught his attention. "The colonel's on the line."

"Yes, Colonel," Ryan said into the receiver that Marcus had handed to him.

"Captain, be prepared to receive orders to move the battery."

"Did we get word we've captured the Green Line?" asked Ryan.

"That's the reports we've been getting," replied Masterley over the crackling line.

"Okay, Colonel. I'll start getting the guns ready to move," he replied. The new gun positions that had once been their targets had already been selected and reconnoitred by the 65th's advance teams. Though badly damaged, they were still suitable for their needs. Ryan hoped the new accommodations would be better than their current ones. They had been dismal so far.

"What's your shell supply like?" asked Masterley.

"We've fired 750 shells in harassing fire, so we're starting to run low. Pack Echelon hasn't been able to keep up because of last night's shelling. We'll be fine until we move."

"Okay. I'll have a word with Pack Echelon. I'll let them know you'll be moving soon," the colonel stated.

"Yes, sir," replied Ryan. Because of the poor conditions, an advance supply dump had been created, and fifty horses and mules had been assigned to keep his batteries supplied. The horses had to make nearly ten trips each day loaded with eight 18-pounder shells in canvas saddlebags to keep up with the guns. Last night, they couldn't get through because of the Huns' counterbattery barrages, until someone realized there were two-minute gaps between salvos. They would time them and try to get the horses through each lift. It had worked pretty well. On occasion, though, a mule would balk, refusing to move, forcing its driver to dive for cover when the shells started landing around them. At least the startled mule would run in the batteries' direction.

"How's the work coming along on the roads?" Ryan asked.

"It's going well. When they've finished, don't twaddle," said Masterley.

"Yes, sir," replied Ryan. The brigade had two hundred men laying wooden planks on the road that they needed to use to get to their new positions. It was a good thing; the roads had been in such poor shape. Moving the guns around was nothing but blood, sweat, tears, and mud.

The other reason for not getting stalled on the roads was to avoid being an easy target for the Hun aeroplanes and guns.

"One more thing: General Morrison may drop in as he goes up to reconnoitre the line."

"What?" replied Ryan in a worried tone. You usually got a warning when the GOC of the Corps artillery planned to show up.

"Don't worry about it. I know that you and your men have been doing a good job. He's pleased as pink."

"If you say so sir," replied Ryan.

"I do," the colonel said as the line went dead.

Ryan stared at the receiver for the moment. Between the two, the Albatrosses and the general, the general made him more nervous.

CHAPTER 25

"Tell General Lipsett I don't mind if he has men conducting active patrols. But I don't want any serious fighting for now," Lieutenant-General Currie said to Colonel Harington. He didn't need to tell Harington that the Corps losses had been severe. His casualty predictions had been spot-on.

"Yes, sir," replied Harington as he made a note. He then handed Currie several sheets of paper. "Here are the overnight summaries. And General Loomis and Colonel Llewellyn have arrived."

"General Macdonell?"

Harington shook his head. "He's being delayed. He said to start without him."

"Send Loomis and Llewellyn in," Currie said as he scanned the intelligence summary. The 2nd Division reported it had been quiet in their front lines, but the rear areas had been heavily shelled. German aeroplanes had been active over their lines. The 3rd reported heavy Allied and German air activity over their trenches. Their rear areas had been heavily shelled as well by 5.9s and 8-inchers. The Huns had been concentrating their barrages in the rear of Korek.

Currie looked up when Brigadier-General Loomis and Lieutenant-Colonel Llewellyn entered his office. While they were neatly dressed and shaven, he could still see the strain on their faces from their recent experiences in the front lines. Some of their strain had been eased. They had been relieved by the 2nd Division, and the 2nd Brigade, positioned at Merville, was now part of the Corps Reserve. "Take a seat, gentlemen." Currie indicated the two chairs in front of his desk. "General Macdonell has been delayed. He said to start without him."

"If you're busy, we can make it another time," offered Loomis.

Currie shook his head. "No time like the present. German spotter planes have been active over our lines, as has their artillery in our rear areas, but our front lines are stable for now."

"We know about the artillery," replied Llewellyn with pursed lips. "We've been dodging them when we drove here."

"Yes, sir," replied the brigadier-general. "I've read the reports. The Hun artillery hasn't let up much. Even before we went over the top, they tried to demoralize us. And once we'd captured our objectives, they tried to sweep us off them.

"It was touch-and-go for a while. If it weren't for our training and tactics, it could have been a lot worse," Loomis said sourly. "The conditions didn't help getting our wounded out."

"I'm well aware of the conditions," Currie replied. "How bad were your casualties?"

Loomis's face became bleak. "A hundred and sixty-eight men were killed. I have 230 missing. And 829 wounded."

Currie grimaced at the news. "How smooth did your operations go?"

"There's always some confusion. A relief took place that shouldn't have. I didn't order it. No one's fault. I have to tell you, my battalion COs did a hell of a job maintaining their organizations, despite the losses and the wet conditions. They also managed to stay in touch with their forward units."

"It wasn't easy," interjected Llewellyn. "The pillbox I was in was small and cramped. The Huns knew I was there and were doing their damnedest. They've built them quite strong. They really gave my HQ a good pounding."

"Hmm," Currie murmured. "The men's morale held up?"

"It did. But the German morale didn't break either," replied Llewellyn. "Their defensive systems of pillboxes and strong points chewed up my men pretty badly. They kept changing their tactics, depending on what we threw at them. They were damn good. They refused to give up anything without a fight."

"I see," said Lieutenant-General Currie. "At least we'll have the winter to reorganize and to build up our strength for the spring campaign."

"Yes, General," replied Loomis and Llewellyn.

"Meanwhile, we'll need to keep the pressure on the Germans. But I don't want any serious fighting. At least not until after the election."

"Sir?" asked Llewellyn in surprise.

"Sir Perley, at Prime Minister Borden's request, has asked Field Marshall Haig that we don't conduct any major operations until after the December election."

Llewellyn glanced at his CO and then back to Currie. "Understood."

He did. Heavy casualties during the election campaign could cause the voters to rebel against the current government.

"Good," replied Currie. "I won't keep you any longer from your men."

"Yes, sir," replied Loomis and Llewellyn as they rose to their feet.

NOVEMBER 20, 1917
HALL OF MIRRORS, PALACE DE VERSAILLES, PARIS

"Dear God!" muttered James when he entered the Hall of Mirrors. He and Samantha were following the crowd flowing through the king and queen's apartments on their tour of the famous Palace de Versailles. Most of the men in the crowd were French army wearing blue-grey uniforms, but there were some in khaki with British, Anzac, and Canadian shoulder flashes. He spotted a few of the newly arrived Americans who were also gawking, like he was, at the Hall of Mirrors.

"Be careful, otherwise you'll hurt yourself," Samantha teased as she squeezed his left arm. He had met her at the port of Calais before they took the train to Paris. When they had arrived in the City of Lights, they had disembarked at the Gare du Nord station, since it was the closest to their hotel on rue Lafayette.

"Have you seen anything like this?" he asked as he made a discreet wave with his hand at the hall. Contrast between where he was now and where he had a been a few weeks prior was startling.

Samantha studied the hall for a moment and then said, "Yes, the Winter Palace in Petrograd. Royalty doesn't seem to like one-bedroom flats."

"They would definitely need someone... Quite a few someones to clean the place," James said.

"It does explain a lot," Samantha said.

"What does?"

"The French and Russian revolutions," Samantha replied. "The amount of money they've spent while the peasants starved."

"Politics," James said with a touch of distaste.

Samantha made a face. "The girls have been talking quite a bit about politics ever since we've been told we're getting the vote."

"So you've mentioned once or twice," James pointed out. He wasn't particularly keen on women having the vote. He couldn't really explain why. They couldn't be any worse than the men. After all, it was the diplomats who had gotten them into this mess in the first place.

Llewellyn's eyes broke away from the cross look Samantha was giving him to stare out of the tall windows at the two large rectangular pools with fountains that were sprouting water skyward. In the distance, he could see the palace's lawns and gardens. What didn't fit into the elegant surroundings of Versailles were the neatly arranged piles of wood scattered along the pools' stone edges. He pointed them out to Samantha. "I wonder what those are?"

"I have no idea," replied Samantha.

"They're covering statues and vases from bomb shrapnel," said a voice behind them with an accent they were both familiar with. When they turned, they saw that it was an American captain. "I apologize for eavesdropping," he said with a grin. "The French decided that all the exterior sculptures, vases, and such on the palace grounds were priceless and needed protection."

"Zeppelin raids?" Samantha suggested.

"A few. Mainly Gotha aeroplanes. The damn things have two machine guns and can carry a thousand pounds of bombs," he replied.

"Thanks for the info," replied James as he took a closer look at the American officer, who was dressed in a khaki uniform, polished brown leather riding boots, and a Sam Browne belt, topped by an overseas cap. Based on his shoulder insignia and the badges on his collar, he was a staff officer.

"What part of Canada are you from?" he asked them.

"I'm from Toronto, and so is Matron Lansdale here," James replied.

"Sudbury, actually," Samantha corrected.

"We're from the same neck of the woods. I'm from Buffalo," he said with a grin.

"Been there a couple of times." James chuckled as he shook the captain's hand. "So you're taking the tour."

"Yeah, I'm taking my boys through. Most have never been off the farm. The tour never gets old."

"Where are you guys set up?" James asked.

"For now, at Invalides," he replied. "General Pershing is spending most of his time with the French and the Brits over at Lady Antoinette's house that they're using as their headquarters."

"When did you come over?" asked Samantha.

"In June," he replied.

Samantha nodded. "The colonel and I have been here since 1914."

"Ah," replied the captain with an understanding nod.

"How have you been finding it?" asked James.

"We're anxious and ready to go," the captain said.

"So were we when we got here. We lost that quick," replied James.

"So I've heard. We had some Brits and Canadians onboard ship when I crossed," he replied. "They were to tell us what to expect."

"Hmm," replied James. "Better than what we had. Have the Brits tried to split your guys up yet?"

The captain gave them a quizzical look. "Yeah, they have."

"They tried the same thing with us," replied James.

"That bad, huh?" the captain asked.

James shrugged. "Some are good. Some aren't."

"How long are you two in Paris?"

"We have a week's leave," replied James.

"We want to see as much of Paris as we can cram in," Samantha said as she waved a Thomas Cook guide.

"Tomorrow we're visiting Notre Dame," James said with a slighty apologetic shrug.

"And he wants to see Napoleon's tomb," Samantha replied in a mockingly exasperated tone as the captain chuckled.

"We were disappointed that we couldn't climb the Eiffel Tower, since it's off limits," James said. "But we have tickets to the Grand Opera and to some musicals."

"I better not hold you up then. Enjoy your leave," the captain said. "Now, I have to find my boys and try to keep them out of trouble."

"Nice meeting you, Captain," James said saluting.

As he and Samantha watched him disappear, she said, "He seemed nice."

"That he did," James agreed. "Who does he remind you of?"

"I know. We've come a long way since then. Haven't we?"

"We have. And I'm afraid we still have a long way to go."

Samantha shook her head and then grabbed his arm. "Enough of that. Let's enjoy gay Paree while we can."

James smiled at Samantha and replied, "Oh, I've got plans for you."

"Hmm," Samantha murmured. "I hope so."

NOVEMBER 24, 1917
AUDITORIUM, QUEEN STREET, KITCHENER

Borden stood at the podium, waiting for the yelling to die down. The hockey arena was packed. They estimated over six thousand had come to hear him speak in support of William George Weichel, the Union candidate for the Waterloo-North riding who was seated behind him on the stage. Weichel's prospects were good, since he had defeated William Lyon Mackenzie King, the Liberal candidate, in the last election.

It was the several hundred Laurierites who had crashed the rally who were preventing him from speaking. As they waved their banners, they chanted, "We want Laurier! We want Euler!" Euler was the Liberal anti-conscription candidate for the seat. In the upper galleries, they had torn down some of the posters that the Unionist organizers had plastered on the arena's walls. The posters that still were up shouted, *On to Victory! Vote for Union government!* or *Conservatives and Liberals unite to win the war!*

The scores of Allied flags hanging from the rafters swayed from the percussive force of the two factions yelling at each other. His Union government supporters were shouting at the Laurierites that they were yellowbacks and slackers. Even the 108th Regimental Band had surrendered when their attempts to soothe the rambunctious crowd with music failed.

The evening hadn't started well and had gone downhill from there.

He had received reports that some of his Union rallies in Quebec had been broken up by agitators. The organizers in London, his previous election stop, had warned him to expect disruptions, but the crowd of four thousand that had come to hear him speak had been well behaved. He had been pleased that so far the Ontario leg of his election campaign was going relatively well. However, he had been annoyed when no one bothered to inform him, until his train had pulled into Paris, that his meeting had been cancelled. Borden also had concerns with the Kitchener rally. While all the references to Berlin had been replaced with Kitchener, a few remnants of the city's former name could still be found; it didn't change the fact that he was campaigning in the heart of German-Canadian Ontario.

Still, he had been surprised by the agitators' reactions when he and his entourage entered the arena escorted by a squad of wounded soldiers recently from the front. Accompanying him to the stage were Dr. Honsberger, the meeting chairman and well-known Liberal; David Gross, the mayor of Kitchener; Henry Mowat, the Union candidate for the Parkdale riding in Toronto; and of course Weichel.

Each had tried to speak before him and had been drowned out by jeers and catcalls. Mayor Gross had made an appeal for fair play while Mowat tried to compliment the crowd on their enthusiasm for federal politics.

Borden didn't like the crowd's mood at all. He glanced at the reporters' table set near the stage and the thin cordon of police officers. They wouldn't be enough, if things turned ugly. All it would take was a spark.

"We have to leave," Borden announced to Dr. Honsberger. Honsberger acknowledged with a stiff nod, concern with the crowded arena written on his face. He motioned to the nearby police inspector, who led them off the stage to the Kitchener Greenshirts' hockey team's locker rooms.

One of the reporters who had been following them, Mike Horne from the *Globe*, yelled out at Borden, "Prime Minister, about the agitators…"

Borden interrupted him and said curtly, "I distinctly see there is an organized effort to prevent free speech tonight. In the circumstances, I don't feel disposed to waste my time."

When they had reached the locker room door, a constable rushed over and whispered into the police inspector's ear. "Prime Minister, please wait in here until the arena is cleared," the inspector ordered.

"Why? What's wrong?" demanded Mayor Gross.

The inspector paused as he glanced at Borden, then at the mayor. "Out with it, man!" demanded the mayor.

"We've arrested several men with revolvers in the crowd," he replied in a flat tone. "We want to make sure there are no others before we escort you back to your hotel."

There was a stony silence as Borden shook his head grimly. Some of his worst fears appeared to be coming true.

CHAPTER 26

Lieutenant-Colonel Llewellyn glanced at his watch, which read eight o'clock, then announced, "It's time."

"Yes, sir," replied Sergeant Ross as he beckoned at the first man in the line. It was a crisp, sunny day, and it was still cold enough that the men needed to wear their overcoats and fatigue caps. Most of them had cigarettes dangling from their mouths. Some were drinking coffee from white enamel cups as they stamped their feet to keep themselves warm as they chatted with their buddies. A few cracked jokes as they waited for their turn to vote.

Since the Richmond Fusiliers were in reserve for the next week or so before going into the line, Llewellyn had been named the presiding officer by Brigadier-General Loomis, before he went on a three-month leave back to Canada, to manage the elections for the camp. He had assigned captains Eastaway, Maddock, and Heathcote as deputy presiding officers. The polling stations had been set up for each company to facilitate the voting. Since there were nearly three hundred men per company, the voting would take most of the day. It meant he had to keep a watch over the polling station from eight this morning to seven this evening.

The A Company polling station had been set up near the mess hall, and the line extended for a half dozen huts. Llewellyn couldn't help glancing at the posters that had been tacked on the mess's exterior. One of them read, *Vote against the government means: You are here for life. A vote for the government means: Another man is coming to take your place.*

Sergeant Ross sat at the first table with boxes of ballot envelopes and a stack of certificates that the men needed to attest and sign. At the second table sat Sergeant Glazer, who was to verify the ballot after the voter had made his mark. Next to Glazer was a grey-white coloured bifolded screen on a table to prevent seeing which candidate the voter had marked.

Behind the two polling clerks, lieutenants Blythe and Holdsworth had been assigned as scrutineers, Craig for the Conservatives and Dawson for the Liberals. Dawson hadn't been pleased when he found out. He had been mercilessly ribbed by his fellow officers. The general attitude in the Fusiliers was pro-government and conscription. The men hated slackers.

Captain Moran gave him a wry smile when Llewellyn inspected the ballot box set on Glazer's table. The box had been sent from London with a lock and a set of keys. After the voting was done, he was to certify the number of ballots in the box before sealing the box with a lock and a wax seal to prevent tampering. Afterward, the box would be sent to the Commissaire Général du Canada in France. There, they would be stored until the actual election day to be counted.

Llewellyn gave the captain a brief glance. He was tempted to say there wouldn't be any dead men voting today but decided against it. When he briefed the election committee on the voting procedures based on the instructions he had received from Brigadier-General Loomis just before he had left last night for his well deserved leave, Moran had suggested they should vote on behalf of the men they had recently lost. Everyone knew how they would have voted if they were still alive. When he had seen the look on Llewellyn's face, he said he was kidding. Llewellyn didn't feel that it was necessary to do that to goose the results. Besides, it was against regulations.

It was also against regulations to have political rallies or meetings. They could be held off-base, but that was rather difficult when the soldiers' movements were heavily restricted and controlled. The political parties were allowed to mail the men political literature and pamphlets. He did notice all the pamphlets he and his men had received were from the Conservatives. He had heard rumours that most of the Liberal material was being stockpiled in England by the postal service. He suspected that was true.

Still, he had lectured his officers and men that he wanted a clean election and that they be respectful of each other's opinions. So far, there hadn't been any serious incidents. He hoped it would continue, and it would be a quiet day.

DECEMBER 4, 1917
CANADIAN CONVALESCENT HOSPITAL, BROMLEY, KENT

Samantha had just come off a quiet twelve-hour shift, and she should have felt tired. Instead, she felt energized and excited as she left the main hospital marque tent. It was voting day, and she saw that a line had already been formed by ambulatory patients, medical orderlies, and nursing sisters that extended several tents. She replied to several morning greetings and smiles as she made her way to the end of the line. She pulled her scarf tightly around her neck when she felt the chill in the slight wind. Midway, Ida Norgrove, standing with Marie Lamerux and Alice Crandal, motioned her over, and said, "We saved you a spot."

Samantha hesitated until the two men behind the three nursing sisters made a space for her. "Thank you," she said as both men gave her a brief smile.

"Isn't this exciting?" said Alice Crandal. She was in her mid-twenties, with a rounded figure and ash-brown hair. She had been a nurse in Victoria before she enlisted.

"I don't see what all the fuss is about," said Marie Lemereux, a Quebec City nurse. She was petite and stocky, with hazel eyes.

"We're the first women to vote," said Alice excitedly.

"I don't know about that," Ida said. "Voting started yesterday."

"At least we'll be among the first," Samantha added. They had all been surprised when it was confirmed women would be allowed to vote in this election. But the government had restricted it only to the nursing sisters and any woman who had a relative in the Canadian forces. Samantha knew it hadn't sat well with some of the women who couldn't vote. The government was gerrymandering it to ensure they would win. And the rumours were they would lose the right to vote once the war was over. For now, though, she was sure all the Canadian women in England would be voting. They all had until the 17th to cast their ballots. One thing was certain: this would be the first time she had ever voted in an election.

It took about a half-hour before they finally arrived at the polling table that was being manned by Sergeant Harris. Lieutenant Lanham, the presiding officer, stood behind him, in front of the poster that read, *The Slacker Must Not Rule Canada Vote Union Government.*

The sergeant gave her a tired, bored smile then asked, "Name?"

"Samantha Lonsdale," she replied.

"Rank and number?"

"Matron, no number," replied Samantha. The Nursing Service didn't assign the sisters a service number.

"Force or service?" he asked automatically. He didn't wait for her to answer before writing *Nursing Service*.

"Are you a British subject?"

"Yes."

"Have you previously voted in this election?"

"No," Samantha replied. But she was curious how they would find out if she had.

"Where did you enlist? And did you live there for more than four months?"

"Toronto," Samantha said. "I was a nursing student at Toronto General for two years."

"You wouldn't know the electoral district?"

"I'm afraid not," she replied with a shrug. "I've never voted before."

"That'll be fine. They'll assign you to one," he stated as he crossed out lines seven, eight, and nine on the declaration. "Sign and date it here," he said, indicating with his finger on the form. Samantha used the sergeant's pencil to sign and date it. He then folded the certificate and inserted it into an envelope. "Go behind the table and put your mark on the ballot you find in the envelope."

Samantha stepped behind the table with a half screen that hid her from prying eyes and removed the yellow ballot from the envelope. Printed on the top were the bilingual instructions on how to compete it. Below were five choices: *I vote for...*, *I vote for the government*, *I vote for the opposition*, *I vote for an independent candidate*, and *I vote for a Labour candidate*.

She paused as she seriously considered her options. There had been quite a few lively discussions with the other nurses concerning the Liberal and Conservative positions. Most of the arguments were about conscriptions. She had seen enough torn bodies not to wish for more. And she had seen the young boys that the Russians had conscripted for the army. It hadn't helped the Russians much. The last she heard, Russia had totally collapsed.

She did, however, want this war to end, so she put her mark beside *I vote for the government* then slid her ballot back into the envelope.

DECEMBER 5, 1917
65TH ARTILLERY GUN PIT, LIÉVIN

"Every man jack of you will vote for conscription or by God there will be hell to pay," Captain Amos announced with his knuckles on his hips as he stared at the men from Ryan's gun crews who had lined up to vote.

It had been a fine day, weather-wise. Ryan had taken the opportunity to check his six 18-pounders' calibrations and registration. Earlier, they had taken part, with the heavies, to pound what was left of Lens. The retaliation from the Huns had been light, which suited him just fine. He had expected more after they had fired a couple of salvos to disperse several of the Boche's work parties.

At least it had been, until the captain had shown up with a polling clerk, a scrutineer, and a pack horse. Tied to the horse's saddle were a locked black leather ballot box and a canvas sack. The sack contained certificates and ballot envelopes. The 65th had been supporting the 2nd Brigade in the line until they had been relieved several days before. It had meant he and his men couldn't leave their posts to go to the 2nd CFA Brigade's polling station at the electric generating plant on the Kingston Road. So the polling station had come to them.

When the captain asked where he could set up, Ryan had offered him his dugout. It was comfortable and reasonably dry.

Ryan knew they were supposed to grant the men privacy when they marked their ballots, but in the confined space it was easy enough for the captain's sharp eyes to spot if a bombardier voted for the government or for the opposition.

He couldn't help noticing that the captain had kept an eye him when he cast his vote. Ryan felt the captain suspected that he was a Laurierite, since he came from Montreal. He was right. However, he disagreed with Laurier on the conscription issue and had voted for the Unionists. Still, he was irritated by the captain's attitude and his attempt to intimidate his men. There was no need to do that. All of his men were already pro-conscription.

He could complain about the captain to Colonel Masterley, but then what? Have all his men's ballots thrown out? That would have gone over well with the 65th and his men. They were being relieved in the next day or so to take part in an artillery test. Masterley said several blocks of concrete had been poured with reinforced steel bars in various configurations to see how resistant they were to 18-pounder shells. It would be a fun assignment for him and his men and an early Christmas present.

He shuddered at the thought of getting on the good colonel's bad side. There were plenty of dirty jobs looking for volunteers.

CHAPTER 27

"What the hell are they doing?" cursed Pilot Francis Mackey when he heard the SS *Imo* returned two blasts, indicating she would not yield the right of way. When he glanced at Captain Aimé Le Médec, who was standing beside him on the bridge of the SS *Mont-Blanc*, he had a similar look of disbelief on his face. According to the rules of navigation, he had the right of way. It was the *Imo* that was supposed to move aside.

The ship he was piloting was in the mouth of the Narrows, and they had very little room to manoeuvre. The straight was only three quarters of a mile wide at this point, and they were only 120 feet from the shore on the Dartmouth side. They had just passed the HMCS *Acadian*, guarding the east side entrance to the Bedford Basin, by a hundred feet. The *Mont-Blanc* was a French-registered 3,121 gross tonnage cargo vessel that had been built eighteen years ago in Middlesbrough, England. She was 320 feet long, had a forty-five foot beam, and a depth of fifteen feet.

Even if he wanted to manoeuvre, Mackey couldn't risk grounding the ship. He knew the Halifax waters quite well, since he had twenty-four years' experience being a harbour pilot. He hadn't been happy to find her holds were filled with 2,300 tons of picric acid, two hundred tons of TNT, ten tons of gun cotton, and thirty-five tons of benzol in metal drums on her deck. The *Mont-Blanc* hadn't been flying a red flag indicating she was carrying dangerous cargo when he and the examination officer had boarded her the previous night. By the time the examination was completed, the harbour had raised the submarine nets for the night. He had decided to stay aboard after the captain invited him to spend the night.

Prior to the war, he knew such a ship would not have been allowed to enter the harbour. Because of the submarine threat, they've been given permission to transit to the safe refuge of the Bedford Basin, where the convoys for the transatlantic voyage were being assembled. The *Mont-Blanc* needed protection. She was a slow ship with a max speed of seven and half knots. He doubted the 90 mm cannons forward and aft would be of much protection, even if they were willing to fire them with the cargo they were carrying. The captain hadn't taken any chances; he had issued strict no-smoking orders to the crew.

This morning he had been pleased that it was a clear day and the waters quite calm except for the wakes of passing ships and boats as the *Mont-Blanc* followed the American tramp steamer SS *Clara* into the harbour. They were the first ships in.

"Give them another blast," ordered Mackey as he continued to watch the *Imo*. He was familiar with the Norwegian flagged ship; he had piloted her several times over the past year. He could see she had *Belgian Relief* in large red letters on a white background draped over her sides to make it clear to the Germans she was a relief ship. The *Imo* was a four-mast ship with a gross tonnage of five thousand. She was 430 feet long, with a forty-five-foot beam and a depth of thirty feet. He noticed the *Imo* was riding high in the water. It told him that her holds were empty. He didn't like the white foam forming on her bow; she was in a hurry.

"Stop all engines and hard to port!" Mackey ordered when he saw that she would cross the *Mont-Blanc's* bow. The captain hurriedly translated the orders into French for the steersman. The heavily laden ship was slow to make her turn. Mackey released his breath when it looked as if they were going to make it with very little to spare. A look of horror appeared on his face when the *Imo* sounded three sharp horn blasts. Her captain was putting her engines into reverse.

When the *Imo's* propeller started to bite her bow began to swing towards the *Mont-Blanc*. Mackey heard Captain Le Médec yelling orders to the steersman. As the *Mont-Blanc* made the manoeuvre, he realized the captain had placed his ship so that the bow would strike the No. 1 hold containing the picric acid, the most stable of the explosives on board.

They all lost their footing when the bow slammed into the *Mont-Blanc*. He could hear the sound of steel plate crunching, screeching, and groaning. When he finally got back to his feet, he could see the *Imo's* bow had sliced nearly fifteen feet into cargo hold No. 1. Barrels of benzol had been crushed and scattered all over the top deck. The gas flowed into the rents to the decks below. As the *Imo* pulled away, black smoke started to rise from the tears in the deck. He could see flames starting to climb the gas waterfalls.

"Fire! Fire!" Mackey yelled in alarm.

"*Mon Dieu!*" yelled the captain when he saw black smoke billowing from the hold. He then pressed the alarm. "All hands abandon ship. All hands abandon ship."

"What about the fire?" Mackey demanded.

The shocked captain shook his head. "There's nothing we can do."

Le Médec and Mackey then made their way to the lifeboats on the Dartmouth side of the ship. Mackey estimated there were nearly twenty men already piled in waiting to be lowered to the water. Mackey noticed the captain was hesitating climbing in until the first officer appeared.

"All the men are accounted, for *mon Captaine*," he said as he clambered on board. As far as Mackey knew, the *Mont-Blanc* had a crew of nearly forty.

Once in the water, they started rowing the hundred feet or so to the shoreline. They tried to yell and wave away the ships that were coming to their rescue, but to no avail. The rescuers didn't have a clue the cargo the *Mont-Blanc* was transporting.

There was very little Mackey could do as he watched the ship drift toward Pier 6 on the Richmond side of the Narrows. Once the lifeboat grounded, he, Captain Le Médec, and the crewmen clambered out and moved inland to escape the blast they knew was coming.

They didn't get far. The shockwave knocked him to the ground, and he was pelleted with debris from the ship. He could see nearby trees were shredded by the blast and the shrapnel. Most of the men from the lifeboat were flattened and knocked unconscious. With his head down, he didn't see the mushroom cloud that rose above the Narrows.

DECEMBER 10, 1917
BELLEVUE HOSPITAL, SPRING GARDEN STREET, HALIFAX

Sir Borden's car stopped behind a truck with red crosses on its sides, disgorging patients. The stretcher bearers were carrying them into the mansion on the corner of Spring Garden Road and Queen Street, with an American flag hanging from the flagpole fixed to the front portico. The house was three storeys high, with clapboard siding that joined the corner brickwork. Borden could see all its front windows that had been shattered by the *Mont-Blanc* explosion were all covered over with clapboard and newspapers to keep out the wind and the elements. He was familiar with the mansion, since it once had housed the commander of the British forces in North America. It had been converted into an officer's mess after the responsibility for Canada's defence was transferred to the Dominion. When he was a student at Dalhousie University, he had attended garden parties on its grounds. And when he had started his Halifax law firm and later had entered politics, he had attended receptions and balls here.

When his driver gasped, Borden turned his attention back to the ambulance. They were gently lifting a young girl out of the truck. She could be no more than six or seven. Both her eyes were covered by bandages. Borden understood his driver's feeling. He and his sister were the only survivors of his extended family of eleven.

Borden stepped out of the car and followed the stretcher into the Bellevue. Once inside the main foyer, he saw an orderly directing the stretcher bearers where they could place their charges. Standing beside the orderly near the staircase that led to the second floor stood Abraham Ratsheky. He was in his early fifties and clean-shaven. Borden could see, through the man's steel-rimmed glasses, fatigue from lack of sleep.

"Welcome, Prime Minister," Ratsheky greeted Borden with a handshake. Borden had met the American banker, philanthropist, and former politician when he had arrived at the Rockingham Junction about six miles outside of Halifax. Both their trains had been delayed by a fierce blizzard and gale force winds that had hampered relief efforts and had deepened the crisis.

Borden had been shocked by the damage the *Mont-Blanc* explosion had caused as he and Ratsheky had made their way to the Halifax City Hall. He had seen similar damage during his visits in France. He didn't expect to see it here. He could see a square mile of the city had been flattened, and the rest of the city had been badly damaged with all the windows being shattered. City Hall hadn't escaped the blast. The only useful office in the building was the City Collector's Office. There, Borden found the Deputy-Mayor; Lieutenant Governor MacCallum Grant; Major-General Benson, the military commander for District 6; Admiral Chambers, the naval commander; Lieutenant-Colonel Bell, the commander of the Halifax CAMC; the chief justice of the Nova Scotia Supreme Court; and the city aldermen were grappling with the catastrophe. Price, the mayor of Halifax, happened to be out of town when the explosion happened. He was running to replace Borden in his old King County riding, and now he was on his way back to the city.

They had been surprised and pleased when the American presented a letter from the governor of Massachusetts offering aid. When the rumours of the disaster had reached Boston, they activated the Massachusetts Committee of Public Safety. The committee had been set up to deal with potential disasters in the Boston Harbour. Within hours, they had sent a train to Halifax with twelve doctors, ten nurses, and baggage cars filled with medical supplies and equipment. Along the way, they had picked up additional doctors and nurses as they traveled through the northern states, New Brunswick, and Nova Scotia. And additional medical teams were coming in from Maine. After the meeting, Bellevue House had been assigned to the Massachusetts medical unit for their use.

"General Benson briefed me this morning on your progress," Borden stated as he returned the American's handshake.

"The men General Benson and Colonel Bell assigned to us, as well as the USS *Colony's* sailors, have done a splendid job in converting the mansion into a fully functional hospital," Ratsheky replied. Major-General Benson had assigned men from the engineers, medical, and ordnance units for the work. "The building wasn't in very good shape when we first entered. All the windows and doors had been blown out. And there was significant water damage. But we managed to treat sixty patients by six o'clock yesterday. This morning, our hundred beds are full."

Borden nodded. "I understand some of the patients are from the Garrison Hospital and the Military Camp Hill hospital."

Ratsheky nodded. "Only the more serious ones. I've been told the hospitals have been overflowing with patients."

"Colonel Bell has informed me that the hospital has only three hundred bed capacity, and they are now treating double that," Borden answered. Included in Bell's report was the estimate: 1,500 dead, and thousands more wounded. The local CAMC unit had six hundred medical personnel available. All the doctors, nurses, and orderlies were pressed into service to assist the local medical authorities. Additional military doctors and nurses were en route from Montreal with much-needed supplies.

"I understand the other hospitals are dealing with the same problems," Ratsheky stated.

"I'm inspecting them shortly, and I'll be visiting some of the patients," Borden stated grimly. Sadly, for him this was a too familiar sight. When he was in France last summer, he had visited quite a few Canadian military hospitals to see the wounded. He never expected to do the same here.

"I'm glad to see everything is in hand. I also wish to express my country's gratitude for your help," Borden stated.

Ratsheky replied, "What are good neighbours for?"

CHAPTER 28

When Sir Robert's car had turned onto his street, his driver hit the brakes and the car slid for a moment before the tires caught dry pavement. He and Laura had to put their arms out to brace themselves so they wouldn't hit the front seat.

"What's the matter?" Borden asked the driver. Laura touched his arm and indicated with her head to look out of the window. He then saw the reason his driver had to stop the car. There were about a hundred men standing in front of the gate of his home. Borden exclaimed, "What the devil?"

It had been a long day, and he was exhausted, since he had been running on adrenaline for most of it. He should have been used to it, since he had been through enough election nights. His emotions ran through the usual gamut of anticipation, nervousness, disappointment, recrimination, and emotional exhaustion as the election results trickled in.

The day started when he couldn't find the polling station where he was to vote, so he had to ask. It seemed that the Liberals were better organized in Ottawa than his Unionists were. After he cast his ballot, he had visited the governor general to discuss the New Year's honour's list. The weather was pleasant enough after lunch that he had taken a long walk for his constitution. He and Laura had taken an early supper because he knew she couldn't eat as they waited for the election results.

They started coming in around six thirty. Nickle had won Kingston by nine thousand votes, and Yates in Peel had a twelve-hundred-vote lead.

At eight, he and Laura, with two of her friends, went to the Senate Chamber in the Victoria Museum. A special wire had been installed in the Senate to receive the election results. A set of blackboards, with ebony button chairs arranged in front of them so visitors and guests could watch, had been set up along one side to tabulate the results as they came in. The throne chair, with the ceiling-to-floor Union Jack behind it, had sat empty for the evening.

He had some concerns initially as the Nova Scotia, New Brunswick, and PEI numbers started coming in. They had deepened when the Quebec ridings results were reported. His fears about the province had come true.

He had lost Québec. Out of the sixty-five seats in the province, the Liberals took sixty-two. He was only able to keep three out of twenty-six seats he once held there.

When the Ontario results started coming in, the tide had started to turn, and it didn't take long before it became apparent that he would win the election. When the vote from the soldiers at the front came in, some of the seats might change, but not by much. He was especially ecstatic that the Liberals had won only two seats in the rest of the country, and they had been reduced to a Québec party.

He had easily won his King riding seat by a thousand votes. Laurier had managed to win a seat in the Quebec-East riding, but he had lost in the Ottawa riding. Candidates were allowed to run in multiple ridings, if they chose.

"Borden! Borden!" A chant started when one of the men recognized him. It was then that he noticed most of the men were wearing khaki overcoats to keep warm in the chilly night. They were soldiers who had returned from the front.

When they had surrounded his car, he realized he would need to say a few words before they would allow him to enter his home. He opened the car door and stepped onto the running board so that the men could see him.

"Our victory tonight is not a partisan victory. It is a triumph of Liberals and Conservatives. The people of Canada have fully realized and splendidly fulfilled their duty. You, the gallant men who have returned from the front after your glorious and heroic service in Flanders, are entitled to Canada's grateful thanks for your service in the campaign just concluded," Borden said.

While balancing precariously on the running board, Borden raised clasped hands above his head in victory. The soldiers' chant turned into a roar of triumph.

CHAPTER 29

65TH ARTILLERY BILLETS, LIÉVIN

Captain Ryan fidgeted as he waited at Whiz-Bang Corner for the tram-line to pass before he could continue down Broad Street to Carlyle Street, where the 65th was billeted. The rail line ran up the Lens Road heading east toward their gun pits and the front lines. A small locomotive was pulling wagons filled with boxes with *Beans*, *Peas*, and *Canned Fruit* stencilled on their sides and petrol tins filled with water. The tram didn't linger; the corner was a frequent target for the German artillery.

"*Dépeche toi salope,*" muttered the old man sitting beside him in the Ford truck as he flicked his hand under his chin at the tram. Monsieur Moreau was a member of the Liévin town council. He was in his early sixties and was dressed in coarse black woollen trousers, a wool jacket, and a grey scarf wrapped around his neck. A black beret was pushed down on his white hair. A lit cigarette dangled from the corner of the frown he was wearing.

Ryan sympathized with the Frenchman. He knew that he preferred to be in his comfortable cottage enjoying the warmth of his fireplace with a glass of red wine while his wife prepared a Christmas goose and la Buche de Noel than spending time with him inspecting billets. The 2nd Brigade had received orders they were being relieved by the 14th Brigade on Christmas Day. Ryan was pretty sure the 14th was not any happier than he was.

Once the tram had passed, Private Mackey put the truck into gear and drove the two blocks to Carlyle Street. The homes on the street were two storey red-brick affairs damaged by the British and German artillery. However, they were still liveable, and they had cellars where men could take shelter when the Huns decided to lay a barrage on them. Stopping in front of the middle cottage, Moreau pushed open the truck's door with Ryan on his heels. Out of the back of the truck, Corporal Hasting and four of his men climbed out with resigned looks. They stamped their feet to get circulation going. It had snowed the previous night, but the light dusting was disappearing.

Ryan was relieved when he saw the small yard was cleared of rubble and the refuse was neatly gathered into bins waiting for pickup. He pulled the checklist out of his haversack he needed to complete before Moreau would sign off. He and Moreau needed to certify that the billets were in good condition, were clean, and any claims for damage to the quarters were properly documented before being submitted to the quartermaster for reimbursement.

So far, it had gone relatively smoothly, with minor damages being uncovered. Moreau had some heated discussions with some of the owners who were attempting to claim damages the 65th hadn't actually caused. Ryan had been pleased his men had cleaned everything up as they packed for their move to Haillicourt. They weren't looking forward to it. They had heard they would be housed in farmhouses and barns, which would not be as comfortable as the billets they had been living in for the past month or two. But orders were orders.

At least once they were done they would have their Christmas dinner before their lorries took them to their new digs. The cooks had assured him they would have a hot turkey meal, pudding for dessert, and beer to wash it down. Ryan was certain his men were looking forward to their liquid Christmas cheer.

CANADIAN CONVALESCENT HOSPITAL, BROMLEY, KENT

"O Lord, let us pray for the victims of the Halifax explosion and say that things are running smoothly in repairing the homes and businesses in their time of need," said Chaplain Deveson as he stood in the front of the mess hall at the table set for the hospital's senior staff. The good chaplain had risen from his seat beside the CO when one of the servers had informed him that all the expected patients were seated.

Samantha had her head down, studying the small gift wrapped in white tissue paper sitting on her plate as the chaplain paused for a moment of silence for the Halifax victims. He then continued, "By your leave, may this table be blessed. Bless us, O God, and we thank thee for Thy gifts which we are about to receive from Thy bounty, Christ our Lord, Amen!"

"Amen," the room replied.

"Might as well open it," said Major Creighton, who was sitting beside her. On his plate sat a flat, rectangular box wrapped in red tissue paper. All the patients and staff had similar boxes in front of them provided by the YMCA.

"What did you get Emily?" she asked as she carefully unwrapped the tissue to reveal a small white box.

"I sent her a silver locket with our photos in it," he replied as he tore the red tissue from his gift.

"She'd like that," replied Samantha. When she had pulled the lid off the box, she found an octagon-shaped turquoise enamelled pillbox.

"That's nice," Creighton said when he looked over.

"It is," replied Samantha. "What did you get?"

He held up to her a gunmetal cigarette case with YMCA engraved on top. He opened the case to reveal that it was filled with cigarettes.

"That's all you need." She knew the major didn't smoke. When she scanned the room, she saw all the patients had received similar cases.

She admitted the hall looked fantastic with the Christmas decorations created by the men in the past few weeks. The white cloth-covered tables had centrepieces with lit candles that gave off a warm glow and were made from green boughs, fruits, and nuts. Green boughs, holly, and garlands of festoons ran up the walls and hung from the ceiling. She was certain there was mistletoe. She was trying hard to avoid it. In the corner, to her right, was a seven-foot Christmas tree decorated with paper ornaments, paper chains, and lit by large electric bulbs. A white angel was perched on its apex.

The servers were coming from the kitchen with their dinner plates. For the evening, the patients' diet sheets had been suspended. She could see some of the men were salivating when they smelled the aroma of roast turkey. The plate that was set in front of her contained a thick slice of white meat, mashed potatoes, and roasted carrots with a dash of gravy.

"This looks wonderful," Samantha said to the server.

He grinned. "Candied apples are for dessert."

"Oh my," replied Samantha. She knew the patients and staff who couldn't come to the mess hall were receiving similar gifts and meals.

"How's the colonel doing?" asked Creighton as he started cutting into his turkey.

"He's doing fine," replied Samantha as she took a bite of hers. "I got a letter from him. He asked for a week's leave, but he doesn't think he's going to get it. We went to Paris last month. It would have been nice if we could spend the New Year together."

She paused to think that last year she was having Christmas in Petrograd at the British embassy. The latest news from Russia wasn't good. The Bolsheviks had taken over the government. At least the Borden government had won the election, which was good news, she guessed.

She shook her head to get rid of the thoughts. "What about you and Emily?"

"She's coming up for the weekend from Shorncliffe," he replied. "We have plans, but she would be glad to see you, though."

"That would be great," she replied. She watched as the men wolfed down their meals then washed it down with cold soda. "The patients look happy."

"Yes," Creighton agreed. "The Christmas concert after the meal I'm sure will please them."

Samantha agreed. One of the local theatre groups was putting on a comedy concert for the men. Anything to keep the men occupied and distracted was good. No one wanted to spend another Christmas here.

SMOKING CONCERT, RICHMOND FUSILIERS' BILLETS, BRUAY

"What are your plans for the men tomorrow?" asked Acting Brigadier-General Lieutenant-Colonel Prower, who was sitting beside him in the front row of the smoking concert. Llewellyn was rather amused by the term. He had to admit the room was thick with grey smoke, which would normally have kept the more refined ladies away as the men talked politics and listened to live music while enjoying a pipe or a cigar. Tonight, cigars and women were rather scarce. Although, he thought, it might change in the future with the women getting the vote.

"In the morning, I'm having the captains lecture on internal economy and run some drills. In the afternoon, nothing much. C Company is having their Christmas dinner," Llewellyn replied as he glanced at Prower, who was in his early thirties, with blue eyes and brown hair. This was the second dinner Llewellyn would be attending this season. He couldn't find a hall large enough to accommodate his entire regiment, so he had a marquee tent, with heaters, raised in an empty field near the billets large enough for a single company to have dinner. It had snowed earlier today, covering the fields outside with a thin layer.

He had skipped the Brigade HQ's dinner at the schoolhouse early this evening. His stomach had room only for one Christmas meal per day. He had to admit the cooks had outdone themselves. The dinner had been roasted chicken, vegetables, and potatoes. Dessert had been apple pie topped with real cream. The general had dropped by after the meal to give the men his Christmas greetings.

All the men had the drowsy, contented, stuffed look. He had noticed a few men surreptitiously undoing some of their waist buttons. The musicians were playing lively Christmas carols, and some of the men had joined in, singing off-key.

"Cancel the drills and inspections for tomorrow and give the men the day off. They deserve it," said Prower.

"Thank you, sir. The men will like that," replied Llewellyn. Prower acknowledged with a grin.

"So, how's your girl doing?" asked Prower.

"She's doing fine. I got a letter from her a few days ago," Llewellyn replied. "I don't think she's received my gift yet."

"The Christmas mail can be slow at times," Prower said.

"Yes, sir," Llewellyn replied. "Have you heard who our new GOC will be?"

"The scuttlebutt says it will be General John Embury," said Prower.

"Isn't he the GOC of the 13th Battalion?" asked Llewellyn.

"That's the one," replied Prower. "Do you know him?"

"I haven't had the pleasure," Llewellyn said as he scanned the room. He couldn't help noticing that fewer and fewer of the originals remained. "When do we expect reinforcements?"

"We're getting a new batch next week," replied the acting brigadier-general.

Captain Eastaway turned his head from the band when he heard the mention of reinforcements. Smoke drifted up from his briar pipe. "With the recent election and conscription being enforced, we should be getting a steady supply soon."

"Yeah," agreed Llewellyn. "But it'll be months before we start seeing them. You know how it is. Selecting the men, giving them time to arrange their personal affairs before reporting for basic training in Canada, and then advanced training in England. We probably won't be seeing them until June at the earliest."

The captain pursed his lips as he shook his head. "With the Americans being worked up, it's only a matter of time before the war is over."

Both Prower and Llewellyn gave him a look. "You've been a captain for how long now?" remarked the acting brigadier-general.

"Yeah," sighed the captain. "I know, I'm an eternal optimist."

THE HOMESTEAD HOTEL, HOT SPRINGS, VIRGINIA

Borden sighed when he studied at the winter scene through the restaurant's window. It reminded him too much of what he had left behind in Ottawa. Laura heard him sigh and gave him a knowing smile. She knew he was itching to hit the links. At six thousand yards, the Donald Ross-redesigned golf course near the hotel was a monster that he and Laura never tired of playing. Luckily, the forecast for the next few days looked good.

"How was your train trip?" asked Mrs. Chelmsford. She and her husband were dining with them in the airy and spacious dining room. Borden knew the Chelmsfords well, since they were Conservative supporters from Toronto. He had been pleasantly surprised to run into them at the Homestead. He shouldn't have been; they could easily afford the cost of the luxury hotel and spa.

"It was rather uneventful, I'm afraid," said Borden.

"Not as much as the election, I hope," Mrs. Chelmsford said as she placed a hand on her chest. She was wearing a very expensive pearl grey silk evening dress that suited her grey hair. "I had such palpations waiting for the results. I didn't sleep a wink for two days before voting day. Mr. Chelmsford can attest to that. I was on pins and needles until the glorious results were announced." Her husband, sitting beside her dressed in black tails with a white shirt and black cravat, hmphed in agreement.

'Thank you," said Borden. "It was a hard-fought campaign."

"Our trip was rather trying," Laura stated. She was wearing a beaded black chiffon evening dress with a string of pearls. She never looked lovelier. "When we left Ottawa, the temperature dropped to minus fifteen. When the train had reached Troy, the water in our rail car froze. It took them nearly three hours to unfreeze the pipes. We arrived in New Jersey just as our connecting train left the station. Our car then had to be taken to New York so we could catch the train to Washington. They had promised we would be on our way by ten yesterday. But when we had arrived in Washington, our rail car was leaking water, so they needed a couple of hours for repairs."

"We took the opportunity to stretch our legs and visit a few of the sites. Robert had called the embassy. When Sir Arthur had learned Robert was in Washington, he was so enthusiastic, he actually hugged him when they met."

"Oh dear, the British ambassador? Really?" said a scandalized Mrs. Chelmsford.

"It was quite amusing," Laura said with a smile. "When the car was finished being repaired, we had to wait for a short while until they attached a couple of cars filled with American soldiers to our train."

"Were they there to protect you and the prime minister?" asked Mrs. Chelmsford.

Laura glanced at him. Neither of them were going to mention the anonymous threatening letters they'd been receiving at their home.

"I think they were going to a military base near here," Laura answered. "We finally arrived here around midnight. It was rather late, so we slept in our rail car last night. Then we checked in this morning."

"That was awful," tutted Mrs. Chelmsford. "And the baths were closed today because it's Christmas."

"I know," replied Borden. "I was really looking forward to taking one of the hot spring baths." It was true. He really needed time to rest and recuperate from the election campaign. He also needed to conserve his strength for the coming year.

CHAPTER 30

"So did we get the white suits for our men?" Lieutenant-Colonel Llewellyn asked Captain Metcalfe, his quartermaster. He was sitting across from him at the table set in the kitchen of the house he was billeted in. He glanced at Madame Serre, the owner of the house, who had just poured coffee for him and his senior officers. She was a handsome woman in her early forties, wearing a black dress that hung loosely on her soft curves. She was of middle height, with a pale complexion that accented her black hair.

"Thank you, madame. *Le petit déjeuner etait excellente,*" Llewellyn complimented her. She gave him a brief smile. She knew he would have to pay extra for the breakfast of eggs, bacon, toast, and black coffee. It wasn't covered by the one franc he paid for the furnished bedroom on the second floor. That only covered fuel, water, and light. Meals were an extra franc per day. He didn't mind, since she was a good cook, but she made him uncomfortable when she entered unannounced as he was taking a bath and then took her time to leave.

When she left, Llewellyn turned to the captain, who was watching Mrs. Serre walk away. "Captain," he said in an amused tone.

The captain blushed slightly then said, "Yes, the white suits. The division has two hundred of them. The problem will be how many of them will be available for us when we return to the line. A lot of the units will want them for their raiding parties."

Llewellyn frowned. White suits were a good idea for the raiders to blend in with the snow as they sneaked across No Man's Land. He knew the units in the trenches had been ordered to increase their patrols to reduce fraternization with the Huns over the holidays and to report results to Corps HQ. "Let's see if we can get a hundred of them for our own men. If the other units draw them from stores, I don't think they'll be returned."

"Yes, sir," replied the captain as he chewed on his toast. "And I just got a memo from First Army about our gardening efforts this spring."

"Spring?" Major Gavin said in surprise.

"Spring here is only two months away," replied Metcalfe. "They want us to plant potatoes, cabbage, turnips, leeks, onions, carrots, and beans."

"Where are we going to plant them? No Man's Land?" Major Gavin joked.

"At least we wouldn't have to plow," said Father Stoats as he sipped his coffee. He was to lead the church parade later this morning.

"What they're suggesting is what the French have been doing. They've been requiring their men to plant small garden plots where they're being billeted," replied the captain.

"I don't know if I like the idea," said Gavin as he rubbed his chin. "I was hoping to be home by next Christmas. Planting gardens makes it sound more permanent than I would like."

"The First Army says it will save on the tonnage they have to transport and relieve some of the stress on the farmers," the captain stated. "Besides, I think the men would like to keep busy. I know they'd enjoy fresh vegetables."

"Well, we can plant them, but will we be here to harvest the fruits of our labours?" Garvin snorted.

"If all the units did it, then it wouldn't be any different from how we deal with stores," replied Metcalfe.

"When did they suggest we start planting, if we have seed?" asked Llewellyn.

"For most of the vegetables, they want them started by March 1st. I'm pretty sure I can get seeds. Potatoes may be a bit of a problem. They're looking for seed for French potatoes, but that might be in short supply."

"Okay," Llewellyn replied. "We'll have to see what we can do in March. It depends where we'll be. I'm sure we have some farmers or gardeners in the ranks that can teach the men to farm. But we'll have to get clearance from the French landowners to make sure that they're okay with it."

"Why wouldn't they be?" asked Gavin.

"I don't know if they'd like the competition," replied Llewellyn.

"Will the ground be firm enough for planting in March?" asked Father Stoats.

"I think so," replied Metcalfe. "I got the latest memo from First Army about the first thaw and what the procedures will be. They want to avoid what happened to the roads last year, so they'll be restricting heavy traffic. When the orders come out, the supplies will be dropped off at the dump, and from there horse wagons will be used to distribute them. They're cutting the vehicles' speed in half, and half loads only."

"We're have to keep that in mind in our planning," remarked Llewellyn.

It meant he needed more lead time if they were planning a major assault.

"And," Llewellyn turned to Gavin, "Corps now wants us to prepare a new standardized trench and wire return."

"Great," muttered Gavin. Like any good officer, Major Gavin hated the paperwork, but he had still mastered it. Successful military operations depended on the details. Also, Llewellyn thought it might be time to push through a promotion for him. He hated to lose him, but he didn't want to hold him back either.

"How did the wire training exercise go yesterday?" Llewellyn asked.

"The training scheme Division provided was helpful, especially the diagrams," Gavin replied. "The men wired a twenty-five section in less than fifteen minutes."

"Good," replied Llewellyn. "Less it takes for the men to put up wire, the less exposed they're to German fire."

He then turned to Father Stoats. "I'm afraid I've gotten word from the French. They won't approve any more memorial monuments."

Father Stoats didn't like it, but he wasn't surprised. For the last few months, the regiment, as many other units were doing, had been collecting funds to build a monument to commemorate their fallen comrades. The French, however, were concerned that too many of them were being built on private land.

"I understand. I'm hoping and praying we won't be in these circumstances next year."

"So do I," replied Llewellyn.

"I've been having discussions with the other chaplains in the division concerning notifications for the next of kin. What we would like is that they be issued from a central record office at Brigade HQ. We would collect the circumstances of the man's death and then forward it to the man's family. What I have been noticing is by the time I've sent my message, they have received letters from the man's friends. Sometimes they contradict what I sent them, which causes confusion. They then write back to me for clarification. It would help, and it would simplify matters, if there were a single point of contact."

Llewellyn paused to consider it and then said, "It makes sense. I'll pass it along to HQ.

"Okay, let's finish our coffee, and let's get to work. We have a lot to do before we celebrate the New Year."

"Well, I have tickets for the Lena Ashwell show this evening," Gavin said with a smile. Ashwell was a British actress who had put on shows for the troops ever since the war began.

"I have had enough of Shakespeare. We're having a concert party in the billet."

Llewellyn wagged a finger at them. "Now, now, both are acceptable ways to bring in the New Year."

65TH ARTILLERY BILLETS, HAILLICOURT

"So, I hear we're having turkey again," Captain Ryan overheard Bombardier Brogan whisper to Corporal Jebson.

"That's what I heard," replied the corporal. "Christ, it's cold."

Both men were wearing overcoats and gloves, as was Captain Ryan, since the stone barn they were sitting in wasn't well insulated. It had snowed the previous night. Not enough to cover the tall grass and weeds outside but enough to make life a bit more miserable. Their fourteen-mile march west to Haillicourt hadn't been pleasant. The horses couldn't find their footing on the slippery roads and kept falling down. Luckily, none were so seriously hurt that they had to be put down.

Their billets at Haillicourt were worse than what the earlier reports had indicated. They were mostly old farmhouses and barns. Considering how tidy they had left their former abodes in Liévin, he and his men were pissed. They were quite colourful in their description of what they thought of the unit that they had replaced.

"Am I boring you?" said a stern Sergeant Liam Winman, fresh from the Corps Training School. He was standing behind the table, on which sat a Hotchkiss machine gun. The sergeant was burly, with a red walrus moustache. His buzz cut below his forge cap was the same colour. He was their instructor on the new weapon that was replacing their Lewises for anti-aircraft work. Their old Lewises were being given to the other batteries as they waited for the arrival of their Hotchkisses.

"Not at all, Sarge," replied Corporal Gilson. "You're doing a good job keeping us awake."

"Knock it off," Ryan ordered as the twenty or so men in the barn chuckled. "The faster he completes his lecture, the faster we get to the mess hall for our dinner." Ryan gave pointed looks to Corporal Jebson and Bombardier Brogan, although his heart wasn't into giving them a hard time. He doubted most of the other men were paying much attention either. It was New Year's Eve. They were cold, hungry, and wishing that the damn war was over. The one thing they were looking forward to was turkey and a glass of cold beer at the YMCA tent.

For now, the 65th was in training mode. All the men were being rotated through the three-day Hotchkiss machine-gun training course. The sergeant had already explained that the Hotchkiss had been invented by an Austrian and that the British got the patents. The Hotchkiss, chambered for the 8mm Label round, was the French Army's main machine gun. The British version was chambered for the .303 round.

The one that sat on the table was nearly fifty inches in length, with a thirty-inch barrel. There were five air cooling fins encircling the barrel near the breach. The gun itself weight nearly forty-four pounds, while the tripod mount supporting it was nearly the same weight. The tripod allowed the gun to traverse and be elevated, useful in its anti-aircraft role.

The Hotchkiss was gas actuated, which meant the expanded gases from fired shells pushed a rod, under the barrel to open the breech, eject the round, and then load the next fresh one. It had a rate of fire of 450 rounds per minute. On the table beside the gun was an ammo box that contained ten strips of thirty .303 rounds.

"The ammo table for the Hotchkiss calls for 1,200 rounds for each gun. An additional 1,200 rounds per gun will be kept with the wagon trains," the sergeant said. "The gun usually needs a three-man crew to keep it continually fed, but in a pinch one man can do the job.

"This particular gun is equipped with a Peycru sight. It has beads for seven aircraft speeds, from 125 to 175 kilometres, to help sight and shoot down Hun aeroplanes.

"Everyone will have a chance to fire the Hotchkiss on the range and spend time with it until you become proficient. Now, let's strip this beauty down. You'll need to learn what each part does and how to keep it clean and well oiled."

Well, thought Ryan as he watched the sergeant strip the machine gun, *this year at least I'm not firing shells at the damned Huns to discourage fraternization. I'm going to spend the night stuffing myself with turkey and getting a good night's sleep for a change. Happy New Year to me."*

CANADIAN CONVALESCENT HOSPITAL, BROMLEY, KENT

Samantha was breathing hard as the band was playing a quick waltz. What made it awkward was that she was more used to following than leading. Her dance partner at the moment was Private Crowley. He was in his twenties, good-looking, with a pencil-thin moustache, blue eyes, and auburn hair. She had to look up to him, since he was taller. His blue patient suit hung loosely from his lanky frame. His left arm that would normally be placed in the middle of her back was pinned up. He had lost it in early October near Mont des Cats. She could tell he felt the same awkwardness, since he was used to leading instead of following her subtle pressure on his remaining arm and back to avoid bumping into the other couples on the dance floor.

Once the waltz ended, Samantha released his grip and said, "Thank you, Crowley."

"My pleasure, Matron," he replied, presumably with a certain relief that he hadn't stepped on her toes.

When a foxtrot started playing, she had to give a shake of her head at a patient with an artificial leg who was approaching her. She hated turning him down, but she had been dancing for the last half hour and needed a break. She was happy to see one of the local girls who had been invited to the hospital's New Year dance smiling at him and then scooping him up.

As Samantha headed back to her table, she smiled as she saw Emily sitting beside her husband. She had come up from Shorncliffe to spend a few days with him. As she had foreseen, James couldn't get leave. She hated not spending New Year's eve with him, especially since he was only hours away. Also, sitting at the table with Jody were her two friends Carmen and Leslie. They were being accompanied by two Canadian captains.

For the evening, they had decided to eschew their nurse's uniforms to celebrate the coming New Year with a touch of colour. Samantha was wearing a crème dress with a flower clasp cloth belt around her waist. Emil was in a chocolate-coloured dress with cafe-au-lait edging. Jody had on a black silk dress shaded with large flower motifs. Leslie and Carmen had decided to wear brighter colours. Leslie was in a light shade of pink with white satin, while Carmen's dress was white, embroidered with soft black and white flowers.

"The men seem to be enjoying themselves," said Jody as she glanced around the crowded hall.

"That they are. They've danced my feet off," Samantha said as she emptied the champagne glass filled with fruit punch. She knew some of the patients preferred something stronger. That was why some of the staff was keeping an eagle eye on the punch bowl.

Still, it was good for the men's morale to have a fun evening, especially when the Christmas concert had gone over well. The men had roast pork with vegetables and Christmas pudding. The pudding was leftover tins from the previous week. After the dinner, the tables were pushed to the walls to create a dance floor.

Most of the patients were in attendance, and even if they didn't want to or couldn't dance, they could enjoy the music provided by the YMCA band. The program called for twenty tunes, a mixture of waltzes, foxtrots, and one-steps.

Samantha knew she and her staff would be busy tomorrow. She expected an increase in medical complaints.

The hall still had its Christmas decorations, and the Christmas tree lights jittered as the couples danced on the hardwood floor. Behind the band, there were two posters: *Old Man 1917* and *Baby 1918*.

"It's almost time," said Major Creighton as he filled everyone's glasses with punch.

When the band paused at midnight, everyone at the table rose to their feet and Major Creighton announced, "To our fallen comrades."

"To our fallen comrades," everyone replied.

"And may there be fewer in the new year," Samantha added.

"Amen!"

HOT SPRINGS, VIRGINIA

"Are your feet warm enough?" Borden asked as his wife shifted her feet under the fur blanket covering their legs.

"I'm fine," Laura replied. "My foot just slipped off the foot warmer."

Sir Robert shifted his feet to give her more room on the wooden-covered steel coal box that lay on the floor of the sleigh. When he did, he inadvertently touched the booted foot of the Mrs. Kelly Evans sitting across from them.

"My apologies," Borden said.

"It's quite all right," she replied brightly. "The weather has been unseasonably cold."

Mrs. Kelly Evans was handsome and in her late forties. She was dressed warmly in a wool winter coat with a scarf wrapped around her ears to keep them warm. On her dark hair she wore a black hat. When he and Laura had dined with the Evanses the previous evening, she had invited them on a sleigh ride to Warm Springs, about four miles southwest of Hot Springs.

The Evanses were one of their favourite couples, and they liked spending time with them when they vacationed at the Homestead. Colonel Arthur Kelly Evans, a Torontonian, engineer, and a retired Canadian officer, had married the widow Lettie Pate Whitehead in 1913. Mrs. Kelly Evans was unique, since she ran the Whitehead Holding Company and the Whitehead Realty Company she had inherited when her previous husband passed away. The Whitehead Holding Company held the bottling rights to Coca-Cola for the entire United States, which made her a very wealthy woman. He had met her two sons from her prior marriage at their home several nights previously. The oldest was an officer in the US Army, while the younger one, not yet of age, had expressed an interest in joining the Canadian Army Officer Training Corps.

"That it has," replied Laura with a grin. "It nearly feels like home."

"I wouldn't go as far as that," Borden chuckled. "Last Saturday they've broken the record in Ottawa with minus thirty-one."

Mrs. Kelly Evans's eyes widened, and Laura gave a shrug as if it was normal. "It's a touch warmer here today."

"A lot of people suffering because of the cold," Borden said.

"It's been a hard winter for the folks here. We're doing what we can to help those in need." The Kelly Evanses were well known for their charity and philanthropy.

The eastern seaboard was in a deep freeze. The papers were reporting that New York had a coal shortage, and the people were suffering there. They were having a major problem distributing the coal from the train yards. In his regular mail and enciphered telegrams, he had received reports there was grave concern about coal shortages due to frozen train engines and tracks. He still hadn't gotten the books he had asked to be sent to him and which had been placed in the mail last Saturday.

However, with the cold weather there was a predictable increase in fires, mainly due to attempts to unthaw frozen water pipes with lamps.

He knew very few were willing to venture out with the potential that the water in the motorcars would freeze and that the horses would balk at going out into the cold. This evening he and Laura were planning to celebrate the coming of the New Year by spending a very quiet evening at the Homestead.

The story continues in

SHEATHING THE BLADE

On November 11, 1918, at the 11th hour, the sword is finally sheathed.

As 1918 starts, the October Revolution has finally taken the Russians out of the war. Spring would be a bloody one as the German divisions from the Russian Front arrive in France.

Brigadier-General Llewellyn and Captain Ryan rested their blades during the German spring offensive. But during the hot summer and the last hundred days, they would be in the thick of battle.

Matron Samantha Lonsdale is back in France. The stationary hospitals in the rear are no protection from the German artillery and aerial bombs as she and her nursing sisters care for the wounded in the final days of the war.

On the home front, in the cut and thrust of politics, Prime Minister Borden keeps his promise to impose conscription. As the war nears its end, in the midst of a flu pandemic ravaging Canada, he fights with the British and the Americans to get a seat at the peace table. A seat paid in Canadian blood.

The blade is finally slid into its scabbard. But for how long will it remain sheathed?

For latest news and updates visit
www.sambiasebooks.ca

www.ingramcontent.com/pod-product-compliance
Lightning Source LLC
Chambersburg PA
CBHW060343030726
47497CB00003B/584